International Acclaim for *Husband and Wife*:

"Shalev is a writer of formidable emotional firepower. . . . *Husband and Wife* is not a book for the faint-hearted, but for anyone prepared to be taken on an emotional white-knuckle ride, to experience with almost hallucinatory vividness the complex and conflicting emotions of a modern woman dealing with a disintegrating relationship, there can be no finer opportunity. Reading work of this caliber in a first-class translation is a habit we should all cultivate."

—*The Scotsman* (UK)

"Zeruya Shalev takes the reader on a breathtaking narrative journey through the hell of a crumbling marriage. . . . Written with a cool eye and a big heart, this is a love story for the twenty-first century." —*Die Welt* (Germany)

"A highly polished and deeply metaphoric account of a troubled marriage . . . a kind of Proustian recollection that carries great weights of meaning."

—*Kirkus Reviews* (USA)

"Shalev explores the chaotic landscapes of intimacy with a rare frankness. . . . [In her hands], the triviality of daily life becomes a real adventure story. This is how we know we are dealing with truly great literature."

—*Telerama* (France)

"Shalev has chosen 'soul-space' as her geography: her plots could be played out in any country of the Western world, her characters could confront their passions and partners in any city. What follows is love, sex, and obsession without borders." —*World Literature Today*

"Filled with a powerful and palpable physicality of love . . . *Husband and Wife* is a bold novel that explores family relations stemming from all ages and civilizations' heart and glue: woman." —*Il Segnalibro* (Italy)

"No short quote could capture the orgiastic design of her prose. . . . One puts the book aside convinced that no other novel could equal Zeruya Shalev's masterpiece." —*Die Zeit* (Germany)

"*Husband and Wife* reminds one . . . of the universe of Ingmar Bergman. . . . Shalev lays feelings bare with a sharp little knife." —*Le Figaro* (France)

"Shalev's language is hauntingly, painfully lyrical, and her understanding of the human yearning for connection and solitude astounds."

—*Publishers Weekly* (USA)

"Shalev succeeds in carving out whole lives and all that comes with them—guilt and trauma, hesitations and love, the growing together of a man and a woman as a couple and their separation through hurt and degeneration . . . an irresistible and thought-provoking novel." —*Ma'ariv* (Israel)

"Shalev's prose, somewhere between poetry and prophecy, flows like a gurgling country brook. . . . She offers such incredible insight into the human condition that it becomes difficult to put down the book."

—*Bookreporter* (USA)

"Zeruya Shalev's fascinating prose has that mythical quality that elevates individual speech into universal discourse. . . . The many allusions to the Bible are but pointers toward more profound levels of meaning."

— *Transatlantik* (Germany)

"A riveting read with an added therapeutic value, such that readers grappling with crises in their own marriages are likely to identify themselves . . . and we haven't even touched upon Shalev's wonderful, rich language or her metaphors and analogies, or the subplots that give the text even more substance and meaning." —*Yediot Aharonot* (Israel)

"Beautifully formed prose merges with rich mythology and metaphor in *Husband and Wife*. . . . This is lyrical, magical and ultimately very demanding stuff, but well worth your effort." —*The List* (UK)

"Captivating, important . . . [this] is the most impressive piece of writing about man-woman relationships of the last few years . . . no line may be skipped or ignored, each seemingly banal detail is significant, just like the details of our life, when we are compelled to consider them. . . . Zeruya Shalev is a fantastic storyteller . . . [and] *Husband and Wife* has by rights won its rank as a best-selling book in Germany." —*Neues Deutschland* (Germany)

Husband and Wife

Husband and Wife

ZERUYA SHALEV

Translated from the Hebrew by Dalya Bilu

Grove Press
New York

Published by arrangement with the Institute for the Translation of Hebrew Literature

Published simultaneously in Canada

Printed in the United States of America

FIRST PAPERBACK EDITION

Library of Congress Cataloging-in-Publication Data

Shalev, Tseruyah.

[Ba'al ve-ishah. English]

Husband and wife / Zeruya Shalev ; translated from the Hebrew by Dalya Bilu.

p. cm.

ISBN 0-8021-4009-2 (pbk.)

I. Bilu, Dalya.   II. Title.

PJ5055.41.A43 B33 2002

892.4'36—dc21   2001058479

Design by Laura Hammond Hough

Grove Press

841 Broadway

New York, NY 10003

03   04   05   06   07   10   9   8   7   6 5   4   3   2   1

FOR MY PARENTS,

Rika and Mordechai Shalev

One

In the first minute of the day, even before I knew whether it was hot or cold, good or bad, I saw the desert plain of the Arava, flat and desolate, growing pale, bushes of dust, melancholy as abandoned tents. I hadn't been there lately, but he had, he only returned from there last night, and now he opens a narrow, sandy eye and says, even in a sleeping bag in the Arava I slept better than here with you.

A smell of old shoes escapes from his mouth, and I turn my face to the other side, to the flat face of the alarm clock that chooses this precise minute to start ringing, and he grumbles, how many times have I told you to put the alarm clock in Noga's room, and I sit up abruptly, sunspots dancing in front of my eyes, what are you talking about, Udi, she's still a child, we're supposed to wake her up, not her us. How come you always know the way things are supposed to be, he retorts angrily, when will you understand that there's no such thing, and then we hear her voice approaching hesitantly, skipping over the notebooks thrown onto the floor, stumbling on the stacks of closed books, trying its luck, Daddy?

He leans over me, savagely silences the alarm clock, and I whisper to his shoulder, she's calling you, Udi, go to her, she hasn't seen you for nearly a week. You can't even sleep like a human being in this house, he rubs his eyes resentfully, a child of ten who's treated like a baby, it's a good thing you don't keep her in diapers, and here she is, her face peeking into the room, her neck stretched sideways, her body still hidden behind the wall. I have no idea how much she's heard, her hungry eyes swallow the movements of our lips without taking anything in, and now they turn to him, hurt in advance, Daddy, we missed you, and he sends her a crumpled smile, really? And she says, of course, nearly a week.

What do you need me for at all, he tightens his lips, you'd both be better off without me, and she recoils, her eyes shrink, and I get out of bed, sweetheart, he's just joking, go and get dressed. With angry fingers I pull the strap of the blind, opposite the bright light suddenly turning the room yellow, as if a powerful heavenly spotlight is being directed at us, surveying our actions. Na'ama, I'm dying of thirst, he says, bring me a glass of water, and I complain, I haven't got time to take care of you too now, Noga's going to be late and so am I, and he tries to sit up, I see him making tired rowing movements in the bed, his tanned arms trembling, his face reddening with effort and insult as he whispers, Na'ama, I can't get up.

She hears this immediately, again she's next to the bed, the hairbrush in her hand, holding out her other hand to him, come, Daddy, I'll help you, trying to pull him toward her, her back bent and her lips pursed, her sensitive nostrils flaring, until she collapses on top of him, flushed, helpless, Mommy, he really can't get up. What are you talking about, I say in alarm, does something hurt you, Udi? And he mutters, nothing hurts, but I can't feel my legs, I can't move them, and his voice dissolves into a puppyish whimper, I can't move.

I pull down the blanket, his long legs are lying motionless on the bed, covered with down, under which his muscles are frozen, stretched out side by side like the strings of a musical instrument. I always envied these legs that never tired, guiding hikers in the Arava and the Judean desert and the lower Galilee and the upper Galilee, while I stayed at home, because walking any distance is difficult for me. You're just making excuses, he would complain, the haversack grinning on his back like a happy baby, you just feel like being alone in the house without me, while I would stand there in embarrassment, pointing sorrowfully at my flat, always painful feet, separating us from each other.

Where don't you feel, I ask, my fingers trembling on his thigh, pinching the tough flesh, do you feel that? And Noga, going too far as usual, slides her hairbrush to and fro, digging red paths on his legs, do you feel that, Daddy?

Stop it, leave me alone, he explodes, the pair of you can drive a person crazy with your nagging! And she sticks the bristles of the brush into her palm, we only wanted to see if you could feel, and now he's sorry, I feel something dull, but I can't move, as if my legs have gone to sleep and I can't wake them up. With his eyes closed he gropes for the blanket, and I spread it over his body with slow movements, flapping it opposite his face, like my mother used to do when I was sick, cooling my forehead with the gusts of her love. His thin hair rises and lands back on his head, together with the blanket, but he moans beneath it as at a blow, what is this blanket, it's so heavy, and I say, Udi, it's your usual blanket, and he groans, it's suffocating me, I can't breathe.

Mommy, it's half past seven already, Noga whines at me from the kitchen, and I haven't had anything to eat yet, and I lose my temper, what do you want from me, take something yourself, you're not a baby, and immediately I'm filled with remorse and I run to her, spilling cornflakes into a bowl and taking the milk out of the fridge, but she stands up with an insulted pout, I'm not hungry, hoists her book bag onto her shoulders and advances to the door, and I stare at her back, something strange peeps at me through the straps, bright childish pictures, teddy bears and rabbits bouncing gaily as she goes down the stairs, Noga, you're still in your pajamas, I suddenly realize, you forgot to get dressed!

She climbs the stairs with her eyes downcast, almost closed, and I hear the bag slamming onto the floor, and the bedsprings creaking, and I hurry to her room and find her sprawled on the bed covered with teddy bears and bunny rabbits, what are you doing, I scold her, it's already a quarter to eight, and she sobs, I don't want to go to school, I don't feel well. Her eyes trap me in an accusing look, watching my heart hardening toward her, contracting like a stone, as a fist of revulsion presses me against the wall. Aggressive crying takes hold of every curl on her head, and I scream, why are you making things even harder for me, I can't cope with you, and she yells back, and I can't cope with you! She gets up ferociously and it seems to me that she is about to open her mouth wide and devour me, but she pushes me out and slams the door in my face.

I take a few stunned steps backward, staring at her closed, thunderous door, and his silent door, and go on walking backward until my back encounters the front door, and I open it and go out and sit down on the cold steps in my nightgown, and look at the beautiful day, wrapped in a golden light, with a gentle breeze shaking tender little leaves and gathering up bright remains of flowers in its train, and honeyed clouds caressing each other yearningly. I have always hated days like this, walking through them like an uninvited guest, on a day like this sadness sticks out more than ever, there is nowhere for it to hide in the great glory, like a frightened rabbit caught in a sudden light on the road it scurries this way and that, slamming again and again into the shining wheels of happiness.

Behind me the door opens, heavy sneakers descend the steps and above them Noga, dressed and combed, and I raise my face to her in surprise, suddenly she seems so mature, bending down and kissing me on the forehead without saying a word, and I too say nothing, watching the receding book bag with burning eyes. A huge, overripe navel orange suddenly drops onto the pavement below, almost hitting her head, and lies squashed in an orange puddle. Who gave it the last push, surely not this barely perceptible late spring breeze, soon children will step into the puddle and their footprints will rot on the pavement until they come home in the afternoon, and Noga too will come home, tired, her pale curls drooping, one sentence on her tongue, a sentence that will begin on the stairs, and I will hear only its end, Daddy, Daddy, Daddy.

I get up heavily, it seems to me that the day is already over, I am so tired, but there are still too many hours separating me from the night. On tiptoe I return to the bedroom, stand silently next to the bed, inspecting the beautiful body lying on it in perfect openness, a body that has nothing to hide. From our youth I remember this body, when it was still smaller than mine, narrow as a bud, and I would walk on the road while he walked on the pavement so we wouldn't have to be ashamed of our common shadow, stooping out of consideration, my eyes fixed on the gray meeting place of the street and the curb, before my eyes I saw him stretch and mature, until one evening he pulled me up to the pavement next to him and put his hand on my shoulder, and our shadow reflected a perfect picture, and I was filled with pride, as if I had succeeded, with stubbornness and faith, in prevailing over the facts of life. With a sinking heart I inspect him, looking for a movement in his limbs, the light blanket lying rejected at his feet, above him the reading lamp bowing its head innocently, as if we didn't quarrel over it night after night. Put the light out already, I would say, I can't sleep with it on, and he would say irritably, but I'm still reading, I can't go to sleep without reading, and I would curse the lamp silently, wishing it a fatal short circuit, and sometimes I would leave the room demonstratively, hugging my blanket and pillow, falling like a refugee onto the living room sofa, and in the morning he would always get his complaint in before mine, you ran away from me again, every little thing makes you run away from me.

His thin legs are still, but his mouth cracks in a sigh, the taut lips of an aging boy lost in his wilted face, swallowed up in the caverns of his cheeks, under the precise lines of his eyebrows looking down sorrowfully at the face whose beauty has dulled overnight, everything exactly the same sandy color, a uniform yellowish gray, like livery that cannot be removed, a uniform of sun and dust, and I try to heal him with my look, anxiety crawling over me like a hairy caterpillar, is this the moment I always knew I would not be able to escape, the moment that breaks life in two, after which nothing is the same as it was before, but like a distorting, mocking reflection, is this the moment, is this its smell, are these its colors, the moment in which all our previous lives would seem to me bursting with happiness, like the orange when it fell, as opposed to this loneliness, crippled, shamed, bedridden forever.

An imaginary hand, long and warm, reaches out to me from the bed, a huge maternal hand, seducing me to sink down beside him, to let him infect me with his paralysis, and I shudder, I can feel my life being drained out of me, gently, drop by drop, collecting in a puddle outside this room, and weightless and airy I try to hold on to the open window, surveying the room as if I am a spring bird which has landed up here by accident. Here is the big wall closet, only yesterday I stood on a ladder and took down the summer clothes and hid the winter clothes, pushing them deep inside, as if winter would never return, and Noga rushes urgently out of her room, always in the middle of a sentence, when's Daddy coming home, she asks, and immediately after that, when are we going to eat, and I say, he'll come home tonight, when you're asleep, and you'll see him tomorrow morning. And will he take me to school, she asks, her nostrils vibrating, and I say, why not, always after an absence of a few days it seems to us that only the lack of his physical presence stands between us, and the moment he returns the void in our home will be filled.

Here's the red rug, the rug of my childhood, with the little threadbare hearts, and here's the bed we bought, hesitantly, years ago, from a divorced couple, and next to it his backpack, dusty and empty, and on the wall a picture of an old house with a tiled roof and clouds sailing over it, and I try to find salvation in the inanimate objects, look, nothing's missing, nothing's changed, and therefore nothing will change in the living either. In a minute he'll wake up and try to pull me onto the bed with his edgy aggressiveness, I know exactly what you need, he'll inform me, why aren't you willing to accept what I want to give, and this time I won't begin to argue like I always do, I won't present him, earnest as a fledgling curator, with the catalogue of my disappointments, I'll take off my nightgown and jump into bed as if I'm jumping into a swimming pool, all at once, without testing the water, why not, we're husband and wife, after all, and this is our only slice of life.

Two

E ngulfed in a torrent of almost boiling water I think I hear an infantile wail, which doesn't penetrate my ear but sticks straight into my heart, between the ribs. Little Noga has woken up, her white forehead is burning, her eyes glittering with fever, and I regretfully turn off the water, part from its calming flow, and try to listen, but Noga's already gone, I recall with relief, and her infancy is gone too, no longer threatening me with its helplessness, and I turn on the tap again, once my mother used to put a clock in the bathroom, only seven minutes, she would warn, so there'll be hot water for everyone, and I would watch the racing hands with hostility, those seven minutes of the warm embrace of the water were so short, and I wanted to grow up and leave home simply in order to take a shower without watching the clock, and now I am ready to begin my shower again, eagerly embracing the stream of hot water, but once more I am alerted by the weak, demanding wail, and I run to him wet, and find him crying with his eyes closed, his nose running. Udi, calm down, everything's all right, I shake his shoulder, my hair dripping onto his tanned face, even his tears are the color of sand, as if he has been sentenced to camouflage himself in the desert forever, and I sit down next to him and try to put his head in my lap, but his head is heavy and cold as marble, and suddenly a scream escapes from his throat, surrounded by a fiery red halo like a bullet escaping from the barrel of a gun, don't touch me, you're hurting me!

I get up immediately and stand in front of him naked, not the provocative, impulsive nakedness I once possessed, natural and confident as that of an animal, but a human, apologetic nakedness, in which a loving eye may find beauty, but it wasn't a loving eye that was glaring at me now, spitting sand in my face. I thought you liked me to touch you, I mutter, trying to call the certainties of the past to my aid, but again the red fire sprays from his throat, don't you understand that it hurts me!

Before you said that it didn't hurt, I argue, unable to adjust myself to the upsets of this morning, still hoping that in a minute everything would return to normal, and we would begin to talk about it in the past tense, where did it hurt you, I would ask, and he would say, what does it matter, as long as it's over, the only thing that still hurts is my prick, he would leer at me, it wants a kiss, and with assertive hands he would help my wet head to cover the distance, which always seemed longer than it really was, between my lips and his penis.

I want a drink of water, he mutters, I've been asking you for water for hours, and I hurry to fill the glass and hold it out to him, but he doesn't stretch out his hands, thin and dry they lie at the sides of his body. Drink, I say to him, and he asks, how?

What do you mean, how, take the glass, I say, full of dread, and he sighs, I can't, my hands won't move. That's impossible, I say in annoyance, only an hour ago those hands strangled the alarm clock, there's no disease that advances so quickly, what's going on here, he's pretending, and violent swings of anger, pity and suspicion quarrel inside me like little girls, each reproaching the other in turn. How can you suspect him, look how he's suffering, but it doesn't make sense, maybe he's acting, but the acting is also an illness, no less worrying, how am I going to cope with all this, until the voice of compassion rises, drowning out the others, which fade shamefully away, and thunders in the house, he's sick, he's sick, a sickness has come and taken him, dragging him down to the depths.

I cover myself with a terry-cloth robe and sit down next to him, trying to feed him the water with a teaspoon, the water slides over the parched soil of his tongue, and makes his Adam's apple dance. Close the blind, he whispers, and I bravely repulse the sun and all its hosts, and lie down next to him in the gloom, stroking the ashen gray hills on his narrow chest, what's happening to you, Udi, when did it start?

I have no idea, he shivers, when I came home last night I was exhausted, I could hardly climb the steps, I thought I was just tired, but now I realize it's something else entirely, I'm afraid to even think of what it might be. Where does it hurt, I ask and he whispers, everywhere, it hurts everywhere, even when I breathe it hurts me, and I stroke his face, the delicacy of his features, their forgotten beauty, glow in the dim light, and the monotonous stroking calms me and makes me feel sleepy, already my eyelids are drooping in a pleasant languidness, it's a long time since we lay in bed together in the morning, perhaps we'll stay in bed like this all day, perhaps I'll hide him like a kidnapped child, and he'll stay at home always, he'll never run away from us on those long hikes of his again, he won't even take a hike to the bathroom, completely at our mercy he'll lie here in bed, he'll make up to Noga for his long absences, he'll hear about her day at school, how the teacher yelled at her even though she didn't do anything, just turned around for a minute to borrow an eraser, why does everybody always pick on her, and I'll leave my job, I can't look after other people anymore, I'll say, I'll take maternity leave without having a baby, but I'll hide his illness, so I won't be forced to take him to a doctor, we'll take care of him ourselves, he'll be a pampered prisoner, a giant baby who can't turn over or crawl yet, we'll keep him for ourselves, not getting better and not dying, he'll be the baby I wanted, the baby who'll make us into a family.

But now a whimper breaks the black silence, rips me from my drowsy cradle, Na'ama, I'm frightened, help me, and I start up, what's the matter with me, what am I dawdling for, we have to go to the hospital, I announce in a brisk voice that jars on my ears too, and he recoils, his shoulders shrink, he's always hated doctors more than illness, I don't want to, I want to stay at home, but his protest is weak, easily defeated by my firm, decisive tone.

Try to move your hands, I suggest, perhaps the spell has been lifted in the meantime, but they don't move, nor do his legs, or his back, his body doesn't stir, only his lips twist, and his eyes dart fearfully around the room. There's no alternative, Udigi, I whisper, you have to be examined, you have to be treated, I don't know what to do, and he says, can't we wait another day, and I object strenuously, as if only a moment ago I hadn't been thinking of hiding him here forever, out of the question, it would be completely irresponsible. But how will we get there, I can't walk, he whines, and I say, alarming myself with the explicit words, we haven't got a choice, we'll call for an ambulance.

His weeping accompanies me as I take clothes out of the closet, I haven't heard him cry for years, not since Noga fell, and now it buzzes terrifyingly in my ears, and I put on a pair of faded jeans, but I change my mind immediately in favor of the suit I bought recently, a light gray pantsuit, and I make my face up carefully and loosen my hair, the more elegant I am the better I'll succeed in chasing the illness away. In the miserable anonymity of the emergency room I'll be radiant and assured, and all the doctors will be convinced that I'm only there by accident, and they'll get us out of there quickly, and suddenly a strange excitement takes hold of me in anticipation of the adventure, we're going out together this morning, not to work as usual, each on his own. I feel his eyes digging into my back in hostile astonishment, have you gone quite mad, he snaps, where do you think you're going, and I turn my made-up face to him, what do you care, Udi, it gives me confidence, I immediately apologize as if I've been unfaithful to him, and he goes on, my shamed voice arouses him, how does it give you confidence to make yourself ridiculous, you're going to the hospital, not to a party, you're going because I can't move, but you're already celebrating because you think you're going to get rid of me.

With heavy fingers I cover my face, as if he's throwing stones at me from his bed, a gravel of filthy syllables, how dare he invade my inner self and pour out his garbage there, how will I get it out of me, how will I prove to him that he's mistaken in me, and why should I prove anything to him, always having to justify myself, as if there's no limit to my guilt. Take no notice of him, Anat would say, just take no notice, in any case he doesn't hear what you say to him, he only hears himself, inciting himself against you, and I would protest, but why should he, he loves me. Precisely because he loves you, she explains like an impatient teacher, and I plead with her as if it all depends on her, but why can't we simply love each other, be friends, why is it so difficult, and she pronounces, that's reality, Na'ama, and now I feel like running to the phone and calling her, like I used to, he said and I said, he insulted me and I was insulted, but I remember immediately, only his mouth moves, he has no power over me, he can't get up and go, he's completely dependent on me. His words are lost without my ears, ridiculous, meaningless, they'll try to reach me in vain, and I leave the room, and go to the phone to call work, but then I see on the fridge in front of me, cling-ing to the edge of the brightly colored magnet that Noga once gave me on Mother's Day, the crumpled phone number of the emergency medical service, and I look at it in surprise, since when has it been hanging there, who knew that we would suddenly need it.

In a smooth voice, as if I'm ordering a cab, I summon the ambulance, and return with brisk, almost provocative steps to the bedroom. I stand opposite his narrowed eyes, even when they're open they look closed, and announce in a matter-of-fact tone, you have to put something on, Udi, they're coming for you in a minute, and he shrinks, averts his face from me, his eyes parting from the inanimate objects, full of dread, clinging to the closet, the closed blinds, the picture of the old house, what is it there on the roof, clouds or the shadow of clouds. I hear the muffled sound of a siren, and I take out a white tee-shirt and a pair of gym shorts, easy to get on, and slip the shirt over his head, his neck is softer now, as if the knowledge that he's about to leave the house makes him feel better, and his arms respond too, only his legs are still stiff and motionless, and I pull the pants up them, under his butt, and then he's dressed, looking ready to go out for a morning jog. This is how he used to come to me sometimes in the evenings, telling his parents that he was going for a run and turning up at my house, short and enthused, and my mother would look him up and down in contempt, as if he was the least of her suitors, offer him a glass of milk, and then she would seat herself regally in front of the television, waiting for the old movies with the leading actress who looked amazingly like her. I was sure that it was really her, the same high cheekbones, the same curving lips, the same smooth brown skin, and I was sure that at night, when she left us alone, she would steal away to take part in those movies, why else were they black and white, if not that they were shot at night, and that was why she didn't get up in the mornings and I had to wake my little brother and dress him and make our sandwiches. It was only years later that I discovered that she spent those hours in bars, sitting with her friends and drinking, and sometimes on the way back they would drop her off at an old house with a tiled roof, and she would wake my father and weep in his arms and promise him that the next morning she would take the children and come back to him, and he would listen to her sadly and say, yes, Ella, I believe you that this is what you want now, but tomorrow morning you'll want something else entirely. Sometimes when she came home she would wake me up too, whisper that if I was a good girl maybe we would go back to live with Daddy, and I would get up early and go to the grocer's and wash the dishes and make the beds, until I understood that I was the only one gullible enough to believe these alcohol-prompted promises in the night.

The knocking on the door is aggressive, impatient, as of police at a house where a criminal is hiding out. Where's the patient, they ask, two stalwarts in phosphorescent jackets, and I squirm uncomfortably in my ridiculous new outfit, he's in bed, I say apologetically, leading them behind me to his radiant boyish smile, which I haven't seen in ages, the smile reserved for strangers, for the tourists who follow him devotedly. What's the problem, they ask, and he says in a calm voice, as if he has fully accepted the situation, I can't feel my legs, I can't move them, and I can barely move my hands too, and they stare at him incredulously, he looks so athletic in his short gym clothes. When did it start, they ask, has it ever happened before, and he says, no, never, just this morning, I couldn't get out of bed. Does it hurt anywhere, they ask, and he gives me an apologetic, sidelong look, everything hurts, even the limbs I can't feel hurt, and they aren't bothered by the contradiction, they take hold of his pulsing wrist, wrap a rubber tube round his arm and listen attentively to the steps of the air fleeing for its life, and then they inform him that he needs more comprehensive tests and they're going to take him to the emergency room of the hospital on duty. Should I pack anything, my voice chokes, a change of clothes, a toothbrush? Good idea, why not, the older paramedic gives me a pitying look, and I smile back miserably, their presence reassures me somewhat, as long as I don't have to be alone with him, and I rush round the house, cramming into my old overnight bag underpants and socks and a robe, just as I did when I gave birth, bent over in pain, the contractions splitting my body in two, and a hairbrush and a bra, and suddenly I look at the bag in astonishment, what am I doing, I'm packing for myself instead of him, and I spill everything onto the bed and fall on his shelves in the closet, and he says, put a book in too, so I'll have something to read, and I ask, which book, and he's already on the stretcher, his feet dangling in the air, my Bible, he says, it's in my backpack.

In a melancholy procession we leave the house, Udi long and limp on his gurney, an expression of utter trust on his face, like a baby being carried down the steps in his carriage by his devoted parents, and I lock the door, leaning on it in agitated farewell, who knows when I'll see it again. Next to the ambulance a few curious neighbors have gathered, what happened, they ask sympathetically, and he, who usually barely bothers to greet them, answers warmly, telling them the events of the morning, and the daughter of the downstairs neighbors, who has just returned from India, tells him about an amazing healer who practices Tibetan medicine, if they don't help you in the hospital tell me, and he nods his thanks, it seems he would be glad to hear further details, but the men in the phosphorescent jackets interrupt this new intimacy impatiently, push him on the waves of sympathy into the back of the ambulance with practiced movements, like garbage removers, and I join him there, sitting on the bench intended for anxious relatives, whose profiles are revealed through the curtains when they pass you in the street with wailing sirens, and you raise your eyes, look at the worried profile and know, their lives have been broken, their fate sealed.

Three

Through the white, long-suffering curtains I see my familiar world waving good-bye to me with broad, hallucinatory movements, parting from me forever. Here's the greengrocer's, wild and colorful as a painter's palette, and here's the new café with its regular morning customers, suddenly I can see them so clearly, I can see everything on their plates, everything written in their newspapers, and soon we'll reach the old café, where I liked to sit with baby Noga, the waitress would give her crisp, lemon-flavored cookies, and she would melt them in her mouth, dribbling sour-sweet spittle down her chin, sending a beaming smile from her stroller, a smile too radiant to be personal, and I would look only at her, at the spit soaking into her neck, and not at the eyes fixed on me, following my movements with undisguised attention, accompanied by a quick hand writing without a pause, as if documenting something whose importance knew no bounds. I try to take no notice, to concentrate only on her, but then he comes up to me, his notebook open, I sketched you, he says, presenting me with my black charcoal face, and I exclaim in surprise, that's not me, I'm not so beautiful, and he protests, you're much more beautiful, people always tell me that I make them uglier, my friends refuse to sit for me because they say I make them uglier than they are. But you made me more beautiful, I laugh, and he examines me and the sketch gravely, as if making up his mind between us, nonsense, he announces, you have no idea how beautiful you are, wait till you see yourself in color, the charcoal misses your coloring, and he retreats abruptly, returns to his table, and his hand races over the paper, his eyes on my face.

The ambulance stops at the traffic light, and here it is on the right, the old café, my stolen mornings, it wasn't him I loved there but myself, in his drawings, but where are the inviting wooden tables, where are the trays with the crumbly lemon cookies, the flames of a blowtorch shine from the door, flames forbidden to look at, or your eyes fill with white lilies, but I look anyway, how can it be possible, they're destroying the café, wrecking the last monument, and I look at Udi in agitation, they're destroying the café, I say, rashly revealing my inner turmoil, and for a moment he smiles a twisted smile, as if he's the one standing behind the white fire. Perhaps I deserve it to be destroyed, because a few months after that meeting little Noga fell from the porch, on all her curls and chubby cheeks and dimples, and her soft belly and tiny legs, dropped like a rag doll from Udi's hands, and I screamed, rushing down the stairs as if I had a chance of getting there before her and catching her in my arms, floor after floor, vow after vow, I'll never fall in love, I'll never be happy, I'll never leave the house, as long as she can walk, my little Noga, as long as she can talk, as long as she isn't hurt, and already we're in the ambulance, like now, only then its sirens wailed and it didn't stop at the traffic lights, she's unconscious, a white wax doll, her face concentrated in terror under the oxygen mask as if at this very moment somebody is telling her a suspenseful story, and the end is not yet clear, and on her face the familiar pleading expression, a happy end, Mommy, give me a happy end, and Udi is crying hoarsely, it's because of you, he yells, because of your artist, I haven't slept for nights, all I do is smoke and drink, I picked her up and suddenly she jumped out of my arms, my hands are so weak,

I can hardly hold a book, so how can I hold a child. I see him recede into the distance, leaving a little pile of bones behind it, before my eyes dozens of Nogas shine like stars in the sky, dancing in front of me in tutus, glittering hoops between their legs, why don't they move their legs, those aren't hoops, I realize in horror, they're little wheelchairs, the sky is full of tiny wheelchairs racing each other down steep slopes, like cars at an amusement park, but instead of the merry laughter of the children, screeching in alarm and pleasure, there is a terrible sound of weeping, Mother, what did you do to me, and I shout, my darling little Noga, I renounce everything, take my legs, I have nowhere left to go, take my heart, I have no one left to love, take my health, I have no need of it, take my life, and my weeping clashes with his, we aren't crying together, but one against the other, as a direct continuation of our quarrels.

And then she opens her eyes a slit, a jet of dark vomit shoots out of her mouth, what does it mean, the story of my life is being written before my eyes in a fateful secret code I have no way of reading, it's a good sign, right? I beg the doctor, she's going to be all right, isn't she? And he examines her doubtfully, and her eyes close again, and I plead, wake up, sweetheart, not yet knowing that she will play with us like this for days to come, look, she's walking, she's eating, we've been saved by a miracle, she seems to be recovering and we sit with her on the hospital lawn, she asks for an ice cream and I run joyfully to the cafeteria, bumping into people on the way and not even stopping to apologize, my daughter has asked for an ice cream and I'll do whatever it takes to place it in her hands, to see her tongue sliding round it. We sit rooted on the melancholy lawn, watching the movement of her lips, concentrating on the ice cream melting in her hands as if if she finishes it the danger will be over, afraid to breathe in our hopefulness, and look, she's eaten it all, she's healthy, maybe tomorrow we'll be able to take her home. At the entrance to the ward we meet the doctor, she's all right now, I inform him, she ate an ice cream, and then the familiar jet of vomit again, the sweet vanilla stream hitting the floor, and again the loss of consciousness, and a low, humble existence takes control of us again, two slaves at the mercy of a capricious fate. Our faces set in resignation, the corners of our mouths crushed and drooping, and every sentence she says bringing tears to our eyes, Mommy I'll grow up, she suddenly says, I'll be bigger than you are, and I'm already weeping, of course you'll grow up, and the fear drills a hole inside me, maybe she won't grow up, who knows what damage has been done to her brain, jolted again and again in its little box, it was a plastic pail that saved her life, a pail of water forgotten outside by the neighbors' maid, and this closeness to danger continued to threaten even after the danger was past, even after we finally returned home, every little deviation terrified me, and I was so wrapped up in her that I failed to notice that at some hidden moment, on that road that led from the catastrophe of the fall to the miracle of her recovery, I had lost him, and what was worse, she had lost him.

We've arrived, he says, and I wake up, momentarily surprised to see him on the bed and not her, the ambulance stops at the entrance to the emergency room, like then, but now nobody runs up with machines and instruments, to take us straight into the trauma room, they walk calmly, as if there is no particular importance to our lives, to our suffering. Dismissed in advance we wait for the door to open, and Udi sends me a strained look, his fingers creeping toward my knees next to them, and I watch his efforts indifferently, what is he trying to play there, an utterly inner tune, and then I understand, he's trying to touch me with his guilty hands, and he mumbles, I'm sorry, and I don't even ask him for what, exactly, for what happened this morning or for what happened then, almost eight years ago, I am so happy to receive this rare apology, a rash happiness, lacking in self-respect, and I put out my hand and lace my fingers in his, and thus holding hands is how our acquaintances in their phosphorescent jackets find us when they open the door, and wheel the gurney out with surprising ease, as if it were empty.

A swarming hive of illness and pain greets our eyes as we are led in, him on the gurney and me on trembling legs, making my way through the crowds besieging the doors, as if some rare product is being distributed, how capricious health is, wandering freely about the streets and refusing to set foot in here, and again I feel ashamed of my new suit, Udi was right, flaunting my elegant health before the sick, provoking fate, provoking him, his body sliding from the gurney onto the bed, where he lies, an aging boy in gym shorts, his body unblemished, not like the woman opposite him, whose leg is swollen and bleeding, or his neighbor on the other side of the curtain, under whose transparent skin you can see the bones being eaten up, a white mask over her mouth, as if there is still something on earth that endangers her more than the devil inside her. Why was I in such a hurry to bring him here, this is no place for him, he's never ill, and I feel like bending over him and whispering in his ear, come, Udigi, let's get out of here, let's go home. Suddenly the tense, stifling house we have just left turns into a kingdom of joy and loving kindness, our gloomy bedroom seems attractive and seductive, come on, move your legs already, they can't really be paralyzed, it would be as if the earth suddenly stopped turning one morning, and I brush his hair back, exposing his high forehead, wavy wrinkles crossing it like hills, Udigi, you remember how you would come to me in the classroom at the ten o'clock break and say, let's run away and go home, and we would leave at once, buying bagels with shiny grains of salt on them on the way, which I would wear on my wrist like a bracelet, and go to my house or yours, whichever was empty that morning, and Udi sighs, I wish I could run away with you now, Noam, the boy's name he would call me then, combining affection with complaint, because I was still completely flat, and my hair was cut short and from a distance we looked like a couple of boys. If you really want to we can, I keep at him, Udi, concentrate, make an effort, and he examines me almost pityingly, you just won't accept anything that doesn't suit you, don't you understand that I can't, as if there's some short circuit, how can I put it so that you'll understand, and I bow my head, it's hard for me to see his mouth biting off the words with such appetite, my eyes are fixed on the floor, the understanding like a darting squirrel, coming closer and disappearing, only the tip of its bushy tail peeping out between the beds, all morning I've been trying to understand and not understand, to approach him and distance myself from him, the contradictory efforts are wearing me out, my hands wander over his skull, from outside everything looks normal, no bumps, no distortion, and the moment it seems to me that I have succeeded in tempting the squirrel with nuts it's trapped, the curtain opens aggressively and a young nurse with a firm, pretty face asks what the problem is.

I can't move my legs, he informs her with a friendly smile, and my hands are weak, and she looks at his hands, one of them is still clutched in mine, and the hint of a sneer flashes across her face at the sight, you think that will help you, says her pretty face, you imagine that being two gives you strength, but disease isn't impressed by such gestures, disease enjoys separating couples. When did it begin, she asks indifferently, and he says, this morning, I woke up this morning and I couldn't get out of bed, the astonishment in his voice is still fresh, and he is ready in his innocence to share it with anyone interested, even the woman moaning next to him falls silent for a moment and stares at him from a bloodshot eye, making room for his absolute astonishment at this fundamental change in the status quo, and it seems that the great space of the hall is filled with the astonishment of Newman Ehud, son of Israel, as would soon be written on the labels stuck to his bed, the popular tour guide, almost forty years old, married and father of one daughter, whose limbs refuse to obey him.

In an inadequate, inappropriate response, she rummages in the pocket of her gown, takes out a thermometer, and holds it out to him, and I hurry to take it from her hand, so I won't have to watch the strange fumblings of his fingers again, and she asks, where are

the forms, and I look round, what forms? You have to go and arrange for his admission, she says, her look as hostile as if she's caught
us stealing into a movie without tickets, and I leave them reluctantly to join the crowded line of people huddled together, standing
shoulder to shoulder while over every head this elemental, innocent astonishment hovers, the astonishment of someone suddenly
finding himself in an ugly foreign country, without knowing if he
can ever get out of it. In a few days they'll get used to it, sit in bitter
resignation next to their loved ones in the different departments,
and only the memory of their astonishment will rouse them for a
moment, like the sight of a blurred childhood scene, almost meaningless, loved for no reason.

When I'm without him, far from his motionless legs, from his
closed eyes that see me from the age of twelve, from his whole being
that defines me more than itself, a moment before it's my turn to stand
in front of the counter and receive the empty forms that will soon be
filled with worrying data, the terrible sadness of the flight of movement from his body, like the flight of the Holy Spirit from the Temple
before its destruction, strikes me like a blow, and the force of the blow
dwarfs me, until all the people surrounding me look like giants, and
I wonder how anyone can notice me at all, like the freckled clerk who
says impatiently, yes, lady. Because I don't exist, the sorrow of this
morning has wiped out my existence, because you'll finish your shift
and go home, and you know what you'll find there, whereas everything familiar in my life has been ground to dust in a single morning,
because my Udi is sick, Udi is paralyzed, he won't leave me anymore
and he won't come back to me.

When I return, my hands full of forms and labels, where all
the details are correct and nevertheless insulting, to Newman Ehud,
son of Israel, with the anxious heart of a mother who has left her
child in the hands of an unfamiliar nanny, I suddenly forget exactly
where he is, opening curtain after curtain, intruding in my panic
on the privacy of as yet unexamined patients, for a moment it seems

to me that I'll never be able to recognize him, they are all colored by the greenish curtains, covered to the chin with wretched blankets, and only his curtains are open, he lies exposed like a child with no shame, obediently taking his temperature, acknowledging me with a bleak nod, on his arm there is already a transparent tube attached to an infusion, and it seems I have been absent for hours, so great is the change that has taken place in him. Now he already belongs here, in spite of his boyish appearance, in spite of his gym shorts and tee-shirt, and I look with hostility at the nurse calmly making the rounds of the patients, as if she has beaten me in a battle for his heart. Let's take the thermometer out already, I say resentfully, it's been there long enough, but he shakes his head obstinately, only when the nurse says so, he hisses through his teeth, and I say irritably, I don't believe you, Udi, you need permission for that, and he says, yes, she said to leave it in my mouth, and shrugs submissive shoulders. He was always so rebellious, he never obeyed anyone, not his teachers in school or his officers in the army, and they always forgave him in the end, how can a person change so much in a single morning, as if the defeat of his legs has brought down the building of his inner self.

I see his eyes transfixed by the brusque, efficient movements of the nurse, the thermometer in his mouth relieving him of the need to speak to me, I've never seen him look at a woman like this before, other women didn't interest him, so he claimed at any rate, and I believed him, he always flaunted his faithfulness at me, a reassuring white flag over a threatening sea, but this demonstrative faithfulness turned over the years into a weapon against me, another way of putting me down, of proving his superiority. He concentrated exclusively on me, only at me he aimed the poisoned darts of his caprices, his jealousies, his inner conflicts, his endless lust, but now when I see him look so yearningly at her I hug my ribs in insult, a chill of loneliness makes me shiver, as if I have just been cast out of my home, without even being allowed to get dressed.

Now she comes up to us and he lets her take the thermometer out of his mouth, with the ingratiating smile of a child giving his mother a present, but even though the thermometer almost stuck to his mouth it was in there so long, he has no fever, ninety-eight point six, she writes contemptuously on the chart attached to his bed, and raises the blanket for a moment, giving me an astounded glimpse of the narrow tube coiling from his penis, leading to a bag hanging under the bed and gradually filling with an orange liquid. Everything the body tries so hard to hide is revealed here with such ease, when did she have time to insert the tube, perhaps it was then that the intimacy arose between them, and now she holds his hand and measures his blood pressure and his pulse, until she finally lets go, writes down the results and turns her back to him, the doctor will be here in a minute, she says, and walks away, not seeing the obsequious smile he sends her, but I see it very well.

When the doctor arrives, insultingly young, a child, so that it's almost embarrassing to admit how eagerly we awaited him, brisk and impatient, he listens smooth-faced to the morning's events, how many times can he repeat the story of the disobedient legs, it doesn't bore Udi, but it soon bores the doctor, whatever little civility he possesses vanishes, and like a child sick of listening to his father's dull reminiscences, he cuts him short, feels the famous legs, heroes of the morning, and then he takes a needle from his pocket and begins to stab. In astonishment I watch the leg swallowing the needle while Udi doesn't make a sound, and the needle goes on traveling up and down his legs, a little hammer joins it, tapping the knees mute as logs, and Udi goes on smiling his obsequious smile, proud as a fakir, until the doctor puts his instruments back in his pocket, looks at the chart on the bed and hurriedly pronounces, first of all we need an X ray, to see if there's any damage to the spine, and we'll proceed from there, and then he's gone.

I drag the bed through the crowded passages, on the glass walls our figures are momentarily reflected, here we are, Udi and I, and the infusion and the catheter, two couples going out for a stroll through the hospital corridors. Where's the X-ray department here, I ask, where's the elevator, how will we all fit into one elevator, one after the other they arrive full, I don't even try to squeeze in, but now they're making room for me, people are hugging the metal walls, holding their stomachs in, breathing shallowly, just so that we can join them, Udi and I, and the infusion with the transparent liquid, and the catheter with the orange liquid, on this downward slide, to the dark X-ray rooms, lit by sickly neon that never goes off, more stable than the sunlight, but at the end of the corridor we see a flickering light, a completely bald child is leaning with his thin shoulders on the switch, turning it on and off, and I see Udi blink his eyes, try to sit up, leave that switch alone, he yells, haven't you got anything else to do, it's impossible to see anything like this, it's ruining my eyes. What's the matter with you today, I whisper to him, what are you yelling at him for, can't you see he's sick, and Udi locks his face, as always when he's criticized, I'm sick too, he snaps, and I go up to the child, hesitantly touch his arm, don't pay attention to him, I say, it's his problem, nothing to do with you, and the child shrugs his shoulders, as far as he's concerned it really doesn't matter, but for me the distinction was essential, how many times have I heard Anat repeat, it's him, not you, they're his problems, not yours, and I would say, but if we're together his problems are mine too, that kind of separation is impossible, and she would insist, deep inside it's possible.

It seems to me that the child is mumbling something, and I bend down to the bald yellow head, what did you say? And he repeats, I'm not a boy I'm a girl, and to me it sounds like some meaningless mantra, but then he straightens up and I see little budding breasts sprouting from the sick body, as if some mighty battle is raging inside it, between the thrust of life and the forces of death, you can almost see two hands wrestling under the shirt, trying to force each other down. He's a girl, he's not a boy, as if this changes the picture completely, he's a girl and he's about the same age as Noga, and the thought of Noga stripped of all her curls, her sweet puppy fat, leaning on the wall and tormenting the neon lights makes me dizzy and I myself lean against the wall, as in an X-ray image I see the colors reversed, the bald head of the boy who's a girl streams darkly like a waterfall at night, and the long neon tubes are deep and hollow as the eye sockets of a skeleton, and in front of me Udi turns black on his wheeled bed, his spine writhes inside his body, vertebra by vertebra, and I see the bitterest of his memories boiling in his blood, tiny sperm tadpoles of doom, and I close my eyes, trying to find rest in the transparent spots engulfing each other in the darkness behind my eyelids.

When I open my eyes Udi is no longer there, and I look around, guilty and worried, where is he, I've abandoned him, and the boy who's a girl looks at me with bulging eyes, and points to the closed door opposite, they've taken him to be X-rayed, and I'm as terrified as if some dangerous surgery is being performed on him behind the door, instead of proving my devotion I abandoned him, exactly when he needed me. Stop trying to prove yourself all the time, Anat would say, can't you see that it's suspicious, what have you done already that you have to keep trying to show that you're a good wife, it only makes him uneasy, and I try to take a deep breath, leaning against the wall and stretching, and my elbow presses the switch by mistake and again the light goes off, exactly when the door opens and Udi's bed is wheeled out, an orderly in a green uniform holds a big envelope in one hand and pushes the bed with the other, and I bring up the rear, suddenly superfluous.

What happened, I ask him, and he says in a hostile tone, what do you think happened, and I try again, what did they say, and he grumbles, nothing, nobody here ever says anything, but there is no bitterness in his voice, only a childish acceptance, and when we return to the emergency room he seems as satisfied as if we're back home, surveying his familiar corner, and I sit down beside him, my hand resting on the X rays, a secret code that will shed light on the mystery threatening us. Let's have a look at them, I propose, trying to make my voice sound full of mischief and adventure, but he, in his new obedience, says, no, they're not meant for us, as if the whole thing is a private affair between the doctor and the nurse, and we're only bystanders, and I can't stand it anymore, I snatch the envelope holding the key to our fate, hug it to my chest and set out to find the doctor.

I would be happy to hear even the nurse's footsteps now, but it seems that we have all been abandoned, like children left without adult supervision, and I go up to the deserted doctors' station and peer into the recesses behind the counter, a mild din can be heard rising from the adjacent room, a buzz of gossip and the smell of fresh coffee, and I approach the almost closed door, in order to fulfil their obligations they have left a narrow crack and I peep through it, the young doctor is chewing a roll with enthusiasm, checking anxiously every now and then to see how much of it is left, the nurse restricts herself to coffee, a few other members of the staff are busy eating and laughing, and I look at them as if they are pictures on a screen, I see them and they don't see me, there is a transparent barrier between us, they are the conquerors, they are the lords of the land and I the least of their subjects. They are in the middle of their ten o'clock coffee break, but for me it's already the middle of the night, I didn't even have a chance to drink a cup of coffee this morning, and the smells make me giddy, but it no more occurs to me to go up and pour myself a cup than it would to join a feast taking place on a movie screen, and I stand and stare, hugging Udi's X-rayed spine, until the doctor notices me and his chewing subsides, is anything wrong, he asks, and I hold the envelope out to him, my eyes hot and imploring, and despite the humiliation, against my will, I feel my lips trembling and I start to cry.

He looks at me flustered, his eyes move back and forth between me and the roll, they all fall silent and look at me, they don't even try to hide their revulsion, and I too am revolted by myself, I wish I could control my tears, but they control me, shaming me in public, lucky Udi can't see me now, he hates it when I cry. Without looking in the mirror I know that my face is red, under my eyes this morning's makeup is running in black tears, and I begin to retreat, trying to hide my disgrace behind the envelope, but the doctor stands up and throws the remainder of his roll into the bin with an accurate aim, his childish face softens as he comes up to me, takes three X rays out of the envelope and examines them opposite the light, and I am afraid to breathe, my eyes are fixed on his face, trying to interpret his expression, to guess the verdict, and then he goes into another room with me trailing behind him, attaches the X rays to an illuminated board and looks sternly into Udi's insides, I can't see any pathology, he says, there's no damage to the spine.

That's good, isn't it, I mumble, and he says, I don't know if it's good or not, we always have to consider the alternative, he can't move his legs, and that's not good. We'll have to hospitalize him for tests, he tells the nurse standing at the door, rapidly listing the names of the tests, it sounds like almost the entire alphabet, and I still wanted to ask him what they were looking for in all these tests, but he has already vanished into one of the rooms, and I can only run after the nurse as she makes straight for Udi's bed, getting there one step ahead of me.

Were you crying, he asks in a hostile voice, and I mumble, of course not, it's just a cold, and the nurse swallows a smile, she doesn't miss a thing, you're going up to the ward, she informs him, and he's taken aback, but a glimmer of pride flashes in his eyes, like a pupil promoted to the next grade, and she's already filling his chart with blue lines, sending me to get the forms signed, and I hurry away, the aging messenger girl of the emergency room, and miss their farewells, because when I return his bed is already standing in the middle of the hall, him looking like some kind of birthday boy, his body covered with the papers and envelopes that have accumulated over the past few hours, like the gifts of generous relatives, and under them all his delicate face peeps out, and perhaps I'm mistaken but it seems to me that between his lips I see the tip of the tail of a secret smile of triumph.

Four

A s we begin our journey to the internal diseases department ambulances drive up at high speed, their sirens wailing in our ears like demanding babies, and we are instantly left to our own devices, all attention turning to the new guest. With embarrassing curiosity I look round to get a glimpse of the new king, and then I see her, on a gurney red with blood, I haven't seen her for years, except in my nightmares, but it's definitely her, it's Geula, and I begin racing with the bed, praying that she won't see me, until I understand, she's half-dead, she wouldn't even recognize her own child now, the veins are cut and the blood's streaming, how would she recognize her own child when another mother is rearing him in her place, little Daniel, with the sharp, peaky face, and all because of me. How many times she threatened, if you take him away from me I'll kill myself, I'll chop my veins into a salad, but we saw the child going crazy, thin as air, covered with blue bruises. She was jealous of him as of a lover, she wouldn't let him go to kindergarten, so that he wouldn't fall in love with the teachers, she hit him if he smiled at another woman, not that I ever saw him smile, she would stand him on a chair and kiss him, pushing her black nicotine tongue into his hollow mouth. We had to save him, we told her to send him to kindergarten, make him food, give him a healthy framework, and she would go berserk, you won't tell me how to bring up my child, clasping him to her like a hostage, if I ever see your mug again I'll kill the kid and off myself. In the end we got a court order, tore him from her body, as in a dangerous birth, and she screamed after me, you think you'll bring your daughter up while I stay without Daniel, you won't have a minute of happiness, and I anguished over it for days, how could I have separated them, and I decided to give up this job, where every decision was right and also wrong and always cruel, and I went to work at the shelter for pregnant girls, and later on I heard that she had tried to appeal, but no court was prepared to give her back her child, and afterward she tried to kill herself, but in that too she failed, and now she's here, after another attempt, pursuing me, the forgotten curses resurrected.

You're crying again, Udi opens one hostile eye, and I can't restrain myself, you remember Geula, whose child was taken away for adoption, they just brought her in, she must have tried to kill herself, and it's all because of me, and he opens his other eye, I always told you that you social workers in that welfare bureau went too far, who did you think you were, God on earth? Waging war on nature? How can you take a child from his mother? And I park the bed angrily next to the wall, we're already far enough away, his reaction infuriates me, but at least it's his from home, familiar to me, not like the new fawning smiles. What are you talking about, I burst out, you and your nature, nature can be horrifying, nature is a catastrophe, that mother destroyed her child, she tortured him, you should have seen his body full of blue bruises, his mouth without any teeth in it.

But she loved him, he declares provocatively, always defending the side under attack, and I say, so what, sick love isn't worth a damn, she drove him insane with that love of hers, and he says resentfully, that's what you used to say to me once, that my love was sick, remember? Nothing interests him unless it's about him, and I try to squeeze a little sympathy out of him, Udi, what does it mean that she's here, it frightens me, it's a bad sign, and he repulses me again, not letting me lean on him even for a minute, what does it mean that I'm here, that's what I'm thinking about, that's what interests me, but not you, you always cared more about all your lame ducks than about me. How can you say such a thing, I protest indignantly, it's so untrue, and already we are surrounded by astonished looks, how can we be fighting here, in the shadow of the dripping infusion, here where we should be united, and I fall silent, leaving Geula behind me, not looking back, able only to guess at the efforts at resuscitation seething around her, the young doctor bending over her dark body full of sorrow and smoke, and when I think of her dangerous love, of her life bitter as poison, I don't know what to wish her.

When I went there he would hide from me like a frightened animal, shut up all day in the dark one-room apartment, with the empty fridge and the brimming ashtrays, once I brought him crayons, and he didn't know what to do with them, in the end he put one in his mouth and started to suck it, and she began to make one of her scenes, what are you bringing him presents for, you want him to fall in love with you, for him to love you more than me, he's mine, get that into you head, not the fucking state's and not the fucking welfare service's, and I would try to explain to her, you're right, Geula, he is yours, but if you don't look after him properly we have to be concerned about him, we're on the child's side, not yours, and she would open her bloodshot eyes wide, me and my kid are on the same side, we're the same body, we're one body, and she would immediately clutch him to her, crushing him to her bony body, you won't tell me how to look after him, and I would leave at a loss, the two possibilities roaring at me in the stairwell, both equally frightening, to take him or leave him, and when I finally decided to recommend adoption, the judge was surprised that I had waited so long. She loves him so much, I tried to defend her, myself, and he said, the question is not whether we love or not, the question is how we love, and I shivered as if he was talking about me, about me and Udi, I had been telling myself for years that he loved me, whereas I should have been asking how he loved me, and whether I liked his love.

And perhaps because I knew the answer I didn't dare go into the question, be happy that you've got a husband who loves you, I would silence myself, it's better to have a love like his than no love at all, but now as we approach the internal diseases department I rebel, why no love at all, why be so defeatist, maybe there is still something out there for me, waiting for me to notice it. You tried once and you saw how it ended, I hurry to put out the little flame, because now it's final and absolute, now our true marriage is taking place, in the shadow of the dripping infusion, because if I haven't been able to leave him up to now, when he was healthy, from now on I'll never be able to leave him, the gates of my life are closed, with no one going in or out, and when I look at myself in the elevator mirror, a stooped figure bending over a narrow bed, with untidy hair and anxious eyes, black makeup smudged around them as if someone punched me in the face, it seems to me that I don't know what to wish myself either.

In the ward we are received with silent indifference, the documents piled on the bed speak for themselves, a cute nurse takes us to the room with the polite expression of a hotel chambermaid on her face, and I am surprised to find a sleepy policeman sitting outside the door, yawning incessantly. I look round apprehensively, what VIP is being guarded here, and to my astonishment I see opposite Udi's bed a handsome youth with long fair hair, fettered with handcuffs to his bed, almost naked, only his leg clothed in bandages, and I ask the nurse, who is he, and she says, he was injured in a fight in jail, but don't worry, he's restrained, and I ask, isn't there another room, and she says, this is the only bed, do you want to lie in the corridor? And I hurry to correct her, I'm not the patient, he is, pointing to Udi lying motionless, his eyes fixed piously on the ceiling, and she persists, you're better off lying here than in the corridor.

Carefully, as if he's a newborn, we hold him and take off his tee-shirt and replace it with a faded pajama jacket, with most of its buttons missing. The nurse's hands are smooth and slender, her nails are manicured, and for a moment I see my hands next to hers and I shudder, the premature sunspots, the lackluster skin, the creased lines of indelible curses engraved by time, and I try to hide my hands, letting her put on his pajama pants alone, the catheter tube hiding modestly in its corner, with a strange indifference I watch her beautiful fingers busying themselves with him, with the body that was mine, which has suddenly been removed from his control and mine, abandoned to the mercies of its new masters, and already his head is resting on the pillow, and his eyes are on the ceiling, ignoring me resentfully, what have I done now, I can't even remember.

I drag up a chair and sit down next to him, my ability to move surprises me for a minute, there are three of us in the room and only I can move, bring a chair, help myself, me of all people, as opposed to all expectations, and perhaps this is what angers him, perhaps he's jealous of the gap that has suddenly yawned between us, unexpected, almost grotesque, jarring as the laughter of fate, and I try to stroke his arm but the sight of my hand disturbs me and I hide them under my thighs, as long as I live I'll never have another pair of hands, or another husband either. Would you like me to bring you something to drink, I ask, and he says, I'm not thirsty, indicating the infusion with his eyes, and I go on, something to eat perhaps? And he says, all I want to do is sleep, Noam, I haven't got any strength, and I immediately soften, he isn't angry with me, he's simply tired, and I put my head on his shoulder, go to sleep, my Udi, I'm here with you, and already his deep, even breathing is covering the words, and a pitiful whine is heard, the whine of a puppy left outside on a rainy night, not from his lips but from the beautiful lips of the prisoner, both of them are asleep, like brothers in their shared room after they have finished fighting.

I steal quietly outside, on tiptoe, even the policeman has abandoned his post, so I can too, and I hurry to the elevator, enjoying the lightness of my movement, only me myself, without a baby carriage, without a hospital bed, I go down to the cafeteria and buy myself a cup of coffee and a roll, sit down with a sigh of relief next to the window, it seems to me that this is the exact same roll the doctor in the emergency room was eating, in the distance I see him entering the cafeteria, and I send him an ingratiating smile, even a woman with a sick husband is entitled to a small pleasure, but he ignores me, I wanted to ask him about Geula, but perhaps it's better not to know, perhaps it wasn't even her, I wanted him to see that I too have a roll in my hand, that I too am a human being, but he doesn't linger, he goes off immediately with a bottle of Coca-Cola, perhaps it isn't even him. I watch his short legs in action, one of them always dancing in the air, he moves with such lightness, and not only him, everyone around me moves their hands and feet as naturally as if they were born walking, and only my Udi, three floors above me, is lying motionless, and again the anxiety rises in my throat, repulsing the mess of chewed roll, as dense and palpable as phlegm, he's sick, a sickness has come and taken him away, drawing him into its fathomless depths.

I pour the rest of the coffee down my throat and run out of the cafeteria, arriving at the ward breathless, Udi is still asleep but the prisoner is writhing on his bed, do me a favor, come and uncuff me, he whispers in a hoarse voice, and I say, I can't, how can I uncuff you, and he says, I know you can, the cop gave you the keys, and I say, no he didn't, I swear he didn't. So what are you doing here, he says resentfully, and I explain, my husband's here, and immediately I inquire sympathetically, what happened to your leg, and to my astonishment he raises his voice, what's it got to do with you, he shouts, who said you could talk to me at all, and I blush hotly, sit down next to Udi and turn my back to him. I hear him call the nurse, this crazy cow is bothering me, get her out of here, and when she arrives, the same polite smile on her face, I make haste to defend myself, as if she's the teacher coming to separate a couple of squabbling pupils, I only asked him what happened to him, and she smiles at me, don't get upset, he yells at anyone who tries to be nice to him, he only knows one language, right, Jeremiah? Where on earth did he get a name like Jeremiah, I wonder, but I don't dare say anything, I hardly dare to breathe, in case I arouse his wrath.

As it turns out, my silence provokes him no less than my speech, and he asks with exaggerated politeness, do you by any chance have a cigarette, and I reply rashly, you're not allowed to smoke here, and he says, who said anything about smoking, I just want a cigarette. I take an old packet of cigarettes out of my bag and hand it to him, and he says angrily, who needs your stinking cigarettes, I don't touch this brand, and I return to my place, hearing him yell, nurse, nurse, I need a cigarette, in a minute I'll open these cuffs and finish off the lot of you. In a minute the policeman will come back and finish you off, the nurse shouts back from the corridor, and he sniggers and turns to me again, what's the matter with your husband? And I say, there's nothing the matter with him, and he laughs, I bet he wanted to get away from you for a bit, but you stick to him like glue here too, let him breathe, or else he'll die in front of your eyes, you can die from nothing too you know, I've seen a lot of people die from nothing.

I steal a look at him, what an appalling trick of God's, to wrap such a warped personality in such angelic beauty, I know I should keep quiet but I can't let it go, there has to be a way to reach him. Look, Jeremiah, I try gently, this is a difficult day for us, my husband's sick, he's come here to get better, I'm worried, don't make it harder for me, and he's silent for a moment as if considering my words, and then he bursts into ugly laughter, I'm making things harder for you?

I was lying here quietly and you came and bothered me with your questions, you think it's easy for me? Tied to the bed like a dog, if my mother saw me now she'd go blind on the spot, and an electric current seems to pass through his body, his snakelike muscles writhe convulsively, trying to get free of the cuffs, and only when the policeman comes in, his paunch preceding him, does he stop twitching and lie quietly like an obedient child, sending me a sullen look from time to time.

Udi is still sunk in his stubborn sleep, why do I suspect him of only pretending to be asleep, taking pleasure in seeing me humiliated, defeated by the hopelessness of the human condition, silently continuing the ancient argument between us, people are garbage, he claims, you're wasting your life on garbage, on the lowest of the low, you'll never reform anyone, you'll never save a single child. You think that if you uproot a child from his home and plant him in a different soil he'll be saved? You can't deceive nature, your pretensions are absurd, outrageous, you people need to reconcile yourselves to nature, accept it. Time after time he would go out on his hikes, sometimes completely alone, sleeping in tents in all kinds of godforsaken places, returning with shining eyes, for three days I didn't see a soul, he would tell me proudly, as if he'd succeeded in evading a dangerous enemy. He never complained about floods, sandstorms, insect bites, he accepted it all with understanding, as part of an intimate dialogue between him and nature, while I sank deeper and deeper in flesh and blood, and it seems to me that he is listening now to this conversation and glowing with an inner smile of triumph, and I rest my head on the edge of his bed, overcome with weariness as if I have been defeated in battle, and as in a dream I hear the conversation being conducted behind my back, it has the logic of a dream, an absurd, threatening, iron logic, either his remand has to be extended or he has to be released, the policeman explains to the nurse, they've just called me and said we have to bring a judge to the hospital to extend the remand, otherwise it's illegal.

What do you mean released, says the nurse in alarm, leave him here without restraints? It's dangerous, there are sick people here, and the policeman says, we can't break the law, if a judge doesn't come by two o'clock to extend his remand we have to release him, and I look at my watch, it's already midday, Noga will be home soon, I have to get there before her, explain what happened, but how can I leave him here, torn between the two of them as usual, which one needs me more, as if I have two husbands. Why did we come here in the first place, where we're even more defenseless than at home, vulnerable and exposed to harm, and again my head drops exhausted to the bed, I know I have to get up now and go to Noga or at least call her on the phone, but it seems to me that the emotion has drained out of my body and without it I'm nonexistent, a random collection of organs, and I remember the mothers that came to the children's house to visit their children who had already been taken away from them, and smiled stiff, detached smiles, because they knew that the moment of parting was near and they were tired of struggling, and in fact they wanted to get it over with already, they were already longing for the freedom that lay in the total petrifaction of their overflowing emotions, for the terrifying happiness of renunciation.

I know that at this very moment she's knocking at the door, and then looking in her satchel for the key, pulling out crumpled notebooks, her pencil case opens and falls down the stairs, spilling all its contents, crayons and pencils and gnawed erasers, where's the key, she's already in tears, she knocks again, Mommy, Daddy, where are you? Finally she finds it, right at the bottom, and pulls it out in relief, and enters the empty house, no note is waiting for her on the table, no meal in the fridge, but I observe her calmly, let's see what she does next, my pampered daughter. What's happening to me, in a moment I've turned to stone, his legs are paralyzed and my heart is, and now he wakes up, his mouth gapes in a yawn, what's the time, he asks, trying to squint at his watch, what about Noga, we have to get in touch with her, precisely when I'm indifferent he shows re-sponsibility, and I say, I just thought of it myself, and suddenly I'm horrified by a wild cry, Daddy!

I look at the prisoner but his mouth is closed and only his glittering eyes roam restlessly round the room, and I hear the thud of panic-stricken footsteps, racing from room to room, who are you looking for, little girl, somebody asks, and she cries, my father, and here's her face in the doorway, her wide-open face, her grape-green eyes bulging in agitation, Daddy what happened to you, she shouts, falling on his still body, ignoring the tubes attached to it, ignoring me, and he tries to hug her but he can hardly move his hands, it's all right, they're only keeping me here for tests, everything will be all right. I pull her to me and put her on my lap, my baby, how did you get here, how did you manage to find us, I was just going to phone, and she sobs, the downstairs neighbor told me an ambulance came to take Daddy, she called a taxi for me and I came here by myself, there's a note of pride in her childish voice, the driver was really nice, he came with me to the information desk, and I say, you must be hungry, let's go downstairs and I'll buy you something to eat, and she shakes her head, no, I won't eat anything until Daddy gets better, overshadowing me in her absolute devotion, holding his hand, while he looks at her with interest, as if he's seeing her for the first time, his fingers stroking her hand with difficulty, and suddenly we're united, like we once were, a united family, waiting tensely for the tests, and all the time the prisoner is watching us with mocking eyes, and I pray, just let him lie there quietly, don't let him frighten her, but he refuses to keep quiet.

Don't worry, little girl, there's nothing wrong with your fa-ther, he says in a surprisingly gentle voice, and she asks him in her innocence, really, are you sure? As if he's the supreme medical au-thority, and he says, you bet, you can trust me, I've seen everything in life, there's nothing wrong with him, he's fine, but if I was you I'd be worried about your mother. Don't pay any attention to him,

Noga, I whisper, he doesn't know what he's talking about, but he goes on, who do you want to die, your mother or your father? And she says in alarm, neither of them, not my father or my mother, and he says, this is life, kid, not a fairy tale, in life one person in every family has to die, so that the others will live, haven't you heard? She looks at him in horror, timidly objecting, but his confidence defeats her. Really? she whispers, and he says, sure, sometimes it's actually the child, like in our family, I sacrificed myself for my mother, he announces proudly, I let my father kill me, and she gets off my lap and advances slowly toward him, but you're alive, she says in bewilderment, and he burst out laughing as if he's just heard a joke, you think I'm alive, ask your mother, she'll tell you I'm dead, and I whisper to Udi, do something, make him shut up, he's driving her crazy. Raise my bed, he requests, and I turn the handle until he's almost sitting, looking in surprise at the gorgeous youth handcuffed to the bed, just ignore him, he whispers, don't let him upset you, and Noga wails, is it true what he says, that one of us will die? And Udi says, nonsense, he's just trying to attract attention, and the young man, who is listening with interest, says bitterly, I want to attract attention? Maybe it's you who wants attention, have you thought of that?

I get up and draw the curtain around us, why didn't I do it before, and we crowd between the folds, his rude laughter reaching us, it won't help you, he says hoarsely, you know I'm right, I'm always right, that's why my father wanted to kill me, I wish I was ever wrong. When are they going to take him away from here, Udi asks, and I whisper, I have no idea, I understand that soon they'll have to take off the handcuffs, if a judge doesn't come to extend his remand, and then an unfamiliar nurse invades our tent, you have to go for a CAT scan, she says sternly, as if she's caught him idling instead of taking his tests, and he looks at her in confusion, he seems to have forgotten for a moment where he is, where his paralyzed legs have led him now.

There's no need for you to come with the child, she says as I straighten up, he has a lot of tests to do, I'll see that somebody takes him down, and in a moment an empty wheelchair arrives and a vigorous young male nurse picks Udi up as easily as if his bones were hollow, and we remain in the room alone with the prisoner, as if it's him we've come to visit, and soon the policeman comes in with the news that the judge can't come, they have to release him. Do what you like, the nurse says from the doorway, as long as you get him out of here, and the policeman says, I can't do that, from the minute he's released he's no longer in our custody, and the nurse asks whose custody is he in then, who does he belong to, and the policeman says, who does she belong to, pointing at me with a thick finger, who do you belong to, he belongs to himself, exactly like you. Does he have a family, the nurse asks hopefully, we'll have to get in touch with his family and tell them to come and get him, and to everyone's surprise he begins to cry, don't call my parents, just not my parents. But Jeremiah, says the nurse, we've already taken care of your wound, you'll be discharged from the hospital soon, someone has to come and bring your clothes, you arrived here from the detention cell with nothing, don't you remember, you don't want to leave the hospital in pajamas, do you, and he says, why should I leave here at all, my wound isn't healed yet, you're throwing me out without giving me a chance to get better, if she had a wound like this, he points at me with his chin, you'd let her stay here for weeks.

Let's go downstairs, Nogi, I say, we'll get something to eat in the cafeteria, but she clings to the empty bed, I'm staying here till Daddy comes back, she announces, clutching the sheet the way she used to cling to her baby blanket, and I plead, Nogi, I'm suffocating here, let's go and get a bit of air, but she insists, we have to stay here for Daddy to get better, and I say with some irritation, it doesn't depend on us, I wish it did.

So why do I feel that it does, she says, frightening me with her certainty, and I give in, all right, if that's the way you feel, but at least let me bring you something, you must be hungry, and she says, I'm not eating anything till Daddy gets better, and I look round in despair, there's nothing more I can do, except hope the time passes quickly, and we wait for him again, like we always do, waiting for him to come home from his trips, tired and dusty, and rejoin our daily lives, for him to talk to us, eat with us, but he's always hungry an hour before mealtimes, or an hour later, and the moment Noga comes home from school he falls asleep, and when she goes to bed he wakes up, eluding us with his resistant presence, increasing her hunger, and I still wonder if he's chosen to evade us in order not to fail again, or if it's a punishment, and who it's intended for, is he punishing me, or himself, for what happened then, almost eight years ago. What was it like before then, I scarcely remember, the years have turned the past into a vague flux, suffused with a golden light and full of reconciliation, baby Noga in his arms, peeping over his shoulder as white as a snowy mountaintop, all his shirts have turned white with her vomit, sucking the warm milk from my breast and burping it onto him, mixing us together, his lips whispering in her ear, talking to her in baby talk, making her dance in his arms, as if her first years with us were one long dance of milk and honey.

In that first winter, the three of us in one room, in one bed, the heater on all the time, and if I went out for a moment the cold in the rest of the house was stunning, as if it were another country, and I would run back and jump into bed, to find Noga lying on his naked stomach, a blissful smile on her face, and I would rest my head on his arm and my hand on her tiny, diapered bottom, sheltered by the shadow of his love for her, falling asleep in a swoon of warmth and sweetness. Like polished mirrors we reflected our love for her to each other, doubling and tripling it, sparks of this love shining on us too, and I was so overcome, so grateful for the warmth of his fatherhood that I became utterly dependent on him, when he left the house I was helpless, I almost turned into a baby myself in her first months, and he was joyful, ardent, murmuring lullabies into my ear, patting my back. Wherever all this abundance had been hiding, it burst out suddenly in her honor, in honor of the little family we had become, close and dependent, isolated as a forgotten tribe, hiding our treasure as if it were stolen. Sometimes friends knocked at the door with belated gifts in their hands and we didn't let them in, because the secret bond between us was so perfect that it could only be spoiled by the outside world, and for months I lacked for nothing, fawning on the two of them as if they were my mother and father who had come back to live together again, because I'd been a good girl.

For years I haven't dared to think of those days, and now they choke me with their concentrated sweetness, nausea rises in my throat, how did his eager hands, which held her in the bath every evening, soaping her smiling little body, brimful of milk, how did they let her slip limply from the porch, and afterward, when almost by a miracle she recovered, I wouldn't let him touch her anymore, I didn't dare to leave them alone, a pitful of venom was dug between us, and she was on my side, I conquered her for myself, the country of her white flesh. To my surprise he gave up in disgrace, he didn't try to fight for her, without consulting me he abandoned his studies in the middle of writing his doctoral thesis and started attending a course for tour guides, leaving home to go on long trips, returning indifferent and estranged, his arms empty of embraces, and when I steal a glance at her sensitive face, her huge eyes fixed tensely on the empty hospital bed, as if she sees terrifying visions there, I wonder how much of all this she knows. What does she remember of her first two years, we never told her about the fall, does she know how much she lost then, fighting all the time for his heart, like a woman whose man has left her, does she know that once all his love was given to her alone?

Stop blaming yourself, Anat would say, sick of hearing me lamenting all the time, if I hadn't fallen in love with that man it would never have happened, I ruined all our lives with that stupid affair, what impertinence, what arrogance to fall in love, and she would scold me, what did you do that was so terrible, why do you think that you deserve such a harsh punishment, and I know that she's wrong, I know that Udi was completely devastated, and everything was ruined, because of what I did Noga lost him, because of what I did we have no more children. You're not responsible for his reaction, Anat would say impatiently, so what if you had a little fling, it's not a crime, you only live once, you never even went to bed with him. But I wanted to go to bed with him, you have no idea how much I wanted to, on that morning that I had described to her over and over again, and she would sigh, wanting doesn't count, for wanting you don't pay such a price.

Light as if I had just been born again I would hurry to him, leaving Noga with my mother and racing down the long street, where just before the bend in the road the gloomy building awaited me, with the studio apartment on the roof full of paints and canvases and a strong smell of turpentine. He opens the door, a paintbrush in his hand and his eyes narrowed, like a nearsighted person trying to read an important road sign from a distance, and although he doesn't say anything I know that he's glad to see me, pointing with his paintbrush to the armchair waiting for me and hurrying to the kitchen, the Turkish coffee in the long-handled little beaker swelling and subsiding as if blown by the wind, and the place fills with the aroma, and the hot little cup is already in my hands, thawing my fingers. He sets the canvas on the easel and begins moving backward and forward, looking at me with his frank eyes, and then he comes up to me and touches my hair, do you have a rubber band, he asks, and I rummage in my bag and find a clip, but he isn't satisfied, he pulls a broad red ribbon out of a drawer and ties it round my head, now we can see your neck, he says, why do you hide it, you've got a neck like a swan, and I sit up straight and stretch my neck, I've never felt so beautiful, and perhaps beauty isn't the issue, what I feel is new, completely new. His brush wipes away layers of frustration, depression and anxiety, creates me anew as I have always wanted to be, a quiet, noble swan, tall and proud, I can sense my body coming back to me from a distant land, sailing on cold blue rivers, this body that was Udi's and then Noga's and is now return-ing to me to be mine.

You want to see, he asks, and I go up to the canvas, how lovely, I exclaim, his colors are clear and deep, the red ribbon merges with my hair, surrounds it like a royal crown, and he stands behind me, his breath on my neck, more coffee? And I answer regretfully, no, I have to get back to Noga, reluctantly removing the crown from my head, bidding farewell to tranquility. Will you come tomorrow, he asks, and I say, we'll have to see, and he smiles, it's okay, I'll be here, you don't have to let me know, and I know that he will always open the door with quiet happiness, with the brush in his hand, and his eyes narrowed, that he'll always be alone among his paints, and I'm already waiting for tomorrow morning, but Noga wakes up burning with fever, and I clasp her to my breasts, stifling my disappointment, she's burning with fever and I with longing, and Udi comes home in the evening worried, how's my little darling, he asks and bends over her, kissing her forehead. The doctor said it's flu, I report im-patiently, and he takes a doll he bought on the way home out of his briefcase, and together they immerse themselves in their game, the dolly's sick, he says, she can't go out until she's better. The next morning I say to him, stay with her for a bit, I have a few errands to do, and I run down his street, look at the building but don't dare go up, I examine the big window, I can almost hear his rhythmic steps going backward and forward, and then I drop in to the greengrocer's and return home with a few oranges. She needs vitamin C, I say, and furiously squeeze orange after orange, and she pleads with him, Daddy stay with us, and he kisses her on her orange lips, if only I could stay with you, sweetheart, I'll come back this evening and by then I want the dolly to be well.

After a few days her fever goes down and I dress her warmly and take her out, even though Udi said she should stay home a day or two longer, my mother gives me a worried look but I don't hang around, I'll come back for her in an hour and a half, I say and hurry off, the desire to see him is already raging inside my body, and I stand panting in front of the door that always opens quickly to let me in, but this time it stays shut. Disappointed, I lean against the cold stair rail, unable to bear his absence, and then a faint noise alerts me, awakening hope, and the door opens hesitantly, it isn't him, I hardly recognize him, a dark stubble covers his cheeks, his hair is rumpled, his pants hang sloppily open, a black undershirt exposes a broad chest and full arms I never imagined. I woke you up, I say in alarm, are you ill? And he smiles, I'm fine now, I'm glad you came, and I try to explain, I wanted to come before, but Noga was sick, and he waves his hand dismissively, you don't have to explain anything to me, I'm glad you're here, sit down, I'll be dressed in a minute, and I sink into the armchair, the blinds are drawn, but even in the gloom I am astonished to see my eyes examining me from the wall, confident and clear. Dozens of gray eyes surround me, and I get up and switch on the light and go from canvas to canvas, one after the other they cover the walls, big and small and medium-sized, and my face is on all of them, my hair swept back, my smile reserved, regal, and in the corner of the room I see myself standing naked, leaning on the wall, tall and slender, and I go up to examine the painting, as excited as if it can tell me something about myself that I didn't know.

He coughs behind my back, puts a hesitant hand on my neck. Don't be angry, he says, and I recoil, why should I be angry, you're free to paint whatever you like, I say, and he laughs in relief, that's what I've been doing all week, painting what I like, you didn't come so I painted you from memory, and already he's in the kitchen blowing into the beaker, and I watch his movements anxiously, as he stirs the coffee, as he sprinkles sugar into it, I've never asked myself what he does when I'm not there, his whole existence was confined to those thrilling mornings with me, and now he leaves me no choice, and I sit down in the armchair, embarrassed, and he stands in front of me, without a paintbrush in his hand, utterly exposed without his weapon, and asks in a hoarse voice, do you want to go or stay?

Aren't you sick of painting me, I ask, and he says, on the contrary, the deeper you go the more interesting it becomes, when I studied painting we would draw the same model every day for three years, from year to year it grew more thrilling, and he takes a paintbrush and looks at me and at the paintings on the walls, but the canvas remains empty as if my presence disturbs him, and I look at the red roofs, fields of roofs flowering beneath us, not far from there I could make out our building, at the bottom of the neighborhood, and then I look at him, he's wearing a white sweater with holes in it over his black undershirt, and for the first time I notice that he's a little stooped, like his building, and his nape is covered with gray curls, and the brush is trembling in his hand, and I hear myself ask, do you want me to get undressed?

He nods wordlessly and leaves the room, and I take my clothes off in mounting excitement, folding them neatly like at the doctor's, and when he comes in I ask, why did you go out, and he says, I don't like to watch a present being opened, I want to see everything at once, and he looks at me with grave attention, limb by limb, and it seems to me that he's disappointed and I quickly apologize, my body's more beautiful in your paintings, and he says, perhaps, but less interesting, I'm not looking for beauty, and he takes the nude painting and rips it up in front of my astonished eyes. Don't be alarmed, he laughs, that's what I do with most of my paintings when I realize how superficial they are, now that I see you I understand how wrong I was, and he turns his back to me and begins to mix the paints, a huge canvas is waiting for him on the easel and he steps backward and forward, completely concentrated, feverishly changing brushes, and I relax in the armchair, the shame gradually leaving me, like a bad memory that suddenly seems trivial, and I examine my thighs, white, almost transparent, tired, smiling at them forgivingly, filled with compassionate generosity, forgiving time, that tower of years like building blocks stacked one on top of the other until the tower collapses, and Noga is always disappointed, why did it fall, why do all the towers fall in the end?

On the canvas in front of me a painful sweetness spreads, winking at me with orange eyes, biting my nipples, and he massages them on the canvas, his lips pursed, bringing them to points with his brush, sweeping down with strong stokes to my pelvis, setting my pubic hair on fire, the paint pours down my thighs, and I am heavy with desire, parting my knees, making room for him, let him come to me now, take off his trousers and fill the aching hollow gaping inside me. I lower my eyes and see his feet approaching me, delicate, feminine feet, and he raises my face to him, dips the brush in water and wipes it on his sweater, staining its whiteness with a ruddy memory, and already he's sending shivers down my neck, sliding down to my breasts, circling giddily round my nipples, painting transparent whirlpools on my nakedness, faster and faster, my whole naked body is one big ring, as if a stone has been thrown into water, a precious gemstone, I'll never be able to retrieve it from the depths, and the soft hairs of the brush caress my pubic hairs, merging with them into one sweet strong flame, breathing in and out, and all the time his face is tight with concentration, seeking a rare color that can barely be seen by the eyes of the flesh, until he hides his face from me, resting it with a sigh on my lap.

Wayward hairs grow on the back of his neck, gray under the line of his haircut, and it seems to me that he's whispering something into my lap, I can't make it out, I put my finger on his lips, what did you say? But he gets up in silence and goes to stand opposite the big window, pulling me behind him, and I stand next to him, leaning my languid limbs on him, and we look out of the window at the roofs, and the narrow curving road, people are hurrying along it, bundled up in raincoats. Suddenly it starts raining hard, lashing the asphalt, and a young man stops, looks in surprise at the cloud bursting right above his head, he hasn't even got a coat, only a brightly striped sweater, just like Udi's, he looks up at the source of the rain and his astonished eyes pierce my shining nakedness, flickering like a candle in the window at the top of the building, and I go rigid, a cardboard cutout on the diabolic firing range of chance, as if I've been electrocuted by his gaze, as accurate as the hand of a sniper who never misses. It's Udi hurrying home to play with Noga, Udi with a bag of oranges in his hand, vitamin C for her red throat, and I fall blindly on clothes that have lost their identity, trying to push a trembling foot into a shirtsleeve, and he seats me on the armchair, his face lengthening sorrowfully, and dresses me like a child, kneeling to tie my shoelaces, and then he picks me up and supports me downstairs, until the cold air outside hits me like a burn on my exposed face, how imaginary is the difference between cold and heat, and the rain jumps on my head as I run home, with a mouth full of explanations, pleas and promises, falling and getting up again, but he won't be there.

Here's Daddy, Noga shouts and runs toward him, and I raise my eyes and see him in the doorway, wheeled to us in a wheelchair, his face drooping, falling sideways, gray and haggard, as if old age has snared him in his absence, and I get up quickly, bend down to him as to a toddler in a stroller, how did it go, Udigi? And he mumbles, they'll only get the results in the morning, his whole body shrinking as if in humiliation, and I ask sympathetically, did it hurt, and he says, no, it was just unpleasant, and Noga announces proudly, Daddy, I'm not going to eat anything until you get better, and he smiles with slack lips, indifferently acknowledging her sacrifice.

Udi, tell her to eat, I protest, tell her you'll only get better if she eats, but he stares at us as if our logic is strange and alien to him, as if he doesn't understand our language. A kick of loneliness makes me recoil, he isn't with us, he's already in another world, and

I watch them putting him in bed, covering him with a blanket, I hear him say, Na'ama, go home, I want to sleep, and Noga protests, but Daddy, who'll be with you, I want to be with you, and he sighs, all I want is to sleep, I don't need anyone when I'm sleeping, if I need anything I'll call you, and I who wanted so badly to get away find it difficult now to accept the harsh sentence, even from his sickbed he banishes us, we'll be cast out forever. Udigi, I try, maybe later Noga will go to my mother and I'll come back to you, and he says, there's no need, it's easier for me alone now, truly, until we get the results I prefer to be alone, it's not against you, he tries to placate me, and I sigh, but not *for* me either. Noga kisses him warmly on his cheek, Daddy Ugi, she whispers to him, like when she was a baby, I want you to get out of bed tomorrow and walk like before, okay? And I bend down and kiss him on his narrow lips, I love you Udigi, you'll see how happy we'll be when you get better, and he nods impatiently, his dry hair sending electricity through my hand.

In the doorway I put my arm around her shoulders and we look back at him sadly, it seems that he's gone to sleep already, and we walk defeated down the corridor, next to the nurses' room Jeremiah waves at us enthusiastically. Have you got a cigarette, he shouts, and I say, no, I haven't, and he comes up to us, still almost naked, I'm free, he announces, just like you, they've gone to get me clothes and shoes from some storeroom, but I haven't got anywhere to go.

What about your mother, I ask, dragged into a conversation again against my will, and he says, my mother won't let me come home, maybe I can come to your house, he asks suddenly, while your husband's here you must have room in the house, take me with you, he begs, I haven't got anywhere to go, and Noga tugs at my sleeve, why don't we take him, Mommy, as if we're talking about a stray cat. Have you gone completely mad, I whisper, the boy's not right in the head, he needs special care, can't you see? And he pursues us, a frightening Tarzan with a loincloth of torn pajama pants, I'll come, you'll see, he yells, I'll follow you home, and I say, I'm sorry,

Jeremiah, we live in a small apartment, there's no room for you, and he shouts, soon you'll have plenty of spare room in your house, and I push Noga into the elevator, the doors close opposite his clenched fist, but his curse has invaded the empty elevator and it reverberates there, beating against the silver walls, soon you'll have plenty of spare room in your house.

Five

All night long I held her close in the big bed, and we slept very little, dropping off and waking up in feverish delirium, nightmare slaps hitting our faces, and between them pockets of happy wonder, look, something's happening, something's happening at last in this life where I thought nothing would ever change, and then condemning fists punch my ribs, the ceiling bends over me with a sullen scowl, in a minute it will cover us like a concrete blanket, bury us beneath it, and I raise my hands, trying to stop it from collapsing, and Noga mumbles, what are you doing, Mommy, and I rouse myself, with a feeling of relief I see the ceiling lift, and immediately I sink again, before my eyes his tests whirl giddily, terrifying details that only in the morning will join together in the verdict, for good or ill. The test tubes red with his frothing blood, the pale shadows of his bones, slices of his back, the recesses of his brain, the dim masses of his muscles and nerves, all this fateful potpourri uniting now against us both like a cruel conspiracy that must be frustrated before morning, and I pray, please don't let them find anything, just something that can be easily cured, ready for new vows, new penances to undertake as long as he gets better, and then sleep snatches me into a savage journey, fierce and violent as a sandstorm, and throws me back even more exhausted onto the bed, opposite Noga's open eyes, were you sleeping, Mommy? And I mumble with a mouth full of dust, no, I'm watching over you. Do you think Daddy's sleeping now, she asks, and I say, yes, I'm sure he is, you sleep too my little girl, and she asks, what will happen if Daddy can never walk again, and before I can reply she falls asleep and wakes up immediately, Mommy I'm hungry, and I get up heavily to make her a sandwich but she refuses to eat, I'll only eat when Daddy's better.

At the entrance to the school, which is fenced in like a pen, I say good-bye to her, to the wayward curls that seem to have shrunk in hunger, drooping limply round her face, to her eyes shining with a dry fire of obstinacy and weakness, I watch her walk alone, groups of children pass her, exchanging giggles and secrets, no one stops next to her, to let her drown her troubles in his. With a heavy heart I continue on my way, on my right I see the ruined café again, white smoke rising from it, dense and curly, workers in pale overalls drift about like angels, weapons of destruction in their hands, to flatten everything, to leave nothing behind. For years I would pass the café in embarrassment, seeking his delicate feet, his white sweater full of holes, with the red stain, his face I could barely remember, seeking not in order to find, like a letter not intended to be sent but nevertheless written with concentration and feeling and care. I never saw him again, as if he never left his house again, bringing the painting up to date, season after season, year after year, adding the traces of the ravages of time, spotting the hands, thickening the flabby thighs, muddying the complexion, darkening the skin around the eyes, and I go past dark and elusive as a shadow, burying my face in the pavement, so he won't see me, and stealing secret glances, it's him, it isn't him, what does he look like at all, one minute every man I see looks like him, and the next I'm sure that even if he walks right past me I won't recognize him, I never really looked at him, I never allowed his features to be engraved on my memory, I never allowed his words to reach my ears, what did he whisper into my lap then, his breath melting the sweet syllables so that they poured onto the soft skin, warm and sticky.

The traffic light changes while I am still staring at the white smoke, my fantasies merging hazily into it as if it is meant for me, a dense curtain over my eyes, separating me from the road signs of reality, and I wait for a signal from the cars next to me, to make sure that I really have to go on driving now, to advance to the verdict, what vows can I still make that I didn't make then, eight years ago, when Noga lay unconscious, I swore that I would never see him again, that I would never fall in love again, what more can I promise now so that Udi will get well, and I can hear Anat's weary laughter already, who needs your sacrifices, who'll profit from your suffering, and I argue with her silently, if it doesn't help, it won't do any harm, and she says, it will do harm, it will harm you, can't you see? And I don't see anything now, sticking stubbornly to the car in front of me, as if it holds my salvation, the white smoke from the café accompanying me all the way like an ominous train, confusing my vows.

In the shadow of the hills I park, far from the hospital, as if I am on my way to a picnic in the bosom of nature, a moment before summer pounces on the mountains with unsheathed claws, they are still covered in a mantle of innocent green, in a few days' time an army of yellow uniformed thorns will defeat it, and after that the fires will come and spread their black blanket everywhere, upsetting the balance in one blazing night. I gulp the sharp morning air, trying to adjure the trees and the grass, advancing slowly, step by step, and already my feet are hurting, I'm not pampering myself, I would always counter Udi's suspicions, it really hurts. He runs on ahead and I trail behind him, insulted, wait for me, but he shoots forward like an arrow, long and pointed, unable to stop after being sent on its way. What will happen to him now, how will he be able to live without his legs, he needs them more than anything else, I would give mine up for him, they're not worth much anyway, and already I imagine myself quiet and noble in a wheelchair, moving from room to room with a melancholy whisper, and tears of sorrow for myself well in my eyes just as I walk into the ward, it doesn't seem to be the same ward at all, all the faces are different, or maybe it's just their expressions, like a landscape that looks completely different in summer and in winter. The nurse with the beautiful hands walks past me, and I ask her tensely, how's Udi, and she says, he's fine, but her look is reserved, as if an unpleasant rumor about me has just reached her ears, and I try to ignore it, have the doctors seen him yet, I ask, and she stops me at the door to the room, you can't go in now, and I recoil, the curtain is drawn round his bed, a heavy shadow leans over him, is he being examined?

Yes, the psychiatrist is examining him, she says reluctantly, sending me a stinging look, and I exclaim in alarm, why, what has he done? Her suspicion immediately wraps me in an obscure guilt, and she says, the doctors will explain, I don't know exactly, and she abruptly turns her neck in a different direction and disappears, and I sit down outside the room, my legs stretched in front of me, threatening to snarl the busy traffic in the corridor. Why a psychiatrist of all things, what did they find, the remnants of any certainty I still possessed crumble between my fingers, Udi would never agree to go to any kind of therapy, together or alone, why should he ask to see a psychiatrist now, and why did she look so reserved, yesterday she was so sympathetic, when we undressed him with four solicitous hands, and today she's avoiding me as if I've committed a crime, and I peek into the room again, a sad old man is lying on Jeremiah's bed, attached to tubes, his face fills with life when he sees me, he thinks someone is coming to visit him, but it immediately empties in disappointment, what does he know that I don't, everything that happened here since yesterday afternoon is hidden from me and revealed to him, the stranger.

I look resentfully at the thin curtain, trying to pick up some key word, what secrets are they telling there, how come I'm suddenly excluded from his world, everyone knows more about him than I do, he doesn't belong to me anymore, he belongs to the disease, and all these people, the nurses, the doctors, even the old man, are his new in-laws, the family of the bride, and in them he confides, revealing his most cherished secrets to them, and I return to my place on the chair at the door, where the policeman sat yesterday, his treachery burning my back, as if a flaming orgy is taking place behind the curtain.

The man who finally emerges from the room doesn't give me a glance, he's tall and broad, a giant, thick gray hair covering his head and thick glasses on his eyes, his back as square as an empty blackboard turned to me as he makes haste to disappear, they all have the same amazing capacity, these relations of the disease, to suddenly melt away, agile and elusive, leaving a train of bewildered insult behind them, and I enter the room, the old man sits up expectantly again and then falls back disappointed onto his pillow, but Udi doesn't move at all, surrounded by his tent, as on his hikes, and I part the curtain with hard brightness, Udigi, what's new, and he answers me with a miserable smile, his face stunned and bewildered, like Noga's. What did they find in the tests, the question escapes me in a shrill squeak, I rehearsed it so often last night that now I lose control, and he says, nothing at this point, and I breathe a sigh of relief, I feel as if I'm drinking water at last after a long thirst and it streams through my veins, bearing a message of comfort from organ to organ. That's wonderful, I say carefully, so everything's all right then? And he says, but my legs aren't all right, and then a frightened whimper suddenly escapes him, they want to transfer me to the psychiatric department, he wails, and I put my arms around him with a feeling of dread, his body under the pajamas is cold and thin, almost that of a stranger.

Why, I ask, why there of all places? And he groans, because they can't find anything wrong, don't you understand, all the tests are fine but my legs aren't fine, and I remember the square blank back, the hasty steps, I won't let them have him, I'll take him out of here, his personality is unique, complex, I haven't succeeded in deciphering it in a lifetime, so how will they succeed in a single day, I have to get him out of here before they destroy him. How are your hands, I ask, and he moves his fingers slowly, a little better, he says, and I fill with happy confidence, then your legs will come right too, you'll see, the important thing is that they didn't find anything serious, all you need is rest, we'll pamper you at home and in a few days it will be all right. Suddenly everything is clear to me, a bright light illuminates the threatening laboratories with their test tubes full of blood and germs trapped in cultures, the X-ray tubes whirling in the CT tunnels, suddenly a knot has been untied, if the body's healthy I can handle the mind.

Why don't I take you out for a while, with the bed, it's such a lovely day, I suggest brightly, and he hesitates, I don't know, the light bothers me, and at that moment the nurse comes into the room, with a number of stern-faced white gowns in her wake, and she says to me, please leave the room, and I protest, I want to understand what's going on here, why doesn't anyone explain it to me, he's my husband, I'm his wife, I add to emphasize the banal words which fall from my mouth to the floor, cheeping feebly at the doctors' feet like baby birds, unable to rise, but the doctors gather round his bed, ignoring me, and only the youngest, who came in last, says to me, wait outside, after the visit someone will talk to you.

I get up tensely and retreat to the door, why did I bring him here, it's not for him, I have to rescue him, and already I'm imagining how I'll smuggle him out of here, wheel him secretly to the car, separate him from the disease, push it out of our lives, and then the phone rings in the depths of my bag and I hear Anat's voice, where are you, she complains, we need you here, Galya gave birth the day before yesterday, and she won't stop crying, you have to come and talk to her, and I say, I can't come, Udi's in the hospital, I let Hava know yesterday, but Anat is clearly not impressed, you can leave him for half an hour, nothing will happen, you have to talk to her or it will end badly, and at that moment I see them emerging from the room, a crowded delegation, impermeable as a secret sect, and I run after them, tug at the gown of the one bringing up the rear, tell me what's the matter with him, and he mutters reluctantly, we're not sure yet, it looks like conversive paralysis. What paralysis, I ask, and he says, conversive, when the body converts mental stress into a physical problem, a conversive reaction, and he looks round apprehensively as if he's just disclosed a closely guarded secret, and hurries off to join the delegation, leaving me with the new word. So that's what she's called, his new woman, conversion, I taste the letters, dark smells rise from it, the smell of torture dungeons in the distant past, the screams of terrified converts, forced to change their religion, to accept the creed of a foreign faith, but what does it mean exactly, and how long will it last, and how does it go away, I think I once learned about this phenomenon, but I scarcely remember, and all the time I can hear Anat's voice throbbing in my hand, gagged by my fist, Na'ama, she cries, you have to come, everything we invested in her is going down the drain, and I turn off the phone and push it back into my bag, closing the clasp on poor fifteen-year-old Galya with her gigantic belly, and hurry into the room.

What did they say, I ask, maybe he knows more than I do, but he seems less interested than I am in the diagnosis, they hardly spoke, they ran through all the results of the tests and examined my legs again. I managed to move them a bit, he adds proudly, look, and indeed I can see a feeble movement in his feet, like a breeze blowing between his toes, and I ask, so what happens now, what are they waiting for, and he whispers, they want to see if there's any improvement in the next few hours, and if there isn't they're transferring me to the psychiatric department, and I hold his hand, Udi you have to make an effort, concentrate, you have to, and he says, I know, I'm trying, and at last I feel that we're together, that we have a common goal, we're fighting side by side, not in opposite camps.

Do you want to go outside for a bit, I ask again, and he shakes his head, no, I want to rest, you go down if you like, and I ask, should I bring you a paper, and he says, no, not a newspaper, have you got a book with you? And I say, no, nothing, and then I remember, yesterday I put your Bible in your bag, and his face lights up at the sight of the shabby book that accompanies him on all his trips, once Noga yelled at him, why do you take it with you and not me, and she threw it on the floor and trampled on it, and I think of her anxiously, she hasn't eaten a thing, you know, I could hardly make her drink chocolate milk this morning, but he's already turning the pages, she'll be all right, one day's fast won't hurt her, and his face relaxes as he immerses himself in the ancient stories. I'm going down for a minute to have a cup of coffee, I say quickly and leave the room, but I don't go to the cafeteria, I go to the car parked in the shadow of the mountains. He won't know that I paid a hasty visit to the shelter, even though he's the one that disappears for days on end, he still allows himself to relate to my work with hostility, as if it's at our expense, as if I'm more committed to the miserable, lonely women with the secret swelling inside their bellies than I am to him.

From the outside it looks like any other house, our shelter, nobody could guess how different it is, and I go in quickly, Anat comes out of one of the rooms to meet me, as always with jeans and a white shirt on her lean body, cropped gray hair round a clean face, which always looks as if it has just been washed in soap and cold water, everything about her is straight and spare, not like my waste-fulness, with my long hair that takes up so much space, and full lips, and round face, and she says, it's great you came, and she doesn't ask about Udi, and I hold back from telling her, because we're no longer friends. Whenever I see her this fact takes me by surprise again, the fact that our friendship is over, it ended one morning, a few months ago, when I came to work with my eyes red from crying, after a quarrel with Udi, and I drew her aside and started to tell her in the usual frantic gabble, he said and I said, he insulted me and I was insulted, she suddenly interrupted me with her clean voice, Na'ama, I really don't want to hear any more, and I protested indignantly, what do you mean, why?

Because it's pointless, she said, you complain about him all the time but you don't do anything, you let him control your life, you're incapable of confronting him and you're incapable of leaving him, maybe you're not sick of it yet but I am, and for weeks I went about stunned and hurt, with no one to confide in about it, and in the end I told Udi, of all people, and he said, why are you so upset, she's just jealous because you've got a family and she's alone, and he couldn't hide his satisfaction. But I knew that he was wrong, and I knew that she was right, and I went on conducting a dialogue with her in my head, her side so familiar to me already that I could say the words in her place, sometimes it was easier for me to formulate her arguments than my own, and that's what was left of our friendship, not a little, in fact, and ever since we've only been colleagues, and like a divorced couple making an effort for the sake of the children, we make an effort for the sake of the girls in the shelter, and I try to hide my hurt, and only sometimes, at the first moment of the day, it seems to me that I've been stabbed in my sleep.

How's Galya, I ask, and she says, not good, she refuses to give up the baby, denies everything we agreed on, and I hurry upstairs to her room, she looks so lost without her mountainous belly, as if she has been robbed of half her body, her eyes shine with a red light and when she sees me she begins to cry again, sobbing into my outspread arms, I'm not giving my baby to anyone, she's mine, I've already picked a name for her, if anybody wants to adopt her they can adopt me too, and I hug her, if only that were possible, I whisper, but you know it isn't, the question is if you can raise her by yourself. Like one more contraction in her labor the convulsive sobbing grips her, I can't give her up and I can't raise her, she cries, and I stroke her hair, we've talked about it a lot, Galya, you know that it's your decision, you have to think about what's best for the baby, and she screams, I forgot everything we talked about after I saw her face, they shouldn't have let me see her, and I look at her face spotted with the first pimples of adolescence, she's a child, barely fifteen, a child who fell into a trap, and I say, you still have time to make up your mind, you're still exhausted from the birth, rest for a while and perhaps things will become clearer, and I glance at my watch, she may have time but I don't. I have to run, Galya, my husband's in the hospital, we'll talk tomorrow, I whisper and kiss her on the forehead, and I hurry out of the room, almost colliding with the director, Hava, who's standing at the door, as if she's been eavesdropping on our conversation, but her authoritative, official face immediately banishes all suspicion. Na'ama, she says in surprise, I didn't think you would make it today, how's your husband? And I say, he's still in the hospital, I have to get back to him, and she releases me with a faintly resentful air, my colleagues always treat family demands with disdain. Will you come to work tomorrow, she asks, and I reply, I don't know yet, it depends on his condition, but when I leave the shelter I am accompanied by the suspicion that this time she actually hoped that I wouldn't come tomorrow, that she prefers to put pressure on Galya without my knowledge, to get her to sign the waiver forms without my mediation.

Luckily for me he's asleep, I'm as flushed as if I've come back from meeting a lover, it seems that over the course of the years I have resigned myself resentfully to his feeling that anything unconnected to him is a betrayal, for years I've been coming home from work with something approaching guilt, and now I've been wondering all the way here whether I should tell him that I paid a flying visit to the shelter or perhaps that I fell asleep in the cafeteria, which would insult him less, but when I penetrate his tent I see him sleeping with the red Bible covering his face, more flushed than me, as if they've cut off his head and replaced it with a fat book, and I heave a sigh of relief and turn round to leave the room, this time making in truth for the cafeteria, only to be stopped in my tracks by a weak, solemn voice from the opposite bed. He walked, he walked, the old man proclaims, as if announcing a miracle, take up your bed and walk, your sins are forgiven, and I ask, who walked, and he says, your husband, he took three steps, with the walker, and indeed, next to his bed the walker stands like a faithful dog waiting for his master, and I ask, when was this, and the old man recounts with the pride of a sole eyewitness, they brought some important professor from another department to talk to him, and then they tried with the walker and it worked, three steps, he repeats in excitement, and now the book sways and slips down sideways, and Udi sits up in bed, with a panic-stricken expression in his eyes.

Everything's going to be okay, I announce, but Udi rejects the good news, they don't believe me that I can hardly move, he complains, they think I'm pretending, and I stroke his arm, don't take any notice of them, Udi, as long as they let you go, the main thing is that I believe you, but in me too the old doubt arises, glancing mockingly at the wheelchair and the walker, a small doubt to be sure, mostly hidden, like a rat in the depths of the kitchen cabinet, never seen, but the certain knowledge of its presence there is so oppressive, it grows so great that in the end it seems that the house no longer belongs to you, but to the rat.

Six

A nd already the hospital is behind our backs, getting smaller and smaller as we climb the hill, full of anxious glee, like children running away from school, breathless with the exhilaration of the moment, but knowing that it will end badly. Udi is sitting next to me, holding in stiff fingers his discharge letter, we waited for it for hours, this letter, while they conferred in whispers behind our backs, suddenly disappearing and reappearing, without a decision, and I put on a show of confidence, let him go home, I know what's good for him, and he stared blankly, his wishes unclear, apparently unwilling to stay in the hospital but not eager to go home either, searching with lowered eyes for some other alternative, but I could see the way they looked at him, I had no doubt that if they didn't let him go today they would transfer him to the psychiatric department, because they didn't believe him, attacking him with insulting questions, chasing him out of their department, which was meant for really sick people, decent people who had earned their attention honestly, and not for someone who had misled them and abused their trust. The perfect test results had exposed the deception, and now he was sentenced to wander in the ambivalent gray area between the sick and the healthy, belonging neither here nor there, and I can see it all in his embarrassed face, he himself is ashamed of his disgraced body, his cheating legs, of this miserable return home, almost as surprising as the departure from it only the day before.

His eyes are frightened, like little Noga's eyes when we brought her home, I sat on the backseat, holding her on my lap, and Udi drove in silence, the back of his neck tight, we were like a broken vase then, fragments longing to be stuck together, and perhaps precisely now it will happen, perhaps now we will be reunited in the bosom of his illness, and I stroke his hand, Udigi, don't worry, the main thing is that we're out of there, you'll rest for a few days and it will all come right, but he fingers the letter discharging him from the hospital, ashamed, like a child bringing a bad report home from school, I don't know, he says, as long as I don't know what it was I can't be sure that it won't come back, I feel unprotected, I don't know how you get cured from something like this at all, but I still cling to the comforting illusion that as long as it's in the mind I can handle it. Don't exaggerate, it happens to everybody in one way or another, the main thing is that it's over, the main thing is that we're home, I announce in relief as I get out of the car, bending down so that he can put his arms around my neck and stand up, he walks so slowly, like an old man at the end of his strength, leaning on me with his feeble limbs, burying his face in the sidewalk, ashamed of being seen in his disgrace, the hero who was carried proudly away on a stretcher, fighting a mysterious disease, returning home in disgrace, thrown out of the hospital.

It seems to me that I can see a curtain parting and the downstairs neighbors' daughter peeping out of the window for a moment, the bells in her hair accompanying our labored steps, and we pause to rest between the stairs, his legs almost folding under him, his joints creaking discordantly, and then our front door opens, there's a blue balloon hanging on it, and Noga comes out, an orange balloon in her hands, we've surprised her in the middle of her preparations for a festive welcome home, and in her surprise she lets go of the balloon and it blows away in the wind, getting smaller and smaller until it's the size of a little orange, caught up in the branches of the Persian lilac next to the building, miraculously transforming it into a proud orange tree. Noga looks from us to the balloon, her sorrow at its loss mingling with her joy at seeing us, until she chooses joy and says, Daddy, you're better, and then she examines him and adds, you're better, aren't you? Otherwise they wouldn't have let you go, trying unsuccessfully to convince herself as his face turns green in front of her and his matchstick legs collapse on the threshold.

With four hands we drag him to his bed, Udi heavy in spite of his thinness, as if his bitterness fills his body and doubles its weight, and Noga sprawls out beside him, so pale that she's almost transparent. Have you eaten anything, I ask, and she says, not yet, I wanted to make sure Daddy was well first, and I say, so come and eat now, you can't go on like this, he's all right now, but she looks at him doubtfully and says, not yet, and then she begins to sob, I ate an apple at school, she wails, I forgot I wasn't allowed to and I ate an apple at recess, and that's why Daddy didn't get well.

I'm sick of your nonsense already, I burst out, when will you understand that there's no connection between your stomach and his legs, you can starve yourself to death and it won't make any difference, and I slam the door shut on both of them and go to the kitchen, luckily there are still a few pieces of schnitzel in the freezer left over from our previous life, and I fry them, and start collecting vegetables for a salad, I'm so tense that I begin to talk to myself, where are the tomatoes, I ask aloud, I saw them a second ago, I look in the fridge and then discover them waiting on the counter, a little wrinkled, surrounding the single aging cucumber, and soon the bowl is full, and I open a bottle of wine, perhaps with its help we'll convince ourselves that the evil has passed, and I put everything on the outsize tray we received as a wedding gift, and like a waitress new on the job I stumble to the bedroom, where they are lying in a gloomy silence, and set the tray down on the bed, encouraging them to eat, pouring wine. To life, I urge, to us, and Noga raises an empty glass, for Daddy to be healthy, she insists, as if she's blown out the candles on a cake and it's time to make a wish, and then she adds humbly, knowing that she's asked for too much, for all of us to be.

All of us together in one room, on one bed, as if outside the room a war is raging and we're in hiding, the plates and blankets overlap, and I eat quickly, as usual, to finish before somebody wants something from me, drinking more and more wine, and a moment before I stretch out on the edge of the bed and fall asleep I see the schnitzel on her plate getting bigger and bigger, whole and untouched, its shape reminiscent of some distant land, almost empty of inhabitants, a conquered, suffering land, and it seems to me as if I'm walking barefoot on the giant, blazing schnitzel, for days and days without seeing a living soul, until I meet a red-robed monk, and he whispers to me with parched lips, escape from here, run for your life, anyone who's caught here is forced to convert, and I ask, where am I, what country is this, and he says, it's called Conversion, haven't you ever heard of it?

When I wake up the room is dark and stuffy, full of crude smells of frying, which push out the cool spring air, next to me I find a greasy plate, and I recoil as if from a living creature, my mother used to say that if you wake up after sunset you won't smile for the rest of the day, and it seems that she was right, and I look at the big bed, at us, a sour, drunken family asleep in the middle of the day, and the celebration I tried to organize here hits me like a slap on the face, what's there to celebrate, it was bad enough before, never mind now. The feverish desire, which hasn't left me since yesterday morning, to get back to our normal routine, to huddle inside it like a dog in its kennel on a rainy night, suddenly seems fatuous, who needs that old life back?

And then I see that my side of the bed is empty, Noga's gone, and I rush into her dark room, she isn't there, or anywhere in the house, where a dim black light prevails, and then I find a torn piece of paper on the kitchen table, I've gone to Granny's, she writes in her clumsy hand, I'm going to sleep there tonight, I took my book bag with me, and I'm astonished, how come she left of her own free will, my housebound little girl, who barely agrees to go to any extra-curricular activities, who sits at home all day like a watchdog, it can't be an accident that she's gone, and I think of her in sorrow and shame, a little girl with a big role that fills her life, to stick the broken vase together, that's what she's been trying to do for the past eight years, and the bigger she grows the bigger the role grows with her, subjugating her childhood, conquering her life.

Heavy snores rise from the bedroom, aggressive as a reprimand, and I return rebuked, stretch my hand out to him, always at the initiation of contact an ancient aversion awakens, preceding everything that will come afterward, the lust or the desire, a pair of merry twins trying to overcome it with a vigorous rubbing of limbs, and sometimes it slinks away, its tail between its legs, and desire celebrates its victory, warm and ardent, and sometimes the desire is vanquished, it seems to flare up, but no, it soon dies down again, how hard it is to light a fire with damp twigs, and all that remains is a faint smell of good intentions that didn't succeed. This was how we lay on my narrow childhood bed, his boy's hands seeking treasures in my body while I hear my father's steps in his rubber clogs, going back and forth, his loneliness echoing throughout the house, and a wave of aversion chokes me until I almost vomit. I sit up in bed and push his fingers away, it's impossible, Udi, how can I enjoy myself when he's so unhappy, but Udi refuses to give up, his limbs thrust themselves on me, his unambiguous will tries to overcome the aversion, and for a moment he seems to succeed, and it hides from him in the depths of my throat, even his long tongue won't find it there, and I surrender, opening door after door to him, pockets of sweetness burst under his hands, but in the morning I wake up with an inflamed throat, it hurts too much to swallow, and my fever rises, and my father calls my mother, she's sick again, she's got laryngitis again, and then they move me, with my sickness, my pajamas and my blanket, from house to house, so little Yotam won't be infected, he's a sickly child at the best of times, and Udi comes to see me after school, squeezing into my sweltering bed, and I mumble, not now, leave me alone, I'm sick, and he goes away offended, without saying good-bye, and I hear the shuffle of the clogs all over the house and I torment myself, is that what you wish yourself, to live in such loneliness, that's what will happen to you if you chase him away.

Sour alcohol fumes breathe on me from his open mouth, and I press myself against him under the blanket, putting his sleeping arm round my shoulders in the illusion of an embrace, try to stroke his body, to awaken desire. How does it awaken, where does it come from, sometimes a single word can quicken it, a provocative smile, but like this, when the body is alone, without any extras, only the still limbs and their mysterious, embarrassing disease, how will it come, but this time I refuse to surrender, I have to try to heal him by the ancient method, Lot's daughters too weren't exactly wild about their drunken old father, in the cave on the mountain, above Zoar, after all the cities of the plain had been destroyed, and nevertheless they made him drink wine and lay with him in order to preserve the seed of their father and he perceived not when they lay down nor when they arose. I lay my hand on his sleeping penis and instantly it stretches and wakes up like a curious baby who doesn't want to miss anything, and I bend over it in sudden delight, here's the only limb in his body that hasn't changed, agile and friendly, I can always depend on it, a faithful ally in a country that has turned its back on me, I never imagined that I would feel so close to it, it seems as if it belongs to me, almost a part of me, and I sit down gently on his belly as flat as a board, and sway from side to side. Here it comes, precisely when I've given up on it, as if it's rising from a deep well, in a swaying bucket, the thick, viscid desire, and I clamp his body between my thighs, no longer caring if he wakes from his tipsy sleep, bending over him, my breasts pouring into his open mouth, and he licks them with his tongue, digs his teeth into the nipples, binds me to him with a cord of pain, sucking all my body into his mouth, my tired, prematurely worn-out body, baking afresh now in the oven of his mouth, and soon it will emerge as fresh and fragrant as a roll, and without any effort or intention on my part, the bucket that has just been drawn up from the well pours over me, lapping me in warm, delicious juices. And now it plunges back into the well, creaking as it blindly makes its way down, its movements are my movements, passive, random, and another cloud pours down, a cloudburst over my head, and I remember the old well at the end of our village, in the heart of the thick mango and avocado planta-tions, where my feet sank into the soft blanket of leaves, dry on top and wet below, mattresses of leaves leading to it, and suddenly some-body shouts, get away from that well, a small child once fell into it, the water drowned his cries, the only child of elderly parents, and I twist and turn, I don't want this water, it's cursed, but the bucket doesn't stop, it rises and falls inside me, with movements that grow bigger and bigger until my ears fill with gurgling, carefree laughter.

You're taking advantage of my condition, he complains in a gratified voice, opening his eyes, and I pant on top of him, and bury my giddy head in his armpit. You couldn't wait until I woke up, he goes on, making me drink wine and raping me in my sleep, you're so famished, where have you been hiding your hunger all these years? And I giggle, how do you know, maybe I've been raping you every night in your sleep, and he gurgles, I wish, and again that carefree laugh, he always becomes completely different after we make love, the bitterness stuck in his throat dissolves, and suddenly he's full of love. My Noam, he strokes my back, poor girl, you were so worried about me, and I am already prepared to weep with relief, it was awful, to see you like that, in the hospital, with all those tubes, and he teases, that nurse in the emergency room wasn't at all bad, and

I bite his shoulder, I saw how she turned you on, and he laughs, bullshit, you know I only want you, and I know that it's true, only it doesn't always sound as good as it does now, usually it sounds like a threat, but now his words caress me inside with soothing movements, the difference between inside and out suddenly blurred. Is this silence I hear inside or outside, how is it that no cars are passing in the street below, and I think about the dreadful silence in that cave, only the whisper of the steam like the steam of a furnace rising from the overthrown land, seeing the corpses of the ruined, smoking cities, the destroyed garden of God, and then he says, you know, on my way home from the Arava I climbed up the mountain of Sodom, did you know that it was hollow inside, that it's both a mountain and a cave? And I answer in a whisper, no, I didn't know. It's the saddest place I know, he says, because it will never recover, even though thousands of years have passed it seems as if nothing has changed there, the sin was so deep that the ground can't heal, it was punished by eternal barrenness, and I am already used to him reading my thoughts, even as a boy he had a kind of intrusive insight, and even if he was sometimes wrong I only remembered the times when he was right, the submissive wonder I felt whenever he continued my private train of thought, or answered a question I hadn't asked.

Don't worry, he laughs in satisfaction, I'm not the last man alive, Lot's daughters thought that all the men in the world were extinct, but this is the opposite situation, I might be extinct soon but the world is full of men, and I hug him, don't be silly, you're the last man for me, and the first too, I add in pious pride, and he drawls yes, but in the middle there was someone else, and his voice grows cold, like his body which suddenly withdraws from me, and I pull him back, Udi stop spoiling things, and he grumbles, I'm spoiling things? It was you who spoiled things, and I crush his shoulder, stop it, that's enough, control yourself, I spoiled things once and you spoil them all the time, Udigi, you have to get better now, try to think only about good things, this bitterness is poisoning you, you're ruining all of our lives. I try to mount him again, it was so sweet before, only me and his friendly, happy penis, but he writhes underneath me, I have to pee, he gets up heavily and leans on the wall, on the doorpost, advancing with dragging steps, it seems as if he will never reach the toilet waiting for him with its mouth open, and I follow him in the darkness, I don't want to switch on the light, to see the dishes strewn around the house, the clothes, the shoes, the old furniture, all the signs of neglect that have taken over our lives, and I look at his narrow silhouette, let's go away tomorrow morning, Udi, we haven't been anywhere together for years, we'll leave Noga with my mother and drive up north, and he leans on the sink, I don't think so, he says, I still don't feel well, but I refuse to give up, this is my goal now, sudden and powerful, to get away from here, to escape from this address, from the bear hug of the old walls, as if an earthquake is making its way toward us. You'll feel better when we get away, I insist, we deserve a bit of a rest, you'll see that it will make you better, and I stand behind him, my hands seeking the consent of his body.

But he looks into the mirror, denying me, feeling the new stubble on his cheeks, his jaw jutting forward stubbornly, giving him a childish expression, why won't he let go, clinging to that old wound as if it's the most precious asset he's acquired in his life. What did you do already, I hear Anat's quiet, beloved voice, and I say, even if it seems small to you, to him it's big, his hurt is big, and she laughs, it's big because he enlarges it, look how he uses it, making you stew on a fire of guilt all the time, your whole life you have to make it up to him, anyone would think he's such a saint himself. He never cheated on me, I defend him, you simply don't appreciate his sensitivity, and she says, I appreciate his sensitivity to himself very well, but where's his sensitivity to you, he was never sensitive to you, he has a need to blame, and you have a need to be blamed. She's right, I say to myself, I won't let him blame me any longer, I won't beg, and I let go of his body, forget it, I say and step into the shower, if you don't want to go with me I'll go by myself when you recover, quickly closing the curtain, and he freezes in front of the mirror, clever Anat, I should always listen to her advice, and then he says, all right, if you want it so much we'll go.

In the morning I vanquish my old enemy, the alarm clock, shutting it up before it begins to shake, and rushing into Noga's room to wake her up, but the empty bed declares her absence, and I stand in front of it in a panic, an empty room immediately turns into a memorial room, the pictures on the wall take on a new meaning. Here she is one week old, her head peeping over Udi's shoulder, her eyes half-closed, and here all three of us are on a checked blanket, they're hugging each other and I'm watching from the side, my hair tied back and my face beautiful, almost as beautiful as my mother in this picture, only she always displayed her beauty and I hid mine, as if it were stolen, and here are her notebooks on the table, I turn the pages in crude curiosity, searching for some unclear information, which has suddenly become urgent, they are almost all empty, isolated sentences imprisoned on the first pages, and after that a white, worrying silence.

I look at the objects frozen in their last race, the clothes flung onto the rug, sleeves gaping as if they have just this moment been discarded, still holding her movements, a fierce longing suddenly stabs me, and I sit down on the rug, how can I go without her, she has to come with us, we'll all go together, but then that "together" sends a tremor through me, with all its tension, to be torn between them again, to see her trying to arouse his love, to be angry with him again for disappointing her, and then with myself, I haven't got the strength for it, and I call my mother, her voice is low and sad, very different from the voice she once had. How are you, I ask, and she says, last night my ulcer woke me several times, but it's quiet now, for a year now that wound in her stomach has filled her world, and she cares for it devotedly as if it were a baby, if only she'd cared for us with such devotion, and I ask coldly, how's Noga, and she sighs, she's all right, but you have to do something about her situation in school. What situation, I ask in surprise, what happened? And she says, what, hasn't she told you? She's completely isolated, the other girls laugh at her for dressing like a boy, and the boys shun her because she's a girl, and I squeeze the telephone hard, so why didn't she say anything to me, the tears are already tickling my throat, and my mother doesn't even try to hide her pride, won't let me think for a minute that I'm a better mother than she was, she doesn't want to worry you, don't you understand?

Let me talk to her, I say, trying to steady my voice, Nogigi, good morning, and she says, good morning Mother, and this formal trio of words stings my ears, good morning Mother, and I say, I'm going up north with Daddy for a couple of days, to rest, and she says, good, as long as Daddy gets better. Granny told me that you're not happy at school now, I venture, but she quickly evades the issue, it doesn't matter, Mother, I'll manage, the important thing is for you and Daddy to go and have fun, and for Daddy to get better, and I apologize, it's only for a couple of days, we'll see you the day after tomorrow and then you can tell me all about it, and she cuts me short, bye Mom, I'm late already, and leaves me alone with her things. Why like a boy, I think indignantly, it's true that she doesn't preen, barely combs her hair, mostly wears Udi's tee-shirts, which cover her almost to the knees, but why should that make anyone laugh, and then I remember that for a long time none of the girls from her class have come round, and the shrill voices haven't been heard over the phone for a long time either, asking, can I speak to Noga, and I haven't even noticed, and now I no longer want to go anywhere, only to disguise myself as a ten-year-old girl and hurry to her school and sit next to her and be her best friend, listen to her secrets and tell her that she's the cutest girl in the class.

Clouds of fragrant steam escape from the bathroom, and I go in and see him lying in the tub, his boyish body covered with transparent water, his hair combed back, exposing pale bays of baldness, emphasizing the precisely chiseled features, and I decide not to tell him anything for the time being, whenever I try to share my concern about Noga with him he stiffens as if he's being accused, defending himself aggressively. How are you feeling, I ask, and he smiles, if I made it here under my own steam that's already something, and I look at him and marvel, all this is mine, in some strange way, a whole person who's mine, I've been given him anew, I've succeeded in stealing him from the seductive arms of the disease, in spite of everything he prefers me to her, and already I am full of foolish pride in my victory, eagerly dipping my hand in the water and walking two fingers over his body, and he tries to pull me in but I elude him, let's wait till we get there, and he chuckles, we can do it now and then too.

The old traveling bag I packed for the hospital, only two days ago, fills up again, I pile in clothes and toiletries without thinking, with a forced gaiety that gradually convinces even me, it seems that almost everything is a question of decision, sorrow and happiness, hostility and closeness, even health and sickness, and only once in a while a dark wave of worry creeps toward me from Noga's room. I peep into it again, it seems to me that stifled moans are hiding there, like the moans of survivors of an earthquake buried under the ruins, you spoke to her only a minute ago on the phone, I remind myself, she's not here at all, but even after we leave the house, turning the key three times in the door, I have to go up again, just to make sure I switched off the boiler, I say to Udi, and run to her room, and look round and call her name, her room is empty and nevertheless it seems to me that we are leaving behind us in the locked house a helpless living creature, begging for help.

Seven

We slide down the great asphalt chute into the dry arms of the desert, Udi drives fast and I press my knees together, the familiar fingers of fear pinching deep in my groin, stinging its absorbent cheeks, and I lay my hand on his thigh, not so fast Udi, you're overdoing it, and he complains, whenever I'm enjoying myself you think I'm overdoing it, but nevertheless he slows down a little, so I can see the Judean desert waving its wand, and I marvel, look how dry it is, a completely different country, and he says, it's simply not irrigated, that's all. But only a few minutes ago everything was still green, I protest, how does it happen so quickly, and he explains with surprising patience, as if to a group he is guiding, about the journey of the rain clouds from the sea to the mountains, rising higher and higher, growing thicker and thicker, until they reach the summit, the city high on the mountaintops, from which the air begins to decline, and where everything changes with terrific speed, the water turns back into vapor, and the vapor turns back into gas, and I ask, and any cloud that hasn't dropped its rain by the time it reaches Jerusalem just dries up, and Udi nods, yes, it will get smaller and smaller until it stops being a cloud. So what will it be, I ask sadly, because suddenly I remember the story he once made up for Noga when she was a baby, about the little cloud

Hanan, the innocent, kindhearted cloud who was determined to bring rain to the parched desert plants at any price, and how he climbed from the sea and swelled and swelled, with the raindrops already heavy inside him, about to tear open his little belly, but the minute he passed over Jerusalem he evaporated into thin air, before he had a chance to drop his rain, and all the thirsty desert plants raised their heads and saw him disintegrating in the sky, his good intentions turning into warm, useless vapors. I would urge him to change the end of the story, let him rain at the last minute, I would plead, let him rain on the border of the desert at least, how can you let him go to waste like that, for all his good intentions, and I would be far more upset than Noga, who didn't really understand the dimensions of the loss, and now I look hopefully at the sky, perhaps today he'll make it, the little cloud Hanan, but it's clear and empty, no puppy cloud is frisking in its courts, indifferently it accompanies us, like a couple grown old without having any children, their bellies are creased with desolate strands of gray but the great sorrow is already behind them.

This is where the border was in the past, says Udi, and I say in surprise, what border, with Jordan? And he says, no, of course not, between the Kingdom of Judah and the Kingdom of Israel, and I have forgotten that there was ever any such division, I look around in astonishment, seeking traces of an ancient wall, but the land is one and the same wherever I look, salty, moonstruck land. Why did they separate, I ask, and he replies, the question is why they ever united, the division between them was a natural, ancient division that preceded the unification, the unification was weak from the start, and I lower my eyes, why does it seem to me that it's us he's talking about, a cold tension grips my spine, icy little animals crawl up it, vertebra after vertebra. What were relations between them like, I ask, and he says, full of vicissitudes, there were wars, reconciliations and alliances, and I strain my memory, Israel was bigger and stronger than Judah, right? So how come it was destroyed first? Precisely because it was stronger it was less careful, he grins, it dared to neglect God, while Judah which was weaker militarily took greater care, it had no choice. So perhaps it's better to be weak, I say, and he nods, from God's point of view, definitely, but that too only up to a certain point, otherwise it's impossible to survive at all.

They were probably stunned over there in Judah, after Israel was exiled, I say, like a couple when the strong one dies before the weak one, and Udi says, the truth is that Israel was only stronger on the face of things, inside it was sick, unstable, there were fanatical prophets there preaching revolt, there was bloodshed, whereas Judah was relatively stable, it never changed its capital or its dynasty. But it didn't help them in the end, they were exiled themselves after a few generations, I say, and he shakes his head, you're wrong, it helped them a lot, even after the exile they remained faithful to the same capital and the same dynasty, and thanks to that they came back here and Israel didn't. I'm sure it was a disaster for them, to be suddenly left alone in the country, I insist, and Udi looks at me in admiration, you're wonderful, he says, and I demur, you're joking, and he strokes my hand lying next to him, no, I'm serious, you see everything in such human, personal terms, I come here all the time with different groups and nobody reacts like you do, I didn't fall in love with you by accident when I was twelve years old, he boasts, I already knew then that you had a special soul, I just didn't know that you would waste it on the wretched of the earth, he adds sourly. Stop it, don't spoil things, I slap his hand, and he smiles at me, look at you, your face has hardly changed, you look so young, and I am confused by all these compliments, I hasten to deny it, nonsense, look at the wrinkles under my eyes, and he insists, you look like a little girl, don't argue with me, and I try to bask in the compliment, a melting sweetness fills me, and I want to close my eyes in the blissful hollow of his love, next to the springlike breeze tickling the window, to close my eyes and hope for the best.

You won't believe what they've got in that monastery, he points to a small building, its dome glittering in the heart of the white plains of Jericho, the skulls of monks murdered by the Persians hundreds of years ago. You want to have a look? He is about to turn off the road, but I shudder, definitely not, and he yields with surprising ease, his mood is improving more and more the farther we get from home, his hair blows in the wind, his face is flushed, it's impossible to believe that only yesterday he was lying paralyzed in the hospital, and I sigh in relief, it really is a miracle, what's happened to him, it's incredible, and I look around curiously, miracles are not foreign to these glittering slopes, out of the mountains dark holes gape at me like hollow eye sockets. Those are ancient caves, Udi explains, you want to climb up there? And I recoil, definitely not, but I go on staring at the empty eyes, they must have seen many wonders, I can't remember what, something to do with the Jordan River, and I ask, where's the Jordan, we haven't seen it yet, and Udi laughs, that's the best thing about the Jordan, that it's almost invisible, anyone who succeeds in seeing it is always disappointed, it's just a trickle, but nevertheless it seems to me that I can sense its presence, accompanying us to the right like the heart's desire, faithful and disturbing, with green-gray steps.

What miracles took place here in biblical times, I ask, and he says, this region is loaded, especially round the Jordan River, a lot of prophets roamed around here hungry for miracles, it was here that Elijah ascended in a storm to heaven, here that Elisha cured the cursed water, here that Na'aman the commander of the King of Aram's army washed his body seven times and was cured of leprosy, not to mention the miracle of the crossing of the Jordan, when the water stood up and a whole people crossed on dry land, but of all these miracles it seemed to me that the greatest and most amazing was the one that had been granted us, and only occasionally did I hear a whisper welling up inside me, quiet as the flow of water in the shrunken river, perhaps it isn't a miracle at all, perhaps it has been an illusion from the beginning.

And people who don't believe in miracles, I ask him, how do they explain all those things, is there another explanation? And he says, nothing on earth has only one explanation, it's always possible to find a rational justification, for instance that there was an earthquake at precisely the moment when the children of Israel crossed the river, and heaps of marl fell into the water and dried it up, but by now I'm hardly listening as I look at his lips polishing the words. I suppose there's someone in every group who falls in love with you, I tease him, and he laughs, why only one, and his hand wanders over my thighs, lingers between them, and this is what I do to them while I drive, he opens the buttons of my pants, and I say archly, how do I know that you don't, and he says, if you don't know that inside then you don't know anything, and I actually thought that I did know, but still, who taught him to open buttons with one hand, while he's driving, however this hardly bothers me now, not when he wants me so much, and I imagine that I'm a young tourist falling in love with the Holy Land and with the fascinating guide who knows it so well.

Udi, be careful, you need both hands on the steering wheel, I scream as the car opposite us honks its horn, we must have swerved into the wrong lane, but he grips me tightly and says through clamped jaws, I prefer to hold your steering wheel, it turns me on a lot more, and in a minute I'm going to start turning it for you, and I protest weakly, not now, Udi, it's dangerous, but his fingers are sending shivers through my pelvis, I writhe uncontrollably, I feel as if I'm lying on the bed of an ancient, salty, oily sea, close to the savage inner life of this land, to the footsteps of the wild animals who prowled here thousands of years ago, and he holds me with sudden, provocative strangeness, as if he hasn't been my husband since the age of twelve, only his hand inside me and his eyes on the road.

Come, he says through his teeth, I'm not stopping until you come, and I say, my mouth dry, have a heart, it could take a year, and he doesn't answer but his long fingers persevere, gathering my whole body round them, sheaving it like a sheaf of wheat in a field, startling hundreds of butterflies from its depths, tiny wings spread inside me, colliding with each other, stroking, fluttering, my throat is hoarse, and I try to whisper, why don't you park on the side of the road, but he takes no notice of me, and by now I take no notice of myself, thousands of wings make me tremble inside, laughing and leaving kisses of nectar in my groin, and when I open my eyes I see to my horror black clouds of butterflies beating against the windshield, and I cry, what's that, and he says, relax, it happens here sometimes, there's nothing anybody can do, I'm trying to drive slowly, and he withdraws his hand gently, and surveys it with a triumphant smile.

I push my seat backward and give the sky an ingratiating look, how pleasant it is to drive like this, it seems as if this wild landscape is visiting my bed, I look at Udi admiringly out of the corner of my eye, yes, a person could still fall in love with him, even I could still fall in love with him, a pang of hunger tickles my stomach, an agreeable anticipation of food, and then I suddenly sit up straight, what about Noga, I forgot to ask my mother if she had stopped her fast, and Udi stares at me in surprise, what's wrong, I thought you'd fallen asleep. I have to find out if Noga ate this morning, I say tensely, and grab the cell phone, but there's no reply at my mother's house, and I don't dare to phone the school, and Udi complains, whenever you're happy you have to dig up something new to worry about from under the ground, and I flare up, it's not under the ground at all, it's above the ground, about one and a half meters above the ground, is that high enough for you? And Udi's already bristling, you're not helping her by tormenting yourself, I promise you that she's eating very well, not that your mother's capable of cooking anything, he pulls a disapproving face, and I can't control myself, don't you care about her, I say, and already my eyes are wet, and he growls, of course I care about her, she's my daughter, isn't she? I just don't exaggerate like you do, that's all, and I'm sick of you testing me all the time.

Disconsolately I stare at the sky, the farther north we go the more it clouds over, but I am no longer consoled by the prospect of rain, what did I do wrong, why is everything spoiled as soon as Noga's name is mentioned, surely it should be the opposite, parents doting on their children together, we ourselves doted on her endlessly when she was a baby, why will this wound never heal, and I feel like saying to him, let's go home, there's no point to this trip, this wound doesn't suit a fancy hotel, it needs to hide at home, until it heals we'll never be happy together, and until we're happy together it won't heal, so let's give up right now. Around us the air is cooling, the colors darkening, as if we have arrived in a different realm, more melancholy but far more real and reliable than the hot and savage realm of miracles and wonders, with the palms and the bananas, the vast cradle spread out between the Judean mountains and the mountains of Moab, and it seems that his face has darkened too, his cheeks hang joylessly on their bones, under his chin a fold of sagging flesh wobbles, an evil spirit is approaching him and I have to stop it, I have to restrain myself again, so as not to awaken the beast of conversion accompanying us, sleeping quiet and dangerous at the back of the car.

When will we arrive, I ask innocently, and he answers dryly, in about an hour, and I suggest, why don't we stop on the way for something to eat, and he says, I'd rather wait, the food there's the best, and it seems that the neutral conversation has relaxed his tension, but not mine, again I feel the cold creeping up my spine, icy worms clinging to the tired vertebrae, hugging them in a freezing embrace.

Do you want to have a quick look at the necropolis, he asks, and all I want is to sit in a warm place with coffee and cake but I don't like to refuse again, he'll snatch the opportunity to say again that nothing eternal interests me, that I don't relate to history. It's a pity I didn't agree to go into the monastery, what's a few ancient skulls compared to an entire city of the dead, and I try to enthuse myself, an entire city of the dead? And he says, yes, a burial city, from all corners of the Jewish world they came to be buried here, and I ask, why here in particular, and he explains willingly, it was already forbidden to be buried in Jerusalem, and also to live there after the Bar Kochba revolt, or even in a place from which Jerusalem could be seen. Altogether, all the burial customs changed after the exile, it was only then that the Jews began to believe in the resurrection of the dead, and I trail behind him into the deep, cold caves, each grave illuminated by a single light, which only serves to stress the surrounding darkness, a private reading lamp for every dead person. At the entrance we are greeted by a little girl who died at the age of nine years and six months, of what it doesn't say, and I stand afraid next to her grave, what do you think she died of, I ask, and he says, what difference does it make to you, there's no lack of things to die from, but her age oppresses me, exactly the same age as Noga, suddenly the long year between nine and ten seems to me terrifyingly dangerous, and I have to know what to beware of.

Proudly he shows me the signs on the graves, the Assyrian bull and the Roman eagle and the peacock, symbolizing eternity, and the seven-armed candelabra, and the goddess Nicea, the Roman goddess of victory, you see how tolerant they were, they weren't averse to using foreign symbols, but I totter behind him freezing and frightened, because all these animals are circling round Noga's head, threatening her life, and I stop listening to his learned lecture, all I want is to get out of there, to be resurrected like these silent, privileged dead, and when we emerge he is as proud and satisfied as if it's his own private plot, the burial plot of his ancient family, and I look with hostility at the cultivated lawns, what has this place, from which you can't see Jerusalem, got to do with me?

What's the matter with you, you're completely gray, he looks at me mockingly, and all I want now is to get back to the car and phone my mother, I'm tired, I say, dialing the number with tense fingers, and finally she answers, I went to see the doctor this morning, they say there's no improvement, she threatens me, and I interrupt her, did Noga eat this morning? Of course she did, she boasts, I cooked her cereal the way she likes it, with chocolate flakes, and she ate it all, and I breathe a sigh of relief, instantly everything seems less threatening, even those burial caves, and I'm so thankful I'm ready to go back in again, and Udi says, you see, when she's far from you there's no problem, it's only with you that she makes difficulties, and I lie back and ask in sudden interest, that surprises even me, how did this place look then? And he says, more or less like it does now, it hasn't changed much, only these cypresses weren't there, but pines, oaks, carob trees, and I look around, so this is what the parents of that little girl saw in the darkness of their eyes, after the long journey with the little body, jolted from time to time by the potholes in the road as if she were still alive, an ancient little girl, even if she'd lived a long life she would still be buried here today, in the depths of the cold stone, there's no lack of things to die from, he said, there's no lack of things to worry about, and I try to rouse my spirits with the words I saw engraved on one of the graves, be strong, pious parents, no man is immortal.

The farther north we drive the more the light retreats, as if the sun has set unseasonably before noon, a dense mist bars our way and we twist and turn with the narrow road over mountains of cloud, at close quarters their touch is strange and hostile, not the expected soft caress. Udi drives laboriously, his forehead almost butting into the windshield, his eyes narrowed, his shoulders swaying from side to side as if he's rowing a boat, one after the other warning signs loom up in front of us, threatening us with aggressive exclamation marks, and beneath us the deep, hungry abyss breathes heavily. A black rain suddenly pours down from the clouds squatting like giant bears over the roof of the car, lashing at the windowpanes, and I move my feet nervously, already I can feel the tug ropes of the abyss coiling round them, while above my head the magnet of the dark sky rules, one more snatched breath and the eternal balance of terror between heaven and earth will be disrupted, and I will be left suspended in nothingness, like between my father and mother when I was a child.

As soon as we get there I'm jumping straight into the pool, says Udi, and I look at him in amazement, what makes him so sure that we will get there, the road is so narrow, and when an occasional car drives past us from the opposite direction we brush up against the mountain, there's a moment when it seems that it's them or us, our whole existence is in doubt and he's occupied with luxuries, but now he turns onto a side road, escaping from the abyss which closes its mouth in disappointment, and already we belong to a different place, a spacious and welcoming estate that absorbs us quickly, like refugees whose wanderings are at an end. The narrow road above the clouds turns into a vague memory, and only the thought of the way back, on the side of the abyss, troubles me for a moment, but I quickly suppress it, so distant does our return home seem, as if by then new roads will be built throughout the land, and all the abysses will be filled with earth.

I stretch out luxuriously on the bed, it's the biggest bed I've ever seen, dwarfing me entirely, I stretch my arms and legs to the full but my hands and feet don't reach the end, and I rebuke myself happily, you see, things don't always go wrong, there are other possibilities besides the worst, Noga's all right, and Udi's recovered, and we have arrived safely, and we're here in this palace with every luxury, and the icicles in my spine melt and turn into a warm solution, and Udi is already rummaging in the traveling bag, not resting for a minute, where are my bathing trunks, are you sure you didn't forget them, and he throws our clothes on the floor, just like Noga, until he pulls out the narrow strip of black cloth triumphantly and puts it on and urges me to hurry up, and I'm still stretched out on the bed, I'll come down in a minute, okay? He wraps himself quickly in a white terry-cloth robe and hurries out of the room, and I stare at the door broadcasting his unambiguous wishes, which immediately become my wishes, and I get up immediately and put on my bathing suit, examining my body suspiciously and covering it with the robe, here too it's like some kind of hospital, everyone wearing white robes.

Panes of clear glass cover the pool like a raincoat, protecting it from the storm, and the pleasant dimness of a winter afternoon hides the bites of age, and I see Udi's arms beating the water, if I told the people here that only yesterday they were paralyzed they would laugh in my face, absorbed in his miracle he advances, not noticing me, we pass each other in the narrow swimming lanes but I ignore him, his existence evaporates, as if we have not yet met, as if I am still in another time, in the small living space I had at my disposal before he took over my life. In the pool at the edge of our village I am swimming now, my tears swallowed up in the chlorinated water, soon the pool will overflow and only I will know the reason why, and at my side I see my parents' eyes accompanying me like two brightly colored fish, back and forth, watching me tensely. Before we all sat on the lawn, my mother cut a big watermelon in two and told us that they were getting a divorce, and from now on we would have two homes, because our father was staying here in the country and she was taking us to the city, and my brother hopped on one foot and shouted, yay, two homes! And I stared at her stunned and started to run, fleeing from the news, hiding from it in the bushes edging the area of the pool, and suddenly I felt a stab in my bare foot and I screamed, Mommy, I've got a thorn in my foot, and my father came running and picked me up in his arms, even though his back was wrecked and he wasn't allowed to carry things, but sticking to the soft pad of my foot was a bee whose fate was sealed, its sting was buried deep inside me and it fluttered for a moment and fell to the ground, and I screamed in fear, Daddy, pull out the stinger, what are you waiting for?

I can't find it, he mumbled and put me down on the warm grass, bending over me, his jaw thrust out like the jaw of a boxer, above it the chubby red cheeks of a baby, I can't find it, and my brother asked if they would have to operate on me, open up my whole body in order to find the stinger, and I lay there, between their legs, the pain of the sting radiating throughout my body, and the sun dived into my eyes, terrifying and ravenous as a yellow vulture, and I felt the sorrow engulfing me until there was nothing left but the pain in my foot, which proved to me that I was still alive, without it I would already have been dead, which at that moment didn't seem such a bad thing to me. Better to die now than to move to the apartment my mother had rented in the city, better to die than to start going back and forth between them, to see him wallowing in his grief, to see her in her disgusting attempts to live, to justify her crime, and I thought that if I died perhaps they would stay together, to preserve what little was left. I won't let them do this to me, I closed my eyes tight, violate my life like Cossacks breaking into Jewish homes and destroying everything, we had just studied the subject in school, and I thought in a panic about school, what was I going to tell my classmates, there was only one other kid in the class whose parents were divorced, and he was a crazy kid anyway and nobody took any notice of him, and now he and I were partners in a ghastly common fate, and a wave of hatred flooded me, making my head spin with its violence.

My mother bent over me, her face worried, not wanting me to spoil her plans, and I turned over on the grass so as not to see her loathsome beauty, digging my fingers into the earth, and she said, calm down, it isn't the end of the world, it will be better for all of us this way, and I screamed, it will be better for you, not for me, it will be worse for me, I'll be miserable forever because of you, you're the bee that just stung me and the sting will stay inside me forever, but at least it's dead and you still think that you deserve to go on living after you've stung me, and then I stood up and hopped on one foot, holding on to the bushes, the folding chairs, falling into the water and diving wildly, strewing tears around me, trying to hold my breath, seeing them in my mind's eye fishing out my dead body, it's so close, it's in my hands, all I have to do is stop breathing, overcome the despicable habit of breathing, and now in this closed, protected pool, with the thin drizzle tapping on the glass above, surprised to encounter the transparent roof, I try again, but not so wholeheartedly, diving to the bottom and holding my breath, and then a hand comes down and pulls me up, what's the matter with you, he says, I've been talking to you for half an hour and you don't answer me, and I stare at him, for a moment he looks like a stranger, the water has darkened his hair, his lips are slack, and I lean on the edge of the pool and pant apologetically, I didn't hear you, I was thinking about something else.

The rain is coming down harder, but Udi pulls me outside, onto the veranda, in the middle of which a black well is bubbling, and we jump into it, the heat of the water stinging our skin, the combination of the heat and the cold makes me come alive and my heart pounds, jolting my body. Purple clouds hide the landscape, here and there a distant light glimmers, sending me signals I don't know how to decipher, and Udi pulls me to him by my hair, kisses my neck, my lips, and I murmur, stop it, someone's coming, and he says, good, she can join us, and she stretches out a cautious foot and smiles, she has curly hair and a long brown body that is immediately swallowed up in the dark water, and I feel uncomfortable in this togetherness, let's go back to the room, I whisper into his ear, licking it to show my intentions are serious, and he looks at the girl for a minute but immediately follows me out, his penis bulging in the tight trunks, and we run down the corridors, sopping wet under our white robes, holding hands in the elevator like youngsters in love, and I say to myself, how simple it is here, not like at home with Noga asleep and all our old scores awake.

A gray light is nestled against the windows, wrapping his body in a dark furry layer, like the ground in the wood at the end of the village, which would cover itself in a fuzzy blanket after the first rain, and I would tread carefully among the baby grasses, looking at the road. Every hour a half-empty bus would arrive and leave the same way, sometimes it would seem to me that the passengers who arrived were the same as the ones who left, refusing to stay in the neglected village, and sometimes Udi got off the bus, short and thin, his straight hair falling into his eyes like a horse's mane, and I would lean against one of the pine trees and examine him in disappointment, almost in shame, this wasn't what my first love was supposed to look like, but his strides as he came up to me were confident, as if they knew that one day he would be tall and handsome, and I would say to myself, in time to the rhythm of his steps advancing toward me, hang on to him, he's all you've got now, because everything around me was coming apart. My mother had rented an apartment for us in the nearby town, opposite the school, but I preferred to go home to the old house, to my father who stared at me as if I were a ghost, his victim's face lengthening, I did all I could to please her, said his face, no mortal could do more. At lunchtime I would open and close the empty fridge in despair, and go out to the orchards, picking oranges in the winter, peeling them and weeping, and in the autumn fleshy red and white guavas, whose smell stuck to my fingers, and in summer plums, and when Udi approached the wood, waving enthusiastically, I would detach myself from the pine tree which had planted a gummy kiss on my shirt, and join my steps to his until we shut ourselves in my room, where he would push me onto the bed and clamber up my limbs as if I were the plum tree, and I would hear my father pacing the empty house and coughing, whole sentences of coughing pouring from his mouth, and my body would close down, how could I be happy when he was so unhappy, and sometimes I would fill with aggressive rage, I will be happy, just because he's so unhappy, and then I would pull the surprised Udi to me, put his hands on my breasts and moan out loud to vanquish the lamentation of his coughs. Sometimes I would hear him crying, through Udi's panting, through the sweaty friction of our bodies, the quiet crying of a neglected baby who knows that nobody will come in any case, and now too, as I fall onto the bed the familiar whimper steals into my ears, and I can't concentrate, his lips annoy me, how do they manage it, pecking my body all over at once, and I push him away from me, that whimpering is driving me out of my mind, why does someone always have to suffer when I am enjoying myself?

With an insulted expression on his face he retreats from the bed, his chin jutting out, have something to drink, maybe it will help you to relax, he quickly opens the bottle of wine waiting for us in the room, as if it's some urgent medicine, maybe you need a new man, he adds sourly, with me you can't escape yourself, I remind you of every minute of your life, and I am quick to deny it, what nonsense, even though I have been thinking exactly the same thing myself, a new love has the power to make things go away, at least at first, there in the studio on the roof among the paintbrushes nothing bothered me, but I drink the wine and try to cheer up, give yourself this gift, give it to yourself, everyone will benefit. I begin to fill the bathtub, the jet of water covers my weak lies, and Udi comes in after me, consenting to give me another chance, and already the foam covers us, clean as new snow, and he contemplates me with a glum, almost despairing look, in his brown eyes a green spot glitters, a little oasis in each eye. If I were a new man you would make more of an effort, he complains quietly, I'm sick of being taken for granted by you, I want you to make an effort too, and I mutter, I make enough of an effort, why does everything have to be an effort, and he says, it hurts me, that you don't really want me, that you're only doing me a favor, to put me in a good mood, or for some other purpose of your own. Of course I really want you, I say, I don't want anyone else, isn't that enough for you? And he closes his eyes, it wouldn't be enough for you either if you were in my place, and I feel like pulling the plug and getting out of the bath and leaving him alone with the residue of the foam, with his never-ending resentment, but the burden of this day rests on my shoulders, we didn't come here in order to quarrel, we came here to love, to feed the exhausted animal of our love whose stomach is shrunken with fasting.

You'll be sorry for provoking me, I say in a seductive voice, and he grins, let's see you, opening a curious eye, and I listen to the beating rain, again a cloud has burst over our heads, like on that morning in the rooftop studio, why did I stand at the window with him then, instead of dragging him to the bed in the recesses of the apartment, tearing off his sweater, snuggling up against his broad chest in its black undershirt, hearing everything Udi didn't dare tell me and saying, me too, me too, me too, how absurd to pay such a heavy price for abstinence, and in sudden rage I grip his slippery penis between my feet, as if it's a fish I have to snare in my net, its mouth full of foam, and I dive down to it, his surprised hands pushing my head down under the water until I almost choke, struggling to push them off and breathe the air. Take more wine, he says, pouring the sweetish gush into my throat, straight from the bottle, and I open my mouth wide, this is how we used to try to trap the first drops of rain, my tongue thirsty for the wine, seeking its traces on the stiff member swaying like a drunk, probing between the testicles, and he presses me to him, the empty bottle against the nape of my neck, the oases in his eyes expanding as he lets out a heavy groan, the fist of his clenched body suddenly relaxing.

Come to bed, he whispers tenderly, wrapping me in a towel and pulling me after him, like a child being put to bed after her bath, and already my eyes are closing but he laughs, this is just the beginning, you still have a lot of surprises for me, and I mumble, really, and he says, you bet, you have to make up for years of indifference in one night, and I turn over onto my stomach, let's sleep a little first, and have something to eat, but he doesn't stop, a cold smooth object rolls down my back, flattening me like a rolling pin, what do you think, will this bottle satisfy you in the meantime, he breathes into my ear, and I say, stop it, Udi, that's enough, but the round mouth of the bottle is already pushing up between my legs, its lips thrusting toward me in a deep cold kiss of glass.

At supper he beams at me over a full plate, I am giddy with the abundance of the food and the drinks, and the smells and lights, and the abundance of love he showers on me, I examine him in wonder, his prickly, attractive tan, his lips proclaiming a lust both delicate and aggressive, he is wearing a denim shirt and pale pants, he chews his food calmly and gracefully, unlike me, my plate is already empty, and he scolds me, slow down, you don't know how to enjoy yourself, and I get up to refill my plate, smoothing my black dress down over my thighs, a man at the next table eyes me but I take no notice, what have I got to complain about, in fact, pits open so easily, all you have to do is give the ground a little kick and suddenly there's a gaping pit that you think will never close. It's true that at first it was me, I didn't want him with all my heart, and I envied my friends who changed their partners while I was still stuck with my little boyfriend from the same class at school, and I thought that if I were strong enough I would try to part from him, look for someone new who would excite me more, but I didn't dare, and he was so keen on me that it was sometimes irritating, too easy. Let her grow a little, my mother would scold him, give her some air, you're suffocating her with that love of yours, even in Yemen people don't get married so young, but he stuck to me, my breasts grew inside his hands, and if an occasional rival arrived on the scene he would succeed in getting rid of him with his childish stubbornness. That's what he was like, a little boy ruling me, I'm the only one who really loves you, he would threaten me, you think anyone else will love you like I do? They'll seduce you and discard you, believe me, and I would sit chastened by his side, considering his words, disappointedly examining his short stature, the silly fringe falling into his eyes, and I would know that outside his stifling house, with his aged, bitter parents, a whole world waited, exciting and turbulent, and only I was unable to either reach it or ignore its existence, until one evening he said, I'm sick of seeing your sour face, I don't need anyone else but if you think there's something better waiting for you out there, go ahead and look for it. I stared at him in astonishment, instead of the enticing magic of freedom I was seized by terror, and a void gaped inside me, like a cavity growing bigger and bigger in a tooth, hammering from ear to ear, and I went home crying, and my mother said, at last he's doing the right thing, don't waste time on weeping, go out and have some fun. I was barely seventeen then, and I felt that my life had ended, all my interest in the world outside evaporated in an instant, in his arms I could dream of other loves but when I was without him all I wanted was to get him back, and as if to spite me he suddenly shot up and broadened out, at recess I would see him in a huddle with other girls, I would see the gleam of pride on their faces, the defiance on his, and I felt like a mother whose son has chosen another mother. With a hollow in the pit of my stomach I would beg him to come back to me, wait for him after school, surprise him at home, but you loved me, you can't suddenly stop loving me, and in the end he returned, after a few months, but something had changed beyond recognition between us, a bitter, demanding suspiciousness usurped everything that had once been natural and self-evident, and suddenly I found myself appeasing him all the time, trying to prove to him with signs and wonders that I had chosen him wholeheartedly and not for lack of an alternative, and without any intention on my part this turned into my life's mission.

With a smile of satisfaction he looks at me as I sit down, pours me a glass of wine, the round mouth of the bottle sends an agreeable shiver down my spine, and he laughs, you enjoyed it, didn't you? And I stroke his hand, it was wonderful, and he says, I've got a few more ideas for you, and I giggle, I didn't know you were so creative, and he says, what can I do, one of us has to be. My mouth is full of fish bones and I don't reply, what do I care if he teases me a bit, when all's said and done he only does me good, reminds me that my body is more than a boring collection of organs with useful functions, that beyond the labor and anxieties of existence there is also the possibility of pleasure, and at that moment a couple about our own age walk past, both good-looking and well dressed, engaged in animated conversation, with a little boy and girl trailing behind them, she's about Noga's age and he is much younger, almost a baby, and I watch them enviously, why didn't we bring Noga along, and why haven't we got a cute, chubby little teddy bear with a running nose like them, and Udi says, don't start now, and I swallow the tiny bones in silence, ever since he let Noga fall he's refused to discuss the possibility of having another child, repulsed my every attempt to bring up the subject, but this time there's a new tone in his words, more indulgent, and I raise my eyes to the window, it seems to me that two benevolent hands are making their way toward us, the old hands of an ancient patriarch, spreading over our heads in a blessing, bringing our heads closer together, and suddenly everything seems possible, even a sweet, stubborn, bad-tempered little boy, like the one who sits down at our table by mistake and immediately bursts into tears, because we are not his father and mother.

Eight

We're not one flesh, one body, but two bodies that have changed places, I am wearing his body and he's wearing mine, each renouncing his own, and it seems as if all our lives we have been striving for this renunciation, ever since we were children in the same school uniform. With a profound sensation of relief I cast off myself, my thorny, restless consciousness, measuring his compact limbs, his fierce desire, it's me he wants and what could be better, it's mastery he wants and what could be easier, from the depths of my body he smiles at me, and his smile is warm and maternal, my love, he says, and I put my arms around his neck, fainting with weariness, with drink, with love, I feel as if I am rocking in a giant cradle, to and fro, the rocking turns into a ritual that seems like sex but it's different, what can it be, it's like a birth, where the sexual organs play a different role, burning in a completely different fire, and this fire licks my groin with its little tongue, the fire of an ancient, painful covenant, the covenant we should have made many years ago, consuming all doubts, frightening and consoling, if you are true to it no harm will come to you.

The dismembered corpses of our doubts lie before us on the sheets like sacrificial offerings, and I kneel on the enormous bed, like a field of cotton it encompasses me, white and generous, and I can run through its vastness and wave my arms, embrace the air of the world with open arms, I have no doubt, the Holy Spirit has passed here, like a bird it entered the window to sanctify us forever, and Udi presses against my back, one minute he's underneath me and the next he's above me, a hungry child falling on the candy of his dreams, and I turn over in blissful exhaustion, tonight I have understood everything, how good it is to be rid of the torturing doubts, now I understand that for me he is like a child or parents, impossible to choose or to free yourself from, and this is what binds us, this is what makes us husband and wife. A wave of compassion engulfs me as I give birth to him again and again, with a sweet resignation as if this is my vocation, until he groans beside me, his body weak and throbbing, and I pull the blanket up and cover us both, it seems full of warm downy kisses, don't sleep yet, its kisses tickle me, you mustn't go to sleep, they whisper, the night is full of desires, tonight is the night when all your wishes come true, you'll never have another night like this as long as you live. I sit up abruptly and look around me, who's whispering here, Udi is already asleep, who's suddenly dripping poison into my ear, the minute he goes to sleep my conscious mind begins to nag again, wake him up, the soft lips of the blanket murmur, don't you know that you must never let a child fall asleep after he's received a blow in case he never wakes up again, he's leaving you now in his sleep, he won't come back to you, you'll long for this night as long as you live, and I press myself to him, don't leave me Udi, his hand caresses me in his sleep, spreading warmth like the red-hot coil of an electric heater, the malicious whispers are silenced and I enter the little hut of sleep I used to tell Noga about when she couldn't fall asleep, and lock the door behind me, no one will bother me here, protected as the night advances, its colors subtly changing on the window, until a terrified roar startles me into wakefulness.

I can't see, he screams, his hands stretched out in front of him, beating the drowsy air like a baby's, Na'ama I can't see, and I wake up abruptly, the pounding of my heart drowning out the words, what is he saying, what does it mean, I've forgotten the language and I don't want to remember it, it's evil, too evil for me, and I mumble with my mouth closed, don't worry everything's all right, and he yells, what's all right, maybe you're all right but I can't see a thing, and I sit up and put my arms around him, calm down and it will go away, in my alarm it seems to me that I can't see either, closing my eyes in solidarity, what will Noga say when we both come home blind, groping after her voice as we stumble round the apartment. Leave me alone, he shakes my arms off his body, I don't need your embraces, and I get out of bed mortified, my whole body is still covered in a thin layer of love, a scab of congealed sperm that peels off easily. Through the window a clear spring day beckons me, a golden bell in the belly of the sun seems to be pealing merrily, calling us to come out into the world, to enjoy its delights, but for us it is all too late, in an instant it has become too late again.

His eyes bulge, almost straining out of their sockets, his hands grope over the bed, in an instant he has adopted the desolate movements of blindness, and I go up to him, don't worry, it will pass like the paralysis passed, the tests showed that everything was fine, and he says sullenly, their tests don't interest me, they make mistakes all the time, I'm sure I've got a tumor that keeps pressing on something else, and I say, that's impossible, that's precisely what they ruled out, it's apparently some stress or mental distress, you have to try to think of what's troubling you, and he jerks his head furiously from side to side, you dare to ask me what's troubling me, he suddenly screams, it's you who troubles me all the time, it's because of you that I'm sick!

A wave of nausea rises in me and I run to the bathroom and stand at the sink, gulping water from the tap, splashing it on my tortured face, the face of a prisoner who has lost all hope of being freed, what's happening here, what's happening to him, he's never been so volatile before, I have to return him to himself, my love, I whisper to the mirror, my love, my husband, it's me who was with you last night, don't turn me into an enemy, don't separate us, didn't you always want nights like this, for us to cover ourselves with layers of love, like warm underclothes in winter, so why are you turning away from me now of all times, and I bend down to the tap again, drinking and drinking and filling with anger, as if murky waters of hostility are flowing from its mouth, no words will help, he simply can't stand happiness, like a child who destroys his favorite toy, so that no one will take it away from him, but I'm nobody's toy, and already I want to yell back at him, how dare you blame me for your sickness, but my voice is inaudible, look at you, absorbed in your own insult when he can't see, that's the problem now, all the rest is luxury, and again I control my rage, collapsing into the bath, only yesterday the foam of our love poured out here, and today barbed wire separates us, a wall that has gone up overnight, arbitrarily cutting our common body in two, at the command of an unknown ruler.

Na'ama, I hear him calling me with the tyranny of the sick, where are you, I need you, and I force myself to come out, wrapped in a towel, what do you want, I ask, apprehensively examining his closed eyes, and he says, for a few days now I've been trying to understand what's happening to me, what's wrong with my life, and this morning it became clear to me that it's all because of the wasted seed, that's why I'm sick. Have you gone mad, I exclaim in horror, what are you talking about? And he says in a cold, confident voice, as if announcing the results of scientific research, about the fact that I go to bed with you, that's what I'm talking about, about the fact that you squeeze my sperm out of me, I can't go to bed with you anymore, the sperm is the essence of life, and I let you drink up my life with all the lips of your body.

I sit down on the bed, stunned, covering my lips with my hand, this is exactly how they slandered the Jews, that they drank the blood of a Christian child, and now the convert, whose nature has been converted by disease, is slandering me brazenly, and in my rage

I see that his face has relaxed, and a new certainty has taken it over, a false and distorting certainty, which makes my blood boil, but you're the one who always wants to go to bed with me, an indignant shriek escapes my throat, the stunned shriek of a trapped animal, so how dare you blame me? I'm sick of hearing that I'm the one who wants it, he says tight-lipped, you're the one who makes me want it, if you weren't with me I wouldn't want it, and I scream, great, so live without me, I'm sick of your accusations!

You won't get rid of me so easily after you've made me sick, he says through clenched teeth, and I tremble all over, I made you sick, you ingrate, I made you sick? But the words stick in my throat, they won't come out, they quiver between my rage-swollen tonsils, who sentenced our moments of grace to so short a life, and what will become of us, and what will become of Noga, and when I think of her the tears rush out, again she is doomed to disappointment, she must be waiting for us to come back to her tomorrow relaxed and happy, to usher her into our happiness as into a glorious palace.

In the corridors the vacuum cleaners are already advancing, hurrying the guests to leave their rooms, to be sucked up into the pipeline of pleasures awaiting them, and only we go on sitting in our room like bleak basalt rocks, strange to each other, strange to the residue of our love on the sheets that will soon be changed, strange to the benign resort surrounding us, and I sob into the wet towel, I can't go on like this, I can't take it anymore, and he snaps, I'm sick and tired of your tears, you only think about yourself, I'm sick and you're sorry for yourself! And I look round the room, what should I do, if I get dressed and go out he'll say that I'm abandoning him, and if I stay here I have nowhere to hide from him, trapped in the sights of a blind sniper, who could kill me by mistake. I return chastised to the bathroom, the sink allows me to lean on it, and again I stare at my face, eyelids already swollen over red eyes, lips slack from crying, this is not how I was supposed to look this morning, this is not where we were supposed to spend the morning, but on the veranda opposite the radiance of Mount Hermon, with cups of coffee and plates laden with delicious food, and then to walk in the fields, to see the flowers blooming, and now we have filled the valley with our bitterness, and I try to repeat to myself, just as I repeat to the women in the shelter, you're not a victim, you always have a choice, you're not a victim, but what choice do I have now that he's bound me to him by his lameness. Again and again I wash my face in boiling-hot water, as you would wash a pot with ancient dirt clinging to it, ugly, black oil stains, you have no choice, I say to myself, you have no choice but to comb this hair, clothe this body, put stockings on these feet, and I get dressed clumsily in the passage, congratulating myself as at some great feat, keeping out the range of his blind vision, and when I'm ready I say to him, I'm going down to have coffee, should I bring you something? He doesn't answer, and I peep in warily, his arm is covering his eyes, his mouth is open, bring me a lemon, he mutters, I feel terribly nauseated and I've got a headache.

So it's only a migraine, I breathe a sigh of relief, my old enemy the migraine, better a known enemy than a foreign invader, how well I know the blinding lights, the numbing nausea, the black, greasy headache, I spent days in bed with it, even on the morning of my wedding day it arrived to spoil the party, until one o'clock I lay on my childhood bed with my eyes closed, a wet towel on my forehead, in the old house that had become the home of my father's loneliness, which had gradually emptied of its contents. Hungry cats had clawed the wicker chairs until they fell apart, like nests nobody needed, and the walls were stripped of their garments, the signs of the pictures my mother had taken still stamped on them, like the marks of dry blows, and only my father's enormous barometer remained, a thermometer of giants haughtily dominating the wall, showing off the glass tube with the heavy dark pool of mercury at the bottom, miraculously climbing, rising and falling, predicting the weather.

He would stand thoughtfully opposite the antique barometer, a rare smile on his lips, like a victorious general surveying the battlefield. No point in hanging out the washing today, he would announce to my mother, when we were still a family, it won't get dry, and she would protest, but the weather forecast said it would be hot and dry, and she would go outside defiantly with the full basin, only to hurry back defeated a few hours later when the sky turned black, her precious washing soaking wet. These were his moments of pride and pleasure, before her marveling eyes he celebrated his victory over the forecaster, that mysterious rival who provoked him daily, as if the two of them were competing for my mother's love, and so precious were these moments to him that he tried to reconstruct them even after she left, trying to impress her with unequivocal messages. Before I went to bed I always asked him, will it be hot or cold, and he would station himself in front of his barometer, study it reverentially, and give me an accurate forecast, which was never wrong. All his confidence, the essence of all the knowledge he accumulated during his life, the essence of his pride, all of them seemed to be gathered in the dense pool of mercury rising and falling in the glass tube, and I with the damp towel draped over my head like a veil, my eyes almost blind, on my wedding day, stumbling to the kitchen to get another lemon, my hands groping in front of me, until a fit of giddiness overcame me, churning up my insides, and I reached for the wall and collided with a hard object that fell with me to the ground, and we both crashed together, me and the giant barometer of the world.

The mysterious solution instantly fell apart into dozens of gray mercury balls, jubilant as prisoners let out of jail, rolling under the beds, all their gravity gone in an instant, all they want now is to play, not to make predictions about the future, and I crawled under the bed, trying to stick them together again, among the sharp splinters of glass, trampling the exploded myth beneath my knees. To my horror I heard footsteps approaching, I didn't dare to raise my eyes, don't worry Daddy, I wept among the ruins, I'll buy you a new one, tomorrow morning I'll buy you a new one, with the money we get for wedding presents, and he said in his quiet, lifeless voice, but there aren't any more like it, it's a rare old barometer, and I insisted, I'll find one, you'll see, I'll find you one exactly like it, I'll get money for wedding presents and I'll take it all and buy you one exactly like it, and the migraine tightened like a vise around my head, how was I going to stand beneath the wedding canopy, and how was he going to stand beside me, the remnants of his pride leaking out of him precisely on my wedding day, and from then on I hid from him in the bustle of my new life, forgetting my promise, and only on the rare occasions when I went to visit him would the shadow of the barometer on the wall haunt me, and I would promise, tomorrow I'm going to buy you one exactly like it, and he would nod silently, and nobody asked him anymore if it would be hot or cold, and so stripped of all his strength he died one night in his sleep, of a silent heart attack, with wayward balls of mercury still playing under his bed.

I'll go down and get you a lemon, I say quickly, before he can stop me, and lean on the door I shut behind me, for the moment I'm free, and if it's only a migraine it's not such a big deal, I can cope with a migraine, but when I enter the dining room and look at the vacationers eating heartily, cramming healthy food into eager stomachs, I realize that I am already in a completely different existence, what's waiting for me today is completely different from what's waiting for them, no trips in jeeps or picnics in the heart of the spring or dips in the pool, and I sit down at a little table for two, there are no tables for one here, and stare at the radiant landscape revealed by the passing of the storm, the valley as blue as the sea, boats of red tiles calmly sailing on it, precisely in such a beautiful place he has to stop seeing, and again the tears, those transparent medusas, sting my cheeks and I bow my head, so as not to see the cheerful chewing around me and not to be seen in my disgrace. The waiter pours me coffee and I thank him tearfully as if he's saved my life, how pathetic I have become in a single morning, and all the time his demanding, ungrateful presence squats on the ceiling dotted with little lights like stars, two floors above me, watching me resentfully, crushing me with its weight. I get up and wander round the buffet, dismayed by the abundance, unable to make up my mind, a young woman next to me fills her plate, her movements greedy inside her robe, she spills carrot juice on me without a word of apology, and I snatch a roll as if I'm stealing it and return shamefaced to my table, scarcely able to swallow, all this luxury upsets me, irritates my nerves, and I escape to the stairs and only outside the door of our room do I realize that I've forgotten to ask for a lemon, they had everything there except for this one little item, the only thing I really needed. Hesitantly I go into the kitchen, where I am greeted by scowling looks, very different from the looks outside, whose politeness knows no bounds, and I ask for a lemon, actually I feel more comfortable there, in the backyard of the sumptuous breakfast, and even when the lemon is in my hand, big and yellow, I am in no hurry to leave, fingering it as if it is a precious fragile-stemmed citron that I must bring to the hut I have laboriously built to celebrate the Feast of Tabernacles, and I carry it carefully upstairs, holding it in front of me as I enter the room, like an offering, which there is nobody to accept, for the bed is empty, the big armchair, the bath, the room is empty of him, of his wrath, of his blindness, and I sit down on the bed and distractedly bite into the peel of the lemon. What's happened here, have I betrayed my mission, have I come too late, or perhaps he has recovered, and hurried after me to tell me that everything is all right now, and to apologize for something said in a moment of blindness, and we will carry on with our lovers' holiday, gliding about in our white robes as carefree as angels in heaven, and this possibility fills me with joy, even if he doesn't apologize I'll forgive him, I decide, the main thing is to go home relaxed, for Noga's sake, not to trap her in the close web of our tension.

I get up and go to the window, this golden day suddenly standing by my side, perhaps we will still make friends, me and the sun and the trees and the flowers, now I see them for the first time, cascades of spring flowers, yellow and purple and red, from a distance they have no names or histories, only bright spots of lively effervescent color. No doubt about it, there's a party going on down there, and I am ready to join in, to mingle with the brief lives of the spring flowers, almost as brief as the life of a match, and suddenly among the trees I see a pale figure swaying in dancing steps, flitting from tree to tree, and then kneeling, bowing down to the ground, as if in some ancient rite, and I am filled with dread and I hurry down to the little wood, and there I find him bowed between the tall chrysanthemums and the shining buttercups, his shoulders shaking, rattling noises rising from him as if from the depths of the earth.

Udi, what happened, I fall on him, crouching down beside him, how are your eyes, can you see anything? And he groans, my eyes are okay, but I can't breathe, I feel nauseous, and I ask, why did you go out, why didn't you wait for me in the room, I brought you a lemon, and he wheezes, I couldn't stay there, I had to get out, there wasn't any air. I look round at a loss, the sun is already burning my back, there seems to have been a coup last night in which summer seized power, and I say to him, let's go back to the hotel, I'll bring you water and something to eat, and he straightens up, leaning on me tall and heavy, but he refuses to move, and I plead with him, Udi, you have to drink something, it will help you, and he mumbles, but it's forbidden for me to go back to the hotel with you, and it's forbidden for me to eat or drink, and I say, yes, yes, as if to a small child, and then I take it in, what did you say? Who forbade you? And he continues in the same submissive tone, completely different from the aggressive tone of this morning, when I was waiting for you I remembered a story from the book of Kings about the man of God who came out of Judah to Beth-el and God forbade him to eat bread or drink water there or to return by the same way that he came. And what's that got to do with you, I ask impatiently, and he says, I feel that it relates to me, I'm not allowed to eat or drink here, I have to leave this place before somebody succeeds in making me sin like they did that prophet, you know what happened to him in the end? A lion slew him, and his carcass came not unto the sepulchre of his fathers. He sends me a frightened, crazy look, and I try to repulse the sticky arms of fear, maybe he's really not right in the head, maybe the doctors were correct, I should have let them put him in the psychiatric ward, how could I have been so foolish as to think that I could handle his mind.

Help me to the car, he groans, I'll wait for you there until you finish packing, I can't stay here any longer, and I lead him to the car which is rapidly heating up, no doubt about it, summer has already seated its burning behind on its throne, and I help him to lie down on the backseat and return disconsolately to the hotel. Why do I have to pack, why do we have to leave, again everything is ruined beyond recognition, my chin sags in a new movement of resignation, how badly I want to stay, to drink coffee in the quiet lobby, or outside, on that bench, but it's really quite clear, it should be quite clear, that the more I want to stay the more he'll want to leave. Maybe I'll refuse this time, I'll tell him that I'm staying till tomorrow as planned, let's see what he'll do then, he isn't really me, after all, so how can he affect my life like this, but I immediately remember that he's ill, I have no choice but to give in to him, perhaps he's ill precisely so that I will give in to him, but that would be hard to prove, and I go into the room, from minute to minute I grow more reluctant to leave, I haven't even had a chance to sit on this armchair, or at the table opposite the window, and with grow-ing regret I throw the clothes into the traveling bag, mixing his with mine. The closet is empty and now to the bathroom, toothbrushes and toothpaste and shaving gear, and here on the night table, face cream and deodorant and hairbrush, and on his side the reddish rectangle of his Bible, and I leaf through it resentfully, yellow grains of sand trickle from the pages, where the hell is that story that's to blame for us leaving here, what did he say, the man of God who came out of Judah to Beth-el, or the opposite, I was hardly listening, I have no idea where to look, I haven't got a hope of finding it, the pages are tricking me on purpose, stinging my fingers, and in my rage I throw the book violently to the floor, as if it contains the roots of the madness that has taken over my life, quickly close the traveling bag, before I can change my mind, this will be his punishment, this book will stay here forever.

Before I leave I scan the room again, to make sure I haven't forgotten anything, peek under the bed, between the towels, and again I see that red brick, the book he was given at the high school graduation ceremony, I remember him going up to the stage, and the principal shaking his hand, reluctant to let go of the outstanding student of his year, ceremoniously presenting him with the book, I lost mine years ago but he kept his, took it with him to the army, and then on all his tours, whipping it out of his pocket and reading it to his tourists, explaining and pointing, and already I want to pick it up in spite of everything, but the distance between us is unbridgeable, especially when I shut the door, frightened but gloating, what does he think, that he can hurt me without me hurting him back, and it seems to me that I can hear a piping cry behind me, as of an abandoned baby, but I'm not sorry, let him be sorry.

Sure you didn't forget anything, he asks, determined to be in control even from the depths of the backseat, and I answer aggressively, if you don't trust me go and check for yourself, and he falls silent, his hollow cheeks flushed red with the heat, like two wilted roses, and I push the traveling bag into the back and sit down as usual in the passenger seat next to the driver, and only then I realize that there's no other driver now but me, that I am supposed to drive down all that dizzying road on the steep mountainside myself, me with my fear of heights and depths. I look at him imploringly, willing him to pull himself together and rescue me, but he lies fainting on the backseat and the driver's seat waits only for me, as in the nightmare that has haunted me for years, driving a car with most of its limbs amputated but it goes on traveling nevertheless, unable to stop, around me the cars roar like hungry lions, cutting into me on all sides, I have no choice but to go on, and I ask in a hoarse voice, is there another road, and he mumbles, there has to be another road, I'm forbidden to return the way we came, and I sigh, he no longer knows what he's saying, and I look at the abyss beneath us, in the sharp clear daylight it looks less frightening but more cruel, waving its wide hips, telling us to give up in advance, to take the shortcut that will spare us the hardships of tomorrow and the next day, minute by minute its powers of seduction increase, like a woman who grows more confident as she feels her victims responding to her wiles.

Nine

ike an ancient lizard, a fossil from primeval times, an extinct
species, he lies motionless in the dark bedroom, separated
from the sun he loved by heavy blinds, his skin fading, his
body covered with scales of dust, as if he is an exhibit in a museum
that nobody comes to see, and only Noga looks in at him almost
wordlessly when she returns from school, hungry and worried, to
make sure that he is still there, lying on his back with his eyes open,
staring at the ceiling.

His long body is growing shorter, his shoulders are shrinking,
day by day he seems to be reverting to the dimensions of his boy-
hood, and when I walk past him in the morning, wrapped in a towel,
to get my clothes from the closet, I am as embarrassed as I was then,
a tall, broad girl with that skinny little boy, because the smaller he
gets the bigger I grow, both of us are returning to the dimensions of
our early youth, as if everything that has happened to us since then
is temporary, easy to deny, for suddenly I have discovered, after years
of thinness, the delights of the refrigerator, compulsively filling my
belly before going in to him when I come home from work, especially with buttered toast, like the stacks my father used to pile up
for us on Saturday mornings, crooked, toppling towers of thin slices
of toast with lumps of butter melting between them, and Noga

watches in astonishment as they fly out of the toaster like burning slaps, how can you eat toast when it's so hot, and I smile apologetically and send her out for ice cream bars, the sweeter the better, I am especially addicted to the ones with the chocolate inside, that take the longest to eat, and we sit opposite each other and lick them, like two little sisters whose parents are too busy to supervise their children's diet. Once upon a time he would scold me, how can you eat that junk, taking the wrapper and reading me the ingredients in disgust, but now he is utterly indifferent to our acts, if we took poison he wouldn't notice, and only my clothes protest, nothing fits me anymore, the jeans haven't got a hope of closing, the new suit despairs of encasing my burgeoning body, and only a couple of hastily purchased, wide, shapeless summer dresses cover my sweating nakedness as I enter the shelter, and the girls look at me in surprise, at first they thought that I was pregnant, like them, and a new sisterhood grew up between us, until they realized that their pointed, arrowlike bellies were quite different from my slack, humiliated one, where nothing floated but lumps of lifeless food.

And the new girls that come to us think that I was always like this, that this is how I really am, and only Hava and Anat sometimes say reprovingly, what's happening to you, Na'ama, what are you doing to yourself, before they hurry off to take care of more urgent matters. Once in a while I catch Anat's eyes resting on me with a compassionate, almost inviting look, but I avoid her, now it's my turn to hurry off, so as not to hear her thoughts screaming at me, deafening my ears, I told you to leave him, you should have left him years ago, and what will become of you now, you see, when you build a house on hollow foundations it's doomed to collapse, you thought that goodwill and guilt were enough to build a family on, and I protest in silent indignation, you won't tell me what to do, you never even tried, what do you know about real life, but she isn't the only one I avoid, I avoid friends with husbands and children too, how can I sit opposite them in cafes, and hear their complaints about their husbands who are always at work, when my life is disintegrating before my eyes, and I have no way of picking up the pieces and putting them together again, like the drops of mercury scattered throughout the house on my wedding day.

When people ask me about him I keep my answers brief and stiff, trying to blur the facts as best I can, and to my relief nobody insists, nobody is really eager to hear about the suffering of his fellows. Some of them say, let time take its course, he'll get over it in the end, and some say, the more you devote yourself to him the longer he'll keep it up, you should try to be indifferent, so he'll understand he has nothing to gain from this madness, while others take the opposite view, you have to support him, make him feel secure, he's your husband, for better or worse, and I listen silently, changing my opinion from one day to the next, one minute to the next, I've tried so hard to please him, to surprise him with small gifts, to pamper him, to cook him special dishes, and the results have been so disappointing that I no longer have the strength to try. When I enter the room he rebukes me with a hostile, demanding look, the demands are undefined and cannot be satisfied, whatever I do only arouses his resentment. When I invite him to come and eat with us in the kitchen he refuses, and when we come and sit next to him he complains that we're disturbing him, when I go to work he complains that I'm neglecting him, and if I take a day off and stay home with him he ignores me resentfully. Sometimes on my way home I hope against hope for a miracle, perhaps he will open the door bathed and scented, wearing clean clothes instead of the stinking rags he refuses to change, and he'll embrace me and drag me to bed like he did once upon a time, quickly before Noga comes home, or just sit on the balcony with a book in his hand, and read his favorite bits out loud to me, nag me with all kinds of stories from the Bible, get in my way when I'm cooking, as long as he shows a spark of life, of interest, in me, in Noga, in the world around him, in all the things that used to fill his life.

But he's always in bed when I come home, and only a murky yellow film in the toilet bowl bears witness to the fact that he was there and didn't flush the water, he refuses to flush because the noise hurts his ears, just as the sunlight hurts his eyes. He refuses to eat too, and only rarely he asks me to make him semolina with grated chocolate on top, the cereal he loved so much when he was a child, and his mother, who was afraid of spoiling him, agreed to make it for him only when he was really sick. No doubt about it, these are our meager moments of grace, when I bring a steaming bowl of cereal to his bed, and Noga joins in, and sometimes I do too, and we sit at his bedside and we all swallow in silence, and he sends us a sad, triumphant smile, like a sick little boy, exposing yellowing teeth.

Sometimes I forget to ask him how he is, because it doesn't make any difference anymore, whether it's his hands he can't move today, or his eyes that can hardly see, or his toes, or his neck that hurts, or his head, the same devastating incapacity seems to be floating through his body, like a cloud in the sky, settling first here, then there, and he too, who at the beginning enjoyed describing his aches and pains in detail, has already stopped attending to them, because what has taken over here is the general tone, the sum of all the details, I'm not well, he's not well, Daddy isn't well yet.

But what's wrong with him, Noga would persist in the beginning, after we came home defeated from our spring vacation, and I would say, it's nothing serious, and she would nag, so why is he in bed if it's nothing, is he well or not? And I would try to reassure her, he's not really well and he's not really ill, and she would reproach me, so why don't you take him to see a doctor, why don't you do something? And I would say apologetically, he won't go back to the hospital, he doesn't want to be examined, I can't take him by force. Sometimes I reproached myself too, do something, don't give in to him, and I would stand resolutely in the doorway, Udi, it can't go on like this, you have to take more tests, to find out what's happening to you, you're becoming addicted to this illness, and he would look at me coldly, I'm not going to any psychiatric ward, if I bother you then you go, and I threaten weakly, I will go, if you don't look after yourself I'll really go, what do you think, that you'll lie in bed all day and I'll look after you like a nurse, and he immediately defends himself, I don't need you to look after me, what do you do for me already, and I look at him helplessly, I'm not keen to take him back to the hospital either, but we have to find some solution, there has to be some cure for this collection of symptoms, and apprehensively I remember the depressing name of his disease, Conversion, as if I've suddenly remembered the name of the other woman.

Even my mother who hardly ever interferes began to pester me, what's happening to him, you have to do something, and one evening she turned up with her friend, a psychiatrist, we just dropped in for a minute, she announced in a meaningful voice, to see what's new, and Udi immediately jumped out of bed and sat with us in the living room, full of smiles, and he made such an effort to prove that everything was fine that the doctor looked at me suspiciously, as if I were the sick one here, and at the door she whispered to me, he looks a little run-down, but I can't see any problem, and I cheered up immediately, sinking into pleasant daydreams of his imminent recovery, but he was already back in bed, exhausted by the effort, and for a week he refused to speak or eat, though in the mornings I would find a cabinet open in the kitchen, a shrinking loaf of bread, seeking signs of his life as if trying to track down a mouse.

Sometimes I ask him in the tone of a kindergarten teacher, so what did you do all day, and he defends himself aggressively, nothing, as if there is nothing on earth worth doing. Ever since his beloved Bible disappeared he refuses to open a book, and I who had regretted it the next day and phoned the hotel and begged them to look for the Bible and send it to me look in guilty remorse at his empty nightstand, how could anyone have stolen a shabby old Bible with sand trickling from its pages. I immediately bought him a new one, but he shoved it into the drawer without opening it, as if his beloved stories were to be found only in the old Bible, and he does the same with the other books I buy him from time to time, he doesn't even open them, he just lies on his back with his eyes open, at night too, with the reading lamp on, heating up the air around him, like the little lights next to the sepulchres in the city of the dead, that only emphasize the darkness.

Every night after putting Noga to bed I open up the living room sofa, cover it with a sheet and lie there like a guest, far from the bedroom that has turned into his sickroom, and there is a certain relief in the night sea of loneliness, to sleep alone, not to consider him, not to wait for the light to go off, just me by myself, in the living room sweltering even at night, the two parts of the sofa drawing my back crookedly into the dent between them, and it's only at daybreak that I wake up in a panic, what's happened to my life, remembering him with a shock, as if I've read something that has shaken me in the newspaper, what does he do all day, what does he think about, what does he want, what is he planning to do, what can he do, but when I go into the room and see his gloomy face, smell his bad smell, I answer myself with his aggressiveness, nothing, he does nothing, he thinks nothing, he wants nothing, and then I remember myself with the same shocked dismay, what will become of me, of the rest of my life, I'm like a deserted wife who can't get married again until her husband shows up, alive or dead, and I try to clarify what remains of my love for him which is almost as old as I am, what remains of all we did, learned, accumulated, all these years, and again that word echoes in my ears, nothing, nothing remains.

Because every feeling is contradicted by another feeling which negates it, and so on and so forth until the love rots, like stagnant water, a stinking swamp swarming with mosquitoes, and the attraction which sometimes flickers like the glimmering of a delightful memory is repulsed by the aversion, when I see him lying on the sheets he refuses to let me change, and the pity and compassion are contradicted by the anger and resentment, how dare he ruin our lives, and even the question that troubled me so much at the beginning, what is the meaning of his illness, is there really something physically wrong with him or is he only pretending, even this suddenly makes no difference to me, for I am equally helpless before both, there's nothing I can do anymore, nothing, only watch the summer advancing, gathering force and cruelty, digging yellow claws into my eyes, mottling my skin with sunspots that will never go away, boiling my blood until steam rises from me, unfamiliar vapors of envy and hatred.

Because I envy almost everybody now, I wander round the supermarket like a sleepwalker, talking to myself between the shelves, and every woman who passes me seems luckier than me, this one fills her cart with beer cans, when the hot evening falls she will sit on the porch with her husband and drink the cold beer, like we did, summer after summer, sometimes slouching on the sofa to watch a disappointing movie on the television, there's a great movie on tonight, he would tell me enthusiastically, but after half an hour he would fall asleep, and I would go on watching alone, faithful to the characters who were offering me their lives, and at the end of the movie he would wake up, smile at me apologetically, pour us more beer, stroke my bare thighs. I even dare to envy the girls in the shelter, those young girls, almost children, whose lives have been distorted like their bodies, with the little bump in the middle, menacing as a growth. Suddenly I grow a hard shell round my heart, and I look at them indifferently, it's true that it's hard for them now, but in a few weeks' time their problem will be solved, the baby hiding in their bellies will be born, handed over to the adoptive parents who have been waiting for years, and everything will return to normal. It's true that every baby they see in the street will make their hearts tremble, it's true that even if they get married and have families, the lost baby will always accompany them, waking them up with its silence at night, sliding down giant chutes between heaven and earth, but in spite of everything they have a choice, their lives are still open, and mine is already closed.

Sometimes Hava looks at me doubtfully during our meetings, and I am afraid that she can guess my thoughts, heretical thoughts forbidden in our profession, because as Anat and I always told each other, in the face of all this suffering our personal problems seemed insignificant, but suddenly with me it's the opposite, my problems dwarf all the problems around me, which I am supposed to deal with to the best of my ability, and now I don't have the patience. I don't have the patience for the familiar discussions, to help them analyze their situation, to present them again and again with the other alternative, to explain the implications of their decisions to them, to visit them in the hospital when they are weak and shaken by the birth, and to reexamine their decision with them, whether to give the baby up or raise it. Suddenly I am sick of giving and giving, and it seems to me that Hava can see all this with her sharp senses and that she is looking at me doubtfully, I'm sure that she's planning to fire me, and I stare at her anxiously, that's all that's missing now, Udi hasn't worked for weeks, my salary is barely sufficient, I think twice before I buy anything, standing at the checkout counter in the supermarket as if I'm in the dock, waiting for the judge to pass sentence, what will happen if she lets me go, what will we live on? When I walk past her closed door I'm sure that she's interviewing candidates for my job, and I pace nervously up and down the corridor and knock at her door on various implausible pretexts, that only make her more suspicious, and me more afraid.

I haven't got the patience even for Noga, I'm sick of seeing the hope in her eyes when she comes home from school, a puppyish hope, the reflection of my own, altogether she is a reflection of my distress, she runs to his room and emerges again immediately, defeated, what's there to eat, she asks in a beaten voice, no longer nagging, when will Daddy get better, when will Daddy take me with him on his trips, and after the meal she shuts herself in her room, staring at the old TV set, whose red light paints the faces of the people with a garish artificial blush. Why don't you ask friends round, I ask her, and she mutters, I don't want to disturb Daddy, and I know that this isn't the reason, they stopped coming months ago. Then why don't you go round to them, you used to go out more, what about Shira, what about Merav, why don't you go and play with them, you can't stay at home all the time watching television, I scold her almost harshly, and she whispers, but perhaps Daddy will need me, she doesn't want to tell me the truth and I don't want to hear it, that she has no friends anymore, that her world has emptied. I'm sick of worrying about her, I want everything to work out, at least for her, for friends to call, to invite her to pajama parties, to a movie, just yesterday I saw Shira and Merav eating ice cream in a cafe, both of them cheerful and slender in brief tank tops and short shorts, and only my little girl is wild and sloppy in Udi's huge tee-shirts and a suffering expression in her eyes, and I look at her resentfully, why are you such a weight on me, can't you even pretend to be happy, how am I going to stop up so many holes at once, I haven't got that many fingers, can't you just pretend to go out somewhere, let me fall apart without you, because I haven't got the strength anymore to keep up a façade in front of you, and I am immediately filled with remorse and I hug her and tell her that I love her, and she squirms uncomfortably in my embrace, recoiling from its phoniness.

Sometimes she switches off the television and goes outside, and then I'm worried stiff that something will happen to her on the way, how will she cross the road with that moony look in her eyes, and I try to persuade her to stay at home, let's have another ice cream, I coax her, and she says, maybe later, and I peep out of the window, hoping to see her disappear into the building opposite, where Merav who was once her best friend lives, but she goes on walking, and then I permit myself to collapse, I get into her bed and cry into her pillow, and then I quickly wash my face and begin to wait, and I know that she hasn't gone to visit any girlfriend but to my mother, who lives not far from us, she only feels comfortable talking to her, she only tells her about her problems at school, and I've been avoiding my mother for weeks, not now, Mother, don't tell me anything now. In the evening when she comes back she seems more lighthearted, and I can't resist asking her, did you go round to Merav's, and she answers sourly, no, to Granny's, and then she gets in her own dig and asks me hopefully, how's Daddy, and I answer sourly, there's nothing new, what about your homework, and then comes the usual ritual of looking for notebooks and times tables, and all the contents of her book bag are strewn over the floor, chewed-up lumps of gum stuck like snails to notepads and textbooks, and I look at her in despair, not knowing where to begin, she's forgotten to write down the homework again, or she didn't have time to copy it from the blackboard, the teacher always rubs it out before she has a chance to copy it down, we'll have to have your eyes tested, I say, and she nearly cries, I don't want glasses, everyone will laugh at me.

Sometimes she stays at my mother's place overnight, and then I go to sleep on her narrow bed, where I sleep the best, and when I wake up in the morning, at the first moment of the day, before you know if it's hot or cold, good or bad, it seems to me that I am still a child in my parents' house before they got divorced, and in a minute my father will come into the room and tell me what the weather is, whether to put on a sweater or a coat, and I luxuriate in bed for a few minutes longer, I don't have to push Noga up the steep hill of the morning, urge her to get up and comb her hair and get dressed, I drink my coffee slowly and shower at my leisure, and then I go into the bedroom wrapped in a towel, to get my clothes, only my clothes are still there, a memorial to my previous life, and he is there as always, a fossilized remnant of primordial times, lying on his back with his eyes open.

One morning I get into bed beside him, straight from the shower, a surprisingly cool summer morning that for some reason fills me with hope, suddenly I feel that everything is simpler than I thought, that everything is after all up to me, and I shake his dry body, to make him come alive, laughing and crying and pleading, Udi get over it, Udigi get well already, let's make love, and afterward we'll have coffee on the balcony and eat breakfast, Udi, please, it's up to us, let's begin again, and it seems to me that his body stirs toward me, he embraces me with his feeble arms, and I kiss his sunken cheeks, gently stroke his penis, surprised to discover that it's still there, I thought it must have rotted by now and fallen off like the oranges in the yard, and I throw off the blanket and sit on top of him, the way he used to like, pressing down on the hard pelvic bones, but his penis wilts beneath me, crumples between my thighs, nothing like this has ever happened to us before, and I whisper, never mind, Udi, we'll try another time, it'll be all right, and it seems to me that his whole body is weeping under mine, begging for help, and I scold myself, why did I even try, why did I force myself on him, now I've exposed his weakness, every attempt to help only makes things worse, only what comes from him will save him, if it ever does come.

He doesn't react, as if he hasn't even noticed what happened, but when I come home at lunchtime he calls me rudely, Na'ama, come here, and I hurry to the room, at long last a sign of life, and he asks, where have you been, his voice dull like the voices of the deaf, and I reply, what do you mean, I've been to work, and he says, but it's already half past two, and I say, I stopped at the supermarket to pick up a few things. So where are they, he asks and I say defensively, I asked for them to be delivered, they'll be here soon, and he laughs hoarsely, the veins on his neck sticking out, I don't believe you, whore, you went to fuck, you went to get the prick I couldn't give you, and I stare at him, stunned, how can I prove to him that he's wrong? You're out of your mind, I mumble, I've been at work all day, I haven't got the faintest desire to fuck, and he yells, liar, I saw how much you were dying for a fuck this morning, you don't care that it makes me ill, as long as you get your prick, and horrified I try to calm him down, Udi, what's wrong with you, I wanted to go to bed with you because I love you, because we're husband and wife, I'm not in the least interested in sex for its own sake, you know that, I never have been, and he growls, you've changed, I've seen you change, when we were in that hotel I understood it, and that's what made me sick, you hear, that's what made me sick, I saw that the only thing that interests you is fucking, you don't care who you do it with, you'd be happy to do it with the delivery boy from the supermarket, if you were really there at all.

I stare at him in shock, my teeth are chattering uncontrollably, the sweat is pouring furiously from my forehead, burning my eyes, Udi, believe me, all I want is for you to get well, and for us to be the way we were again, that's all, and for a moment he examines me in surprise, as if weighing my words, and then he bursts out, you want them to take me away, that's why you keep nagging me about doctors, they promised you to hospitalize me and that's all you're waiting for, to throw me out and bring someone to fuck you every night, and I leave the room and lie down on the living room sofa, the tears and the sweat mingling in a sour, stinging solution, and then the delivery arrives, with the smiling boy, who disappears before I can open my purse, he has no idea what he's suspected of, and Udi shouts from his bed, make me something to eat, if you still remember what I like at all.

I try to cheer myself up, perhaps he's returning to himself in spite of everything, if he has an appetite, and I decide to make spaghetti and meatballs, for two hours I stand in the kitchen, and when the food is ready I go to him, do you want to eat in bed or will you come to the table? He looks at me disdainfully, you won't make up for your cheating with your fancy meals, I'd rather die of starvation, and I leave the room in silence, my hands trembling with the desire to hit him, to tighten round his neck, to tear off his limbs, I grab the saucepan and eat the boiling dish straight out of it, without even using a fork, my hands red from the fresh tomato sauce, my mouth burning, I swallow without chewing, without tasting, until I reach the bottom of the saucepan, scraping with burning fingers, fatty bits of red meat collecting under my fingernails, and then I realize that I've eaten it all, without leaving anything for Noga, her favorite food, how could I have done this to her, and I stumble to the bathroom and kneel down next to the toilet, I can't keep all that food in my stomach, and I push two fingers down my throat, it seems to me that when everything comes out I'll be purified, but nothing comes out, the meatballs stick to my stomach like unwanted fetuses, and I push my fingers deeper and deeper until my throat is scratched and bleeding, what have I done, what have I done, red tears drip into the toilet bowl, and I get up and wash my face, I hardly recognize this filthy face, it isn't me, what has he done to me, turned me into an animal, a wounded bear, it can't go on like this.

I'll never go into his room again, I swear to myself, I'll move all my clothes into the living room and be finished, there's nothing for me to do there, let him take care of himself, let him hate himself instead of me, and in the evening he comes out of the room, hanging on to the walls, thin and trembling, I can't see anything again, he says, where are you? And I whisper, I don't feel well, Udi, I can't help you, and he creaks in a hoarse voice, you break so quickly, there are women who look after their husbands for years, and you break after one month, suddenly you don't feel well either, trying to compete with me, after you made me sick, and I don't reply, I feel faint, I can hardly hear him, dull syllables smashing on the floors of the house, I must be careful not to tread on the shards with my bare feet, and his outburst peters out, like a dead cat jerking, a kitten run over in the street, he jumps a few more times but in fact he's already quite dead, and I too, buried beneath him, not expecting anything, and only the fear still sends an occasional jolt of life shuddering through me, what will happen if they fire me from my job, what if something happens to Noga?

Little by little, almost imperceptibly, the forgotten fantasies of his recovery give way to fantasies of his death, and I wake early in the morning and stand on tiptoe opposite the closed door, seeing in my mind's eye the thin, stiff body, frozen as a mummy, shining with a heavenly radiance, commanding me to live, and I fill with pure sorrow, free of anger, almost pleasurable, like the sorrow that accompanies the first love of youth, the feeling of relief competing with the pain of the loss, how easy it is to love him when he's dead, and I imagine how I'll climb the stairs to the rooftop studio after the days of mourning are over, how I'll stand in front of the parade of my painted faces, without saying a word I'll take off my clothes, my painted nude will turn me on, and there on the armchair all the vows will be canceled, completely canceled, they won't exist anymore, and I'll tighten my thighs round his waist, the curls on the nape of his neck will coil round my fingers like silver rings.

With a faint creak I open the door, our double bed is almost empty, he lies on the edge as if he's been kicked there, one leg hanging in the air, his night face full of suffering, how abandoned he looks at the edge of the bed, like a helpless child in the prison of his sickness, and suddenly his eyelids flutter, I see him smile in the bitter moonlight, Na'ama forgive me, he whispers, I don't understand what's happening to me, I don't know what to do, I need help, and I lie down beside him, stroke the transparent hairs on his chest, Udigi, I only wish I could help you, if we were only together we could drive the illness out, but it comes between us and makes you hate me, and me hate you. I know, he whispers, you'd be better off if I was dead, and I don't trouble to deny it, in any case these dawn murmurings will soon be swept into sleep, and I myself won't know if they were really said, when I hurry to the car in the morning, tired and worried, and a clear tinkle of bells will greet me, as if a flock of sheep are grazing between the buildings, and then I'll see the neighbors' daughter coming toward me with shopping baskets full of groceries, the one who was in India, and she has bells on her ankles and her hands and in her hair, and I'll gaze at her with an unclear thirst, and then I'll remember, tell me, didn't you once say there was some kind of Indian doctor that you could recommend? And she'll laugh, not Indian, Tibetan, and I'll say, it doesn't matter, as long as she's good, and she'll say, she's not just good, she's amazing, she can bring the dead to life, and I'll say eagerly, give me her number, I have to try her, and she'll ask, it's for your husband, right, I haven't seen him outside for a long time, and I'll say, yes, he isn't getting any better, do you think she'll be able to help him? And she says, sure, she'll get him out of it, just be careful, and I ask I surprise, careful of what, of her? And she'll say, no, not of her, just be careful, because the Tibetans say that it's dangerous to put an end to suffering.

Ten

When I open the door to her she looks to me like a beggar-woman, young and skinny, with a big basket in her hand and a dark, hungry face, and I'm already on my way to my purse when she says, I'm Zohara, and just then her basket begins to squeal, and she takes out a little baby and immediately pulls out her breast and starts feeding it standing up, holding it firmly in her thin arm. Loud gurgles of pleasure break out of the baby's throat and I marvel at the amount of milk gushing out of that shriveled breast and I examine her in surprise and disappointment—this is the woman who's going to save us? She seems more in need of salvation herself, just like one of the girls who come to us at the shelter, young and lost, burdened with her heavy basket, and after all my efforts to persuade Udi to agree to see her, it took me hours of coaxing, why not give it a try, what have you got to lose. I've got nothing to gain either, he grumbled, all that voodoo and witchcraft isn't for me, and I protested, it's an ancient, natural form of medicine, what do you care, just give it a try, and now what—I'll show this black girl into his room and he'll kick her out in a second and never agree to see anyone again, and I count her steps resentfully as she moves calmly around our living room, circling the armchairs with quiet steps until the baby falls asleep on her shoulder, and then she puts it down in the basket and asks with surprising authority, so what's the problem?

There's the problem, I point to the closed door, he hasn't been functioning for weeks, and I fill her in reluctantly on the progression of his illness, I'm wasting my time, it's clear to me that she won't be able to help him, but she listens gravely, nodding her head, her eyes fixed on my face, I'll go to him, she says, leaving the living bundle on the living room carpet like Moses in the ark of bulrushes, and marches confidently to the door, which immediately closes behind her. I sit down on the carpet next to the sleeping baby, and examine its plump, fair face, so different from its mother's, bending over it curiously, I haven't examined a baby at such close quarters for ages. So that's how you really look, I whisper, excited as a spy who has succeeded in penetrating the enemy camp, because even though I tirelessly repeat to the girls in the shelter, this is a living creature we're talking about here, full of needs, just one big need, it seems that I too have unconsciously grown used to seeing the tiny creature in their stomachs as something abstract, a supernatural being, alternately monstrous and messianic, a fist from heaven smashing their youth to smithereens. I pick it up carefully in my arms, unbelievable how light it is, its face connected by a tenuous thread to a tiny, weightless body, as if it's still a darting tadpole of sperm, and I sniff it, seeking the famous, soothing baby smell, but instead I smell something deep and salty, the smell of private parts, and I recoil as if I've smelled my own insides. How can that be possible, I wonder, shocked, haven't they even cleaned it yet from its embarrassing passage into the world, and again my resentment flares against the young mother, how will she take care of Udi if she doesn't even bother to wash her own baby.

I put it back quickly into the straw basket, before it comes apart in my hands, and luckily it goes on sleeping quietly, as if it hasn't yet been born at all, and I go out onto the porch, today it's actually not quite so hot, friendly clouds soften the sun, the summer seems to have taken fright at its own intensity and decided to let up a little, and I stare at the little street, the Persian lilac opposite sends me a wilted, apologetic wave, and I smile at it, never mind, I haven't got much to offer either. Only a few weeks ago her starry flowers blossomed giddily about her, weaving a tapestry of perfumed purple threads, and now not a trace of them remains, and she is left yellowing and humiliated, exposed to the glare of the sun, which sends me back inside, and I tiptoe past the closed door, a strange silence comes from the room, as if they've both fallen asleep in there, and in me the anger rumbles, that's my Udi in there, my husband, once I would write my name on his earlobes, what gives her the right to seclude herself with him and leave me outside, to look after her baby. A cough rises from my throat as if I've swallowed smoke, the smoke of an embarrassing jealousy suddenly flaring up, I have to put a stop to this intimate communion, and there's only one way to do it, and I go back to the living room and shake the basket, until the pink mouth gapes and a feeble cry of complaint rises from it, and then I hurry to the room and open the door, without knocking, and see her sitting on the edge of the bed, her fingers encircling his wrist like a velvet bracelet, while he sits erect with his legs crossed, his arms bristling with tiny needles, as if he's turned into a hedgehog, and on the crown of his head, where his hair is growing thin, a stick of incense burning calmly, like a little horn.

She lets go of his wrist and quickly leaves the room, beckoning me to follow her, and I obey furiously, it's my husband, it's my house, who does she think she is telling me what to do, and follow her shamefacedly to the basket which is already quiet, the baby was crying, I stammer behind her back, I thought it was hungry, how can I let such a young girl shame me, and in my house too, and I immediately ask her impatiently, so what's the story, when will he get better, and she smiles calmly, I hope not too soon. What did you say? I examine her in stunned surprise, and she repeats, I hope that the illness won't be in a hurry to leave him, and you too, if you care about him, should hope with me, and I ask in a near shout, why? What you're saying doesn't make any sense at all, and she explains quietly, stressing every word, every illness is an opportunity, Na'ama, your husband hasn't even begun to realize the opportunity that's been given him here, he mustn't waste this illness of his, because it will be a long time before he gets another opportunity. I stare at her in astonishment, I don't get it, who does she think she is turning everything upside down, since when is illness good and recovery bad, and suddenly she seems monstrous to me, with that angular face of hers and that forward-jutting jaw, why did I let her into our house, and I beg her, as if it all depends on her, listen, Zohara, we can't go on like this, this strange disease is ruining our lives, our daughter is depressed, I'm a wreck, I can't cope at work, things can't go on like this, and my voice is already disintegrating, and I'm so ashamed of crying in front of this stranger, but she listens to me with that profound seriousness of hers, moving her lips as if she's measuring the words with the ruler of her tongue, and saying firmly, but this is completely unnecessary, you have to change your attitude, both for you and for your daughter this is a chance to develop, for you too this illness can become a source of inspiration and liberation from suffering. What are you talking about, I burst out, what inspiration is there in a person who rots in bed all day long and does nothing but complain and blame, and she looks at me patronizingly, try to understand, she says, both of you cling to each other too tightly, in order to benefit from the situation you must let go, relax your grip, think of two clods of earth ground up in two clenched fists, nothing will be left of them, and I protest indignantly, we barely talk to each other, you call that clinging? And she says, clearly, look how hard you're taking it, it's your choice, reacting like that. What do you mean, taking it hard, I ask, vacillating between dismissal and astonishment, any woman would react like me if her husband behaved like him, and she rocks the baby and says, are you sure? And this direct question awakes a doubt, and

I say, I suppose you wouldn't take it hard, you would celebrate if something like this happened in your family?

I'm not asking you to celebrate, she says, but it's possible to carry on as usual, there's no need to fall to pieces, it's possible to accept what happens without anger, without blame, to believe that every difficulty is intended to strengthen us, and I object, but that's inhuman, how can you not be angry when your whole life is disrupted, and she says, the Tibetans believe that the one who hurts you is your greatest teacher, giving the baby a rebuking look, as if her words are directed at it rather than me, and then she adds earnestly, sometimes we cling to our bad habits and when change comes we tremble with fear, without understanding that it is our only chance, and I protest, that's just an empty slogan, there are good and bad changes, you can't convince me that all bad things are actually good, everything depends on the circumstances.

But what are circumstances, Na'ama, she says in excitement, as if this is precisely the question she's been waiting for, how far can we allow ourselves to be dependent on circumstances, like a slave on his master, today you're happy because everything is all right for the time being, tomorrow you'll be miserable because something goes wrong, and your happiness will turn into a distant memory—the question is, what is our basic character, our true nature, how can we live when everything changes, like the light, from moment to moment? So what do you suggest, I ask, and she answers quickly, I suggest that you try to reach the thing inside you that doesn't change, that isn't dependent on circumstances, and to draw your strength from it. You can't be a slave to deceptive external reality, you have to lean on the steady thing inside you, and I ask, so what is this thing inside me, it doesn't seem to me that I possess such a thing at all, and she opens her eyes wide, of course you do, it's your true being, your basic, whole, enlightened nature, and I say, in genuine surprise, really, so how do I reach it?

I'll explain next time, she smiles, and I'm glad to hear that there'll be a next time, that she's not deserting us yet, with all her surprising news, that she's offering me something to wait for, and I ask willingly, how much do I pay you, and she says, at the moment nothing, we'll talk about it at the end, and I wonder what this end is, it seems that she intends to settle in, deep inside our lives. The end of the illness? I ask hopefully, and she corrects me, the end of the process, as if it's a question of linguistic distinctions, and then she returns to his room, with the baby in her arms, forgoing my baby-sitting services in advance, and after a few minutes she comes out heaving a sigh of relief, like a midwife after a difficult birth and a successful delivery. I'll come here tomorrow at sunrise, she announces, there are a few tests I want to perform on you all, and I ask in surprise again, what do you mean sunrise, actually at sunrise or just early in the morning? And she says, actually at sunrise, this is the time when the energies are strongest in the main channel of the body. What time does the sun rise, I ask, and she shrugs her shoulders sternly, I have no idea, and thrusts out her slender wrist which is bare of any timepiece, as if the watch has not been invented yet, I simply sense the sun waking up, and I listen to her in shame, in an instant I have turned into the dull, insensitive representative of progress, helpless and frightened in the face of nature.

Ehud will wake you, he knows when the sun rises, she says, so they've already fixed it up between them, they appear to understand each other very well. She puts the baby carefully down in the basket and I can't resist asking, how old is it? She's exactly thirty days old, she replies proudly, and I'm surprised that she counts the time in days, as if we're talking about the days of a period of mourning. And you've already gone back to work? I ask, hidden disapproval in my voice, and she says, not really, I turn most people away, but when you called I couldn't say no, and I ask, embarrassed, so you're treating him only now, and she says, yes, only him. I accompany her to the door with an oppressive feeling of uneasiness, but it doesn't reach her, from the stairs she sends me a smile full of good-will, it's very important to sleep well before the examination, to eat light foods, to avoid all tension, try to relax at least for tonight, don't try to hold on to what cannot be held.

I hurry to his room, repeating her instructions to myself, relax, relax, and he seems to be repeating instructions of his own, he looks more relaxed, and I ask, how do you feel, and he says simply, I feel better. What did she do to you, I ask, and he says, I don't know exactly, she took my pulse all over my body, examined my tongue, stuck needles and magnets in all kinds of places, and he rubs the top of his head, and that incense, it was soothing, and I think of all my efforts to help him, my frightened, pitying efforts, all of them in vain, and here she comes and burns a pagan fire and he feels better already, and I ask sourly, and what else, did she talk to you about your basic nature? And he says, no, she mainly asked questions, she didn't say much, and I see that he isn't interested in going into details, I sit down on the edge of his bed, taking over the place where she sat, and it seems to me that something has changed in the room, a sweetish smell is coming off the walls, obscuring the smells of neglect, even his dry body suddenly smells of a pleasant perfume, as if he himself is a slender stick of incense, burning calmly.

Wake me at sunrise, I ask him when I go to bed, but to be on the safe side I set the alarm clock too, how proudly she held out her watchless wrist, as if I and not she was the primitive one, and I open out the couch in the living room, another moth has been roasted on the halogen lamp, a cruel altar that claims its sacrifices every night, and its corpse joins the long line of former victims, filling the room with a smell of charred flesh. No breeze comes to blow the smell away, and so it squats over me as I sleep, covering me like a blanket of evil thoughts, and as I twist and turn beneath it the alarm goes off, it's five o'clock in the morning, and I growl at it with hatred but immediately drag myself out of bed, like an obedient schoolgirl getting up for an early class. Inside the house the darkness seems absolute but on the porch a misty blue greets me with a cold caress, and I sit down with my coffee on one of the chairs, who would have believed that this is the way these sweltering hamsin days begin, like a baby born beautiful growing ugly in the space of a couple of hours. The trees sway in the breeze, darker than the sky, each moving in its own character, like human beings, the cypresses glum and heavy, the poplars dancing like excited young girls, even before the sun rises the darkness flees, only from the houses it peeps out, from the shadowy windows, where heavy sleep covers eyes like black patches. I raise my eyes to the east, a few branches flutter like the arms of swimmers drowning in the sea of pale air, on the roofs the ramshackle crosses of the television antennas crowd, commanding the sleeping concrete kingdom, trapping the moon between them, a whitish balloon still clinging to its borrowed light, but its entourage of stars are already fading, swallowed up in the mouth of the sky like lemon drops sucked to nothing, leaving one last glimmer, like tiny scars, behind them.

The sky is already light but there is still no sign of the sun, everybody seems to be waiting for it, the mother we can't do without despite her wickedness, the brightening trees, the birds breaking into their loud chatter, and I gaze at the east in suspenseful anticipation, a few warm rays touch the curls of the poplar and turn them to gold but the sun is still missing, hiding behind the trees like a great eye hidden in a tangle of hair. I'm waiting in vain, what did I imagine, that I would see it rising, in the middle of the city, round and red like once upon a time, over the mountains I loved so much, in the empty countryside, when there was nothing between us, only the transparent, caressing air, and already I feel angry, what did I get up so early for, it's impossible to see the sunrise here, and why didn't she give me an exact time, I'm sitting here by myself on the porch for nothing, waiting for the sun, waiting for the doctor who believes in disease, I hate them both, I need them both, and then I see her running out of breath in the street below me, a bride late for her wedding, a slender girl all dressed in white, her long hair loose, softening her face, the straw basket in her hand as if she's hurrying to the market, apparently there's no father around to look after the new baby, and a wave of pity floods me, look at her, instead of worrying about her own problems she's helping us, not like you, looking askance at the girls in the shelter, and I move aside so she won't see me watching her run, her body tight, all of a piece, not like mine, all my limbs separate, each like a body of its own.

We missed the sunrise, I say to her in an accusing voice, and she smiles serenely, still panting from her run, don't worry, this is exactly the right time. But by the time the sun rises above the roofs here it's already full, it's impossible to see the sunrise from here, I complain, and she says, trust me, Na'ama, and she puts the basket down on the carpet and examines me sorrowfully, as if I'm the patient here, she doesn't even ask about him, and I'm in no hurry to wake him either, I sit down opposite her and let her touch me with her long, dark fingers, seeking treasure underneath my skin, lingering on my wrists, each in turn and then both together, crossing her hands, changing between right and left, and then feeling behind my ears, pressing down and letting go.

What are you doing, I ask, and she explains willingly, I'm listening to your pulse, the blood circulates in the body and tells us by means of the pulse what's happening there, and I protest, but I'm healthy, there's nothing wrong with me, it's him you came to examine, and she says, the wife's pulse reveals the condition of the husband too, the Tibetans believe that you can tell by the wife's pulse whether the husband will live or die. Really, is the bond so tight? I ask in alarm, and she smiles a secret smile, as if it all depends on her, yes, and you can learn about the condition of the parents from the child's pulse too, and suddenly she gives me a penetrating look, quickly scans my face, pulls up my eyelids and examines my eyes, pulls my tongue out of my mouth, and all the time with that secret smile on her beautiful lips, now that I'm so close to them I can see how beautiful they are, like he was close to them yesterday, close to her smell, actually the smell is strange, unpleasant, of private parts, like the smell of the little baby. So what's with my pulse, what does it tell you, I ask nervously, and she ignores me, presses my fingers and listens, how did you sleep last night, she asks suddenly, and I'm surprised, it's a long time since anybody asked me such a friendly question, I slept okay, except that I worried about missing the sunrise all the time. She goes on asking question after question, her hands hovering over my fingers all the time, simple questions, so simple that I'd forgotten the answers to them, like childhood friends scattered in all directions in the hurly-burly of life, reminding me of a distant time when I was still new to myself, what my favorite colors are, and what I like to eat and drink, what spices I use, what season I prefer, what I suffer from more, heat or cold, and my answers appear to fascinate her immeasurably, even though she takes no notes it seems that she will remember them to her dying day, and then she asks, and what do you like to do? And I stare at her for a moment, as if the words are incomprehensible to me.

She looks at me with questioning eyes, velvety black eyes fringed with a thick brush of lashes, and I giggle in embarrassment, what do I like to do, I'm so used to thinking of what I have to do that I've completely forgotten what I like, and I shrug my shoulders, I like to be with them, I point my chin at the doors closed on the sleeping Udi and Noga, but she isn't satisfied with this pious answer, try to concentrate, she says, it's very important, what do you like to do with yourself, without any connection to your family, without any connection to anyone but yourself, and her question gives me a melancholy feeling, like someone orphaned long ago remembering that once upon a time she really had parents. What did you like doing when you were a child? She tries to help me, and I make an effort to remember, paging through the album of yellowing photographs stored inside me, it was so early on that Udi burst into my life, with his wishes that were always stronger than mine, his loves and his hates, what was there before him, and then I remember, like the first breath of wind breaking a hamsin the memory approaches, and I say hesitantly, almost shyly, when I was a child I liked to lie on the lawn and look at the clouds.

She is thrilled by my reply, she looks at me admiringly as if I am the incarnation of the Buddha on earth, wonderful, she says, and did it calm you? Yes, I say, encouraged, I think so. And when did you do it last, she asks, and I smile apologetically, years and years ago, before my parents got divorced, afterward it didn't appeal to me anymore, and she nods sympathetically, and suddenly I long to lay my head on her shoulder and burst into tears, and cry all day, because it's clear to me that she understands me, not even Anat understood me so deeply, and one moment I want to be her daughter and the next her mother, as long as she never leaves my life, as if the sentence of loneliness passed on this house had suddenly been lifted thanks to her.

And when you looked at the clouds, she goes on, did you ever think about the sky? What do you mean, the sky, I say in surprise, and she asks, does the sky love the clouds, and I stammer, I have no idea, I never thought about it. What does the sky do when the clouds pass over it one after the other, she asks, some of them vanishing without a trace, others changing shape, and I say, nothing, what can it do, it just watches, and she nods happily, right, and don't you think you have something to learn from the sky? I can already feel a bone of mockery tickling my throat, listening to her as she declares quietly but importantly, as if she is announcing some great tidings, that's how we should be, Na'ama, like the sky watching the clouds pass by, without trying to cling to them, without trying to stop them. But it couldn't stop them even it wanted to, I object, and she says, right, just as we can't cling to our mates or our friends or even our children. Her dark look rests on the sleeping baby, on the furniture crowding the living room, on the floor covered with curls of dust, we have to be as free as a drop of mercury that falls on the floor and never gets mixed with the dust, have you ever seen a drop of mercury on the floor, she asks, and I say in a whisper, yes I have, I wish I hadn't.

What will happen if you let go, she asks, what are you afraid of, and I mutter, it's obvious, isn't it? Losing control, being left with nothing, take your pick, and she nods scornfully, yes, that's how people think in the West, but the great Tibetan teachers believe that if a person lets go of everything he gains true freedom, and then compassion will dawn within him like the sun rising above your head this morning. It didn't actually rise, I flaunt my disappointment from this morning, but she looks at me sternly, you saw night turn to day didn't you, and I remember the dark, cool blue that greeted me when I stepped out onto the porch, actually I prefer the night, the sun is too aggressive for me, I say. She looks at me seriously, almost imploringly, quickly, she urges me, before everyone wakes up, you have to listen to me, and it's true, I think, everyone is still asleep, her baby, my daughter, Udi, a spell has been cast on the house, it's not so early anymore, almost seven o'clock, but still it seems as if the whole city is sleeping and only we are awake, and again I ask her, what do you need so urgently with me, it's him you came to heal, and she says, and if I saw someone lying on the pavement and groaning in pain, wouldn't I go up to him? And alarmed by the comparison, I say, don't exaggerate, and she answers me sternly, I'm not exaggerating, Na'ama, I saw your husband and I see you, I can help you both, but Ehud, in the last analysis, is capable of helping himself more than you imagine, while you don't even try to take care of yourself. Why, did you see by his pulse that I'm going to die, I giggle nervously, and she cuts me short unsmilingly, listen to me, Na'ama, but I'm in no hurry to obey, I always thought that Tibetan medicine was all kinds of ancient remedies from the Himalayas, and medicinal herbs, and acupuncture, I protest, and she suppresses her anger, almost insulted, and says, I have a bagful of medicines here, we'll come to that later, first I want to talk to you, listen to me and you won't be sorry, quickly before everyone wakes up and the day begins.

Listen, she brings her lips close to my ear and says in a confidential, prayerful whisper, there are different aspects of consciousness, our ordinary consciousness is like the flame of a candle on the threshold of an open door, exposed to harm from every wind, falling victim to external habits and conditioning, creating waves of negative feelings and wallowing in them, but on the other hand we have latent within us the true nature of consciousness, think again of the sky and the clouds, the sky is our true nature, and the clouds are the confusion of our ordinary consciousness, they don't belong to the sky, they never leave traces on it, and I listen to her mesmerized, all around us are closed doors, everyone behind them seems to have given up the ghost, but it doesn't even sadden me, the idea that we will be left alone in the world, she and I, it gives rise in me to a sweet serenity, because all at once her words have connected me to an ancient calm so deep that death seems small beside it.

Look at this house, she says, and I look around me, taking in the shabby armchairs, the bookshelves, the gray walls spotted with our fingerprints. How long have you lived here, she asks, and I say, nearly ten years, we came to live here before Noga was born, and she says, but it's not your real home, and I say in astonishment, what do you mean, of course it's my home, I have no other home, and she says, but this house could burn down in five minutes, it could collapse in an earthquake, your real home is inside your mind, only there are you safe, only there are you mistress of your own happiness.

And then the quiet between us is broken by the familiar squeak of the door and Noga bursts out of her room as if the house is on fire, looks around with a swollen, apple-cheeked face, and asks, what's happened, and I get up and put my arms around her and say, nothing's happened, I'm talking to Daddy's doctor. She examines

Zohara suspiciously, but immediately she smiles, a hopeful, innocent smile, you're his doctor? she asks, I'm glad he has a doctor, and
then with all her eager, uninhibited impetuousness, will Daddy get
better? I blink imploringly at Zohara, just don't let her start telling
the child that her father hasn't yet plumbed the depths of his illness, but she smiles at her and says reassuringly, don't worry, of
course he'll get better, health is right there inside him, he only has
to find it.

Noga stretches in relief, sits on my lap, warm and heavy, stuffed
with sleep, and Zohara comes up to her, as long as you're here, I'd
like to check a few things, and she says in alarm, why, is Daddy's
illness infectious? And Zohara says, no, no, don't worry, I just want
to see how it's affecting you, and she examines her with the movements that have already become familiar to me, pressing and letting go, her lips moving as if in prayer, and Noga holds out her limbs
tensely, until the deliberate movements turn into a gentle stroking
of her hair, you're fine, dear, don't worry, everything will be all right,
and Noga breathes a loud sigh of relief, as frank and externalized as
her previous tension, everything I try to hide is exposed in her with
such rashness that she sometimes seems to me like a caricature of
myself, and I urge her to hurry up and get dressed, it's already a
quarter to eight, and when she shuts the bathroom door behind her
I am alarmed to see Zohara looking at me in concern. She isn't in
a good state, she whispers to me, she's too tense, she's weak, not
focused, she can't function properly in school or with other children, and I feel my head spinning on my neck, the bad news has
reached me at last, and it's worse than I thought, and I whisper, what
can we do? And I immediately add, I told you his illness was destroying us, and you talk to me about opportunities.

I haven't changed my mind, she whispers, and I'm not sure
that before the illness the child was in such great shape either, there
are deep-seated problems here, which the illness brings out, and
perhaps it's for the good, but you have to get strong for her sake,

when she feels the change in you her condition will improve, and I'm already prepared to change on the spot I'm in such a panic, tell me what to do and I'll do it, just tell me what to do, and she announces, I've told you enough for today, think about everything we've said, but this isn't enough for me, what will become of us, I have to change immediately, I have to change before Noga comes out of the bathroom, I'm ready to turn into a toad if it'll help her, my eyes are fixed on the bathroom door, the window is broken from an old quarrel, bandaged with masking tape as in a time of war. So what shall I do, I whisper, maybe I won't go to work and I'll spend all day looking at the clouds, but the sky is blazing, no cloud would dare to come near it, it's impossible to even look at it with your eyes open, and she gets up and puts her hand on my shoulder, calm down, she says, try to relax, try to find a way to the serenity inside you, don't be afraid of changes, they shape us, like the sea shapes the rocks, try because you have no alternative, and now Noga comes out, her eyelids swollen, and I'm sure that she was crying in the bathroom, tensely I watch her clumsy movements, dragging her bag, draped in a huge shirt, and I say to her, as I say every morning, Nogi change your shirt, you can't go out like that, it looks ridiculous, and she says, of course I can, and she explains to the doctor, I only wear my father's shirts, he likes me to wear them. Taken aback by this preposterous explanation I survey her with disapproval, a huge walking shirt, white legs in sneakers peeping out below it and a fan of yellow curls above it, what's the wonder that she has no friends, that everyone avoids her, and again the familiar anxiety creeping up my spine, but Zohara's fingers climb up after it, there's a chase taking place on my back, and I freeze, listening to the fingers massaging my spine vertebra by vertebra. Don't forget, she whispers to me, without anger, without blame, without negative feelings, only infinite calm, like the sky, and I can't control myself any longer, I turn around and embrace her, lean on her with all the heavy weight of my body, with all the odors of the night that have not yet been washed away, not ashamed of anything, wanting only to cling to her strong, compassionate slenderness, and she puts her arms around me, planted in the earth like a tree trunk, dark and firm, I'm not alone anymore, she'll help me, she'll watch over me, her hands stroke my hair, look how she came out of the sunrise to save me, how she brought light into my dark life, everything was crooked and now it will be made straight. Enclosed in her arms I whisper, just say that it isn't too late, and she whispers, it's never too late, there is always hope, even the day before death it's not too late, and I'm ready to be consoled even by this, and now footsteps approach us, clumsy shoes intrude on our embrace, Noga's hands clutch our waists, hot and sticky, Zohara goes on murmuring, without anger, without blame, it's never too late, there's always hope, and I hug Noga like in the kindergarten, when the parents were called to join the children's circle, and Udi would remain in his chair and I would rush in to cover up his indifference, feeling his eyes digging into my back, moving uncomfortably to the childish rhythm, in the forest in the forest in the forest we'll dance we'll dance. I turn my head and see him standing there, leaning against the wall, pale and haggard, we didn't hear him coming out of his room, contemplating our tight little circle, which comes apart immediately, and the three of us look at him in embarrassment, how typical of him to survey us like that, not to join in the rare harmony but to disrupt it in a second, but I repeat to myself, without anger, without blame, hurrying to pour the cornflakes into the bowl, come and eat, Nogi, but she says, I'm not hungry, fawns on him with exaggerated movements, almost knocking him down, Daddy, the doctor says you're going to get better, and he puts out a limp hand and rumples her hair, I'm glad to hear it.

I hurry to the bedroom to get dressed, snatching a dress with a silly flower print, all my pretty, thin clothes have been pushed to the margins of the closet, you have to make a real effort to pull them out, and only a few big, loose dresses offer themselves, ashamed, and

I'm ready in a minute, dragging Noga behind me, come, I'll take you so you won't be late, and at the door I glance back at them, she's bending over the still quiet baby, her hair falling into the basket, black and frizzy, her dress clinging to her body, and he lowers his eyes, avoiding mine, and I say, thank you, thank you, Zohara, see you soon, I can't find the words to express the love swelling in me for her, and she smiles, call me this evening, not forgetting the pact between us, but when we go downstairs I suddenly feel an uneasy sense of exclusion, as if they, there behind me, he and she and the baby, are the real inhabitants of the house, and we, Noga and I, are a couple of nervous, unwelcome guests, at whose departure the householders breathe a sigh of relief.

Eleven

On the way to the shelter I forget to count the traffic lights compulsively, I suddenly forget to be afraid, as I have been every morning over the past few weeks, afraid of the director Hava, of the wails rising from the rooms, of my inability to help. A new spirit accompanies me from traffic light to traffic light, driving the old car forward, as in the first days of falling in love, when love still wraps the body in a coat of oiled chain mail, repelling all arrows. I am not alone this morning, she is here next to me, protecting me with her body, as brown and hard as a tree trunk, with her calm voice, with her utter serenity. In the side mirror I see a radiant scrap of sky following me, and I know, this is the sign, reminding me to be like it, remote and full of compassion, no one can really hurt me, just as no one can hurt the sky.

When I walk quickly to the shelter gates it seems to me that eyes are watching me and I look round, violent men sometimes hide here, lying in wait for a girlfriend sheltering in the shelter, threatening to kill her if she gives up the baby, and even parents have been known to lie in wait for a daughter who has disappeared after bringing disgrace down on their heads, but there is nobody spying from the bushes, only a young girl crossing the road not far from me. I look immediately at the middle of her body to see if an embarrassing secret is signaling there, I can't see anything but this doesn't mean a thing, the body knows how to deny, to collaborate enthusiastically with the mind. I had better ignore her, perhaps she just lives somewhere round here, but she doesn't take her eyes off me and I make a mistake and send her a little smile, I know it's a mistake, because everyone who comes here has to make her own way to us, and I'm in a hurry to get to a staff meeting, but the sky covers me with its compassion, and now she approaches me with careful steps, yes, she's pregnant, judging by the care with which her foot meets the pavement, the tearful smile, the smile of an unwanted pregnancy, the complete opposite of the complacent smile of a wanted pregnancy, and I glance at my watch, it's already half past eight, the meeting is starting now and Hava is looking sternly at my empty chair, but I look at the girl coming toward me and my heart goes out to her, she's older than most of our girls, in her middle twenties at least, well dressed, in a short black dress and matching high-heeled sandals, red hair cropped short, almost shaved, bright red lipstick, exactly the same color as her hair, on her fleshy lips, what on earth is she doing here, this is no place for her, she's coming from somewhere else entirely, and I go up to her as naturally as if we have an appointment, meeting her halfway, can I help you?

You're from there, right? she asks urgently, indicating our gate with soft doe eyes, and I say, yes, I work at the shelter, and she says breathlessly, I've been hanging round here for two days already, trying to make up my mind whether to go in or not, I'm afraid that if I go in you won't let me out again, and I protest, nonsense, nobody is forced to stay here, this isn't a prison. And what happens to the babies? Her voice is tight with tension, and I say, in most cases they're given up for adoption, but that's not compulsory either, and she says, so if anyone wants to bring up her baby herself she's allowed to do it, you don't force her to give it up? And I am so used to these questions, but today everything seems new to me, like the questions I was asked early this morning, what do you like to do, what's your favorite color, do you prefer heat or cold, and I say, if you want to raise the child, and we gain the impression that you can handle it, then there's no problem, we'll even help you.

What do you mean you gain the impression, she recoils, her pretty face falls, and if you gain the impression that I can't, then the baby will be taken away from me? And I explain, we just recommend, the judge decides, according to the good of the baby, but this only happens in extreme cases, and she says, then I'd rather not go in at all, this way I'm free, what gives you the right to decide for me, and I say, it depends what your circumstances are, most of the girls here have no choice, they haven't got anywhere to go during their pregnancy, and no possibility of raising the baby, clearly if you want to bring up your baby and are capable of doing so, it's better for all concerned, we won't stand in your way, on the contrary, and I glance at my watch, I have to go inside, the meeting will soon be over and I'm still standing here, Hava won't pass over it in silence.

Why don't you go home, I suggest, calm down, think it over, we're always here, it's your decision, but she clings to me, wait, don't go, grabs hold of the hem of my dress, I have to decide today, I can't drag it out any longer, you have to help me, and I say, then let's talk about it inside, and she hesitates, I'm afraid they won't let me out, and the truth is that I too feel more comfortable sitting out here on the pavement in the shade far from Hava's watchful eyes, and she sits down next to me, I'm already in my seventh month, she chokes on her tears, I can't believe that this is happening to me, my whole life is ruined.

Do you know who the father is, I ask, and she sobs, of course I do, we've been having an affair for a year, but he's married with children, he's much older than I am, I work in his architect's office. When I found out I could still have an abortion but I hoped he would leave home and move in to live with me, he drove me crazy, changing his mind every other day, making promises and choosing a name for the baby one day and completely ignoring me the next, and in the meantime it was too late for an abortion and I still believed that if I faced him with a fait accompli he would come round, but a few days ago he announced that he didn't want the child or any further connection with me and that was final, and I don't know what to do. My parents are religious and I can't allow them to find out, it would kill them, my mother's very sick anyway, and I can hardly hide my stomach anymore, and I hate him, I can't understand how he could have done this to me, ruined my life and deserted me, how am I going to bring up a child by myself, I'm barely twenty-two, I'm too young to be a single parent, and I haven't even got a profession yet, I've only started studying this year, and I haven't got any money, and there's nobody to help me.

I sit listening to her gasping sentences, merging into her distress, again the familiar feeling of another's pain thrust onto my shoulders, sacks of despair and insult, the picture fills with colors and sounds, I can hear the hoarse quarrels, see the blazing nights, they well up in me like memories, and again the raging helplessness that overwhelms me at such moments, how can I help her, the situation is really difficult, however you look at it it's difficult, and I say weakly, you know, you can always prove paternity and demand child support, but she shakes her head tearfully, I don't want anything from him after what he did to me, if he's capable of leaving me like this I don't want his money or his child either. Her hands beat her frightened, hidden stomach savagely, and I put my arms around her shoulders, my eyes fixed on her feet next to mine, the toenails painted red to match her lipstick and her hair, how beautiful feet can be, I marvel, encouraged by her well-groomed appearance, things can't be all that bad if she can still pay attention to every little detail, and I say, try not to poison yourself with negative thoughts, it will weaken you and you need strength now, you need to prepare yourself for the future, any decision you make will be hard but possible, we'll help you.

The trouble is that every decision is impossible, she wails, nothing I can do will be right, if I keep the baby my life will be ruined, my family will ostracize me, no man will want me with a baby, I don't even want myself with a baby, but if I give it up I'll never forgive myself, I'll never stop thinking about the crime I committed, giving up my own child, and I'll be punished for it all my life long, and I won't have any more children. God forbid, I say quickly, why do you deserve to be punished? If you give the baby up to give it a better life, you'll be doing something mature and noble, which certainly doesn't deserve punishment, but on the contrary, only admiration, and she's immediately on the alert, so you think I should give it up, you'll force me to give it up. Of course not, I say, it's your decision and yours alone, it's up to you, I can only help you to see the whole picture, and I rise wearily to my feet, it's already nine o'clock, in a minute the meeting will be over, and suddenly I see this morning sparkling in front of my eyes again, the sunrise that didn't happen, the cool blue light, Zohara's hair panting on her shoulders as she ran down the empty street, and I ask her, what's your name, and she whispers, Yael, and I look at her with the same concentration as I was looked at this morning, listen, Yael, you don't have to decide today, you have another two months at least, but try to change your attitude, try to think of what's happened as an opportunity, not a disaster, try to get something good out of it. Something good, she cries in protest, just as I did yesterday, what are you talking about, how can anything good come of it? And I say, I don't know enough about your life, perhaps it will enable you to free yourself of unhealthy patterns of relationships with men, perhaps it will bring you closer to your parents, mature you, it's still too early to tell, go home, try to relax, and if you want our help we're here, but she clutches at my dress again, nervously crumpling the flowers blooming on it between her fingers, drowning me in a stream of words, but I haven't got anywhere to go, I can't hide my stomach anymore, and if my roommates find out it will get back to my parents, I haven't told anyone about it, not even my best friends, if I give the child up for adoption I don't want anyone in the world to know, and I nod my head, the fewer people that know the better, but from now on it will be harder and harder to hide.

So what should I do, she wails, I'm afraid to come to you, I'm afraid you'll try to influence me, I'm afraid of the other girls, and I say, Yael, I really have to go now, think about it for a few more days, and she raises her wet eyes to me, stretching her lips imploringly, but I simply can't stay with her any longer, I punch in the familiar code, the gate opens and I send her a busy smile, I'm here if you need me.

She follows me with a disappointed look, now I too have abandoned her, but I don't look back, even though they need me a lot less in the shelter, I should have stayed with her, in any case the meeting's over, and I am already thinking of going back to her, but then Anat comes down the stairs toward me, in the distance she looks like an aging boy in her narrow jeans and cropped gray hair. Where were you, she says, Hava's looking for you, and I sigh, I knew she wouldn't let it go, and she adds, you remember that Etti gave birth yesterday, you'd better go to her later with the forms, and I go inside without answering her, whenever I walk into the shelter I marvel at its beauty, like all the girls when they first arrive, three elegant, spacious floors, I wish I had a house like this, they say, and sometimes so do I, but today I don't linger in the hall, I go straight to Hava's office, where I find her sprawled in her reclining plastic chair, a kind of beach chair she brought in because of the problems she has with her back, her reading glasses make her eyes bigger but she removes them when I come in and puts the pile of papers on her knees.

Good morning, she announces brightly, did you just wake up? And I think of the azure beginning of this morning, whole seasons have passed since then, and I stammer, no, far from it, I took my husband to have tests, and she sighs, how is this going to end,

Na'ama, and I am about to justify myself but she attacks with unexpected warmth. I see how hard it is for you, she says, why don't
you take a short vacation, a week or two, take whatever time you
need, take care of him until he recovers, and then come back to
work, so that you won't be torn between him and us all the time,
and I am embarrassed by her sympathy but I shake my head firmly,
no, that's the last thing I need now, to be stuck in the house with
him all day, how can I take care of him until he recovers, I haven't
got a clue how to take care of him, or when he'll recover, and to
her I say, thank you, Hava, but I prefer to carry on like this, and
she puts on her glasses again and examines me with huge, magnified eyes, I know you think I'm too strict, she says, and perhaps you're
right, but I have no alternative, none of us has any alternative, we
can't allow ourselves to overidentify with all the misery around us,
identification is the easy way out, we have to rise above it. Would
you like a cup of tea, she asks and rises heavily from her chair to
brew her insipid herb tea, and I look at her big, swaying body, seeing its vulnerability for the first time, what's happened to her all of
a sudden, Hava with her perfect life, her rich husband and beautiful home and successful children, and she seems to hear my thoughts,
I have hard times too, she says, I've had all kinds of problems lately,
but I don't let them take me over, Na'ama, and you devote yourself
to your trouble, and I say, I don't want any tea, thank you, and she
sighs, pushing a gray curl off her forehead with a surprisingly feminine gesture, just be honest with me and with yourself, if you feel
that you haven't got anything to give at the moment then take some
time off, and be careful of overidentification, she adds sternly, when
we have a sorrow of our own it draws us like a magnet to the sorrow
of others, and that's extremely dangerous.

I leave her office exhausted and look around me, trying to
sense the general mood this morning, everything here is so sensitive and fragile, every birth upsets the equilibrium, every form that's
signed, immediately they gather round, how is she, what did she

decide, there's always someone to denounce, if I had conditions like hers I would never give up my child, and someone else retorts, it's a good thing you haven't, poor kid to be brought up by you. I see Ilana standing at the sink, washing the dishes roughly, splashing soapy water all around, and Hani sitting at the dining table, balls of pink wool in her lap. I have to finish this sweater before the birth, she tells me agitatedly, I have to leave something with my baby, and Ilana bangs the dishes together defiantly, stirring up trouble as usual, she won't need that sweater, believe me, she snaps, she'll have plenty of sweaters in her new house with her new parents swimming in money, you and me should only have so many sweaters, I bet they're all folded up already waiting for her in a new chest of drawers with pictures of Snow White on it.

But I want her to have something from me as a memento, Hani insists, I want it to be her favorite sweater, and Ilana laughs her jarring laugh, what an imbecile you are, they'll throw it straight into the trash, they don't want any memento of you, all they want is to forget you, aren't I right? She turns to me with her dull little eyes, and I say, Ilana, I understand how hard it is for you, but don't interfere with Hani's efforts to help herself, it's important to her to leave something with the baby and that's just fine. But why a sweater, says Ilana, let her leave a letter in the adoption file, that's what I'm going to do, and when she opens the file, when she's eighteen, she'll come back to me, they're just raising her for me in the meantime, and I say, eighteen years is a long time, more years than you've lived, you can't know what your daughter will feel, whether she'll want to see you or not, and she says, that's why I'll write her a nice letter, so that she'll want to find me, I'll write that I've got tons of money, or that I'm a famous model, and I smile in embarrassment, not knowing whether to laugh or cry in front of the stout, short body, the compressed face. Ilana, I say, her wish to see you has nothing to do with things like money or glamour, you have to base the relationship on the truth, you have to tell her how old you were, and about all the difficulties you had at the time of her birth, which are the reasons you're giving her up, so that she can have a better life, don't try to prettify anything.

You won't tell me what to do, she says, turning resentfully back to the sink, and I hurry to the office, with Hani trailing behind me, you know what I want, she says, I want to dress her in the sweater myself after the birth, and when the adoptive parents come to get her they'll see her in the sweater I knitted for her, I want them to tell her about it when she grows up, that her real mother knitted a sweater for her, and I smile at her, all right, Hani, I promise you that's what we'll do, don't worry, but she clings to me with the wool and the knitting needles, I want it to be the first thing she wears, you see? And I say, sure I do, but you'd better hurry up, your stomach has already dropped and you've hardly even begun, and when I look at her I am astounded again at this cruel choice of nature's, pregnant women had always seemed imposing to me, superior, officers in nature's army, and since the day I started working here I haven't been able to stop wondering at this crude joke of hers, recruiting child soldiers, almost babies themselves, into her army, and loading additional babies onto their narrow shoulders, and again I am angry with Udi, whenever I have a bone to pick with nature I am angry with him, her eager advocate, and I think furiously of his emaciated body covered with needles, and the smoke of the incense rising from his head.

When I enter the office to take the forms their deliberate, naked words confront me, the terrible words of renunciation, formulated as dryly as if they concern the renewal of a passport or the changing of a name, I put them into my bag and take a package containing soap and body lotion from the gifts cupboard, and when I bump into Anat in the corridor I say to her, tell Hava I've gone to the maternity ward, and she says in surprise, already? You've just arrived. I want to get it over with, I say, just keep an eye on Ilana, she's in a lethal mood, and Anat smiles, she's not the only one, and only at the gate I remember to wonder, who did she mean, me, Hava, maybe herself, what does it matter, the only thing that matters is that Yael isn't here anymore, she's disappeared on her high heels, taking the fear of her future with her, without leaving me any way of contacting her, only the shadows of burning leaves caress the pavement in the spot where we were sitting.

But this place where life begins, this brightly lit corridor, lacking any mystery, these limp bodies that hide nothing, their painful gaits, aching but proud, like that of war heroes who know that there is a point to their pain, this place draws itself to me with strong arms, and as I walk among the tottering women I am seized by the certain knowledge that I will never be like them, I will never limp down this corridor stooped and happy, I will never have another baby. There were years when I still thought that it would work out, that Udi would come round in the end, but now I know for sure that it won't happen, and the knowledge that all is lost hits me like a blow, I will never be given a second chance. I sink onto a chair next to the wall, exhausted, as if like many of the girls around me I have just given birth, for I too have painful stitches, ancient stitches that have become infected and refuse to heal, but then a woman in a hospital gown dragging a baby in a transparent box on wheels sits down opposite me, and I get up at once, her gaze follows me without curiosity but it fills me with uneasiness, as if I am an impostor, and I hurry to Etti's room at the end of the corridor, with a forced smile on my lips, this is always the most difficult moment, what exactly am I supposed to congratulate her on, how can I wish her mazal tov, when the day of birth presages the day of separation. Ettileh, good for you, I venture, I hear you were a real heroine, and she looks at me with sullen eyes, it was a nightmare, don't ask, he stuck to me like a tick, and I stroke her bony arm, it's terribly hard but with time you'll forget, and she says, like a leech he stuck to me, thirty-six hours, he wouldn't come out, with all the inducings and everything else, it hurt like hell, it almost finished me, I don't know what I did to him to make him stick like that, and I ask, have you seen him already, and she says, what are you talking about, I never want to see him, he disgusts me.

But Etti, I coax her, he's your baby, he came out of you, and she says coldly, that's why he disgusts me, if he came out of you he wouldn't disgust me, don't you understand, he's nothing, just like me, he isn't worth a damn, and she stretches her skinny arms indifferently, utterly detached. I'm dying to get out of this hole already, she grumbles, and to be alone, without you people watching me all the time. What will you do when you're alone, I ask, even though I know the answer, she'll shoot heroin into her arm and lie on her stinking mattress and feel like the queen of the world, and I look at her sorrowfully, her face is completely dark, her neck is wrinkled, this isn't the first child she's given up, in her youth she gave up a baby who must be at least twenty years old today. She isn't a whore, she claims, she only goes with men to get money for the drug, and if it results in an unwanted baby, like the side effect of a necessary medication, then you get rid of it and carry on. I thought I was too old for this to happen, she sniggers, and I hold her hand, she looks ageless, sexless, perhaps there is some dent in her tough skin, a moment of understanding, and I say, let's go and see the baby, you have to know who you're parting from, it's important for you to see that he's a sweet little living creature, not a monster, and she recoils, leave me alone, Na'ama, I don't want to see the little leech, and I surprise myself by volunteering, then I'll go myself and describe him to you, and she shrugs her shoulders, if you haven't got anything better to do with your time.

With a heavy heart I go into the neonates' room, like freshly recruited soldiers they lie there on parade, crib after crib, and I remember how I would lift little Noga out of her transparent crib, the tiny heart-shaped face, the pouting rosebud lips, and once I got mixed up, I stood amazed in the middle of the night opposite a different little face, and only then I looked at the label and discovered that he wasn't mine at all. Here he is, Etti's baby, there's no mistaking him, he looks so much like her, an angry little elf, his hands trembling, not only them, his whole swaddled body is trembling, and the nurse sighs behind my back, he's in withdrawal, poor little creature, he was born addicted, we're detoxifying him now. It will be all right, little elf, I whisper to him, stroking his crumpled cheek, we'll change your fate, we'll plant you in a different soil and you'll flourish, and a ferment of pride suddenly awakens in me, raising my head high, you see, I turn to Udi in a whisper, we save lives, soon this child will get new parents who will raise him with love, take care of all his needs, instead of seeing his mother screwing strange men and shooting up he'll see cartoons and play with Lego and read books.

And what will you do if he falls into bad company in high school and begins shooting up heroin, I hear Udi arguing with me, imagine if he lands up in exactly the same hole as his mother, maybe she'll even supply him, or he her, and I retort angrily, anything can happen, but we're giving him a chance at another life, if he stays with her his fate is sealed, and I think of Noga in her transparent box, what would have happened if different parents had taken you home, perhaps a different father wouldn't have dropped you from his quarrelsome arms, from his vengeful heart, perhaps another mother wouldn't have infected you with her guilt, imposed a hopeless repair on you, Udi's right, knowledge is a grotesque illusion, the eyes of the flesh are covered with an opaque film. I stroke the tiny hand in farewell, and suddenly his fingers grip mine with surprising strength, and a bleat escapes his lips, what is he trying to tell me, that in spite of everything he wants to stay with his mother who loathes him? a moment before I take the forms out of my bag and the nurse comes up with a bottle, he's hungry, poor mite, she says, picking him up and freeing my fingers, his eyes are closed, they haven't even opened yet, so why do I feel as if he's looking at me, and I hurry away like a criminal, and return to Etti who's waiting for me with her eyes shut, the resemblance between them is startling, there'll be no way of ignoring it if they walk the same streets, but why should they walk the same streets.

Ettileh, he's really sweet, I say, he looks just like you, and she waves her hand contemptuously, I'm not interested, for all I care he can look like you, and I hand her the forms, I want you to read them first, and she grumbles, get off my back already, I don't care what's written there, I don't want him, I told you, but I insist, you have to read them, Etti, this isn't a small thing that you're giving up, you have to understand what it means, and she says sullenly, it means that at this time tomorrow I'll be free, but I refuse to give in, slowly I read the thundering words aloud, they smash against her skin without leaving a trace, and then she takes my pen and signs, her eyes half-closed, a bunch of threads of blue ink at the bottom of the page, and the job is done, even when it's easy it's hard, and I sigh, her indifference depresses me despite making things easier, with no need for hesitations and explanations, coaxing and consolation. She pulls a packet of cigarettes out of her locker and hurries me on my way, come on, let's get a move on, I'll go to the lobby with you and we can sit and have a smoke, and when we pass the neonates' room she doesn't even give it a glance, walking past the parade of swaddled babies without curiosity, without guilt, as if it's not her little cub quivering there, wanting her milk, her love, and when we sit down in the lobby I can't resist saying, Ettileh, isn't it worth the effort to try and break your habit, look at the price you pay, we could help you, isn't it worth a try?

Get off my back, Na'ama, she hisses at me, I'm not interested in stopping, I'm not interested in anything, except the drug, it's my only reason for living, it's my baby, it's the only thing that makes me happy, and suddenly a wheezing nicotine laugh sprays out of her, I'm taken, see, I'm the mother of the drug, see? The laughter shakes her empty stomach under the hospital gown, it pursues me when I say good-bye to her and stand waiting for the elevator, looking back at her admiringly, almost enviously, the way she sits there, crossing one emaciated leg over the other, puffing gray smoke at the baby she will abandon tomorrow, perhaps she's right, at this time tomorrow she'll be lying on her filthy mattress and she'll be the queen of the world.

Twelve

The sun I awaited so eagerly early this morning now pursues me inimically, menacing me from all the car mirrors, three glaring suns following me with three knives, not allowing me to turn right or left or back, to return to the shelter or to go home, only to drive straight on as if I have been hijacked, to a place which is exclusively mine, where there is no need to take care of anyone, and I race ahead before I can change my mind, seeing in my mind's eye the sky shining on me through the treetops as I lie on the grass, my limbs relaxed, empty of hunger and thirst, expectation or insult.

The farther I drive the narrower the roads get and the greener the landscape becomes, even in the heart of summer there are still shining lakes of green here, orange groves examining me curiously with their eyes, I haven't been here since my father died, and before then too my visits were few and far between, the encounter of my adulthood with my childhood always gave rise in me to a feeling of inevitable catastrophe. Whenever I came to visit him I would begin to limp, as if an old fracture in my bones had never healed properly, but today I go back gladly, because this is the only place I have left, because my father and mother are waiting for me here with lunch, sitting opposite each other at the big table, glancing anxiously at the clock on the wall, where is she, why is she late. Here I am coming home from school, their separation has not yet thrown my life into disarray, she is still imprisoned in a secret cage of dangerous ideas, sometimes she roars at night but I still don't hear her, only the nocturnal conversations of the jackals sometimes give rise in me to an obscure fear. On this road I walk home, between the citrus groves, a black country road, bare of traffic, sometimes in the evening I walk along it barefoot, and although it's dry and rough I can feel soft currents under the asphalt, remnants of warmth flowing toward me from the depths of the earth as I walk up the densely growing, always clouded avenue of oaks, here I would rest at the side of the road, gathering acorns, hoarding the hard fruits in their crumbling cradles.

I park the car on the old guava orchard, now covered with asphalt, trying to aim for the spot where my favorite tree once stood, the red guavas heavy with sweetness shining between its branches like lamps, and run to the house, wait for me, Mommy and Daddy, don't start to eat without me, don't clear the table, don't wipe the crumbs with a cloth, here I am back from school, my notebooks neat, my textbooks clean, today I'll look after Yotam so you can go out. How sudden it was, I didn't suspect for a second, she seemed so happy with us, her little family, she was so beautiful at lunchtime in her checked apron with the beads of perspiration blooming on her lip. We were all in love with her, little Yotam who lived inside her dress, who cried when she moved away, I who worshiped her and imitated her every gesture, and my father who was much older than she was, and whose only wish was to please her, and they never fought and spoke quietly and politely and everything seemed wonderful, until it transpired that it wasn't enough for her, this life, cooking boiled chicken and mashed potatoes every day, sitting at the lunch table opposite an aging man who bored her. She was still young, she wanted to live, to be an actress, to dance and sing, she didn't want to rot in this remote village in an old house, a miserable Jewish Agency house as she called it, and now I stand before it, all the houses around have changed beyond recognition, like children who have grown up, adding rooms and stories until they are unrecognizable, and only our house cringes in its modesty and mortification. Here are the remains of our little garden, the solitary poinciana tree planted in the middle, the birthday tree I used to call it, because on my sixth birthday I ran round and round it, holding on to its rough trunk and whirling round and round until my head was spinning and all the guests merged together into one big smile full of tongues and teeth. I was holding a little handkerchief in my hand, a white handkerchief I had received from one of the neighbors, and it filled me with indescribable joy, I waved it again and again, as if I were on the deck of a ship, waving good-bye before setting out on a long voyage, whose dangers could not yet be guessed.

Under the birthday tree I now stretch out, its branches divide the sky into blue bits, swaying like seaweed, changing ceaselessly. How I loved to lie here in the dark, the clamor of the house like a reassuring buzz in the background and me under the tree, listening to the singing of the clouds, a soft dim choir high above me, a song without sorrow or gladness, without meetings or partings, we go past you, they'd sing, but we'll be here after you, we'll never be born, we'll never die, we'll never remember anything, we'll never forget. They climb on top of each other, they stretch their languid arms, they lie luxuriously on the bed of the sky, they swallow the moon and immediately vomit it up whole, unharmed it escapes their grip, they join together and immediately part again, spreading out fearlessly over the kingdom of heaven, changing shape, conjuring valleys and hills, bays and snowy peaks. Nearly every evening I would go out into the garden, even in winter, lie down on the lawn and stare into the depths of the sky, at the immeasurably fascinating events taking place there, over which I had no control, as if I ever had any control over what happened here, on earth, in the little Jewish Agency house, and gradually peace of mind would descend on me, a magical, marvelous peace, unrelated to anything that had happened that day or would happen the next day, this was apparently that infinite consciousness, that naked, radiant simplicity, and now that I remember it I call it to come back to me, I try to coax it, to tempt it, but what do I have to offer it, and how can I trust it, if precisely at the moment of my greatest need it stopped coming, it left that house just like my mother did, at the same time on the same day. Again I try to remember the things I was told this morning, relax, she said, learn from the clouds and the sky, connect to the calm inside you, how tempting it sounds, if only I could, but there is no calm inside me, Zohara, on the contrary, sometimes it seems to me that there is more calm in the world spinning round me than there is inside me.

Ashamed I stand opposite the locked door of my home, someone bought it years ago but they never lived in it, and until its rooms are peopled our heartbreak will remain there, treading on the shaky tiles, fingering the mark of the barometer on the wall, the rage of the abandoned house, and I follow its footsteps from outside, circling the house where my childhood lived. Here the red plum tree stood and next to it the yellow plum tree, husband and wife we called them, because in the course of the years they joined together, and the tips of their branches intertwined until we could not tell them apart, and only in the summer, when the fruit ripened, did we know which branch belonged to the red tree and which to the yellow, and we would climb them, straining and stretching to pick the warm fruit, and let it melt in our mouths like candy, and here, opposite the window of our room, the giant acacia tree once stood, which shone in the spring like the sun, strewing our dreams with gold. Here's the east porch, opposite the blue mountains threaded together like a necklace of sapphires, here my father would sit in the afternoons in short khaki pants, leaning back with his legs crossed, chewing black grapes and predicting the weather, the lenses of his glasses glittering gleefully, and I would sit at his feet on these steps, my arms full of kittens. They would suddenly appear as if out of nowhere in the depths of the bushes, frisking among the ferns, their tails dancing between the light and shade, and I would lie in wait for them on the steps, anticipating their first leaps into the world, tempting them with saucers of cream, sniffing warm, milky fur. Here's the west porch, where the pigeons lived, cooing and gurgling under the roof tiles, soiling the porch floor with their droppings, and my mother would yell, get rid of those pigeons with their germs before they make us all sick, and my father would gaze helplessly at the nests, torn between his pity for the pigeons and his wish to please my mother. Sometimes he would pluck up the courage to pull down a nest or two, though he'd secretly transfer the eggs to another and so never succeeded in getting rid of the pigeons, but after she left, on his first night without her, he fell furiously on the nests and tore them down, together with their eggs and fledgelings, it was a proper pogrom, and the news must have spread throughout the pigeon population, because they never dared to return, and even now, nearly thirty years later, there isn't a pigeon to be seen on the porch.

Strangely enough, although nobody lives here the lawn is still fresh and green, like a grave secretly tended by devoted admirers, yes, this was the grave of the rest of his life, wandering through his emptied rooms, lamenting her leaving without anger, as if he agreed with her, as if he would have done the same thing if he had been in her place. I always thought that if she had left him for another man it would have been easier for him than the way she did leave him, for all the other men in the world, she offered him no focus for his anger, which was weak in any case, so that he remained defeated in a battle in which he never took part, what did he have to do with wars, all he wanted was peace and order, a quiet life without any surprises, even the weather never took him by surprise, but she did surprise him, she of all people, who had been so happy when he rescued her from her poor, hardworking, hard-hearted parents, from the two little brothers she had been forced to bring up, happy to have a home of her own, a husband of her own and later children of her own, who would have believed that it wouldn't be enough for her.

Immediately after she left a procession of women came marching down the narrow path, broad-hipped, no longer young women who tried to convince him that it would be enough for them, but he only wanted his wayward girl, all other women seemed dull and boring to him, just like him, and he didn't want himself, but her, and he was ready to take her back the minute she said the word, but she didn't say the word, even though nothing worked out for her, not the singing or the dancing or the acting, she wasn't young enough, or attractive enough, it turned out that only in his eyes was she a star, but amazingly enough she didn't break, she held her head high in her failure, surveying the ruins of her life with satisfaction, as if this was her great achievement, to have dared and failed. For years I meant to ask her how she coped with the disappointment of her failure, and after paying such a high price too, but now she is completely different, so quickly did her beauty fade, her dreams vanish, that she appears to have turned into another woman entirely, and it seems that this bony old crone with the broad clay face knows nothing about that young woman who broke my life in half, and there would be no point in troubling her with ancient rumors.

Again I pass their bedroom window, trying to peek through the slats of the closed shutters, to push aside the curtain of hibiscus swooning in the heat, and I want to shake the wooden shutters until they open their parched mouths and tell me what happened there inside their bedroom, the smallest room in the house, with the pullout bed, she sleeping on the big, high one and him on the low, narrow one that was pushed under her bed in the morning so they would have space to move in the tiny room. Helplessly I stand before the secrets of the shutters, this room has always given rise in me to an obscure sense of oppression, a nagging pain in my throat, and suddenly I hear a howl coming from inside it, and my jaw drops in astonishment, it's impossible, nobody lives here, how did some poor creature get inside, and how will it get out, when all the shutters are closed and the doors are locked, and I walk round the house again, trying to peep inside and not seeing a thing, and again I hear a cat hissing in the bedroom, and I'm sure that it's my fault, that I am the one who left a kitten there many years ago, a kitten which by some miracle has managed to survive to this day, and now it's begging me with the remnants of its strength to rescue it, and in my panic I run away again, propelling myself down the narrow path, my hand rummaging in my bag, where are my keys, all I want to do is get into the car and get out of here, why did I come here in the first place, nobody needs me here, they need me at home now, Noga must be worried stiff, why haven't I come home from work yet, it's already late, and he's scolding her instead of reassuring her, and the thought of the two of them alone in the house without me weighs on me all the way home.

A hot, pungent smell of frying onions greets me as I hurry up the stairs, my muscles hurting as if I've run all the way, the neighbor across the landing again with her enviable cooking, but no, the smell is bursting out of our kitchen, combined with a sight that for the past weeks I have seen only in my imagination, Udi stirring the pan with a big wooden spoon, he always looks so reluctant when he's doing something in the kitchen, standing on one leg with the other foot resting on it, wearing underpants and a torn blue tee-shirt, which I've been nagging him for years to get rid of, but he refuses, and rightly, he looks like a boy in it, young and thin, suddenly he looks much younger than me, he looks healthy, the ancient medicine of the East has saved him in the twinkling of an eye. Noga is standing next to him bowed over the marble counter, cutting up tomatoes, her lips pouting with effort, everything is hard for her, not to drop the tomato, not to cut her finger, but her eyes are wide with happiness, and I look at them in astonishment, as if I have landed by mistake in another family, the similarity to my frequent fantasies is stunning and paralyzing, almost insulting, and instead of being delighted I feel superfluous, what's going on here, I come flying back to them with my heart in my mouth, and it turns out that they get along much better without me.

You came too early, Mommy, we're making a surprise for you, Noga complains happily, and I go up to him and peep into the pan, something's burning, Udi, I say, bits of blackened garlic are floating around between the still hard wedges of onion, how many times have I tried to explain to him that you only add the garlic when the onion turns yellow, but he refuses to listen, clinging to the belief that his stubbornness will prevail and that the garlic will adapt itself to him, like me, like Noga, and when I see the blackened crumbs I fill with rage, he never learns anything, stirring the blazing pan, standing like a stork on one leg, and instead of admitting his mistake he begins scolding Noga, blaming someone else as usual. What's happening with the tomatoes, how long does it take you, can't you see that everything's about to burn? And she meekly offers him the watery slices, and I can't stop myself, Udi, the onion isn't done and the garlic's already burnt to a frazzle, how many times have I told you to put the garlic in after the onions and not to fry them together from the beginning.

He shrinks as if he has received a blow, the pan shakes in his hand as he lifts it, in a minute he'll brandish it like a tennis racket and hurl it to the floor with the whole greasy mess, and I quickly take a step backward, dragging Noga behind me, but he only bangs it down on the leaping flame and yells at me, so you cook if you're such an expert, I'm sick of listening to your moaning, nothing I do is good enough for you, and already he's back in the bedroom, slamming the door behind him, and I run after him, in a hurry to cover his words with mine.

You're simply impossible, that's what you are, you're incapable of hearing one word of criticism, I yell, what did I say, all I said was that you should put the onion in before the garlic, is it worth ruining everything for that? And he's already in bed, pulling the blanket over his face, I ruined it? His voice is crushed under the blanket, I ruined it? At last I feel a bit better and I try to give you a surprise, to prepare a meal with Noga, and you come in with that tense face of yours and instead of being happy that I'm capable of standing on my feet at all, you're annoyed because I didn't put the onion in before the garlic? Anyone would think I'd committed a crime, you should try to look at yourself from outside occasionally, you think you're a big saint and everyone persecutes you, but let me tell you that the reality is completely different!

I look sadly at the blanket covering him, black and red checks filtering his words, they're right, those checks, why was it so urgent for me to teach him to cook now of all times, the first day he got out of bed, and I bend down to placate him, but then a shout comes from the kitchen, Mommy, something's burning, and I charge back to see the flames licking the sides of the pan, everything's burnt, now even I can't tell the difference between the onion and the garlic.

What's the matter with you, can't you even turn off the gas, I yell at her, you're nearly ten years old, girls your age cook whole meals, and she tries to turn the knob with clumsy fingers, almost tearing it out of its socket. I've already turned it off, can't you see that I've turned it off, I scream and run to the porch, I can't breathe for the smoke, and she runs after me, her multicolored eyes shooting rays of blue hatred and green hatred spotted with yellow at me, why did you have to come back at all, she bawls with her mouth wide open, we were happy before you came. I have never heard her say anything like this before, but now that the words have been said a strange feeling of relief descends on me, a wild feeling of freedom, no doubt about it, it's a lot less oppressive than receiving a compliment. You're right, I whisper, I should have stayed there on the lawn and looked at the clouds instead of hurrying back here, nobody needs my sacrifices, and again I fill with guilt, like the smoke filling the house, and I cough hoarsely, and contemplate the afternoon heat flooding the porch, it's a pity it's not night yet, what will we do with the rest of the day, it drags like a wounded leg, it needs to be bandaged, taken care of, I haven't got the strength for it.

It seems to me that I hear the phone ring for a moment and stop, he must have answered it, to my surprise I hear his voice in the distance, since the day he fell ill he has taken no notice of its ringing, and now he approaches us, making his way through the smoke, and sits down next to me, I put a conciliatory hand on his knee and ask softly, who was it on the phone, and he says, it was Avner, he has to guide a tour in the Negev tomorrow, and he has the flu, he wants me to substitute for him, and already I feel insulted, again he's running away from us the first chance he gets, the minute he begins to feel better.

But Daddy, you still need to rest, Noga pleads, you're not better yet, and he says, it will help me to get better, I have to get out for a bit, but I know that if we were sitting at the table now and eating the meal he prepared, he wouldn't have answered Avner at all, and Noga knows this too, and she gives me an accusing look and says, I'm hungry, why don't we go out to eat. You two go, he shrinks, I want to rest, and I grumble, if you're strong enough for a trip to the Negev, you're strong enough to come with us to the restaurant across the road, and he sighs but he doesn't object, I see budding signs of moderation in him today, he holds back from exhausting his rage, and this is ostensibly desirable but gives rise in me to a strange melancholy of parting, like the melancholy at the end of summer, because in spite of all the complaints about the heat of the sun it's hard not to be offended when it grows cold. Great, we're going to a restaurant! Noga shouts, but her enthusiasm wanes when she sees my worried face, and I follow him to the bedroom, an embarrassing question at the tip of my tongue, do you still love me, watch him pulling on a pair of shorts over his underpants, like two flags waving on his shrunken thighs, flapping as he walks, tensely I follow his movements, he hasn't left the house for weeks, and I pray for him not to change his mind, or fall, making this little celebration of his recovery vanish before our eyes.

Where are my sandals, he asks, and I begin to search the house, it's been a long time since he needed them, where can they be, they're not in the closet drawer or under the bed, I search feverishly, as if our lives depend on it, what did they look like, I scarcely remember, two brown leather straps, and he begins to lose his temper, I can't go barefoot, he leans against the wall, apparently it's hard for him to stand, how will he be able to guide a tour tomorrow. I'm going back to bed in a minute, he threatens, I have to rest, he rakes his fingers through his greasy hair, and Noga begs, wait Daddy, wait, and she runs to her room, rummages in the closet, with me behind her, what are you doing, why should they be in your closet? And she blushes, I hid them once, swear you won't tell him.

Her clothes fly wildly out of the emptying closet, and I whisper, have you gone completely mad, why on earth did you hide them? And she wails, I dreamed that he left us, a few days ago, so I took his sandals, so he couldn't go without telling me, but I don't remember what I did with them, it was in the middle of the night, I was half-asleep, and I stare helplessly at the heap of clothes, there's nothing to be done, there's a curse on this trio, that's what we are, a trio and not a family, we can't even manage to go out together, and I lie down exhausted on her bed, watching her efforts indifferently, I too have suddenly grown milder, I'm not responsible for what happens here, I'm only one of three, what was the game we played as children, slapping dirty hand on hand, pulling them out, shouting, one out of three is out!

I shift uncomfortably on her mattress, trying to straighten it, strange lumps are growing out of it, what's the matter with this mattress, I snap, it's brand-new and look how crooked it is, I sit up and try to lift it, I don't believe it, Noga, just look what you did, under the mattress two brown straps peep out at me, thick, flexible soles, how on earth could you sleep like this, on top of his sandals, and she blushes, mutters in a whisper, just don't tell Daddy, remember, and I say, don't worry, and I wave the sandals in pretended triumph. We found them, Udi, I announce, let's go, but he answers me with a jarring snore, two saws sawing each other into little pieces, he no longer hears me or himself, he's fallen asleep on the living room sofa, his long narrow back examining us doubtfully, his bare feet clinging to each other like orphaned kittens.

Thirteen

What am I doing here between the bushes, hesitating at the gate, almost pressing our entry code and retreating again, walking up the street, returning to the car as if I've forgotten something, trying to give her an opportunity to call me, to suddenly pop up from some corner, yes, no doubt about it, it's her I'm waiting for, it's her I thought about all night, not Udi, who went on sleeping on the living room sofa, vacating our double bed that I abandoned long ago, sour with the breath of his illness, and I had a hard time falling asleep in the strange bed, as if I'd landed up in some filthy bachelor apartment, and I thought only about her, not about Udi and Noga, on purpose to punish them, about her shamed belly and hurt eyes and tangled fate, and the longer the night lasted the more clearly I understood the depth of her distress, how could she sleep at all, the blow of his abandonment churning in her stomach and filling her bed with hate, how could he have jumped out of the ship of her life, leaving her to the cruelest of decisions, and I hoped that she wouldn't come back to me, for how could I help her, but now I'm waiting for her, scanning the empty street, a river of boiling asphalt, with thirsty cars crouching on its banks, what will she do, she has no one to turn to, and I have let her down. In the end I have no choice but to go inside, and I press the secret numbers of the code reluctantly, the girls are already clearing away the breakfast dishes, the smell of greasy omelets and salad with lemon rises from their clothes, I snatch the last roll from the breadbasket and furtively dip it into a plate full of leftover salad and little triangles of omelet, I don't even care whose leftovers they are, as if they are all my children here, and here's Hani smiling at me in embarrassment, even more embarrassed than I am at catching me red-handed, falling on the leftovers like an alley cat. Is this your plate, I ask, and she nods hesitantly, but she's obviously lying to make me feel less uncomfortable, and I smile at her and pick up a cold triangle of omelet in my fingers, to show her that I stand behind my decision, just as I urge them to do, and it seems to me that I see a gob of Ilana's spit sparkling there, she always sprays spit from her mouth, but I have to swallow it, my stomach is already turning over, and with an effort I ask her, how's the knitting getting on, and she proudly waves a pink cloud in the air, in a few days I'll finish it, I can't give birth until it's finished, and I say, wonderful, and give her an absentminded pat on the shoulder.

In the distance I hear Anat's voice telling the girls to hurry up, don't tell me you forgot, she comes up to me, we're going to the maternity ward today, and of course I have forgotten, every now and then we take them to see the delivery rooms, the newborn babies, like you take children to the zoo, and they walk round heavy and glum, pressing their bellies against the transparent cribs, as if trying to connect the visible babies to the mystery inside them.

How did it go yesterday with Etti, she asks, her clean blue gaze on my face, and I say, smooth sailing, no problems at all, and take the signed forms out of my bag. Go and give them to Hava, she urges me, she was angry with you for not coming back here yesterday, and I hurry to Hava's office and submissively hand her the forms with the precious signature, as if making an offering to a greedy goddess, a wretched human sacrifice, a little child. Were there any problems, she asks in a satisfied tone, and I murmur, none at all, it all went off smoothly, and then I leave before she can read my rebellious thoughts about the dubious success which smells of failure, and I know that the lenses of her reading glasses are following my steps sternly and that a disapproving frown has appeared on her forehead.

Na'ama, someone's waiting for you at the gate, Anat calls from one of the rooms, and I ask, who, trying to hide the happiness dancing inside me, and she says, I have no idea, they asked for you to come down on the intercom, just keep it short, we're leaving in a minute, and I charge down the stairs, it has to be Yael coming to try me again, this time I have to help her, suddenly it's clear to me what she should do, and I'll tell her in no uncertain terms, without any hesitation, sometimes out of the maelstrom of doubt a moment emerges when you have to act firmly to prevent a tragedy.

But no one is waiting for me at the gate, I look round expectantly, a man in a blue shirt is sitting on the opposite pavement, his head between his knees, how hot it has suddenly become, I can hardly open my eyes, seeking her blindly in the glare, Yael, I'm here, I whisper into the silence, don't be afraid, I'll help you, and only when I come close to him do I recognize first the sandals, two brown straps that only yesterday I waved in the air like a trophy, and then the tee-shirt that I've been nagging him to get rid of for years, and I shout, Udi, what are you doing here, trying to hide my disappointment, my growing panic, what happened to the trip to the Negev?

He raises a gray, sweating face to me, it was called off, he whispers, I couldn't remember anything, and I sit down next to him on the pavement, what couldn't you remember, I don't understand, but it's already clear to me that it's bad, he's never stopped a tour in the middle before. I took them to Lachish, he groans, all the time I was sick I longed for that tell, and I wanted to teach them about the history of the city, the letters that were found there, I know them all by heart, and suddenly I forgot everything.

But Udi, it happens to everyone, I put my arm around his shoulders, trying to ignore the smell of sweat breaking out of his body, you just have to wait a little and it comes back, and he says, you think I didn't wait, I called a break and they sat down to eat and I walked round by myself and tried to remember where I was, but when they gathered round me I forgot everything again, I didn't have a clue what to say to them, and his head sinks again, I'll never guide a tour again, Na'ama, you have no idea how humiliating it is, and I feel my stomach contracting in anxiety, what will become of him, what will become of us, what will we live on, but I immediately pronounce in a firm voice, this isn't the time for decisions, Udi, you have to calm down, you probably got out of bed too soon, and he groans, you know what it means to send people away in the middle of a tour, you know how they looked at me? What's going to happen, Noam, what are we going to do?

I get up heavily and give him my hand, dragging him behind me like a reluctant child who doesn't want to go to kindergarten, the leftover omelet I furtively swallowed burning in my stomach, as if the sun is continuing to fry it in the depths of my body, and my gorge rises, this time he really is broken, his hand lies limply in mine, what will become of him, he was always so proud of his memory, whipping out dates, historical processes, sites and names, what will he have left now, the bitterness will swell into a tide and pour out of his throat and engulf us all, and already I see Noga and myself trying to keep afloat in the swamp of his bitterness, heavy algae sticking to our legs and pulling us down, with nothing to hold on to, her curls are black with mud and I try to cling to her hand with the remnants of my strength, Nogi don't sink, but her hand is slippery, it escapes my grasp, finger after finger. You're hurting me, Na'ama, he pulls his hand away, and I rouse myself, help him into the car, sit down heavily beside him, I haven't got the strength to go upstairs and tell anybody, in a minute Anat will discover for herself that I've disappeared, that she has to shepherd the girls on their excursion alone in this heat, another working day gone down the drain, two working days, his and mine, both of us are already outside the healthy, functioning world, beyond the pale. Locked in the speeding car, our breath whistles between the closed windows, all I want is to get home quickly, but what will we do at home, what else is there to do that we haven't already done, who will help us? What would the healer with the baby say now, is this good news too, is this too an opportunity, I think of her with resentment, as if it's all her fault, and then in a burst of hope, that's what we'll do, we'll call her, and she'll come at once, and fill the house with her innocent smoke, so that at least it will seem as if we're doing something, and I say to Udi, as soon as we get home we'll phone Zohara, sure that he'll object, but he nods in agreement, I was just thinking the same thing, and then his face comes alive as he says, for we cannot see Azekah.

Who, I ask, and he says, Azekah, a large fortified city in Judah, it's the line I love best in the Lachish letters, all morning I was trying to remember it and now it's come back to me: May Yahweh cause my lord to hear tidings of peace, this very day, this very day! And let my lord know that we are watching for the signals of Lachish, according to all the indications which my lord hath given, for we cannot see Azekah. I listen reluctantly, what good are those ancient letters to me now, please let Zohara be free, and come quickly, so I can leave her with him and go back to work, I can't go on like this day after day, and when I call her from our house she is free, and she listens to me with hurried affirmations, confirming my frantic report, as if this is exactly what she expected, and everything is proceeding to her satisfaction, and promises to come immediately, and he hurries to the bathroom, mumbling the remembered lines to himself, like a bar mitzvah boy learning his Torah portion by heart, washing his humiliating forgetfulness away in the water, and I look at him, sitting in the tub with his knees up, his bones pressed together, and when he opens his eyes and sees me a smile of helpless embarrassment spreads over his face. Something seems to be missing in him, and I scan his body anxiously, like a house after a burglary, what has he been robbed of, how misleading the revealed limbs are, the important thing is inside, concealed under the faded blanket of skin. No, all his limbs are there, and nevertheless something is missing, something that held them in a tight grip, sex, that's what it is, the sexuality that compressed him into one stubborn, assertive will has suddenly disappeared, lost its control over his body, and without it he is almost insignificant, a creature without a purpose. What does he want now, whenever I got into the bath with him before a movement would start to stir throughout his body, as if a wind were blowing through him, and now he looks at me indifferently as I undress, his body is still, I'm getting out in a minute, he says, but I send out a groping foot and sit down opposite him, there's room for both of us, Udi, have you forgotten?

My white hips which have grown wider lately press against the sides of the tub, blocking the water like a dam, and it crowds up behind my back, mocking my fat, he actually liked it when I put on weight, but now he seems not to notice, what does he want, what is it that unites his limbs into one purpose now, perhaps the desire to be well, perhaps something else, a hidden wish that threatens me because I have no part in it, because it no longer depends on me, what will fill the space that has grown empty now?

He soaps himself punctiliously, lathering his whole body, bending over his feet and scrubbing each toe, even between his toes, as if he has been wallowing in filth, muttering unintelligibly from time to time, utterly absorbed in a conversation with himself, now I remember, he announces triumphantly, To my lord Yoash: May Yahweh cause my lord to hear tidings of peace this very day, this very day! Who is thy servant but a dog that my lord hath remembered his servant? Thy servant Hoshaiah hath sent to inform my lord Yoash: May Yahweh cause my lord to hear tidings of peace, for the heart of thy servant hath been sick since thou didst write to thy servant. And let my lord know that we are watching for the signals of Lachish according to all the indications which my lord hath given, for we cannot see Azekah.

Once I remembered what was written on every potsherd, now it's all muddled up in my head, he smiles apologetically, and I ask, what are they, those potsherds, and he says, the Lachish ostraca? The earliest personal documents in Hebrew to be found in Palestine, dating from about the time of the prophet Jeremiah. So why can't they see Azekah? I try to show an interest, and he explains gladly, Azekah was a fortified town not far from Lachish, on the way to Jerusalem, and it had apparently already been conquered by the Babylonians, and therefore it was impossible to light signals from it, and the writer had to watch for signals from Lachish, and he is waving his hands about enthusiastically, drawing me a map in the thin foam between us, here's Lachish and here's Azekah and here's the little fort the letters were sent from, and here's Jerusalem which will also be destroyed soon, sitting in the cooling bathwater and delivering an impassioned lecture, as if he's standing on the heights of the ancient ruins, everything the tourists missed this morning I'm getting now, a private guided tour I never asked for, and I force myself to listen even though I haven't got the faintest desire to do so, I have far more important things to think about, far more urgent than some affair that took place two thousand five hundred years ago, but he doesn't notice my indifference, he goes on telling me enthusiastically about some prophet from Kiryat Ya-arim whose prophecies of destruction weakened the will of the people and the army in the last months of the Kingdom of Judah, and the king and his men want to kill him, and Hoshaiah, the writer of the letters, is pleading with his master to prevent the catastrophe. The water is already cold, outside it's so hot but in the tub I'm shivering with cold, as if I'm getting sick with something, and I ask without interest, so what happened to him in the end, that prophet, and he says, apparently he fled to Egypt, but they brought him back and killed him, imagine, they thought that if they eliminated him they would repudiate his prophecy, and I say, so he died without knowing that he was right, that his prophecies of destruction would come true, and Udi nods, yes, it was only after the Kingdom of Judah was destroyed that it was possible to distinguish between the false prophets and the true prophets, all the ones that prophesied peace and quiet were proven wrong, and only Jeremiah and that other prophet, whom nobody believed, proved to be true prophets.

Why are you so interested in dead prophets, I complain, and he says, I'm interested in the past, and the past is full of the dead, both the false and the true prophets, their bones are mixed, they cover each other, you remember the story of the man of God who came from Judah and the old prophet from Beth-el who led him astray, and how they were buried in the same grave?

My teeth are already chattering, but he doesn't even notice, the past heats his blood, not my breasts spread out before him, floating in the water like fat fish that have given up the ghost, their one eye open, he would always chase my naked body all over the house, reaching for me with all ten fingers, whenever I got into the bath he got in after me and tried his luck, and I would snap irritably, a person can't get undressed in this house without it being construed as an invitation. You should be pleased, he would retort, wounded, would you prefer me to be indifferent? And I would answer in the depths of my heart, maybe I would, but now I don't know which I would prefer, my teeth are knocking into each other, no, it's not my teeth, someone is knocking at the door, it sounds so close, almost as if it's the bathroom door. I jump out of the tub and wrap myself in a bathrobe, I feel as if a stranger is prowling round the house, seeing us naked, and now the front door creaks open, a dark figure moves in the doorway, I'd completely forgotten that I asked her to come, my memory's gone too. How quickly she came, I marvel, hasn't she got anything to do with her time, and I go to the door, come in, Zohara, thank you for coming, examining her enviously all the while, a tricot dress clinging to her slender body, no one would guess that she's just given birth, I'm the one who looks as if I've just had a baby, with the old robe and wobbling fat, but there's no point in arguing, the proof is in her arms, a fair baby girl whose features are gradually growing clearer, like an ancient text hard to decipher, and again I say, thank you for coming, I wouldn't take a baby out in this heat for anyone, a note of reproof underneath the appreciation, and all the time the doubt gnaws at me, why is she so devoted to us, is he really so sick?

He doesn't look sick at all, hurrying into the living room, a towel wrapped round his waist like a skirt, and she looks curiously at us both, it's obvious that she's gotten us out of the bath, but we don't look close, that's for sure, only very clean, soaped, shampooed, without the glow of physical intimacy. Her black eyes encompass us with impersonal compassion, broad and all-embracing, and she puts the baby down on the sofa, building a wall of cushions round her, her hair caressing the little body, long dark ropes down to her waist, today she's almost beautiful, still too angular but it's hard to take your eyes off her, every movement she makes flows serenely out of the one before it. She doesn't seem affected by my implied criticism, or by my thanks either, she isn't thinking of herself at all, I suddenly realize, she isn't thinking about what my every word says about her, but about what every word of mine says about me, she hasn't come to be judged, she has come to help.

It isn't a failure, Ehud, she says to him quietly while she rummages in her bag, fishing out little cloth bags, lining them up on the table, don't see it as a failure or a punishment, everything that's happening to you now is only a reflection of the past, and he passes his hand thoughtfully over his hair and asks with a shy smile, what do you mean by that? What you are now is what you were, she replies, what you will be in the future is what you do now, do you understand, the results of our actions ripen slowly, they catch up with us long after we forget what we've done, every bad action comes back to us, it leaves shadows of self-loathing behind it, but those shadows belong to the past, Ehud, the pain you are experiencing now is the completion of the results, the ripening of the fruit, and there is relief in knowing that it's already the end of the process.

What do you mean, the end of the process, he says, maybe it's just the beginning, and she smiles, that depends on you, if you change your inclinations in the present, you can change the future. Look at your body, she says, her eyes measuring his bare chest, lingering on the red towel, the negative feelings accumulate in the centers of energy of the body, the seeds of hell can be found in the soles of the feet, where anger accumulates, the seeds of the hungry ghosts are found in the base of the spine, where greed gathers, the seeds of jealousy hide in the throat, we're going to work on purifying these areas of your body, she promises, this is actually an exercise which is usually performed after death, but we're going to do it ahead of time.

But how do you do it, I burst out, it seems to me that I haven't spoken for hours and my voice comes jerkily out of my throat, how do you purify, how are you changed, they're only words, and she looks at me calmly, we can only change through suffering, suffering spurs our spiritual capacities, it wakes us up, forces us to release the wonder imprisoned within us. As we advance along the spiritual path all our old ideas about ourselves and the world evaporate, and then a completely new way of looking at things develops. You may have begun to recover but you haven't changed, she turns to him in gentle rebuke, you set out on the tour this morning with negative feelings, you have to change now, or else you'll pay the price in the future. Aren't you exaggerating a bit, he sniggers, who hasn't got negative feelings, and she opens her eyes wide in pretended astonishment, I'm exaggerating? Have you any idea of the influence exerted by every thought you've ever had, every word you've ever uttered, every feeling you're ever felt, how they affect the weather, the plants and the animals, the earth and the air, not only other people, and he hangs his head in shame, his mouth a little open, his hands loosening their grip on the towel, and I look at the sagging towel in suspense, in a minute it will drop to the floor, but I immediately turn my eyes in her direction, looking only at her, in any case we stand naked before her.

I heard anger in your voice, Na'ama, her rebuke shifts to me, you were angry with him for disturbing you at work today, you're angry about all these weeks that he hasn't been functioning, you have to cleanse yourself of this anger, you have to awaken the compassion within you, not the pity, which is a violent, patronizing emotion stemming from fear, and I defend myself immediately, looking at him uneasily out of the corner of my eye, it's just that I got such a fright when I saw him this morning, it isn't easy when something goes wrong nearly every single day.

But you have to understand that you have no reason to be angry with him, only to thank him, she says, through his suffering he awakens your compassion, thereby granting you the greatest gift of all, you know that in Tibet they say that the beggar who asks you for alms or the sick old woman needing help could be Buddha in disguise, crossing your path in order to arouse your compassion and lead you to spiritual transformation.

I examine him doubtfully, a hostile skinny Buddha in a red towel skirt, a Buddha without light, trying to avoid my eyes, once we would exchange gossipy glances, secret skeptical smiles, but now we are estranged, as if we have never met, two students landing by accident in a private lesson with the same tutor, united only by her rebukes.

So how do we arouse our compassion, I ask, and she answers immediately, for every question she has a ready reply, she never pauses for a minute to reflect, try to see him as you see yourself, not in the role of husband or father, but as a free being, just like you, with the same desire for happiness, the same fear of suffering. Try to imagine someone you love very much in the same situation, let's say your daughter, imagine what you would feel for her, and now take this feeling and transfer it to him, but I push her words away, God forbid, I couldn't bear to imagine Noga in his situation, and she says in a reassuring voice, you're quite wrong, Na'ama, the thought would only liberate Noga and help her, you still don't really understand how powerful and miraculous the action of compassion is, it blesses everyone who takes part in it, the one who awakens it, the one who is awoken by it, and the one at whom it is directed.

Again I examine her with suspicious admiration, sitting erect opposite us, stretching her neck toward us as we stand before her, one hand lying on her baby's back, her hair floating hazily in the hot wind coming from the porch, her voice welling moist and fresh from her throat, and I feel as if I could go on listening to her forever. Thus the children of Judah must have listened to the prophecies of consolation and encouragement, so what's the wonder they wanted to silence the somber prophet, destroying their happiness with his threats, O daughter of my people, gird thee with sackcloth, and wallow thyself in ashes, make thee mourning as for an only son, and bitter lamentation, for the spoiler shall suddenly come upon us, for death is come up into our windows, and is entered into our palaces, and it seems to me that I have to do it for her sake, to flood myself with compassion, and I try to imagine Noga lying paralyzed in bed, suffering from a mysterious disease. No, it's not compassion that awakens within me but a great fear, and I glance quickly at my watch, today she's coming home early, she mustn't see Udi here like this and realize that something has gone wrong again, she was relieved this morning to see that our hateful routine had returned, I have to catch her before she comes home, take her for a walk or something, and suddenly I feel doubt, like the sun going in and out of the winter clouds, darkening and illuminating the landscape, it moves inside me, changing my colors, and I look with animosity at the little bags she is holding in her hand, taking out brown pills, like the turds of small animals, the Dalai Lama blessed these pills, she tells him, and he looks at them admiringly. I turn my skeptical back on them and go to get dressed, hearing their muffled conversation as I do so, your enemy pulse is strong, she warns him, that means you will soon come across an enemy, or that you already have an enemy in your life, and he says, there are always enemies, the problem is to recognize them, it's only with hindsight that we know who really endangered the Kingdom of Judah, Babylon or Egypt.

I'll pick Noga up at school and take her out to eat, I don't want her to see you at home now with the doctor and start to worry, I say to him, and he looks at me with a frown, recoiling from me as if I am the enemy, and Zohara says, you can go, if you like, even though I don't think you should hide things all the time, she returns the pinprick I thought she hadn't noticed, and I say, it isn't all the time, I just don't want to worry her, that's a form of compassion too, isn't it?

They flock out of the gates, in wild, stormy torrents, I can hear the roar even through the closed windows of the car, here and there I recognize a familiar face, children who once came to our house, a year ago, maybe two, shutting themselves up in her room with the television, emerging occasionally to ask for a drink, leaving sticky puddles of raspberry cordial behind them, and I want to stop them and ask, why did you stop coming, why are you ostracizing her, come back, I'll bring you whole trays full of raspberry cordial to the room, Coca-Cola, ice cream, snacks, whatever you want, just come back. They don't recognize me, imprisoned in their clamorous worlds, even if I were lying next to the road they wouldn't notice me, and already the stream is thinning out, a weakening torrent, here are Shira and Merav again, inseparable, both wearing the briefest of dresses, almost identical, but where's Noga, why is she missing? Perhaps she came out first and I missed her, and I am on the point of turning round and driving home when I see her in the distance, what relief I suddenly feel, almost joy, she isn't alone, she's talking to someone, there's someone interested in what she has to say, a little taller than she is, with round glasses and thin hair, who on earth can it be, he doesn't look like a child, he's an adult, who can it be, he talks and talks, waves his hands in the air and she is silent, her eyes downcast, and not far from me they stop, I see her smiling good-bye at him and walking away, and he gets into a car parked nearby, and I go on staring at her receding figure until I rouse myself and open the window and shout, Nogi.

The book bag bounces on her back as she turns to face me, Mother, she says in surprised rebuke, what are you doing here, why aren't you at work? Just as I said to Udi only a few hours ago, a series of surprises we're giving each other today, he surprises me and I surprise her, that's family life for you, every event gives rise to a chain reaction, and I answer with false cheerfulness, I finished early today so I came to take you out to lunch in the mall, and perhaps we'll buy you a dress, you can't go on wearing those rags all the time. But my cheerfulness fails to infect her, has something happened, why did you finish early, she insists, looking at me with an expression of disbelief, and I say, nothing happened, Anat took the girls to see newborn babies, and I wasn't needed. She gets into the car next to me, and I can't resist asking, who was that man, and she says, Remi, the history teacher, I told you about him, and I nod, she must have told me while I wasn't listening, how hard it is to listen to them. He's so young, I marvel, he looks almost the same age as you, what did he want? And she shifts uneasily in her seat, nothing special, but I saw the way he was waving his hands about, and now it's my turn not to believe her, and I say, what was he so excited about?

Nothing, she says sulkily, he thinks I don't show enough interest in his subject, so he was trying to arouse my interest, to make me see that everything we study is connected to our lives, and I say, really, how exactly, remembering Udi's impassioned lecture over the pale foam in the bath, and she replies evasively, I haven't got a clue,

I didn't understand what he was talking about. I examine her doubtfully, neither of us really believes the other, and I only hope that
she isn't going to fall in love with this childish history teacher,
anything can happen for lack of a functioning father figure. So what
do you want to eat, I ask, and she says, I'm not hungry, I want to go
home, and I say angrily, but I am hungry, I'm a person too, you
know, and I can feel a scream rising inside me, all I've done is put
myself into an unnecessary trap, Zohara was right, why try to hide
things, she can feel that something's wrong, but it's clear to me
that I can't retreat now, and I step on the gas, stealing a sidelong
look at her, her head is bowed, her lips twisted as if she's about to
vomit, but I refuse to give up, I park aggressively at the entrance
to the mall and get out of the car, hearing her footsteps trailing
reluctantly behind me.

Once she loved coming here with me, extorting little presents
from me, what's happened to her all of a sudden, she isn't an adolescent yet, so what is it, and I try to give her a hug but her body
stiffens, what's wrong, Nogi, I ask, and she says, nothing, I'm tired,
I want to go home, but I push determinedly through the crowds
taking refuge here from the heat, holding her hand so she won't get
lost. Long lines of people are waiting hopelessly at the food counters,
the only place with empty seats is the pizza joint at the end of the
mall, and I sit down exhausted on a plastic chair, pulling up a chair
for Noga, and chew the hard, lukewarm pizza, so that's why the place
isn't full, there's a reason for everything, including her hostile
silence. So how was it at school today, I ask, and she answers auto-
matically, all right, and I persevere, what do you do at recess, and
she lowers her eyes, sucking cola from the bottle, nothing special, I
go outside or I stay in the classroom. I saw Shira and Merav, I say,
and she says dully, what about them, and I whisper, you used to be
a trio, remember, you never moved without each other, what happened? She shrugs her shoulders, trying to maintain a façade of
indifference, I don't remember, she says, they started to get on my

nerves, I'm not interested in them anymore. Convenient as it is for me to hear that the choice is hers, I don't really believe her, did you have a fight, or did it happen gradually, I ask, and she replies, I don't remember, lowering her eyes, above them her thick, untidy eyebrows stare at me, and I ask, have you got any other friends, and she says, here and there, and I don't know if she's deceiving me or herself, but a pang of sorrow silences me suddenly and I have nothing to say, all I want to do is weep, lay my head on the table and weep unclear, unjustified tears, what is it compared to real, terrible trouble, it's nothing, only my Nogi, my only child, apathetically chewing her pizza, her skin soft and milky, a few new freckles have settled on her snub nose, her golden curls swelling round her head like a halo, Nogi who has nothing to say to me, who hides her loneliness from me, who keeps me at arm's length as if I have some dangerous disease, or she does. Once we were so close, she wanted to look like me, talk like me, dress like me, she was my little double, and we walked hand in hand, here in this shopping mall, stopping to window-shop, and she would pick things out for me to try on, and sometimes I would take the three of them, her and Shira and Merav, and I would have fun spending money on them, buying them stickers, hair ribbons, ice creams, seeing their pleasure and excitement, and now this silence rising from her, flooding the marble spaces, it seems as if every corner where she rests her eyes answers her with a tense silence.

But suddenly sirens shriek in our ears, so close it seems that the ambulance is racing terror-stricken through the mall itself, wrecking the shops, crushing the milling crowds, and I am about to jump up and take shelter when the wail recedes, swallowed up in the expressway, and Noga raises her eyes to me, I was in the hospital once when I was small, wasn't I? And I say with affected calm, yes, it was a long time ago, you were only two, do you remember it at all, and she says, I remember something vague, you bought me an ice cream on the lawn and I threw it up. Yes, that might have happened, I giggle nervously, even though I remember every detail of that day vividly, and she asks, what was the matter with me, and I falter, nothing, nothing serious, and she insists, so why did you put me in hospital if it wasn't anything serious? Because it seemed serious in the beginning, I invent, it looked like meningitis, but it turned out to be just a virus, and she looks at me in disappointment, let's go home, I've got tons of history homework.

Noga, wait, I shout at her receding back, let's buy you a dress, and she grumbles, I hate dresses, but I hurry into one of the stores and begin searching through the hangers, what do you care, just try it on, so you won't look so different. Here, I pull out a blue dress with a pattern of yellow chrysanthemums, this will be a perfect match for your eyes, you have to try it on, and she says, it's exactly like your dress. Then let's be twins, I nag her, once you liked looking like me, and she pulls a face but stomps up to me, snatches the dress with an expression of disgust and goes into the changing booth, while I accompany her with yearning eyes, once I would go in with her, help her to undress, but now I don't dare, she frightens me, I suddenly realize, as if mines planted in her body are liable to explode if I get too close, and then the door opens and I look at her pityingly, the dress is so unbecoming, why did I force her to try it on, her legs are too thick, her shoulders stooped, she's different, she's not like Shira and Merav, it's not as if she can put on a dress and be like them.

How do I look, she says in an enthusiastic voice, suddenly she needs to please, and I say quickly, you look lovely, but she stamps her foot in front of the mirror, I look disgusting, I'm fat and ugly, and escapes into the changing booth, and the sales assistant comes up to me, it suits her beautifully, and I look at her glumly, what's becoming of me, just as I don't believe a word she says Noga doesn't believe a word I say, lying to her like a sales assistant in a dress shop, and when she emerges humiliated from the booth, hidden behind Udi's tee-shirt, I say to her, it really didn't suit you, and she bursts out, nothing suits me, my body's disgusting, and I hug her, you're just beginning to grow up, your body isn't formed yet, it takes a few years, but I, like her, think enviously of the tanned, slender Shira and Merav with their smooth hair and with earrings nestled like sweet, sparkling secrets in the lobes of their ears.

Now I too want to go home, I'm desperate to get there, I can't wait, here we're exposed, only at home will we be protected, but all of a sudden the mall darkens, as if the sun has gone down in the middle of the afternoon, and someone shouts, the power's failed, there was a short caused by the overload of the air conditioners, and the crowds stampede for the exits, as desperate to escape as they were to take shelter from the heat, a fire has broken out in a shop at the end of the floor, greedily licking at the Italian shoes, and the smell of burning leather fills the mall, and I grab hold of her arm and pull her behind me, coughing and gasping, pushing and being pushed, with signs and wonders the ancient Tibetan warning is coming true before my very eyes, how great is the power of every word we utter, every little lie is capable of setting the world on fire.

When we finally reach the car, sighing in relief, I say to her, Daddy's already at home, his tour was cut short, and she raises her head, she doesn't even ask why, she knows she won't get a satisfactory answer, and she mutters, great, he can help me with my history homework. So battered are we by our excursion that even he seems like a support, in a minute he'll open the door and dispel the tension that has accumulated between us, but when I climb the stairs behind her I see her feet freeze on the threshold, as if a horrifying sight has met her eyes, and I stand beside her and see Udi walking up and down the living room holding a fair-skinned baby in his arms, her eyes half-closed, her tiny mouth dribbling milk onto his shirt, while he rocks her and says, shush, shush, shush.

She's asleep, he announces with a silly smile, I put her to sleep, as if he's talking about the achievement of his life, and I look around, where's her mother, and Noga yells, and where's her father, has she got a father at all? You're waking her up, Udi scolds us roughly, it took me an hour to put her to sleep, and I see Noga's lips trembling, I try to put my arms around her but she pulls away and runs into her room, slamming the door as if nobody in the world is sleeping, but she rushes out again immediately, what's going on here, there's someone sleeping in my bed!

I asked you to be quiet, didn't I, he scolds her, can't you show some consideration? There's no limit to your selfishness! I rush to her defense, you're so insensitive, Udi, how can you talk to her like that, and the baby moves her bald head and opens her mouth wide, shrieks of despair break out of her throat one after the other, like shofar blasts, and he looks at us with furious animosity, we've ruined his achievement, and he murmurs soothing words into her ear, but it's too late, she won't go back to sleep, and neither will her mother, standing disheveled and sleepy in the doorway, what happened, she asks, for the first time I see her deprived of her serenity, and Udi complains, she was already asleep in my arms, but she woke up when they came in. She goes up to him and takes the baby, there really was no need, we agreed that you would call me if she cried, she must be hungry, and he says, I like conquering their hunger, I used to walk up and down with Noga for hours too so that Na'ama could sleep, and Noga looks at me for confirmation, and I say, yes, all his shirts had white stains on the shoulders, and she drops her eyes, it seems that this information only deepens her sorrow.

You're hungry, my sweet, Zohara sits down quickly on the sofa and pulls a smooth brown breast with a black nipple out of her dress, I stare deliberately, shamelessly, amazed at the absolute darkness giving rise to the white jet, and he too stares, mesmerized, as if he has never seen a woman breast-feeding before, and even Noga, the three of us watch her intently and without embarrassment, as if we are in the theater, making no attempt to hide our gaze, while she sits on the stage of the sofa like an Amazon, the shoulder of her dress dropped, revealing a single muscular breast, her eyes fixed on the sucking mouth and her forehead glistening with sweat. You must be thirsty, I say, handing her a glass of cold water, and she drinks it eagerly, and again I feel sorry for her, she was so thirsty and didn't dare ask for a drink, and I invited her, she came to help us, and she did help, Udi looks completely recovered, and already she is lifting the baby to her shoulder, smiling at me apologetically, the treatment demands such powerful energies, I had to rest, I could hardly stand on my feet, and immediately I am on her side, all the resentment is gone, of course, Zohara, you don't have to apologize, I'm so grateful to you for helping us, and she looks at him, are you feeling better, Udi, she asks, and he beams, yes, much better.

When I see her standing at the door, the basket slung over her shoulder, I am afraid that she is already slipping out of our lives, and I try to detain her, why don't you stay for supper, I offer, even though supper is still a long way off, and she says, I'm in a hurry now, perhaps another time, and Udi too approaches the door, gives her a tender, grateful look, and she smiles at him, don't be in such a hurry to get better, remember that your illness has a purpose, it can't be hurried, and as I watch her going downstairs I can't resist asking, so when will you come, and she replies, next week, but the week passes and she doesn't come, and another week passes, and an inexplicable uneasiness grips me whenever I think of her absence, as if someone has set an unsolved riddle before my eyes and the answer eludes me.

Fourteen

When I go outside in the morning the heat clings to me like a fur coat impossible to remove, reminding me of Noga's rabbit costume one Purim that covered her from head to foot, and when I tried to take it off after the party I found that the zipper was stuck, and she was sentenced to remain a rabbit forever, and she stamped her feet, I'm not a rabbit, I'm a little girl, I want to go back to being a little girl, her curls wet with sweat, until I was forced to cut the beloved costume off her, and the lumps of fur fell to her feet like pieces of a real dismembered rabbit. But the sticky air surrounding me cannot be cut away, I hang up the washing at night and take it down in the morning, boiling, Udi's underpants burning in my hands, his shirts, his trousers, suddenly I notice that most of the washing is his, after weeks when he never changed his clothes, when he refused to let me change his bed linen, a frenzy of cleanliness has seized hold of him and the washing machine fills up every day, as if there is a new baby in the house, and I do the washing gladly, there is no sound more encouraging that the singing of the washing machine, a strenuous prayer of cleansing and purification, a wringing out of good intentions.

The noisy, normal metabolism of this body called a house, with the three crowded chambers of its heart, has a calming effect on me, and I sit among the washing on the porch at night, every now and then a smooth sheet or the hem of a dress strokes my hair in the feeble breeze, keeping me company in my loneliness, because Udi is already sleeping, he goes to bed early every evening, right after Noga, both of them gather up their troubles and disappear into the silence of their beds, with only the busy fans sweating their electric sweat in the rooms.

In silence we eat our supper, yogurt soup and salad, and hardboiled eggs chilled in the fridge, I even gave up my beloved toast in order not to add to the heat. It's impossible to eat in this heat, Udi complains, but he takes care to sit with us, watching with an intent frown as we crack the eggshells and greedily gulp the cold soup, as if he is gathering data for some mysterious research he is conducting, and Noga steals wary, sidelong glances at him, from time to time she asks him to help her with her homework, and I stand eavesdropping at the door, perhaps something else is being said there, among the textbooks and notebooks, something I have been waiting to hear for years, but their conversation is matter-of-fact, everything has become dry and matter-of-fact between us, it seems that nobody dares to feel.

So what, I console myself, this is good enough, as long as it doesn't get any worse, there's been enough friction between us, better to keep a distance, although sometimes, sitting alone on the porch, I admit to myself that nothing joins us now except for the threat of some passing danger, as if the three of us have landed by chance in the same shelter in a time of war, and as soon as the war is over we will each go our own way, and if we bump into each other in the street we won't even blink, no one will want to remember the humiliating days of hiding. It seems that even the ties of blood are evaporating in this heat, boiling and bubbling under the thin cover of skin, I even look at Noga sometimes in surprise, what has she to do with me, she doesn't even look like me, growing more and more different as if to spite me, her body grows before my eyes wild and secret, and one night she calls me in alarm, my chest hurts, under the nipple. I wake up heavily, feel her chest with sleepy fingers, what is it, a little nut is hiding there, hard and round, a nightmarish nut, and I whisper to her, it's nothing, Nogi, go to sleep, trying to hide my anxiety, but I can't go back to sleep, my throat is full of painful nuts, lumps of terror preventing me from swallowing. Is it the thing I don't dare name, can there be a growth in the breast when there's no breast yet, I have to take her for a checkup, and early in the morning I can't restrain myself and I wake Udi, sit trembling on the edge of his bed, and he mutters in his sleep, nonsense, it's probably her titties starting, and I feel my breasts, no hint of a nut there, I don't remember that they began with that kind of pain, and in the morning I pounce on her the moment she opens her eyes, feeling urgently with my fingers, yes, maybe he's right, I heave a sigh of relief, it seems to me that I can feel a little nut hiding on the other side too, and the nipples are swollen, and I tell her the good news, it's nothing Nogi, there's nothing to worry about, it's just your titties starting, but to my astonishment she bursts into tears, she's inconsolable, as if this is terrible news, worse than any terminal illness. I don't want titties, she kicks the bed, nobody in my class has titties yet, what do I need it for, now they'll laugh at me even more, and I stroke her sadly, she really doesn't need this so early, at her age I was as flat as a board, now she'll have something else to hide under Udi's shirts, and all the joy of relief evaporates, and I call Udi to the rescue, tell her that it's natural, tell her that breasts are beautiful, I plead with him, and he says coldly, of course they're beautiful, and I know that both of us are thinking at that moment of Zohara's smooth, muscular breast with its coal-black nipple.

But the days go by and she doesn't come, with muffled longing I wait for her, with tender expectation, whenever she stands in front of me my resentment rises, but in my thoughts I almost love her, warm and wise and merciful, I see her sitting with the baby at her breast, the infant's sucking noises merge with the chirping of the birds and the howling of the cats, an integral part of the sounds of the cosmos. Thinking of her gives me a pleasant feeling of confidence, that if anything goes wrong again she will come back to rescue us, and when she fails to come I begin to worry, perhaps we have offended her, perhaps something has happened to her, I never realized how dependent I was on her.

What's with Zohara, I ask him one evening, and he says, she's fine, she called a few days ago, I told her that everything was all right. So she isn't going to come? I ask, disappointed, and he says, I don't think so, she's busy with her baby, and she isn't needed here anymore, and I say, right, she really isn't needed, and nevertheless I feel betrayed, as if I've been abandoned, and I ask with a resentment that surprises even me, does that baby have a father at all? I have no idea, he shrugs his shoulders indifferently, what difference does it make, and I say, it doesn't make any difference to me, but I'm sure it makes a difference to her, and he says, don't be so sure, I've always said that your ideas about the family are out of date, and again an ancient rage against him convulses me but I stifle it, it's impossible to fight with him nowadays, he doesn't seem to have the passion or the interest, or perhaps the love, to feed a quarrel. He's quiet, calm, he doesn't complain about anything or ask for anything, and we conduct ourselves circumspectly, the very opposite of the way we have behaved all our lives, vehement, burning with hurt, with insult, with frustration, and I who have always been easier to placate try to welcome this new order, even though I sometimes feel a nagging fear, which I immediately try to calm, he's simply making an effort to change, to cleanse himself of the old patterns, the negative feelings, perhaps there's some stage at which you remain without feelings at all, like with an organ transplant, but soon the positive new feelings will take root in him and then everything will come right.

The same dullness surrounds me at work, when I arrive at the shelter in the morning the girls stare at me apathetically, lounging on the sofas with their swollen legs stretched out in front of them, until Hani greets me enthusiastically one morning, I finished the sweater, and waves the pink cloud in my face. How lovely, I exclaim admiringly, it's perfect, and she pats her stomach, my baby's perfect too, it will suit her, remember that after the birth I have to put it on her myself, and she takes an elastic band covered with pink velvet out of her pocket, and I'll make her a topknot with this band, and Ilana who has kept quiet up to now begins to laugh, what a moron you are, you don't even know that babies are born with hardly any hair, what are you talking about, a topknot, buy her a doll, Na'ama, she turns to me, that's what she needs, a doll, so she can dress it and comb its hair, not a baby, and I say, Ilana, don't insult her, everyone chooses their own way to keep in touch, and Hani fawns on me, right, this way I'll be able to recognize her, by the sweater, whenever I see a baby in the street I'll look for this sweater. She'll have another thousand sweaters, Ilana snorts contemptuously, your baby's going to be rich, it'll be her most pathetic sweater, and Hani nearly cries, this is pathetic, this looks pathetic to you? And she waves the sweater in the air, I only wish I'd had a sweater like this when I was a baby, I never had anything new to wear in my life, only rags handed down from my sisters, and Ilana won't let go, you're still a baby yourself, you should give the baby to your mother so she can bring it up like your sister, but Hani recoils, what are you talking about, my mother hasn't got any patience for anyone, screaming and slapping all the time, I want a good mother for my baby.

How do you know that the woman who's adopting her will be a good mother, Ilana teases her, you think that if she's got money it means she's got a heart? And I intervene, don't worry, Hani, we check the parents out very thoroughly, these are people who want a baby very much, they have a lot of patience and a lot of love, and Ilana pulls a disbelieving face, they're making fools of you, you haven't got a clue what they're really like. Then why are you giving your baby up, if you don't believe them, Hani asks, and Ilana announces triumphantly, because I don't give a damn about this baby, that's why, she wormed her way into my belly without my wanting her and ruined my looks, and because of her I can't be a model, and I try to suppress my scorn, she's found herself someone to blame, but Hani has no such scruples, you, a model? With your figure, with your face? She almost chokes with laughter, slapping her belly, and Ilana yells, shut your mouth, you whore, you'll be sorry you laughed at me.

I hurry them upstairs for their prenatal exercises, and go to look for the new girl who arrived yesterday, her parents brought her in, beaten black and blue, yelling that they didn't want to hear anything more about her or the Arab bastard in her belly. I find her sleeping in her bed, and I contemplate her sadly, the first days here are always the hardest, the sudden separation from familiar surroundings, the painful end of denial, it really is best to sleep through them, and then I go up to the office to do some paperwork, and little by little a new serenity descends on me, things seem to have settled down a little, I can afford to breathe a sigh of relief. I'm able to concentrate, to keep the right distance, lucky that Yael didn't turn up, she touched my heart too much, who knows what's happened to her, perhaps her man came back to her in the end, and they'll raise the baby together, and already tears of happiness well up in my eyes, and even an embarrassing envy, how happy they will be, how happy we were, lying in the double bed with Noga gleaming between us, bending over her pale body, nibbling her feet, soft and fragrant as twin Sabbath loaves, as she kicked at our faces, her laughter ringing, and when I get home from work I look with hostility at her feet, wrapped in thick socks and sneakers, and she asks at once, where's Daddy? And I shrug my shoulders, I have no idea, he must have gone out for a walk. Sometimes he goes out to practice walking, and he comes back thoughtful but healthy, without any complaints of pain, I have to call Zohara, she really saved him, and when

he comes home I say, let's call Zohara to thank her, it's not nice
that we only phone her when we need her, and he frowns, thank
her for what? And I say in surprise, what do you mean, for what,
look how you've recovered, look how well you walk, have you
already forgotten the weeks you lay in bed? And he says coldly, but
it's not thanks to her, you think that's what helped me, her sermons
and the blessings of the Dalai Lama?

His ingratitude fills me with revulsion, and I stride indignantly
to the telephone, where's her number, it was here on the fridge, I
think I remember it by heart, and I dial the number hesitantly,
Zohara, it's Na'ama, and she replies, how are you, but her voice is
clipped, frozen, perhaps she's offended that I didn't call before.
We're fine, I announce emotionally, I wanted to thank you, Udi's
back to his old self again, and immediately I'm sure that she will
say, he needs to change, not to go back to his old self, but she doesn't
say anything, it's clear she has no interest in continuing the conversation, but I persevere, I don't want to lose her. How's the baby,
I ask, and she says, fine, and I suggest shyly, why don't you bring
her round one day, you promised to come for supper, and she cuts
me short, she doesn't even wait for the end of the invitation, all
right, one of these days, and I put the receiver down in disappointment, not knowing how to interpret her coolness.

I told you there was no point in calling her, Udi snaps, and I
retort crossly, you're not exactly my model in the field of human
relations, I felt the need to thank her, and if it made her uncomfortable that's her affair, not mine, and I open the fridge angrily,
the vegetables are finished again, he lies round the house all day
and it never occurs to him to fill up the fridge, I have to do everything when I come home from work, and I grumble, why didn't you
do the shopping, once you were already roaming round for hours,
there's nothing for supper, and he says, I'm not hungry anyway, and
I burst out, terrific, so you're not hungry, what about us? You can't

only think of yourself, you're part of a family, whether you like it or not, and he says in pretended innocence, so do I have to be hungry when you're hungry?

You have to think about everyone's needs, I yell, in the evening people have supper, it's not so complicated, and he grumbles, you and your bourgeois ideas, and by now I'm almost screaming, you raise a family on other ideas, children need to eat supper, people who work all day get hungry, and he shouts back, so eat your fucking suppers, am I stopping you from eating? And he rushes out of the house, slamming the door behind him, and I sit down in the kitchen, stunned, what did I say, is it so much to ask, hoping that Noga didn't hear us, her door is closed, the television is on full volume. Now I don't feel like eating either, I can do without supper, I can do without vegetables, without bread, I can do without him too, and I lean against the fridge, the motor chugging noisily behind my back, how long have I got before she bursts into the kitchen and demands, when's supper, not much, but I need the time just to sit down, to listen quietly to the chugging of the fridge, and when he comes in a few minutes later with shopping bags, I am as moved as if I have received a magnificent gift, ready to make peace on the spot, he isn't so bad after all, something else must have upset him, maybe the conversation with Zohara, he didn't want me to talk to her, there's no point in even asking why, the main thing is that he's already chopping vegetables, instead of apologizing. I'm glad that he came back, I'm glad that I won't have to sit alone opposite the glum Noga, but she's still glum, for some reason, and he's still tense, his jaws go up and down as he chews, making a disagreeable creaking noise, and I can't wait for the two of them to go to bed, they weigh on me so heavily, then I can sit on the porch among the fragrant washing, here and there an empty sleeve will caress me, because he crams his winter clothes into the machine as well, long-sleeved shirts and corduroy trousers, and a few sweaters.

Among the damp vapors I breathe a sigh of relief, how pleasant this empty silence is in the night, with nothing to be disappointed in anymore, and suddenly I see a shirt and a pair of pants advancing toward me, as if they're grown arms and legs, they are arms and legs, he's inside his clothes, I've grown so used to seeing empty clothes at this hour of night that I stare at him in wonder, as at some prodigy of nature, and at that moment the phone rings, before I have a chance to ask him why he isn't in bed, and childish crying rises from the earpiece, Na'ama, she sobs, and I ask, Hani, what is it? And she moans, I've given birth, they took me to the hospital after you went home, and I exclaim, mazal tov, how did the birth go? But she takes no notice, as if this is of no importance, the sweater's ruined, she sobs, Ilana unraveled it. Are you sure, I demand, appalled, how do you know? And she says, I took it out of my bag to put it on my baby, and it was all unraveled, just bits of wool, that's all that's left of it, I'll kill her, she's a monster, and I say, Hani, calm down, tomorrow I'll bring you one just like it, I'll search the shops until I find one just like it, and she screams, there's nothing like it, I knitted it myself, I'm not handing over my baby without the sweater, I'm not giving her up, in all my life I've never had anything of my own, I'm not going to give her up, and I plead with her, calm down, Hani, I'll come right away and we'll talk about it, we'll find a solution, the important thing is that you're well, that it all went smoothly. I look in embarrassment at Udi standing opposite me, one of the girls unraveled a sweater the other one knitted for her baby, I try to sum up the drama for him, that Ilana, I knew she had to be watched, and I stand up quickly, I have to go to the maternity ward, I say, but he stands in front of me barring my way, he smells nice, don't go, he says, I have to talk to you.

Happiness takes me by surprise, it approaches me with hesitant steps, he has to talk to me, he still has something to say to me, I felt so extraneous sitting here every evening opposite his closed door, perhaps we'll sit on the porch together like we used to, smoking and drinking cold beer, and he'll stroke my thigh, steal cool fingers under my dress, and I'll kiss his beautiful forehead, the green oases in his eyes, I missed you Udi, I'll whisper into his mouth, and the words will sweeten his tongue, and return to me wetly, so did I, so did I, and nevertheless I say, I have to go, I'll be back in less than an hour, but he stands his ground, I'm going soon, and I say, then we'll talk when you come back, I'll wait up for you, and he says quietly, but I'm not coming back.

Why, I ask in innocent surprise, has some war broken out that people don't come back from? I look at him like a little girl whose father has been called up in the middle of the night, and he says, Na'ama, I'm leaving, and I stare at him, still not understanding, who are you leaving? And he says, I'm leaving home, I'm leaving you, I can't go on like this, and apparently I start to tremble, because he grips me firmly by the shoulders and says, calm down, Na'ama, it will be better for you too, you'll see, we both suffer being together, and I stammer, but why, is it because of the vegetables? Because of supper? Then we don't have to have supper anymore. It's not because of the vegetables, he says, pulling up a plastic chair and sitting down on it, for a moment it seems that he is trembling too, but no, he looks composed, pale but determined, I've never seen this face before, I've known him for over twenty years and I've never seen this face before, refined and at the same time vicious, the face of a particularly dangerous criminal, his jaws creak when he talks, what is he saying, I can hardly hear, he's delivering a prepared speech, he must have been working on it for a long time, practicing opposite the mirror in the closed room, but I sink into the cloud of the cruelly unraveled sweater, the strands of wool coil round my neck, how could she have done that to her, she worked on it for weeks, weaving all her unhappiness into the pink wool, and now it was all unraveled, beyond repair, beyond repair, and he shouts, can you hear me, listen to me, Na'ama, and I try to look at him but my head sags crookedly as if my neck is broken, it droops down, all I can see are my kneecaps, huge round nuts, pressed together. What difference does it make to him if I'm listening or not, let him go and make his speech to someone else, let him go into the empty streets and prophesy to the trees and stones, and he says, listen Na'ama, I have to make a change, he raises my chin gently, my head is full of steel nails, how can his slender hands lift it up, I know that this illness is a sign, he says, I've been given a warning which has a deep meaning, it took me a long time to understand it but now I have no doubt, I have to make a change in my life.

But how do you know what change, I whisper, it seems to me that I'm whispering but he says, don't shout, and lets go of my chin, which immediately drops, and I mumble to my white knees, why this change, perhaps you should do precisely the opposite, and he says, I've been thinking about it for months, I know there's no alternative, this framework of ours is sick, all there is between us is tension, negative feelings, I can't go on living in an atmosphere like this, I keep on disappointing you, disappointing Noga, I can't go on like this, I'm not prepared to live for another forty years in the shadow of your anger, and I raise my head abruptly as if a spring in my neck has been stretched and yell, so in order not to disappoint us you're leaving? That's what you do instead of trying to mend matters? Is that how you cope with problems?

Some things are beyond repair, he says, you have to face it, we're not talking about an unraveled sweater that can be knitted again, there's something profoundly wrong between us that we haven't succeeded in putting right, I'm not blaming you, we're equally to blame, but you can go on like this and I can't, and suddenly he opens his mouth wide in a yawn, exposing teeth as sharp as barbed wire, and I look at the movements of his mouth grinding up my life, and of all things it's this yawn that makes me start to cry, how can he yawn now, showing me my place in his life with this insulting gesture, after I've been the center of his life for twenty-five years, a quarter of a century. You don't love me anymore, I sob, and he says, I don't love our life, I don't love my life, I have to make a change, and I say, but what about me, what about your love for me? And he whispers, I don't feel it, ever since I got sick I don't feel it, and I weep, what will I do without his love, how will I be able to live without it, I'm not prepared to give it up, I have to try to awaken it again. But why necessarily this change, why do you have to leave, why can't the three of us go away together, leave everything behind us, try to make a fresh start somewhere else, that's the change you need, Udigi, we'll sell this apartment and go away, you won't have to go on guiding tours, you'll be able to finish your doctorate without any interference, and already I plunge into this happy vision, encouraging myself, he won't refuse, I'll succeed in persuading him. Udi, you don't understand, I say firmly, almost coolly, it's like prophecy, you hear voices inside you, you don't know who to believe, you don't know which path to take, it's only after the fact that we can tell the true prophet from the false one, it's true that we have problems, but how can you imagine that this is the solution, to leave everything and go, to run away from the problems, what kind of miserable solution is that? How can you even think that you're free to go? I've never felt free, I've never even considered the possibility, it was clear to me that things could only be put right from the inside, and you'll see that this is what you have to do, this is what will make you well. You've never faced what happened to you with Noga, I continue enthusiastically, more and more convinced of the justice of my words, you preferred to wallow in the mire of guilt and accusations instead of rebuilding your relationship with her, and with me, that's what you have to do now, Udi, believe me, I know you better than anybody, don't be tempted to take the path of destruction, it could lead to tragedy, Noga won't be able to cope with it, I'm afraid to even think of what will happen to her, and I hold his hand with all my fingers, I don't care if I have to beg, to humiliate myself. Udi, it's so clear to me that you're making a mistake, try my way, the change has to come from within the family, give it a few months, you can always leave, and he shakes my fingers off his hand, his composure is melting away, you see why I can't go on living with you, he bursts out, I can't stand your bossiness, you're the only one who knows what to do, you always think you're right and everybody else is wrong, so maybe I'm wrong, he yells, but it's my mistake, and I'll pay the price.

You'll pay? I yell, if only you would pay the price alone, what about me, what about Noga? You still don't understand what it means to be a family, everyone pays a price, everyone is connected, you think you can cut off the connection? And he says, stop educating me all the time, stop using Noga to punish me, you won't tie me to you with bonds of guilt, I'm not prepared to sacrifice my life for this greedy goddess called a family, no one benefits from the fact that I'm suffering, certainly not you or Noga. I feel that my life's in danger, I have to save it, why do you think I got sick? Nothing happens by accident. It was my anger at you that made me sick, because I didn't dare be angry with you I was angry with myself, I punished myself because how could anyone be angry with a saint like you? And I simply can't believe my ears, you're angry with me? You've still got the nerve to be angry with me? I gave my life for you and for Noga, for years I've been covering up for your deficiencies, if it was anger that made people sick I'd have been dead long ago. I never asked you to cover up for me, he yells, I never asked you to make sacrifices for me, and you won't force me to sacrifice whatever remains of my life for you, to rot here in a prison of guilt, I have to get away from here, to cut myself off, if it goes on like this I'll die, and I scream with a hoarse throat, cut yourself off? How can you cut yourself off from your daughter? And he says, it's been years since I had any communication with my daughter, and it's all your fault, you're always supervising me, testing me, you have no idea how much damage you've done to my relationship with her, and I shout, I've done damage? All I tried to do was salvage something.

I'm not doubting your intentions, he sighs, but it turned out badly, and I don't know how to put it right, Noga's a big girl now, she doesn't need me on a day-to-day basis, I need time to think about what to do with her, and I stare at him tensely, suddenly I have nothing to say but I'm afraid of keeping quiet in case he gets up and leaves, as long as he's here there's still hope, I have to wear him out with words and then he'll stay to sleep, and I'll lie next to him and hold him tight, and perhaps in his sleep I'll succeed in getting him to make love to me, like when we came home from the hospital, and in the morning he'll understand that he has to stay with us, that this is his place. His irises dart round restlessly in the narrow prison of his eyes, his pale lips are tightly clamped together, I've succeeded in sowing doubts in him, I note with satisfaction, but then he stands up and begins hastily pulling the washing off the line, and I am encouraged by this act of domesticity, leave it, I say, we'll do it tomorrow, it's not dry yet, and then I see, it's only his own things that he's taking down, the sweaters and the long-sleeved shirts, preparing himself for winter, he isn't coming back, and I feel my face flooded with blood, dense and violent as lava, it seems as if my eyes, my cheeks, my lips, my nose are all quivering inside blazing red lakes, and I tear down the still-damp clothes and fling them in his face, now I understand, I scream, I don't care if all the neighbors hear, you waited until I finished washing your clothes and now you're going, you dirty swine, you miserable coward, I washed your entire wardrobe and now that I've finished you're leaving, and he says through clenched teeth, shut up already, you petty bitch, that's what you're worried about now, the wear and tear on the washing machine? I'm worried about the wear and tear on me, all the years I've wasted on you, from the age of twelve we've been together, and now you decide to leave, when I'm almost forty? When I was still young and attractive you didn't dare, and now you're brave? Egoist, exploiter, I yell, tearing more and more washing off the line, trampling on whatever falls from my hands, how can you do this to me, by what right, suddenly you feel like having a new life? You think this is a holiday resort, where everyone does what he likes, you know how many things I wanted to do and didn't, you know what I've given up for this family?

So now you've got the chance, he says in a whisper, and I scream, now? Thanks a lot! For me it's too late, I haven't got the strength to start a new life now, and you won't start one without me, you hear, up to now we've done everything together, you can't begin again without me, and now my hands are on his shoulders, closing in on his throat, I could strangle him, in my fury I'm capable of anything, but he pushes my hands away, calm down, he says coldly, and I know that this outburst repels him but I don't care, I suppose I should have sat with my legs crossed and listened to his prepared speech and parted from him nobly, perhaps that would have made him want to return, but I rage like an animal, kicking, cursing, exactly like the girls at the shelter when their babies are taken away, he's mine, he's mine, they scream, and I scream too, you're my husband, you can't leave me, and suddenly among the flying sparks of my screams a mute picture shines at me, yellowing with age, of two crop-haired children holding hands in a little room, and I remember how I used to write my name on the lobes of his ears, and when the letters blurred I would go over them again, with a blue pen, and he would laugh, you don't need that, Noam, presenting his ear to the brand of the pen, I'm yours forever.

His fingers hurt me so much that I let go of his throat, drop my hands and follow him to the bedroom like an obedient dog, behind the pile of laundry, and he takes his knapsack out of the closet and begins folding the clothes with his crooked folds, at the end of arguments I've always broken and gone to his aid, and now too I sit on the bed and begin to fold, shirt after shirt, and he looks at me in embarrassment, it was more convenient for him when I yelled and cursed. Where are you going, I ask, and he says, I don't know yet, first I'll go south for a while and then we'll see, I have to think about everything quietly, to be with myself, and I try to find encouragement in his words, it isn't for real, he's just going on a trip, in a few days he'll be back and everything will come right, I won't even say anything to Noga, but then he says, I left Noga a letter, I tried to explain a few things to her. A letter? I flare up again, what do you mean, a letter? You drop a bomb on her and I have to absorb the blast? You have to talk to her and be here when she reacts, not leave a letter and run away, but he says, I can't, I'm doing it in my own way, and I yell, there's no such thing as can't, you're too easy on yourself, you have to make yourself do it, and he snaps, so when you leave you can do it in an exemplary way, I'm such a failure in your eyes that I don't even know how to leave. But that's precisely the difference between us, I yell, I would never leave, I wouldn't be capable of going off as if I didn't have any obligations, you don't even say where you're going, how to get in touch with you if anything happens, and he says, I'll call in a few days to tell you where I am.

I watch the clothes being swallowed up in the belly of the knapsack, the corduroy trousers I bought him last winter in the store across the road, the beautiful denim shirt Noga and I gave him for his birthday, the striped sweater he wore that morning under the broken cloud, how can he leave when all his clothes are marked, and again I fill with rage, I'll never forgive you, I declare, and immediately feel ridiculous, he doesn't care how I feel, that's what it's all about, I have no power over him, if he cared he wouldn't be leaving, and as expected he takes no notice of my declaration, goes on feeding his hungry bag, the new, dust-covered Bible, which has never been opened, he leaves behind to rot with me here, and I try to think urgently, what else can I say, I have to find something that will arouse his doubts, that will keep him here tonight, and then I suddenly understand, the words have lost their power, I have lost my power, nothing I can say will change his cruel, heartless decision, something I was never afraid of because it simply never occurred to me that it could happen. After so many years in which one word from me could provoke his rage, his fear, his pleasure, tonight I can threaten, blame, plead, and nothing will change, and when I realize this a murderous exhaustion descends on me, the exhaustion of a terminally ill patient who no longer has the strength even to mourn for himself, and I push aside the superfluous garments, the ones that didn't fit into the knapsack, and curl up next to them, close my eyes swollen with weeping and feel as if I'm sleeping, but at the same time I hear his footsteps, the familiar sound that will soon no longer be heard here, becoming as rare as those of an extinct animal, who remembers the footsteps of the dinosaurs on the ice-bound desolation of the planet, and it seems so inconceivable to me, that soon the only footsteps to be heard here will be Noga's and mine, that I want to share my astonishment with him, and I raise my head and whisper, Udi, but he answers by turning the key in the door, and I leap from the bed gasping for breath, he can't leave like this, without a kiss, without a hug, when he left for a week we would part with a kiss, and now he's leaving forever, and I run to the door and try to open it, but it's locked, my key is probably hidden in the depths of my purse, and I can't run after him down the stairs and pull him back inside, like I sometimes did when we fought, and I hurry to the porch, wait a minute, I try to shout but only a hoarse whisper comes out of my throat, wait a minute, I still haven't said the most important thing.

He's already striding up the street, tall and obdurate, the huge pack on his back, like a tireless tourist, in a minute I won't see him anymore, even if something terrible happens I won't be able to contact him, I have to stop him, but my voice creaks when I scream at the receding backpack, full of his clothes, and all of a sudden I feel the enormity of the catastrophe and I scream, leave a few tee-shirts for Noga, how could I have failed to think of it before, but the street is empty of his presence, his vigorous strides, only the trees stand opposite me, the silhouettes of the cypresses, the Persian

lilac, the poplar, breathing in relief in the night, freed for a while
of the tyranny of the rule of the sun. Soon it will come back to reign
over them, but in the meantime they confer in whispers behind its
back, and I stare at the deserted street driving into my heart, and a
terrible pain tears me apart, where is he hurrying at this hour of
night, how does he intend to get to the south at all, the simplest
things are hidden from me, suddenly I know nothing about him after
growing accustomed to knowing everything, and this reversal is so
extreme, so unexpected, as if all my blood has been drained out of
me, and I lean over the balustrade, dry sobs tear at my throat, the
barks of a dog run over by a car, Udi don't go, I bark at the empty
street, come back to me, I can't live without you, Udi, my Udigi,
come back.

It was here that I sat and waited for the sunrise, here that I
saw Zohara running in her white dress to save us, why did I make
such an effort to cure him, it would have been better for him to
remain imprisoned in his illness, and when I think of the inevitable
sunrise I shudder, Noga will wake up in the morning, what will I
tell her, how will I face her, I have to find his letter and hide it until
I pull myself together, and I stumble into her room, I've been leaning over the balustrade so long that I can't straighten my back, and
I walk with a stoop, like prehistoric man in his cave, steal into her
room, treading on the piles of clothes and the notebooks thrown
onto the carpet, where's the goddamn letter. I hear her sigh, turn
over in her sleep, she turns her face to me and it's beautiful, calm,
the wonderful eyes closed, the lips parted in a mysterious smile, the
face of not knowing. She doesn't know yet that tomorrow morning
her life will be broken, and this certainty, that I know the full cruel
truth about her life and she doesn't, is so shocking to me that when
I stand over her bed I feel like God looming over his mortal crea-
tures, not just knowing but also guilty, I could have prevented it
and I didn't, and I grope over her desk with trembling fingers, so
many papers, where is that goddamn letter, I have to hide it, I want

her to get up in the morning and go to school as usual, I can drag it out for at least a week before she realizes that something is wrong, and in the meantime he may regret it, but it's impossible to see anything in the dark, and I return to the kitchen to look for a flashlight or a candle, I can't seem to find anything today, only a box of matches, match after match licks my fingers and falls black and weightless onto the rug, in a minute I'll set fire to the room, as long as that letter burns, without leaving a trace. No, it's not on the desk, maybe it's on the rug, lying in wait for her among her clothes, did he take the trouble to put it in an envelope, or are we talking about a piece of paper here, and I crawl on the carpet, groping blindly, and suddenly she sits up in bed, Mommy, what's going on, and I say, nothing, Nogi, go back to sleep. But what are you doing here, she insists, and I say, I just came to tuck you in, and she lies down again, I can smell fire, she whispers, I dreamt that the house burnt down, and I pick up the burnt matches and murmur, sleep, sleep.

I have no alternative but to wait for the first light of dawn, at sunrise I'll steal into her room again and find it easily, I encourage myself, as if this will change everything, and I go back to bed, curl up again among his faded clothes, shivering as if my skin has been stripped from my body, burning with cold, a consumed, blackened match, disintegrating underfoot, and I grope around me, seeking his long limbs, his head resting on this pillow, plotting dastardly schemes. Worn out by hatred I beat the mattress, Udi how could you do this to me, hating you means hating my life, hating Noga, hating myself, we're all entangled with each other in knots that can never be untied, and now you attack us with sharp scissors, scattering the corpses of our lives like severed limbs after a road accident, until it's impossible to tell what belongs to who, that's what you've left me here, in your sickbed, and I seize the pillow furiously, sink my chattering teeth into it, the smell of his cheeks and hair, the smell of the saliva dribbling from his mouth in his sleep, suddenly I see Geula's little Daniel before my eyes, how we took him from her to the children's home, and how he begged us to bring him the pillow she slept on at night every morning, and he would snuggle up to it like a kitten, sucking it as if it were soaked in milk, and suddenly I am seized by hunger, to the bottom of my empty body, and I jump out of bed and rush to the kitchen, where I stare into the fridge. Here are the vegetables he left me as a souvenir, cucumbers and tomatoes and peppers, but they're on his side, not mine, I'm looking for something warm and sympathetic, that will embrace me inside, and I take out milk and Quaker Oats and begin to cook myself some porridge, stirring the heating saucepan wearily, I'm so tired, but the hatred won't let me sleep, it will wake me every minute, now it's clear to me that I'll never sleep again, I'll drag out the rest of my life without ever closing my eyes again.

Standing over the bubbling saucepan I try to work out how much time I have left until I can part from this life, which has become so burdensome, like a sentence I have to serve, at least ten years, I calculate in disappointment, until Noga turns twenty, and then my anger rises against her again, because of her I have to go on living, night after sleepless night, if it wasn't for her I would be able to fill my belly with pills and be done with this agony, how can you live after you've been stripped of love, that's exactly what he's done, stripped me of the skin of his love, which even if it wasn't always felt was rooted in my consciousness, we don't feel the earth turning either but still we know it does.

Again I smell burning matches, maybe I left one in Noga's room and it's gone up in flames, but no, it's the oats burning at the bottom of the saucepan, I can't even cook cereal anymore, and I taste it, a repulsive black taste, as if I'm eating smoldering coals, but I don't care, as long as I fill my belly, I swallow it down straight from the saucepan, breathing in the bitterness of the fumes, my whole mouth one big burn, it hurts so much I don't feel the pain, I'll only feel if I stop and I don't stop, I scrape the bottom until there's nothing left and stumble back to bed, perhaps my full stomach will put me to sleep, I have to sleep, and my hands grope hesitantly between my legs, perhaps this will help me calm down and fall asleep, but a wave of nausea floods me when I touch the bush of hair, a kind of frizzy beard, a rejected hairy animal, its lips drooping in humiliation, it is his, it reminds me of him, of his fingers, his tongue, what has it got to do with me, and I run to the toilet, crouch over the bowl and throw up a stream of burning cereal, like a dragon spitting the fire of its hate at those coming to slay it.

Fifteen

e won't pee here anymore, I tell the open mouth of the toilet bowl that swallowed his waters day after day, year after year, staring at him submissively as he stood before it with an unsheathed penis, frothing its jaws with golden showers, he'll have another toilet to urinate in, and already its insult merges inseparably with mine, the insult of the porcelain tiles surrounding the sink, the window broken in one of our quarrels, its cracks bandaged with masking tape, the towels hanging on the arched necks of the hooks, all the deserted spaces of the house, the old furniture I've been meaning to replace for years, the dusty carpets, the countless objects, necessary and unnecessary, accumulated over the years, and all of them ruled by the high hand of Noga's insult. Like an orchestra attentive to the slightest movement of a demanding conductor we all gaze at her dark room, whence a smell of burning rises, as if a bereaved bear is lying there, threatening to rise to the full height of its grief and devastate everything in its path.

With half-closed eyes I glance at my watch, hardly an hour has passed since he left, if time drags so slowly, how will the whole night pass, and the nights to come, the rest of our lives, and I get up with difficulty, how can I shorten this night, how can I induce consoling sleep, perhaps a hot shower will help, but the strong jet

of water almost knocks me over and I lean swaying against the plastic
shower curtain, how I loved taking a shower here in the dark, after
we made love, and he would come in and send me a smile I couldn't
see with my eyes, only soak up with my wet naked body, and now I
wash this body with disgust, a rejected body, what has it to do with
me, for it was Udi who always mediated between us, it was he who
loved it, and now without his mediation it is alien to me, even soaping it makes me shudder, the prickly armpit sagging to the heavy
breast, the belly that was once taut and is now flabby, the full thighs
and the great dread between them, and finally the flat feet, broad
as a duck's, which always caused bad blood between us, because I
walked slowly and he ran ahead, and I aim an almost boiling stream
of water at them, and they hop frantically as if on blazing sea sand,
but I don't care, their pain is not my pain, just as this burning sensation belongs to my throat and not to me, and between the pain
at the bottom of my body and the pain at the top are only a shaky
scaffolding, rusty nails, the filth of humiliation that no knife can
remove, how could he leave, simply get up and go with his pack on
his back as if he were free, as if I were some site on a dusty map that
could be abandoned, a dried-up creek he left behind in order to
search for a better one, taking with him all I had, all I thought I
had. If only I knew where he was I would go to him now, without
even drying myself, I would persuade him, I would threaten him,
what he's done is clearly illegal, people can get thrown into jail for
less, abandoning a wife and child after so many years.

Sometimes he would wait for me with the towel spread out,
wrap me in it like a baby, it never occurred to me that it could end,
I never imagined that even these few luxuries would be taken from
me, and again the weeping bursts out of my bruised throat, I thought
it had gone and now it's back again, hiding between the blankets,
lying in wait for me because I am all on my own, without a shield
or a savior, an easy prey, a snail without a shell, a soft slimy slug,
and I cover myself with the wet blanket, sleep won't come, it won't

give me even a moment of grace, it won't come, but apparently it comes in the end, and even stays too long, because suddenly Noga's pale face looms above me, Mommy, it's late, she whispers, and I sit up abruptly, my head almost colliding with hers.

The letter, I think in alarm, I never had time to destroy the letter, and I quickly scrutinize her face, what does she know, she looks worried but she always looks worried now, her eyes slide away from each other, like two grapes scattered on a plate without any connection between them, and she averts them from me and goes to her room, and I get up with an effort, my body hurts as if I've been wrestling all night, my face is swollen, my mouth dry and bitter, all I want is to go on sleeping, send her to school and go back to bed, but she isn't dressed yet, sitting on her bed in her pajamas, an overgrown little girl covered with clowns and teddy bears, and I try to feel her out, is everything all right, Nogi? But she doesn't answer, she knows, there's no doubt about it, she found the damn letter before me, and I stagger to the kitchen and make myself a cup of coffee, staring at the empty house, Udi isn't here, that I can't hide, the sun is already attacking the porch, crossing it with sharp rays, illuminating every corner of the house, broadcasting the news of his absence.

Noga, come and eat, I say in a creaking voice, putting an empty plate in front of her chair, and here she comes, still barefoot, you know it's not, she whispers, nothing's all right, and I say, show me the letter, I can barely conceal my eagerness, but she shakes her head defiantly, I threw it away. What did he write, I ask, pouring coffee into my cup with trembling hands, and she stammers, I didn't understand exactly, that he has to get well in a different place, that he has to change his life, that he loves me, and all at once I realize the tremendous advantage she has over me and I am seized with violent jealousy, he loves her, in his flawed, incomplete way, but still he loves her, and not me, he doesn't love me anymore, and I burst out, so why did you throw the letter away if you didn't understand it, I would have explained it to you, and she says, I threw it away on purpose not to show it to you. But why, I shout, why don't you want to show it to me? And she says, because it's for me, not for you, with the same pathetic pride, the same miserable importance that I felt last night when he said, don't go, I want to talk to you, and I like an idiot said to him, we'll talk later, not understanding anything, and apparently she too doesn't understand, directing a new hostility toward me, instead of recognizing our common fate we're quarreling like beggars over a last crust of bread, but to my surprise I feel more comfortable with her hostility than with her love and I hurry her up, eat your breakfast, it's late, I'm not interested in heart-to-hearts with her, and she chews her roll with a strange voraciousness, pouring herself more and more milk, everything she does this morning seems strange to me, but I don't want to go into it, all I want is for her to leave the house and let me have a few hours to pull myself together. He needs to get better in a different place, she repeats, her lips white with milk, the main thing is for him to get better, right? And I say, right, almost grateful to him for the vague phrases, and now she's already at the door, parting from me with a stiff bye, Mother, and I kiss her on the forehead, quickly lock the door behind her, three loud turns of the key, just don't let her change her mind, just let her go to school and leave me by myself.

I quickly roll down the blinds, obliterating the stubborn slits of light, and fall into bed, where a damp black pit is waiting for me, only in its depths can I rest, spread out my aching limbs, all I want is to stay here all day, without having to worry about anyone, that's all I want, this is my playground, only here am I safe, outside the playground is a busy, dangerous road, Mommy and Daddy don't allow me to go out because there is no one to watch over me, there is no one to look after me now, a terrifying monster crouches over me, holds my wrists down to the bed, crushes my body beneath it, its revolting breath in my mouth. What will become of me now, I've never been alone, I was always with him, against him, for him, opposite him, underneath him, on top of him, behind him, I always tested myself in relation to him, and now that he is out of it the whole picture wobbles, in a minute it will smash to pieces before my eyes, and all my life will not be enough to pick up the pieces, like my father's precious barometer, when I crawled all over the floor on my wedding day, under the bed, chasing the little balls of silver mercury. I should have canceled the wedding, it was a sign, I should have married someone who wouldn't have left me in the middle of my life, when I'm not young enough anymore to start a new family and not old enough to die.

I try to remember other men but I can't, vague shadows loom up in front of me, I never dared to really look at anyone else, all my life I never dared to open more than one eye, the other was inflamed with fear, glued together with yellow pus. What was I so afraid to see, the radiance of the world or its gloom, giving up friends, boy-friends, another child, and for a moment I feel sure that if only I had another child now everything would be different, there would have been three of us, Noga and I and the little boy, three is a family, and two is cold comfort, and already I can sense the child who was never born at my side, his limbs soft and chubby, with all his babyish strength he clambers over me, strokes my hair, nestles against my breast, and I shift in bed, it seems to me that we are lying on the beach and the sand is warm and soft, covering my entire body, and Udi rises from the sea, shaking his salty hair over me and laughing, look what I brought you, he holds out his hands, but the sun dazzles my eyes and I can't see what he has in his hands. What is it, I ask, completely blind, and he says, can't you see, can't you see how much I love you, and I shout, the baby, take care that the baby doesn't run into the sea, he doesn't know the meaning of fear, and Udi laughs, what baby, there's no baby here, only you and me, because I'll love you forever, never believe me if I say I don't, and I moan with joy, rolling in the sand like a huge cat, I don't care that I'm blind, as long as I'll be loved forever. How glad I am to hear it, I whisper to him with my mouth full of sand, because I just dreamed that you stopped loving me, you have no idea how much I cried, the sea overflowed with my tears, and he laughs dismissively, his laughter rings in my ears. Stop laughing, it's not so funny, I say, but he doesn't stop, the ringing goes on from behind the closed door, and I wake up abruptly, it's already twelve o'clock, and the tele-phone doesn't stop ringing, I forgot to call the shelter, they must be looking for me, better not to answer, but perhaps it's Udi, per-haps I've conjured him up with my dream, how could you believe that I've stopped loving you, he'll laugh, and I pick up the phone, listen expectantly, and an unfamiliar voice screeches in my ear, Na'ama, your daughter's sick, come at once and take her home. Who is this, what's wrong with her, I almost bite the receiver, and she screeches, I'm talking from the secretary's office, she has a fever of nearly a hundred and four, I gave her aspirin but the fever won't come down, we've been trying to contact you for an hour, and I throw on a faded housedress and run just as I am, without combing my hair or washing my face, wet from the sweat of the sea, and drive with my eyes half-closed through the sun-struck streets.

Here she is, sunk in an armchair in the secretary's office, her cheeks red and her eyes glittering as if she is lovesick, her overgrown body suddenly shrunken, and I put my arms around her, kiss her burning forehead, I gave her another aspirin but it didn't help, the secretary reports in agitation, like leeching a dead man, she smirks, her lips painted dark red, almost black. Has someone examined her, I ask, isn't there a nurse here? You're out of luck, this isn't the nurse's day, she answers and looks at me suspiciously, we looked for you every-where, at work they said you hadn't turned up and at home nobody answered the phone, and I mutter, I had some errands to do, but her gossipy, made-up face examines me skeptically, my wild hair, shabby dress, swollen eyes, and I shrink under her gaze, it's so obvious that I was abandoned last night, that I'm a woman without a man, a woman without justification, anyone can humiliate me.

Come along, Nogi, let's go home, I whisper in a promising voice, as if home is a sheltered and healing place, and she raises her glittering eyes to me and begins to cry, I can't walk, I can't stand up, and the secretary says, she behaved like a heroine up to now, but as soon as Mommy comes we want to cry, right, sweetie? We like to worry Mommy, don't we? I bend down and try to pick her up, all I want now is to get out of here, her arms wrap round my neck with frightening weakness, like the hooves of a trapped animal, her body is hot and heavy, and I hold on to her and advance at a snail's pace, my spine feels as if it's disintegrating under the load, ground to dust by her weight, and I sob, Udi, look what's happened, help me, I'm going to fall, I can't go on.

Along the sides of the corridor children stand watching us silently, making way for us with frightening reverence, what do they think, that she's dead? That she won't ever come back? There's no end to this corridor, no end to this loneliness, only me and my sick child, and our weighty tragedy, crouching like an animal, this sorrow obliterates every human feature, once I cared what I looked like, how I sounded, now I groan aloud, snot weeps from my nostrils, all I care about is getting to the car, laying the sick body on the backseat, but I'm not going to make it, my feet are crushed under our common weight, in a minute I'll collapse in the middle of the corridor, a pile of limbs that have lost their vitality, and then I hear short steps coming quickly toward me, a bald child is running next to me and shouting, wait, let me help you, I haven't even got the strength to turn my neck, he's not a child, just a short man, and I remember, the history teacher. He grabs hold of her legs, the lower half of her body is in his hands now, he pulls her like a wheelbarrow, the small relief only emphasizes the pain that has accumulated in my body, and I hang on to her arms, hurrying to keep up with him so that the lower part of her body won't be torn from the upper part due to the lack of coordination between our steps.

When we reach the car I'm breathless and choking with the effort, and he slips deftly into the backseat and drags her in after him, and to my surprise he remains there, her legs on his lap, and I lay her head on the seat, feeling her forehead again, she's breathing heavily, her eyes are closed as if she has lost all interest in her surroundings. Thank you, I say to him and wait for him to get out of the car, his presence makes me feel awkward, but he insists, how will you carry her up to the house alone, and I say again, thank you, I didn't think of it, and on the way I wonder, how does he know that there are stairs, how does he know that there's nobody to help me, and he seems to sense my surprise and says quietly, Noga told me this morning, and I ask aggressively, told you what, and he says, that her father left home, and when I hear these words coming from the mouth of a total stranger, their validity is brought home to me, as if I have just heard them over the radio, at the top of the news, Noga's father has left home.

This is how he used to carry her upstairs when she was a baby, she always slept in the car, and she would clasp his neck with sleepy pride, while we mounted the stairs in silence, so that she wouldn't wake up, and we would have a little time to ourselves, hushing one another, he would lay her on the bed and I would remove her shoes, and we would quickly close the door before we put on the light in one of the rooms, and if she didn't start crying immediately we would breathe a sigh of relief, slaves granted an unexpected respite, and then we would pour ourselves a glass of wine or beer and go out to the porch, or sit embracing on the sofa, secretly missing her, but now she is in these short bald arms, he appears to weigh no more than she does but I can't be choosy today, climbing up behind them to catch her if he drops her, his legs stagger on the steps but he keeps climbing, his face pink with effort. I direct him quickly to Noga's room, a somber guide of very short tours, and there he deposits his feverish load on the bed, wipes the sweat from his brow, on his finger is a wedding ring that looks brand-new, as if he got married only yesterday, and I bend over Noga, we're home, I whisper, and she groans, my head hurts, I want to sleep.

Go to sleep, I kiss her flushed cheek, you'll feel better when you wake up, and I take off her shoes and cover her with a thin blanket, it's only the flu, I try to reassure myself, what else can it be, and he follows me out of the room, takes a glass in the kitchen and fills it with water from the tap, I forgot to offer but he takes care of himself, I can't get rid of the impression that he's been here before, his eyes look round without curiosity, round clear child's eyes, and I invite him to sit down, I feel uncomfortable standing opposite him, especially since he's shorter than me and I have to look down at him, and he says, I have to go, I have a class in a minute, but nevertheless he lingers, something is keeping him, he feels sorry for me, I suddenly realize, he simply feels sorry for me, I'm someone people feel sorry for, and I haven't even got the strength to pretend that I'm not really like that. He's already on his way to the door with his short steps, he takes hold of the handle and whispers, confidentially, Noga is a special child, and I say wearily, as if I have received a compliment, thank you, and then I rouse myself and say, in what way, and he waxes poetical, she has a lot of treasure in the depths of her soul, like a magnificent ship drowned at sea, we must help her bring it up to the surface, and I ask, and if there's nobody to help her, and he says, it will all be lost.

So is that what you're trying to do, I stare at him with a sour smile, and he says, no, not really, I just talk to her sometimes at recess when I see that she's alone, I try to draw her out, I feel sorry for her, she's so withdrawn, she seems to be guarding something all the time, and I say, maybe it's her treasures that she's guarding, so they won't be taken away from her, but his words are only increasing my anxiety and I want him to leave, with his exaggerated concern, let him worry about his new wife, not my daughter, and I say, thank you for your help, and he nods, if you need anything get in touch, Noga has my number, and I say of course, even though I have no intention of getting in touch with him, I feel uncomfortable with him, it seems to me that he knows Noga better than I do and this makes me feel uneasy and guilty, but when he goes downstairs I feel abandoned again, left alone with the little girl whose father has left home, what kind of a mother am I, who can't keep a father at home, who chases him away, and doesn't even know where he's gone? I have no way of summoning him to sit at his sick daughter's bedside, to feel her forehead, to peer into her throat, to consult with me about what to do, and I return defeated to her room, her golden curls fill the pillow, cover her dear face, sleep, my love, I murmur, sleep soundly and wake up well, but suddenly she sits up and points at the door with a trembling finger, as if she's seen a ghost, who's that, she shouts and laughs wildly, who's there, and I put my arms around her, there's nobody there, Nogi, what do you see, and she falls back on the pillow, mumbling broken syllables, as if she's reverted to her infancy, before she learned to talk.

She's delirious from the fever, I say to myself, I have to bring her fever down, and I push two more aspirin into her mouth and hold a glass of water to her lips and she swallows obediently, my head's splitting, she mumbles, I can't see anything, and suddenly I realize that this isn't just flu, what are the symptoms of meningitis, I try to remember, something about the neck, try to bend your head, I whisper, feeling the nape of her neck, and she cries, I can't, I can't move my head, and I'm out of my mind with worry, I rush to the telephone, repeating Zohara's number like a prayer, she's the only one I trust, the only one who can help us.

Answer already, I beg, strangling the receiver, and in the end she answers, in a muffled voice, as if I've woken her up, not the fresh crisp voice I know, and I shout, Zohara, Noga's sick, please come and examine her, and she hesitates, her voice is weak and strange, almost inaudible. It's a little difficult for me now, she says evasively, but I won't let go, wild weeping breaks from my throat and floods the receiver, Zohara, I'm afraid it's something serious, just come and tell me what to do, and she is silent, what's the matter with her, she always came so eagerly, as if she was only waiting for an invitation, and now she says reluctantly, I'll try to come, as if the way from her house to ours has grown long and full of danger. At a loss I go back to Noga, the aspirin has had hardly any effect, and I put a wet towel on her forehead, soon the doctor will come, I whisper, and she wails, I want Daddy, call Daddy, and I feel my heart freezing in sorrow, a jagged iceberg is sliding down my spine, Daddy's on a tour, I say to her, I can't get hold of him, he'll probably call later, and she groans, her breath full of broken, swollen sounds.

I cuddle up next to her in the bed, shaking with sorrow, how could I have thought that it had passed over quietly, that she'd gone to school and everything was all right, that I could devote myself to my imjury, my loss, what do I matter, nothing matters anymore, I'm ready to spend the rest of my life alone as long as she gets well, that's all I ask for. The heat of her body next to mine is so intense that it seems to me that I too am feverish, under the thin blanket I press myself against her with my anxiety, my vows, abandoning myself to the flames of her fire as if I am being burned at the stake, the two of us will die here together, deserted, abandoned, we have no life without him, that should have been clear to me from the beginning, for that was how we lived, as if we had no life without him, we'll burn together until we go out in silence, like bonfires dying down with the departure of the revelers, and I nestle into her arms as if she is my mother and I am her daughter, she the sun and I the moon, ready to go to sleep and never wake up again, but suddenly quick footsteps ring out in the house. He came back, I exult, he heard her cries and came back, he's not capable of really leaving, like us he has no life without the other two, we are all the sick limbs of one body, but then the slender figure enters the room, she always surprises me, even when I am expecting her.

How is she, she asks, her voice still reserved, and I get out of bed and whisper, she has a high fever and a severe headache, her neck's stiff, she's in a bad way, I sum up and add in a broken voice, everything's in a bad way, Udi left home, she can't take it, I can't take it, he simply got up and went, he didn't even say where he was going, all because of that damn illness, I sob, abandoning the last shreds of self-respect, all I want is to collapse in her arms, nestle there like her baby, and she examines me with a concentrated, unsurprised look, it's natural for you to feel like this, she whispers, but it's possible to feel differently too. How differently, I suppose this is an opportunity too, I demand aggressively, and she says, obviously it's an opportunity, there is a relief in loss, imagine coming home one day and finding that you have been robbed of everything, everything, you have nothing left, there's no point in even trying to recover what you once had. In one instant the agitated consciousness disappears, the paralyzing thoughts, and you sense a profound calm, almost a moment of grace. Suddenly you realize that the struggle is over, because it's pointless, that you have to let go, because you have no alternative, you lose everything but win a profound peace. Look around you, Na'ama, she whispers, the walls of the house are collapsing, but this makes it possible for you to see the landscape that has been hidden from you all these years, and I listen to her in mounting despair, how can she parrot her silly, automatic parables now, what have they to do with me.

Come and see what's wrong with Noga first, I urge her, I can't believe that I once drank in her words so thirstily, and she goes up to the panting bed, her look opaque, without all the spiritual enthusiasm I once liked so much, her hands gravely feeling the delirious body, try to bend over, she whispers to her, bow your head without bending your legs, and Noga screams, leave me alone, you're hurting me, and Zohara lets go of her instantly, I can't examine her properly in these conditions, she says, it could definitely be meningitis according to the stiff neck, but I can't do the tests, you must take her to the hospital or the clinic, and I stare at her in disappointment, my faith in her was so great, I was sure that all she had to do was touch Noga with her fingers to make her well, where are her magic powers, her fragrant incense, her reassuring promises, without them she is an ordinary person, dark, parched, helpless.

I'm sorry, she whispers, and flees the room, with me behind her, still expecting the customary pronouncements, her sharp chin is so close to me that I feel it is about to wound me, the birth of a man is the birth of his sorrow, she says slowly, softly, I have to come close to hear her, there's an ancient Tibetan story about a woman whose only son sickened and died, and she wandered the roads, carrying his dead body in her arms, and asking everyone she met to help her bring him back to life. In the end she met a wise man who told her that the only one in the world who could perform this miracle was the Buddha. So she went to the Buddha, laid the body at his feet and told him her story. The Buddha listened to her and said, there is only one way to cure your suffering, go down to the city and bring me a mustard seed from a house that death has never visited. The woman immediately ran to the city and went from house to house, but she didn't find a single house that had not been visited by death. After she had been to all the houses in the town she understood that she would not be able to comply with the Buddha's demand. So what did she do, I ask anxiously, and Zohara says, she said farewell to the body of her son and returned to the Buddha, and asked him to instruct her in the truth, she understood that life is an ocean of suffering for us all, and that the only way to escape is to take the road that leads to freedom.

So what do you want from me with your frightening stories, I burst out, after waiting in suspense, naively expecting a happy end, what freedom are you talking about when my little girl is sick and my husband's left us, and she says, but these are the most important moments in your life, the moment when the doors of enlightenment are opened, you have fallen now from a great height, but you have landed on the ground of truth, and the fall is not a tragedy but an opportunity to find a refuge within you, to understand that in the last analysis nothing is either good or bad, and there is no point in getting overly emotional. We must live without attachment and without anger, she declaims, we must attain perfect balance, neither clinging to happy experiences nor collapsing because of sad events, not allowing turbulent emotions, good or bad, to take hold of us, and I listen to her impatiently, my indignation rising until I can no longer ignore it. But what will be left of me without my emotions, I interrupt her, they're all I have, you want me to be as unfeeling as a statue, without any emotions? Then let me tell you that it won't work, what you're saying is monstrous, I burst out, how come I never saw it before, what does it mean to live without attachments, do you want me to let my daughter die, to look at the clouds while she suffers? What is all this serenity you talk about worth if it comes in place of feeling? It's simply one more step toward death, that's why you're all so happy to die, because as far as you're concerned there's no big difference between life and death, but it doesn't suit me, you understand, I'm ready to feel sorrow, because otherwise I won't be able to feel joy either, I don't want to give it up and I never will.

She examines me with open disapproval, her velvet eyes dark, you're completely wrong, Na'ama, I'm not telling you to neglect your daughter, I'm talking to you about something else entirely, about inner freedom, you know that mothers in Tibet send their children to be educated in India, they part from them for years, sometimes even forever, but they do it wholeheartedly because from their point of view the physical presence is marginal, mental closeness is what's important, and mentally they aren't separated. So what are you trying to tell me, I ask, are you talking about Noga or about Udi, and she says, we'll talk about it some other time, you're too upset now, and I have to get back to my baby, I have to feed her, and I look at her lean breasts filling with milk under her blouse, ashamed of my outburst, I've succeeded in chasing her away too, leaving me alone with my sick child, hurrying off to her healthy baby, I never even noticed that she'd come without her, suddenly she's got someone to baby-sit for her, and I accompany her to the door and stand at the threshold surveying the sweltering living room, the sun seems to be squatting on the ceiling, vomiting all the heat it has accumulated since the morning on it, and I remember how Noga and I came in only a few weeks ago and saw Udi walking up and down holding the fair baby in his arms, rocking her and murmuring, shush, shush, shush, how our legs trembled on the threshold, and then I understand.

Sixteen

wake, awake, stand up, O Jerusalem, which hast drunk at the hand of the Lord the cup of his fury; thou hast drunken the dregs of the cup of trembling and wrung them out. There is none to guide her among all the sons whom she hath brought forth; neither is there any that taketh her by the hand of all the sons that she hath brought up. These two things are come unto thee; who shall be sorry for thee? Desolation, and destruction, and the famine, and the sword: by whom shall I comfort thee? For the Lord hath called thee as a woman forsaken and grieved in spirit, and a wife of youth, when thou wast refused, saith thy God. For a small moment have I forsaken thee, but with great mercy will I gather thee. In a little wrath I hid my face from thee for a moment; but with everlasting kindness will I have mercy on thee, saith the Lord thy Redeemer.

On the rug at the foot of the bed I lie, a worn-out dog wallowing in the bones of the ancient verses, in the book he left behind him, a common fate uniting the three of us on this night of terror, none of us needed anymore, not the furious book buffeted on its waves of wrath and consolation, not the sick child with the treasure ships drowned in her depths, not the rejected wife of his youth. Ephraim compasseth me about with lies, and the house of Israel with deceit, who would have believed that this would be the end of our love, the end that accompanied it from the day it came into being, in the bloom of our youth, that tagged on to all the words of love and longing and jealousy and hostility, that peeped out from under our marriage bed, lying in wait for the right moment, no one would have believed, of all the members of the wedding who accompanied our lives, that a strange woman would appear and succeed in diverting the river, in directing the stream of his love toward her. Legions of cruel light have invaded the world, not leaving a single mystery, now I understand the meaning of his frequent, aimless wanderings, the meaning of his frowning brows every evening, when we sat at the table to eat, and he examined us with his darting eyes, moving restlessly about the rooms like a spy in enemy territory, the meaning of the door that closed so early at night, hiding his elusive shadow, for a moment I am comforted, perhaps it's better this way, I can almost understand this abandonment, he was ill, she saved him, I almost fell in love with her myself, with her dark quietness, her surprising insight, I too would have preferred her to myself, and there is a relief in understanding, compared to the endless bewilderment, but I immediately protest, what has she to do with him, she's a total stranger, and we grew up together, he isn't only my husband, he's my whole family, all my memories, I have nothing without him. Why didn't he tell me the truth, for weeks he hid it from me, what are all the words we exchanged over the years worth, millions of words passing from hand to hand like coins in a shady business deal, if at the most important moment everything is concealed. I would have understood, I would have told him that it's only natural for a new love to arise from time to time, it happened to me too, all these years I denied it and now I'm ready to admit it, and nevertheless it never occurred to me to leave, it was clear to me that I had to give him up, and not even with any great difficulty, and now I'm not even asking you to give her up, just to stay with us, not to remove your protection from us. Perhaps we'll clear a room for her and the baby, we'll all live together, we'll raise the baby together, anything not to separate, but I immediately take it back, that's what you wish yourself? all these years you've been making concessions and making concessions and now you're prepared to concede his love too, as long as he stays with you, weep ye not for the dead, neither bemoan him, but weep sore for him that goeth away, for he shall return no more, nor see his native country.

Noga whimpers in her sleep and I sit up, feel her forehead, swallow her boiling breath, her sickness squats on top of me, heavy and terrifying, in the morning I won't have any alternative, a white ambulance will park outside our house, its doors will open wide, men in phosphorescent tunics will load her body onto a stretcher, only a few months ago I accompanied him on this journey, when summer had just begun, a kind of frightened practice drill for what awaits me tomorrow, but tonight she's still mine, I'm not ready to hand her over yet, with the power of my love I try to heal her, with the power of his love, he has to come back tonight, if he doesn't come back tonight he'll never come back, this house will no longer be his house, this child will no longer be his child, my body will no longer be his body, in the place where I loved him an ugly scar will grow, a barbed-wire fence will stand forever between us, if he doesn't come back tonight, when she is suffering in her sickness, and I lean my head against her bed, weeping into the blazing hollow of her shoulder, before the sun rises he will deny me three times.

She puts out a sweaty hand and feels my face in disappointment, where's Daddy, she whispers, I want Daddy, a bad smell comes from her mouth, the smell of burnt porridge at the bottom of the saucepan, and I say, Daddy will come as soon as he can, and I hurry out of the room, she'll die if he doesn't come, she'll die, and I grope for the telephone in the dark, I'll call her house, I'll tell her that the child will die if he doesn't come at once, and I begin to dial the number, I don't care if I wake the whole world up, as long as my child is saved, but the minute her sleepy voice answers I hang up, the words escape my mouth and echo through the house, I can't force him, she has to get well without him, she mustn't be so dependent on him, and I go and sit on the porch, cool breezes pierce the heat, the show is over, I suddenly understand, the curtain is torn, the stage has crumbled, the limits of my ability have become clear, I no longer have the power to prettify the world for her. For years and years I've been exhausting my strength in these vain efforts, stretching my body to its full length, to cover up the rifts, from year to year it's grown harder, and now the moment I feared has arrived, the moment when it's impossible to cover up anymore, because the truth, fierce as fire, has consumed with its breath the flower beds I planted with an anxious heart. I stand up heavily and return to her room, the darkness in the depths of the house is dense and oppressive, covering her white face, her lifeless curls, and in a broken voice I whisper into her sleep, before I can regret it, he's left home, Noga, he'll come only when he chooses, he'll call only when it suits him, the time has come for us to stop waiting.

But early in the morning, a mantle of majestic blue light still covering the room, I seem to hear an insistent knocking at the door and I wake from my restless sleep, Behold, I will bring them from the north country, and gather them from the coasts of the earth, and with them the blind and the lame, the woman with child and her that travaileth with child together; a great company shall return thither. They shall come with weeping, and with supplications will I lead them; I will cause them to walk by the river of waters in a straight way, wherein they shall not stumble; for I am a father to Israel, and Ephraim is my firstborn. The verses of consolation I have been reading all night stand up next to me and cheer, like the dead at the moment of their resurrection, refrain thy voice from weeping and thine eyes from tears, I can't straighten my back and I hurry stooping from the room, my heart beating wildly, he's come back to me, my Udi, he couldn't really go away, we're one people, even if two kingdoms, we will make a new covenant between us now, for I will forgive his iniquity and remember his sin no more. Why is he knocking on the door instead of opening it, overnight he has turned from a resident to a guest, where's his key, and I approach the door, filled with absolute happiness, from the day I was born to this minute there's nothing I wanted more than his return this morning at sunrise, to redeem Noga from her sickness and me from my sorrow, to be a family again, and I deliberately draw out this moment of his knocking on my door, delicate, timid knocks of sorrow and regret, open to me, my sister, my love, my dove, for my head is filled with dew and my locks with the drops of the night, until they suddenly peter out and I hasten to turn the key, in case he changes his mind and leaves, in case he slips away, and my eyes burning with tiredness narrow at the sight of the old back slowly descending the stairs, at the sight of the face turning toward me, a dark, wrinkled face, covered with black sunglasses, and I open my mouth in a wail of disappointment, it seems to open wider and wider, until the lips tear as in giving birth, so great is the disappointment that rends me, his not coming shocks me even more than his going, and my whole body bows down in a cry of despair, Mother, what are you doing here?

I came to help you, she says, the stairs bringing her back to me, and I stretch out my arms to her in an endless fall, here I am hugging her knees in childish dismay, Mommy don't go, stay with us, Mommy why are you getting all dressed up, why are you wearing high heels, why are you putting on makeup, her knees hurry from room to room with me between them, tangled up in them, trying to trip her up, Mommy stay, Daddy's so sad without you, we're so sad, stay with us, and here are her hands on my hair, I have to, I have no choice, she says, it will be all right, everyone will be better off, but no one was better off, certainly not her, did a malicious false prophecy echo in her ears then too, a voice calling her to get up and go, and now her voice is hoarse from smoking, her hands rumple my hair, you should start dyeing it, she says, look how many white hairs you have all of a sudden.

It's not all of a sudden, I mutter, it's just that you haven't stroked me for a long time, and I hang on to her and stand up with difficulty, a hooked beak gapes at me in a hungry smile, black wings spread out before my eyes, and then close, and I wave my arms to and fro to chase them away, I'm not quite dead yet, I shout, leave me alone, I can't die, I can't die yet, and my mother embraces me, that's enough, stop crying now, I didn't realize I was crying, and then a cry rises from inside the house, a cry that darkens the beating of the wings around me in its despair, Daddy?

It's not Daddy, I say and hurry to her room, morbid vapors rise from it, but she is sitting up and pointing at the door with a contorted smile, her eyes bulging and opaque as the eyes of a doll, Daddy's back, she shouts, and immediately lies down again, as if frightened by the sound of her own voice, dropping her head to the pillow and sinking into a delirious sleep, breathing heavily. Has she seen a doctor, my mother asks sternly, and I say, not really, and she yells, what are you trying to prove, why haven't you called a doctor, do you want her to get worse so that you can show that he's a murderer too? And I yell back, I don't need you to preach to me, I need you to help me, you said you came to help me, and only then I remember to ask, how did you know?

Udi called me, she says, a note of pride stealing into her voice, and I ask in suspense, where did he call from, and she replies, he said that he was in the south, in the Arava I think, he asked me to be with you, and I raise my voice again, did he know that Noga was sick, did he say anything about it? And she shrugs her shoulders, I have no idea, I could hardly hear him, but I examine her doubtfully, it seems to me that she knows more than she's letting on, and I plant myself in front of her, eager for every scrap of information, like a hungry dog in front of a pot of meat whose lid he can't remove.

I trail behind her to the kitchen, studying the tiles, anything not to look at her, for years I've been averting my eyes from her, avoiding her gaze, there is so much to hide, the endless anger against her and the spiteful glee, the sorrow for her beauty and the sorrow for her life, and the fear of being like her and the fear of being like him, like my father, and it seems that tonight the pendulum that has been swinging over my head all my life has finally made up its mind, I'm like him, on the side of the abandoned, of the ones who take the blows, not those who deliver them, I'm on the side of the victims and not the victimizers, that's my place, and I'll have to get used to it. At the beginning it seemed completely different, Udi would denounce my genes, you're faithless like your mother, you'll throw me out in the end like she threw him out. And for years I tried apologetically to prove that I wasn't like her, that I was faithful, and now the truth had come out, he who was always above suspicion turned out to be the cheater and I had won, actually I had lost, and I fill with shame before her at having been beaten like this, my inferiority is so striking in comparison to her, the beautiful heartbreaker, while I am the heartbroken daughter, and I can no longer hide my disgrace, I lay my head on the kitchen table, I'm so ashamed, Mother, I suppose I seem as pathetic as Daddy to you now, and she says in a gentle voice, you're quite wrong, Noam, I almost envy you, it is better to be on the side of the abandoned, and I raise my head in surprise, ancient crumbs of bread sticking to my cheek in a moist trail along the track of my tears, you're talking nonsense, Mother, I wish I'd left him, I'm sorry for every day I stayed with him, how could I let him decide for me, that's what makes all the difference, and she says, sometimes it's a lot more convenient when someone else decides, and I say, bullshit, you don't know what you're talking about.

Believe me, Noam, she coaxes me, the one who has the decision made for him recovers a lot more quickly than the one who decides, you'll soon get over it, you'll be able to have a better life, but he'll remain with the whole burden of the responsibility, all the guilt, the doubts, he doesn't know yet what's in store for him, you'll see that you'll get over it long before he does, but to me all this sounds like a fiction, something out of her imagination, because I saw him, I heard him, he's completely in control, cold and calculating, and I'm falling apart, but nevertheless her words succeed in surprising me, and I peek at her with lowered eyes, she always managed to confuse me until in the end I gave up trying to understand her, everything about her is contrary, illogical, she seems happy when she's unhappy and vice versa, for years I've been avoiding her and now he's sent her to me, on this sick morning, still controlling my life from a distance, so that I'll sit opposite her in the kitchen, my face freckled with sticky bread crumbs, abandoned and sulky as a child, and say to her, why did you do it to me?

Her light eyes stare at the door for a moment, as if waiting for someone to save her, but she immediately recovers, I didn't do it to you, she says, it wasn't against you, it was for me, mothers are allowed to live too, it's not a crime. With all due respect to children, she continues with an effort, as if trying to convince herself, you don't have to commit suicide for them, and I feel my face turning white, just as my father's did when she scolded him, and I ask, was staying with my father like committing suicide? Aren't you exaggerating a bit? I don't understand how anyone could leave such a good husband, and she says, stop it, Na'ama, there's no point in discussing your father now, but I persevere, now that I've dared to ask I'm not about to let her get away without answering me. Of course there's a point, I want to understand how you could permit yourself to leave a man who loved you so much, who only wanted your happiness, who only wanted to be with you and your children, who came home from work with baskets full of shopping, and washed the dishes and made the food and read us stories, and never got angry, and never made accusations, he was an angel, wasn't that good enough for you, what did you think, that you deserved to have God himself in bed with you?

You think it's such a pleasure to live with an angel, she says through gritted teeth, living next to an angel turns you into a monster, don't you understand? He was too good, his goodness was inhuman, it was impossible to be angry with him, always trying to please, sacrificing himself until you could go mad, it was scary, as if he was atoning for some crime, can't you understand? And I shake my head, no, I don't understand, why is it so difficult to accept goodness for what it is, why do you only believe in evil, and she says, listen to me, Na'ama, it took me a long time to understand too, at first I couldn't believe my luck, but gradually I started to feel as if I was going mad, he tormented me with his saintliness, and I protest, he tormented you, what are you talking about, he was incapable of harming a fly, you remember how he took pity on the poor pigeons? And she says, I'm talking about things that are hidden from the naked eye, all saints turn into martyrs in the end, and that's what happened to him, that's what happened to me, I found myself in the role of the torturer, he was so pure that I became dirty, and I shake my head indignantly, I don't believe this, how can you blame him, you're just like the worst men, who blame their wives for all their own shortcomings.

You know what it's like to go to bed with a corpse, to make love to a corpse? she pounces on me, he was so lifeless I had no choice, I started to look for life outside the house, and even then he wasn't angry, on the contrary, sometimes I thought that he actually enjoyed living through me. Because he loved you so much, because he was so happy with you, I plead, we were all happy until you ruined everything, and she takes my hand, clinging with all her strength to the talk she has entered into so reluctantly, like going into a filthy room, but the moment you begin to clean it you can't stop, how come he was so happy when I was so unhappy, his happiness showed a total lack of sensitivity, he didn't see me at all, and I wasn't only unhappy, I was guilty too, for being the one who spoiled everything, for being the one for whom nothing was ever enough, when in fact all I wanted was to live, I had to save myself, not for a career, believe me, simply in order to be a human being. You know what a human being is, it's good and bad together, and he took all the good for himself and burdened me with all the bad, but it wasn't real, it was all false, both his role and mine, and I bow my head and close my eyes, as if she's telling me a bedtime story, a good one that puts me to sleep without any problems, my head sways and it seems to me that we're standing facing each other in the yard of the old house, I'm holding two newborn kittens in my hands, still blind and slimy, and she's shouting at me, leave those kittens alone, now their mother won't want them anymore, you must never touch such small kittens, because of you they'll die, because of you they won't last the day, and I drop them in alarm, and now I yell at her, I don't buy it, for the sake of your little children you could have lived with a man who was too good, that's not such a tragedy, and she lowers her eyes, her eyelids tremble, I thought you'd be better off without me, I thought I was only harming you, he was such a wonderful father.

But after she left he stopped being our father, he was so sunk in his sorrow that he didn't notice our existence, all his devotion drowned in that ocean of grief as if it had never been, she's right, it wasn't real, and all these years all my anger was directed solely against her, and even now it's hard for me to part from that anger, like a coat you're afraid to take off though the weather has changed, and I examine her bony fingers as she lights a cigarette, the lines above her upper lip crowd together, surrounding the pale stick, her movements are still theatrical, as if dozens of people are watching her every minute of the day, in spite of the marks of age, in spite of the bites of the ulcer, in her stylish embroidered dress she still looks striking, how beautiful she was then, falling on us with wet kisses like a winter wind, appearing and disappearing, scheming schemes.

Maybe I was too good too, always trying to prove that I wasn't like her, to calm Udi's fears, and after that morning it was no longer possible, an endless atonement for a sin that never happened, and when I think about it suddenly, about the most beautiful morning of my life, for the first time I allow myself to take pleasure in its details, I don't understand why I didn't stay there, standing at the window when the first rain began to fall, why was I in such a hurry to run after Udi, a pointless pursuit that went on for nearly eight years, to placate him and please him, I should have stayed there, let him fight his wars by himself, make his decisions by himself, not stationed myself immediately in front of him to absorb his frustrations, to take my punishment before I had a chance to sin, the way I ran after him demonstrated guilt, weakness, defeatism, everything that had made it possible for him to leave me tonight. You know that he's got someone, you know that he left me for someone else, I say quietly, and she shrugs her shoulders, her blue eyes glitter in her dark face, it doesn't make any difference, it really makes no difference, he left for himself, she says, and I say, you know that I wanted to leave him a few years ago but I stayed, you know that there was somebody who loved me? And she strokes my shoulder, you'll still be loved, Noam, I promise you, but it sounds completely unreal to me, that there was once a man, with curly hair on the back of his neck, who loved me enough to let me go. I remember how he crouched, bending over my thighs, and I touched the nape of his neck, and then he raised his eyes to me, one was blue and one gray, and both were sad, what did he promise me then, what did he try to say, and I wail, instead of staying with him, instead of enjoying his love, I ran to appease Udi, to get Noga, to stick us all together, but ever since then nothing's worked.

It wasn't working so well before then either, she says, and I protest, nonsense, don't you remember how happy we were when Noga was born, how good it was until I spoiled everything, and she laughs, you call that good? He was as jealous as a child of the attention you gave her, he wanted you to devote yourself entirely to him, don't you remember how he was sick when she was born, and I say in astonishment, what are you talking about, he fell in love with her at once, he would walk round with her in his arms for hours, bathe her, get up for when she cried at night, and she says, but that was part of his power game too, he wanted to humiliate you, to show you that even here he was better than you. You're going too far, Mother, I say, and she admits, maybe I am a bit, I wasn't living with you, but I was here often enough to see that even before her fall there were problems, and I listen to her in a kind of daze, as if I am hearing good but dubious news, from an unreliable news agency, and suddenly it seems to me that there is a fire in the house, breathing from a gaping mouth, a wave of heat advances on me and a weak voice says, what fall, and again it demands to know, what fall? And I heave a sigh of relief, Noga is getting better, here she is standing on her feet, leaning against the wall, her eyes clear, but how long has she been standing here, how much has she heard, and my mother drops her eyes, I know that she saw her approaching but she went on talking anyway, and I put out my arms and draw her to me, and sit her on my lap, her body is limp and babyish, and I feel a pleasant tingling in my breasts as if restorative milk is collecting there for her, and I press her to me and whisper, you fell out of Daddy's hands, you were two, a bucket of water forgotten downstairs by the cleaning lady saved your life.

Seventeen

As in a time of war, when all the men are called up to fight on the front and the women stay with the children in the rear, we live, three women in one house, where everything is completely changed, and where it seems as if no man has ever set foot. At night I offer my mother the double bed, whose very image fills me with sadness, and open up the sofa in the living room, the old bed of my loneliness, for I was abandoned long before he left, and its hairy arms reach out and draw me into another tormented night, the sun seems still to be beating on the concrete shell above my head, and I am seared by its dark rays engraving tattoos of jealousy in my flesh. I see him in her bed, his body that grew up in my arms moving lewdly against her supple body, long and narrow as a snake's, and I knock on his back, let me be with you, don't leave me alone, I promise not to be a nuisance, just let me sleep here next to you, but he is so absorbed in her that he doesn't even notice me, it's hard for me to imagine what he looks like at this moment because I was always too close to him, with my eyes too tightly closed. I can't see him from the side, only feel the tenderness that comes from him at moments of intimacy, a rare and surprising warmth like the touch of a sunbeam on a rainy day, how does he make love, I try to remember, conjuring up his body on the sofa by my side, how is love made, how do the hands reach out, how do the lips part, how does the clenched body, withdrawn into itself, open, how does this miracle happen, I am so far from love that I can hardly see it even in my mind's eye, for nights on end I lay here by myself, with him in the other room, behind a closed door, why didn't I creep into his bed in the middle of the night, like a child into the bed of its parents after a bad dream, why didn't I nestle between his limbs like she does now, pushing her black milk-filled breast to his mouth, and he sucks and sucks, and I beat the mattress, he's mine, he's mine, he's not allowed to suck the milk from another woman's breast, but suddenly this vision changes into a worse one, and whenever I close my eyes I see them lying in a big bed with the baby ensconced between them, and then I quickly switch on the light, trembling with rage, no, it's impossible, he wouldn't lie in bed with a strange baby, he wouldn't betray his own child, but then I see him again, walking up and down the living room, holding the fair-skinned baby in his arms and murmuring to her, shush, shush, shush.

So my father's steps would plow through the black earth of my nights, again and again I would hear them all over the house when I tried to fall asleep, drawing sleep toward me on a thin thread, like a kite, come, come down to me, and when it was almost there his listless steps would tear the thread, and I would grope with small, tired hands, to mend it. Night after night I would curse my mother, wishing her ill, wishes that all came true, that she would remain alone until the end of her life, that she would grow old quickly, that she would become ugly. Yotam would wake up and cry, I want Mommy, and I would make room for him in my bed, for his chubby body that was growing thinner from day to day, nobody but me noticed that he had stopped eating, that he had stopped smiling, and I would say to him, don't cry, tomorrow we're going to Mommy, but when she came to take us I would run away to the citrus groves, I couldn't get used to the new apartment in the town, I couldn't leave my father alone, even though he was so absorbed in himself that he barely noticed my existence. In the evening I would call him to eat, watch him dunking dry bread in a cup of yogurt and chewing it slowly, as if in his sleep, aren't you going to your mother, he would ask, and I would say, I'm staying with you, even though he didn't ask me to, even though I may have burdened him with my presence. When I did go to her my hatred would cool, it was easier to hate her from a distance than from close up, and now too when she's sleeping in the next room her presence casts a strange peacefulness over me, of tender feelings hidden in basements, in dovecotes, in attics, that suddenly dare to emerge. For years I withstood the temptation, I refused to love her, my father's murderer, even after he died, I only agreed to give her Noga, not myself, I saw with satisfaction how she was spending her life opposite old movies on the television, opposite the movie stars she once outshone in her beauty, everyone said so, and now for the first time a breach had opened up for her, and she had stepped in straightaway, without wasting any time, and here she is, polishing up her new image, a combination of sorrow and resignation, pride and restraint, as if she is a sad, respectable widow and not a cruel murderess, but my anger against her is dwarfed by my anger against Udi, and that too is growing pale and tired.

I force myself to think in small steps, not about the rest of my life but about the next minute, concentrating on Noga's recovery, little by little and with great difficulty she parts from her illness, as if they are a pair of lovers whose bodies cling together, refusing to detach themselves. Most of the time she sleeps, and even when she wakes sleep accompanies her, sitting next to her in the kitchen as she swallows a few spoons of chicken soup, a little lukewarm tea, and goes back to bed like a sleepwalker. Hypnotized by fear I watch her, as if she is a suspicious object at the bus stop, looking at the bed bowed beneath the weight of the warm limbs, the feathers of fair hair, the tangle of bedclothes, as if a completely different person will finally emerge from between the sheets. I am glad of her sleepy silence, so fearful am I that she might share her sorrow with me, I marvel at my mother's ability to welcome her brief awakenings warmly and naturally, and one night when I am making up my bed on the sofa my mother advances on me brandishing a cigarette, you're doing the child an injustice, she says, stop feeling sorry for her, your pity makes you shrink from her, and I nod my head in silence, her words oppress me in their accuracy, but what shall I do with them, how can you stop worrying, how can you stop pitying, if you stop worrying you stop loving, no? Because that's love.

This little girl needs to be loved, she goes on, not to be protected or pitied or feared, are you capable of pure and simple love? And I shrink before her, her stiff clay face surrounding eyes that are young, irritating in their surprising vitality, and I avert my eyes to the wall behind her, where an ancient picture is hanging, in a dusty frame Yotam and I are frozen in a clumsy embrace, I'm bending down to him and offering him a cookie and he's smiling, and behind us is the old house, an illusory shelter roofed with red tiles, and I say, maybe I really don't know how to love, love is a luxury, you can only afford it when everything's all right, and everything is never all right. I look sadly at my little brother, his passionately expressive face, like Noga's, comes closer and closer to me, him I really loved, he growled in my arms like a wild little bear, I was the wolf and he was the bear and together we romped wildly in my mother's high bed, until it became my father's bed, and sank beneath him, and Yotam almost disappeared inside the scaffolding of his bones, and nobody saw, only I tried to save him, and perhaps it was then that love turned into a roar of panic, and I am on the point of hurling all this at her, I suppose you know how to love, but what's the point, that was how Udi always threw the ball at me as if it was on fire, without pausing for a moment to think of what it held, and suddenly I think of him in a kind of surprise, once Udi was here, edgy, tense, his narrow eyes darting, chasing each other over the triangular ground of his face, and now he's not here, and for a moment I don't care where he is. The tense, tiring expectation of his return has given way to a strange indifference, for I have a little girl here and I have to learn to love her, far from his sharp, jealous, complaining shadow, and again I look at the photograph, we had no idea of what was hiding underneath those red tiles, but so what, what's wrong with illusions, why do children have to have the truth shoved into their faces and be told to cope with it?

The years of the lie were far better than the years of the truth, I say to her, think of how happy we were, couldn't you have kept it up for ten more years? And she lowers her head, her still-dark hair tied tightly back in a ponytail, stretching the ravaged skin of her face, you think I didn't try? The easiest thing is to lie, but it's not right, even a child can't live long in an illusion, and I protest, Yotam could have, it's what he's been doing ever since, unable to cope, wandering round the world like a ghost ship, maybe Noga's like him too, maybe she won't be able to either, and she says, Noga will be able to, she has a good mother, better than the one you had, and I cringe, shrinking from this wretched compliment of hers, and I say, let's go to bed, Mother, and she pulls me to her, and strokes my face very slowly, as if she's blind, her fingers smell of perfume and cigarettes, and when I lie down on the sofa I think that he never stroked my face so gravely, with complete attention, and perhaps I shouldn't have given up on this either.

And this is only the beginning of a hot, dark torrent of resentment, welling up from the depths and engulfing me entirely, heavy with resentment I move about the house, feeling it kicking inside me like a developed fetus, how had I allowed him to take over slice after slice of my life, how had I abandoned my studies because of his nagging jealousy, you already have one degree, he would complain, why do you have to hang round the university as if you haven't got a baby at home, how had I given up my girlfriends, he was sure they were inciting me against him, I would always arrive at my get-togethers with them with tears in my eyes, because of a quarrel he would deliberately provoke when I was already at the door, and little by little I grew accustomed to this isolation, just him and me and later Noga, and my work which he also viewed with skepticism, a kind of imprisonment which I came to accept, which became almost pleasant, to live without temptation, without stimulation, and it seemed to me that if it was easy for me to renounce things they obviously weren't important in the first place. Why was it so convenient for me to renounce my power, to yield to his will which was always stronger than mine, even before the guilt which he squeezed to the last drop, like an orange, even before that I lived in a constant state of apology, shrinking from my beauty instead of basking in it, and now what's left of it, not much, not enough for what I need for the rest of my life. But the thought of the rest of my life is so threatening that I kick it violently away, what has it to do with me, just let me get through this hour, and the one waiting after it, which will wipe it out immediately, every hour wipes out the one before it, every new day its predecessor, that's the only reason they arrive, meekly offering themselves, days nobody needs, for our house is closed, no one comes in and no one goes out, only my mother sometimes goes down to the store, and the thud of her steps on the stairs makes me tremble, like the turning of the key in the door, like the rustle of the plastic bags on the kitchen table, but I look at her and keep quiet, all three of us are silent most of the time, only the most essential words escape with difficulty from our dry mouths, like corks from narrow bottles of wine, preferring to disintegrate inside their necks rather than to expose themselves. Even the washing machine is still, and the telephone too hardly ever rings, and if anyone does call, mainly from work, my mother announces in a firm voice that I am ill, convincing even me, and I go to sleep with a vague feeling of incipient illness hesitating between my throat and my back, my stomach and my head, Udi come back, I mumble, Udi come back. Early in the morning he always answers my pleas, tiptoes into the dark room, wakes me from a hard sleep and throws his gifts at me, usually he brings shoes, three pairs of identical sandals and two pairs of slippers, all for him and not for me, and I ask him, what do you need all this for, I just bought you sandals, and he laughs happily, he's so happy that I don't want to spoil it, I laugh with him at the joke, five pairs of shoes on one night, what a fine harvest, and in the morning I wake up in a disappointment that gradually shrinks, at first it fills me to bursting, stretching my skin like a balloon, but little by little it disperses through the house, slips through the cracks in the shutters, until the alarm clock infects me for a moment with its joy, at last I'm not disturbing anyone.

And when I feel rapid breaths caressing my face in the middle of the night I repeat, he's back, he's back, and nevertheless I turn my face to the other side, I could never fall asleep when we were facing each other, examining each other with our eyes closed, but then I hear Noga whispering, I can't sleep any more, I've slept so much, and I make room for her and she nestles up to me, the smell of sickness enveloping her even though her forehead is only lukewarm, and for a moment the earth seems to tremble, until I realize that her body pressed to mine is shaking in a storm of weeping, and I feel annoyed, why has she come to trouble me, where am I going to get the strength to calm her, but suddenly a strange, resigned serenity descends on me, perhaps it's not my job to calm her, simply to be with her, and I coil my arms around her and my weeping coils round hers and we cry together, like two orphaned sisters who have survived a catastrophe.

But we have a mother. In the morning we wake to the smell of strong coffee, fresh salad and omelets, and the two of us, after not eating for days, fall on the table, giggling like girlfriends who have spent the night confiding their deepest secrets to each other, and my mother looks at us in satisfaction, the way she sometimes looked at me and Yotam, Noga fawns on her and I see how much they resemble each other, not in their coloring but in the generous and noble cast of their faces, the high cheekbones, and the chiseled lips, how beautiful she is, in her bright pajamas, her curls tied in an untidy knot, how pleasant it is to be her sister, without the endless burden of motherhood, and after breakfast I fill the bathtub and sit on the toilet seat next to it, peeking at her changed body, the baby fat has melted in the fever and left her tall and slender, the new breasts rising from her chest stiff as cones, and she wets her hair until it reaches the middle of her back and says to me, come on, you get in too. No, I showered last night, I say, but I immediately take off my nightgown and get in, my body too is lighter, knees facing knees we sit, sunk in a pleasant embarrassment, barely touching, only the warm water conveying caresses and laughter and snatched kisses, her presence at my side fills me with an unfamiliar serenity, I'm not alone, I have a daughter, and this time the knowledge blunts the loneliness instead of intensifying it. I like feeling the currents of water stirring between us, responding to her movements, and in the kitchen my mother is washing the dishes, like on a Saturday morning in the old house, and in a minute she'll wrap us in big towels, and I hear her answering the phone, yes, she's better now, she says and comes into the bathroom with the phone in her hand, presents it to Noga with a flourish, and I sink into the water until it covers my head, I don't want to gather the crumbs from their conversation, and her excited voice reaches me muffled, telling the tale of her illness like the recounting of some heroic exploit, magnified from moment to moment in the telling.

So when will I see you Daddy, she asks in the end, as if in the expectation of well-deserved praise, and then she nods and passes me the wet telephone, and he says in a soft voice, Na'ama, I'm sorry, I didn't know that she was sick, and I sigh in relief, it seems to me that this was all I wanted to hear, the certain knowledge that refutes all my suspicions, if he'd known he would have come, and I'm glad that he sounds so far away, that a wide expanse of land separates us, he hasn't denied us, he simply wasn't around, he wasn't hiding from us in her house, perhaps he didn't even leave for her, it was all my wild, dangerous imagination. The only thing that matters is that she's well again, I say, and how about you, where are you, and he says, I'm still in the south, I'll be back in a few days and I'll come to see Noga, and I say, fine, no problem, smiling into the receiver, but suddenly I recoil and let it fall from my hand, watching it turn over like a little submarine at the bottom of the tub, because behind his soft voice, which stings me with a pang of loss, I seem to hear the distant, muffled crying of a baby.

Eighteen

nd on the eighth day we rise from our mourning and go out into a world distorted beyond recognition, a steep crater has opened up almost beneath our feet, a giant maw frozen in a ghastly yawn, one step ahead of us wherever we go, one short step on our part and we'll fall in and be swallowed by its depths. Hand in hand we descend the stairs, opposite the brazen face of the morning sun, my mother waves us good-bye with emotional, exaggerated movements, as if many years will pass before we meet again, and Noga leans on me, weak and tottering, the only shirt he left her flapping round her like a black flag, signaling a stern warning with her every movement.

Next to the school gate I say good-bye to her, embracing her with a pounding heart, as if she is six years old and this is her first day of school, and then I continue on my way, emptiness spreading inside me as I leave her behind, it seems that only the walls of my body have remained as they were, and between them is a desolate void. This is what the village pool looked like at the end of summer, after they emptied out the water, and once Yaron, the neighbors' son, dived headfirst into the hard, deceptive void, and afterward he lay for a whole year without moving, his neck in a brace, and everybody said that it would take a miracle to make him walk again. On nights when the moon was full I would steal over there, climb the gate, and gaze down from its heights at the transfigured pool, like the ruins of an ancient Canaanite city it looked back at me, dug into the earth, surrounded by black cypresses, somber and majestic, as if it had forgotten the shouts and laughter of the children in the clear water, the golden glints between their fingers, the redness of the watermelons bursting with sweetness on its banks. So I too will forget the comforting murmurs of closeness before falling asleep, the pleasant relaxation of Saturday mornings, making family plans for the day, even the faintest of gestures, like the echo of the male pulse on the mattress, the presence of another, even if it was hostile, separating me from myself, and which boiled down to the knowledge, now unbearably precious, that if I slipped in the bathroom in the middle of the night there would be someone to hear the thud, all this will be forgotten in the course of time and I will turn into a cold, petrified monument to a little family of three that had once existed and was no longer there.

A young woman runs past me, her hands behind her neck, her face sweating, and I try to guess if she has a man or not, for a moment it seems to me that a woman with a man is surrounded by a shining halo, like a royal crown, and I, who had no longer been conscious of the presence of this crown because it had become part of me, now feel its absence keenly, how it was torn from my hair, ripping off pieces of my scalp. With insulted fingers I feel my head, dragging my feet up the shelter steps, in a minute Hava will summon me and I'll have to tell her, even if I don't want to she'll drag it out of me, and then she'll use it against me, I have no doubt, she'll have one more reason to look down on me, a woman rejected by her husband. Silent as a thief I steal into the elegant building, the girls are absorbed in their breakfast and pay no attention to me, some of them are unknown to me, one week in a place like this is a lifetime, Hani has left already and I am glad to see that so has Ilana, and when I remember them the shadow of that night pounces on me, the night when the pink sweater was unraveled and so was my life, and I nearly fall, hanging on to the banister, dragging myself up to the second floor, all I want is to hide in my office, not to see a living soul, but the sound of stifled weeping follows me, and I feel my lips to make sure that it's not coming from me, the sound is so familiar that it seems to me I hear myself crying in the distance, wailing at the shadow of his back disappearing up the street. Embarrassed I peek into the rooms, opening door after door, until I see on a tangled bed, next to the window, bare limbs gathered sorrowfully around the sharp hill of a stomach, a bowed head covered with cropped red hair, the eyes of a wounded doe widening at me in surprise, and I sit down next to the bed and say in an agitated whisper, Yael, what are you doing here, when did you arrive, I had no idea that you were here.

I arrived a week ago, she sobs, I've been going crazy here without you, I was afraid you'd never come back, and I hold her hand, I thought about you a lot, I whisper, I hoped that things had worked out with him, and she sighs, nothing worked out, he's not prepared to leave home, and I can't bring up the baby alone, I can't be a single parent at the age of twenty-two, with nobody to help me, and suddenly I hear myself saying urgently, I'll help you, Yael, I'll help you raise it. She sits up slowly, staring at me in astonishment, and I smile back at her in embarrassment, it's too late to go back, and there's no reason to go back either, even Udi is bringing up a little baby now, so why shouldn't I help this charming child, who captured my heart as soon as I saw her, and already I imagine how excited Noga will be, and how we'll all mobilize for the sake of this baby, take it for walks in its carriage, warm the house for it in winter, put it down in the middle of the living room carpet, where it will smile and kick its little legs, and we won't feel Udi's absence anymore, we won't even think about him, because a tiny life will grow before our eyes and console us, sing, O barren, that thou didst not bear, break forth into singing and cry aloud, for thou shall forget the shame of thy youth and shall not remember the reproach of thy widowhood any-more, but she falls back onto the bed in confusion just as Hava's authoritative voice conquers the corridor, and I stand up hastily and say, I have to go to a meeting, I'll see you later.

At the conference table I am as wary and silent as a double agent, listening tensely to the evaluations of her situation and ca-pacities, of the future of the inconsiderate fetus, it seems that the two courses of its future are running the length of the table like two parallel railway lines, who can tell which train will reach its desti-nation quicker, and my finger wanders restlessly over the table, how come nobody thinks of the middle way, it doesn't occur to anybody that I could raise it with her, with them everything is extreme and hopeless, like the choice between a fatal disease and a traffic acci-dent. My finger comes back to me clean, not even a speck of dust in Hava's domain, and she turns to me unexpectedly and asks, what do you think, Na'ama, and I stammer, it's too soon to say, I'll work with her until she gives birth and then we'll see, trying to speak calmly even though I feel as if I've suddenly gone mad, or else that I was mad before and now I'm sane, but Hava keeps her eyes fixed on me, she sees everything, are you all right, she asks impatiently and immediately adds, I want to see you after the meeting.

With clamped lips I follow her, determined not to cry, to maintain my dignity, and she asks, so what happened, you've been through a difficult experience, and I say, Noga was sick, we were afraid it was meningitis, I say "we" on purpose, even though the word rebels in my mouth, sticks between my teeth, as if I have dared to use an aristocratic title which has already been stripped from me, but she waves her hand in dismissal, what else happened, Na'ama?

Udi left home, I say, and to my surprise I don't cry, as if I have said the heat wave's over, and she rises solemnly from the chair she's just sat down on, congratulations, she says warmly and shakes my hand as if I've just announced that I'm getting married, it's the best thing that could have happened to you, it's the best thing that can happen to any woman, but especially to you, I was afraid he wouldn't have the guts, it's more than I expected of him, I must say, she concludes calmly and resumes her seat on the shaky beach chair, steadying it with her weight, and I stare at her in confusion, she isn't considerate enough to put on this show simply in order to cheer me up, she must really believe in what she's saying, and I ask weakly, what's so good about it, and she says, can't you see? At last you'll be able to look after yourself, to put yourself at the center, for years you've been revolving around him, considering him, taking his problems on yourself, it's high time to put an end to it.

But what am I, Hava? My voice trembles between the walls, how can I feel good with myself when even he left me, how can I put myself at the center when I feel rejected, humiliated, pathetic? She waves her hand dismissively, you're adapting yourself to his yardstick again, and even that without a drop of sophistication, if he left that means you're worthless? Maybe it's just the opposite? Maybe he isn't able to contain your full value, maybe he feels guilty and defective next to you, maybe he lives in the constant fear that you'll leave him? It's so simplistic, the way women interpret men leaving them, he left so it means he doesn't love me anymore and I'm not worth anything, while the reality is much more complex, and you know that I'm not trying to comfort you, I have no problem with saying harsh things when necessary.

With my heart pounding I look at her face which is no longer young and was never beautiful, how dear she suddenly is to me, perhaps she's right, I hope she's right, she's usually right, clever, unexpected Hava, I was sure I would leave her office a hundred times more humiliated, and now I feel almost proud, making for my office with a light step, even if I believe it one minute a day it will be a revolution, and perhaps it will grow and flourish, this little seed she's planted inside me, until I believe in it all day, and maybe even all night, and then I'll be happy. And already I imagine myself happy, before my eyes a vague memory dances like a butterfly, all I have to do is put out my hand and catch it and it will never escape from me again, and a broad smile splits my face from ear to ear, and it stays there when I hear a knock on the door and before my astonished eyes a strange man appears on the threshold. Very few men ever put in an appearance here, brokenhearted fathers, or frantic, hurt young husbands, but no one like this has ever been seen in the shelter before, with his neatly combed black hair and fashionable shirt, and I try to wipe the silly smile off my face but it refuses to go away, he probably thinks he sees before him a happy woman, sitting alone in her room, full of herself, and I have to correct this mistake, but it immediately transpires that a more comprehensive mistake has been made here, because he examines me in embarrassment and says, you're Hava, at which my smile turns into actual laughter, it seems so amusing to me that anyone could think I was her, and I gurgle, I wish I were Hava, all my life I've wanted to be Hava, and he says with surprising gentleness, I'm sure Hava would like to be you.

You couldn't be more mistaken, I protest with relish, you'll see how wrong you are when you meet her, she's very satisfied with herself, she doesn't want to be anybody else, and he says, if you tell me where to find her I promise to look into it, and I accompany him excitedly to her door, stealing a sidelong glance at his face as I do so, he's not so handsome in profile, there's something disturbingly aquiline about the tip of his nose and chin, but nevertheless I don't go back to my room but hurry to the bathroom instead, and look tensely in the mirror, where I get a pleasant surprise, the red knit flatters me, lends my pale face a delicate, milky radiance, and the hair I shampooed this morning glitters like strands of gold. Maybe Hava's right, maybe it really is the best thing that could have happened to me, I already look a lot better than I did a week ago, and then I remember, she's sitting opposite him now, what does she want with him, what does he want with her, he's too young to be the father of a pregnant daughter, what can he be looking for in this sad place, but he seemed sad too, ashamed, he's not here for nothing, and I return to my office, where I leave the door open, so I'll see him on his way out, maybe I'll be able to delay him, and I sit there in suspense, reluctantly contemplating the papers that have accumulated on my desk in my absence, until I hear him leave Hava's office. He walks past my door, a little stooped, his eagle's profile gloomy, as if he's just heard bad news, but his face softens as he turns to me and says with a faint smile, I still prefer you, and I thank him with exaggerated enthusiasm, as if I have never received a greater compliment than this, and immediately rush to her defense, she's a hard woman but a wise one, I stick to the subject since as yet we have no other, just one common acquaintance whom he met for the first time today, who knows in what context.

Wisdom after the event can't help, he says, and I hasten to reply, but we're always both after the event and before it, surely, and he says nothing, leaning heavily against the doorpost as if he needs its support. What brings you to us, I ask, already prepared to take all his problems aboard, like a dirt truck that has emptied its contents and is looking for a new load, and he sighs, great foolishness, or bad luck, sometimes it's hard to tell them apart, and I look at him sympathetically, it's the same with me, great foolishness, or bad luck, which have left me abandoned in the middle of my life. To my regret he doesn't sit down on the empty chair opposite me, or unburden himself either, beyond this brief, generalized reply, but nevertheless he doesn't leave, thoughtfully surveying my room, the expression of anticipation on my face, he seems as surprised to find himself in a place like this as I am to see him here, and then he opens his mouth and it seems that he is about to say something to me, something that will change my life, but then the sound of the familiar crying bursts out of one of the rooms, rolling down the stairs and making its way to my ears, and he pales as if his life is in danger, and makes off at a run, without even saying good-bye to me, and I stand astounded at the window and watch him rushing out of the gate and running with broad strides until he reaches a silver car, where he stops and turns back to look at the shelter with an expression of undisguised horror on his handsome face, as if the entire building, with all its rooms, is about to collapse on his head.

Unable to restrain myself any longer, I burst into Hava's office without knocking, close the door behind me and lean my back on it, panting, and she slowly removes her reading glasses and says deliberately, Na'ama, what's wrong now, you look upset, and I realize that there's no point in trying to hide anything, it would be a waste of effort, and smiling like an adolescent girl I ask, who was that? And she sighs, you don't want to know, you have enough problems already, and I say, you're absolutely wrong, I have to know. It's the new girl's father, the one who was waiting for you all the time, she says, and I say in surprise, Yael's father, he doesn't look as if he could be Yael's father, and she waves her hand crossly, not her father, her baby's father, and since the father is known we have to get his signature on the consent to give the baby up for adoption, are you satisfied now?

Not in the least, I say, not even bothering to close the door behind me, how can I be satisfied when he's lost to me twice over, and I return disappointed to my office, trying to remember everything Yael told me about him, the only thing I remember clearly is that he refused to leave his wife, the only man who had no problem leaving his wife lately was my husband, and there's no way to sweeten the pill, including all of Hava's theories. Maybe I should send her to tell this man that he has to do his wife this favor, that it's the most wonderful thing he can do for her, but even if it happens it's Yael's life that will be changed, not mine, it seems that nobody's going to change my life, it's in my hands now, for good or for ill, but nevertheless during the few minutes he stood leaning against my doorpost something passed between us, I can't have been mistaken, my sorrow kissed his, it happened halfway between the door and the desk, and we both saw it. We both had that brand on our foreheads, the brand of the sorrow that fell on us so suddenly, taking us by surprise although we'd been waiting for it all our lives, because in the secret of our hearts we no longer believed that it would come, we hoped that we would succeed in ransoming it with a thousand little cares, and this surprise connected us so strongly that I can still sense the vapor of his embarrassed breath in the room, and again I go to the window, reconstructing his look, the silver flash of his car driving away, and the pain of the missed opportunity bites my neck, and when I turn my face back to the room she's standing there, her stomach almost hiding her face, which is already growing ugly with the prenatal swelling, and she whispers, he was here, wasn't he?

Yes, I say, he came to see Hava, you know that we need his consent for adoption, and she sinks into the chair opposite me with a sigh, flushed with insult, so why didn't he come and see me? He knows I'm here, and I say, it really is insulting, but apparently it's hard for him, and she bursts out, hard for him? So what is it for me? When I had to drop everything and come here, hide here like a leper, suffer for months with this pregnancy, he made the mistake and I paid the price, it's so unfair. What mistake, I ask weakly, trying to disguise the passionate interest I feel in every detail, and she snaps, you know what mistake, he promised to be careful, he told me to rely on him, and now he's acting as if I did it to him on purpose, and I think of the dark man with the shining eyes under the sullen brows, with the face moving between warmth and sternness, and with embarrassing yearning I think, she went to bed with him, she saw him without the white shirt and the pressed trousers, he kissed her, stroked her, made love to her, and already I'm prepared to feel jealous of her even though she is filling the room with her self-pity.

I don't understand him, she sobs, he loved me, I know he loved me, this pregnancy ruined everything, I don't understand why he didn't leave home and come to live with me, why he can't love this baby like he loves his children he worries about so much, why he can't leave his stupid wife, and I feel how every word she says hurts me, every word proves how superior this man is to my Udi, how lucky the stupid wife he refuses to leave is, I'm on her side now, the side of the wife of his youth, not that of the young mistress, and I say in a low voice, I know I mustn't say it and if Hava heard me I'd be fired on the spot, Yaeli, but my husband left me a week ago.

She covers her mouth with her hand and stares at me in astonishment, the complexity of things suddenly closes in on her, stinging and buzzing like a swarm of mosquitoes, and she puts her other hand on her stomach, listening in quiet despair to the murmur of the fetus, as if it is all she has left, and I approach her and put my hand next to hers, I'm sorry, I whisper, my story has nothing to do with it, just try to understand that at this stage of life every step a person takes destroys something. I'm sick of taking him into consideration all the time, she says resentfully, I'm allowed to think only of myself, my life will never be as simple as it once was either, and I say, that's true, but you have to be realistic, apparently he isn't going to leave home, the question is what you can expect from him nevertheless. She looks at me in surprise as if this question has never crossed her mind, her head sways as if in prayer, for him to go through it with me, she murmurs, for us to decide together what to do with the baby, instead of which he ignores me, doesn't answer my calls, just think of the fact that he was here and didn't come up to see me, and when I remember his hurried flight the moment he heard the crying I am ashamed for him, I bow my head and close my eyes, the proximity of the stomach quick with life fills me with longing and sadness, and I hear her voice in the distance, you have to help me, Na'ama, help me. That's what I'm here for, I say, it takes time, you know, and she whispers, I want you to talk to him, to explain to him that he can't cast me aside like this, that he's responsible for everything that happened, I won't be able to cope without him, it's the hardest decision of my life, I can't do it alone, and I declaim, you're not alone, we're with you, but she persists, please, Na'ama, get in touch with him, just try, I have a feeling that he'd listen to you. It's unbelievable, I say to myself, the girl's gone out of her mind, she's actually pushing me into his arms, and she gets up resolutely and takes a piece of paper from my desk, this is his number at work, she writes rapidly, please try, and she walks out of the room, leaving me with the patch of white paper on the desk, and I stare at it, Mica Bergman, it says, with seven numbers next to the name.

I won't call him, it's unprofessional, my job is to help her strengthen herself, not beg for mercy on her behalf, and nevertheless the new name hypnotizes me, Mica, it's too glittery for him, an unfamiliar name, I don't know anybody called Mica. You're in trouble, Mica, I shake my head sympathetically, memorizing the number, a malicious fetus is threatening your life, and you're scared to death, and while I'm still vacillating by the telephone it rings, and I pick up the receiver, for a moment I don't recognize the voice, the most familiar voice in the world to me, dusty and bleak, with a faint new note of apology, Na'ama, it's me, he says, how are you?

How could I not have recognized Udi, it's as if I'd failed to recognize my own voice, and he says, I'm back, and immediately elaborates, back from the trip, in case I imagined he'd come back to my arms, but I don't even have a chance to get it wrong, the words of prophetic consolation I repeated at Noga's bedside are echoing in my ears, thy sun shall no more go down, neither shall thy moon withdraw itself, for the Lord shall be thy everlasting light, and the days of thy mourning shall be ended, how I'd prayed then to hear his voice, but now I'm as empty as the old swimming pool, he'll break his neck if he tries to jump into me.

Where are you, I ask, and he says, not far, Avner's gone away for a month and he left me the key to his apartment, and I swallow the words in relief, even though I know full well that the relief is illusory, that the truth was revealed to me on that fateful day and nothing will obliterate it, even if he isn't living with her and the baby he already belongs to them, and he asks, when does Noga get out of school today, I want to pick her up, and I say, in a little while, at a quarter to two, and he says, then I'll bring her home this evening, okay? And I mumble, fine, no problem, still holding the receiver in my hand even though his voice is no longer there, imagining her joy at the school gate, the smile spreading to the tips of her curls, the fawning, awestruck hug, and I have no part in their joy, even though I gave all I had for these two, almost all my life, and now they'll go out to eat, maybe to a movie, for years I nagged him to take her without me, to devote a bit of time to her, I didn't think it would happen like this.

My head drops heavily to the desk, I have the whole afternoon free, nobody needs me until this evening, for years they both needed me so much, I was torn between them like a piece of old cloth, and now I'm extraneous, and I'm so used to being needed that I don't know what to do with the time that has been freed, this is something else I'll have to learn, exactly like learning a foreign language, and I wonder what I'm going to do until this evening, glancing at the patch of white again, a bright cloud on the somber sky of my desk, and I can't resist it, I dial the number quickly, before I have time to regret it, and to my surprise he answers himself, and I ask, Mica Bergman, and he announces almost proudly, that's me, his voice brisk and businesslike. This is Na'ama, we met this morning at the shelter, I say, hearing with relief how his voice opens up to me, oh, he laughs, you're not Hava, and I smilingly admit, right, I'm not Hava, and he says, how can I help you?

I breathe uneasily into the mouthpiece, am I really so transparent to him, after all, I'm the one who's supposed to be doing the helping, and hurriedly adopt a more formal tone, I wanted to talk to you about the situation, as the person taking care of Yael, and he sighs softly, what will I do if he says no, but then he says, okay, not-Hava, I'll be glad to talk about the situation with you. When,

I ask eagerly, and he asks, are you free this afternoon, and I reply immediately, yes, this was all I wanted, wasn't it, to find something to do this afternoon, and he says, I feel uncomfortable coming to the shelter, let's meet in a cafe, there's a nice place not far from there.

We'll pretend I'm building a house for you, he says when he arrives, even before sitting down opposite me, smiling mischievously, as if we're playing a game, as if undecided destinies are not lying open on the table between us, and he takes a large sheet of paper out of his briefcase, and I look curiously at the squares and rectangles drawn on it, living room, it says there, guest toilet, study, children's room, bedroom, and everything is clear, orderly, reassuring. What a lovely house you're building for me, I sigh, I only wish it were true, that I was a fine lady with a well-ordered life and nothing to do but consult her charming architect about the size of the guest toilet, and he asks in a pleased voice, do you like it, and I say, very much, looking sidelong at the bedroom, and he looks at it too, taking a pencil out of his pocket and drawing a big bed in the corner, and opposite it a closet, his fingers as accurate as they'd have been if they'd had a ruler implanted in them, and next to the bed he puts a little dressing table, I've never had a dressing table, my few cosmetics are strewn over the top of the washing machine, where they jump about with every wash, and above it an oval mirror. Is the mirror big enough for you, he asks, and I say, yes, what about the window, I bet you like big windows, and I nod, and he inserts a long window in the wall, reaching almost as far as the bed, and then he surveys his work with satisfaction and asks, is there anything missing, and I say, nothing, and then I say, everything, because I remember that it's not for real.

What does your bedroom look like, he asks sympathetically, and I think of the shabby room with the closet attached to the wall, and the red carpet, the carpet of my childhood, with its fraying hearts, and the picture of the old house with the red-tiled roof and the clouds sliding down it on the wall, and under it the bed we bought years ago from a divorced couple, and lying on it is Udi, his mouth cracked in a shamed sigh, his long legs still, like on the morning when they lost their movement, and when I remember that morning I feel as if I am ostensibly recovering from an incurable disease but that everybody knows that's impossible, because the disease is incurable, and I too really know that it's only a respite whose days are numbered, but nevertheless we all collaborate in maintaining the illusion that I have recovered, until it is no longer clear who's deceiving who, and I'm afraid that he's going to ask whom I share the bedroom with, but he is silent, glancing with a neutral expression at my hand, the wedding ring is still there, slender and lusterless, and then he asks, do you have a big mirror in your bedroom, and I say, no, nor a small one either, and he nods gravely, now I understand. What do you understand, I ask, and he smiles, when I saw you this morning I said to myself that you have no idea how beautiful you are, and now I understand why, you simply haven't got a mirror, and I smirk, that's exactly what that painter said to me years ago, once in a decade a man appears in my life, informs me that I'm beautiful, and goes away. How easy it is to breathe after receiving a compliment, my whole life seems instantly transformed, even my sorrow seems suddenly beautiful, and I sit back and relax, really, there's no more charming sight than a beautiful, sad woman, except perhaps a beautiful, sad man, like the one sitting opposite me, I'm supposed to be angry with him, I'm on her side after all, but I want him, I know it and he knows it and there's no point in hiding it.

When the coffee arrives we clear the table of the beautiful rooms we'll never live in and he says, go ahead, talk, and lights a cigarette, fixing me with chastised eyes, actually they're dark, almost black, but with a dim radiance shining out behind them, as if someone has left a bulb burning in the recesses of his head and it is lighting him up from inside, its comforting rays even bursting from his mouth, and then he taps his ear, I'm listening, and I notice that his ears are surprisingly small, clinging to his head like frightened baby snails, at last I've found a flaw in him. Nervously I take the cigarette he offers, what's happening to me, I can't get a word out, and he smiles, what's the matter with you Na'ama, this would never happen to Hava, I'm sure Hava always knows what to say, and I laugh in embarrassment, again our only common acquaintance, but actually we have another one, the one in whose name I am here, and whom I am supposed to represent. What should I say to him, I vacillate, that he should leave his wife like my husband left me, hurt his children like Udi hurt Noga, and he sighs, let me help you, Na'ama, I'm not usually so helpful, but you make me feel a desire to help you, I'll talk about the situation in your place, you should tell me that I'm behaving like a swine, that I can't abandon Yael in this condition, that I have to take responsibility for my actions, that I have to support her and help her raise this child I didn't want, and I'll tell you that you're right but I can't do it.

What do you mean, you can't, I suddenly get tough, you men are spoiled rotten, who cares what you can do or can't do, there are some things that you have to do whether you like it or not, and he bows his head, I am sure that he will defend himself by going on the attack, like Udi, but his temperament is different, I feel so guilty that I can't look at her, he says quietly, such a sweet pretty child, I've ruined her life, and I look at him and imagine Udi and Noga embracing at the school gates, behind my back, it was guilt that made him keep her at arm's length, and instead of comforting him I magnified his guilt, and I ask with real curiosity, but how can you escape, it will haunt you even if you don't see her, and he says, you'd be surprised, people can detach themselves. So how come I can never detach myself from anything, I ask in childish complaint, but immediately I fall silent, covering up the complaint with another, graver question, so why didn't you terminate it in the usual way, why didn't you take her to have an abortion, and he sighs, you know how I pleaded with her, threatened her, nothing helped, every time

I made an appointment for her she canceled it, she thought that this way she would force me to leave home.

What, she got pregnant on purpose? I ask in astonishment, and he says, no, of course not, but once it had already happened she couldn't give up the chance, I'm not blaming her, it was out of love, but I don't have to tell you what a curse love can be, and I smile bitterly, I'm not interested in how he knows what I know, but on the other hand I am very interested in the differences between their versions, and I wag my finger at him rebukingly, she told me that you were the one who couldn't make up his mind, that you kept changing your mind until it was too late, and now it's his turn to smile bitterly, that's an outright lie, I told her at the outset that I didn't want the baby, that I would never leave my wife, I told her that if I didn't have any other choice I would acknowledge paternity and pay child support but that I could never live with her, I swear to you, I never vacillated for a second. Believe me, he's almost begging, I did everything I could to put an end to it while it was still possible, once we were even on the way to the doctor and she jumped out of the car, you simply can't imagine how crazy it was, I ran after her in the street, I was almost run over, I couldn't believe it was happening to me.

I listen to him with my eyes closed, it's hard for me to look at him, my heart goes out to him so much, I've become so used to being on the side of the women, but now the borders seem to be blurring, the pain is the same pain, even if it's borne differently, it's common human bad luck, which makes no distinction between men and women, and again I think of Udi, what would he do in similar circumstances, but immediately I remember what he's already done, left me for less than a baby, for a woman with a baby that's not even his, and when I open my eyes I see him looking at me curiously, his tongue wetting his lips, and he whispers, what are you thinking about? Suddenly everything came together, I say hesitantly, suddenly I realized how connected we all are, it should bring us closer but instead it estranges us, and he smiles, it doesn't estrange me, I felt close to you from the moment I saw you sitting in your office and smiling with sad eyes, and don't get the wrong idea, I don't usually find it easy to come close to people, and I say, I wasn't talking about you and me, I was talking about humanity in general, and he declares solemnly, ah, humanity, that's your field, I don't know anything about it, I only know how to build homes.

Or to wreck them, I say and immediately regret it, and he clamps his lips and takes his wallet out of his pocket with a sharp movement, I've chased him away, he's going to pay and leave, but instead of taking out a banknote he takes out a snapshot and hands it to me, a strange family snapshot, usually in photos like these everyone is clustered together, in the garden, or round the table, looking at their empty plates, but here they're all in motion, as if they're playing catch. At one end of the photo a brown boy is smiling at me, dimples in his cheeks, and not far from him a little girl in a sundress, with dozens of thin braids sticking out all over her head, and at the other end a tall, mannish woman in shorts is trying to catch up with them, my interest is naturally focused on her, one tanned leg resolutely thrust forward, she has big blue eyes in an attractive face, but her shoulders are broad, her haircut mannish, making a disagreeable impression, I expected him to have a completely different wife. I'm prettier than she is, I conclude in surprise, but nevertheless she has him and I have nothing, and again I study the photograph, the vigorous movement of the leg which seems hopeless, she'll never catch up with them, but what difference does it make, they all look content, calm, only he, the photographer, is not content, nervously lighting another cigarette, do you understand, he urges me, and I ask, what exactly am I supposed to understand?

Our lives are free, he says, that's the only way we can live together, she never asks me where I've been, I never interrogate her, over the years we've learned to free ourselves of both the truth and the lies, she knows that I come home because I want to see her and the children, not because I have to, and that's enough for her, and for me, we've learned to believe in actions, and that's how we live, without guilt and blame, without prying into each other's souls all the time, and that's how we bring up our children, in a family where there's room for everyone, and the more he talks the more humiliated I feel, as if he's holding a mirror in his hand and showing me my life, fundamentally false, choked with guilt, resentment, ancient bonds, a combination of a prison and a torture chamber, where everyone is both inmate and warden, torturer and tortured. Suddenly I feel that he is utterly alien to me, what have I to do with him, what have I to do with this polished propaganda speech, for one minute sorrow penetrated his life, and I entered through the same breach, but soon his sorrow will be banished and he will return to his comfortable, rationally managed life and I will return to mine, and again he wets his lips, I'm sorry, he says, I didn't mean to hurt you, and I bow my head, it isn't you, it's reality, it does that, you know. He puts his hand under my chin and raises my face to his, angling it like a mirror, I don't know what to do, he says, sliding his tongue over his teeth, I should never have started it, but she was so sweet, she would stay behind in the office on purpose until everyone left, ask my advice about all kinds of things, provoke me, so I had a little fun with her, I never imagined that it would end in such a mess.

You forgot the facts of life, I say sternly, and he sighs, give me a break, Na'ama, you know I go over that one time in my head every night, curse myself for not holding back, one lousy time, after she'd flaunted herself in front of me all day in a miniskirt without any panties on, and the minute we were alone she sat down on my lap, and I rummaged in the drawer and saw I was out of condoms, and in the end I said, okay, so we'll go back to the old methods, and bingo, it happened, there isn't a night that I don't go over it in my head, and I lower my eyelids modestly, why on earth is he sharing all these details with me as if I were his confidante, but at the same time I'm busy reconstructing the scene with him, it sounds so pro-vocative, despite the unhappy results, and then I realize that this was precisely his intention in telling me, to stimulate me, to let me know that he was open to all comers, and that if I were to flaunt myself in front of him without any panties on, it would happen. For a moment I feel angry, who does he think he is, what does he take me for, but the next I steal a forgiving look at him, how can I be angry with him, his frankness is so disarming, and in fact, why not, I'm free now, not only deserted, not only abandoned, there's another side to my plight, exciting and unfamiliar.

In a transparent gesture I look at my watch, and he grins, do we have any time left to talk about the situation? I nod quietly, feeling more excited than I have for years, and he brings his face up close to mine, at close quarters his skin is coarse and pitted, just like the leather wallet lying on the table between us, and do you want to talk about the situation here or somewhere else, he asks, why don't we go to the place where the situation began, and I whisper, all right, suddenly my doubts and hesitations are over, I follow him spellbound, for the first time in my life not thinking about the consequences, or the price to be paid, simply following a man I'd never met before this morning, and my whole body wakes up, new currents of life stream through it, this body that was exclu-sively Udi's, and that perhaps, by means of another man, will come into my possession again, and I don't think of Udi or Noga or Yael, only about the seductive grace flowing generously from his every movement. Drive behind me, he says, it's very near, and I get into the car and drive behind him, as if there's a thick cable joining us, he's the tow truck and I'm the damaged car attached to his rear, without the freedom to indulge in doubts.

Next to a small, well-tended building we stop, two potted plants greet me with a bright smile in the stairwell, and I follow him into an elegant and, more crucially, empty office, today everybody in the office gets off early, this was our regular day, he says, and I laugh, suddenly everything seems delightful and entertaining to me, everything I had shrunk from for years, even the thought of the fat soon to be revealed underneath my clothes, embarrassing as stolen goods, the appalling private body odors, all the things that only Udi could love, no longer bother me, for the first time I am experiencing what every girl goes through in her youth, and it's a lot less frightening that I thought, a lot more simple.

His hand brushes my shoulder, directing me to his office where the floor is covered from wall to wall by a bright red carpet, exactly the same color as my blouse, and his voice gurgles in my ear, when I saw you this morning, you know what I thought? And I nod because I know what he's going to say, I thought how much I wanted to see you lying on this carpet with your lovely yellow hair, and he comes closer to me and strokes my hair, he's so close that his lips are almost touching my cheek, and briefly I pull back, in a minute his mouth will cover mine, and all the traces of the food we've eaten today and the words we've spoken today will mingle, how strange that one little organ should perform so many functions, there should have been a special organ just for kissing, what have I to do with the remains of his food, the remains of his words, and his lips breathe on my ear, don't run away, Na'ama, he whispers, don't worry, we won't do anything if it makes you nervous, I just want to see you on the carpet. I look at the carpet beneath my feet in embarrassment, how am I going to get down there, but he sits down lightly and pulls me after him, lays my limbs down one by one, precisely as in a drawing, arranges my hair around my head, he radiates an innocent enthusiasm that wipes out my reservations about myself, his admiration seems exaggerated but it's so reassuring, covered with the sweetness of a daydream like the icing on a cake, an illusory sweetness there's no point in arguing with because it's not real anyway, all you can do is lick it, until all the icing is gone and the cake is left without it, dull and naked, but I don't care, I've worried about the future enough, I made all kinds of secret agreements with it that only I kept, now the future can worry about itself.

I'm not asking you anything, he says, looking at me with his eyes lit up, but you can tell me everything, and I try to smile but a little tear is already staining the carpet when I say, my husband left me exactly a week ago, I've never been with another man, the shameful declaration escapes my lips, but he isn't put off, he strokes my lips with the tips of his fingers, he'll come back, you'll see, he whispers, I promise you that he'll come back, and I'm ready to believe him, touching his handsome face, even from close up he's beautiful, even if not so young, I never guessed how deep the frown marks between his stern brows were, but his smile is warm and sensitive before his lips press mine, let me love you, he whispers into my mouth, into the evening descending on the room, a soft summer darkness, faintly perfumed, with the smell of fresh fruit wafting from it, warm plums just plucked from the tree, melting in the mouth like candy, as he gently peels off my clothes, you're so white, he tells me, your skin is so smooth. Without his shirt he looks heavier, accustomed to Udi's boyish body my hands measure the breadth of his back in surprise, but it feels pleasant to the touch, no reservations poison me. How simple it is, I marvel, to make love to a perfect stranger, without all the old grievances and resentments of a life in common, how come it never occurred to me that you can only really love a stranger.

His finger travels provocatively over my body, it seems to me that the roots of my hair are shuddering with pleasure, splitting the dry earth of my scalp, don't be shy, he whispers, show me how you really are, and I become lighter and lighter, as if I have just shed a heavy load, sacks full of baggage, a minute before the ship went down I threw all I possessed into the sea, and now I am standing alone on the deck, with nothing left to lose, concentrating on the journey of his finger, now it rests for a moment in my mouth and I lick it like a cat enjoying a juicy fish bone, and now it hides itself from me in the depths of my body, and his abrasive tongue is at the bottom of my neck, and already he is completely naked, standing on his knees before me short-legged as a dwarf and drawing me toward him, and I am trembling round his hot, surging penis, in a minute it will break, smash to pieces, like my father's giant barometer exploding at my feet on my wedding day, and I hear him cry out, gasp, don't run away from me, Na'ama, I can feel you running away, and I say, I'm here with you, and he shakes my shoulders, disappointed, you're not, you're not, and immediately I make haste to comply, to prove to him that I am, my whole body goes round in circles to please him, circle within circle like a target board, with his hypnotizing penis stuck in the middle, and nothing can change this, not my father's sorrow, not Udi's unfaithfulness, nor Noga's hurt, this is the one and only fact, and with a wild fling of freedom I throw back my neck, raising the blinking barrier to let the sugared coaches of pleasure through, and here they come, one after the other, like the train cake I made for Noga's second birthday, three gorgeous coaches covered with chocolate icing, which she didn't even get to taste before she fell.

So that's what I had to tell you about the situation, he suddenly announces in an alarmingly loud voice, as if a loudspeaker had been turned on in the depths of his throat, the white shirt already making its way to his shoulders, his face shifting like the face of a child who has received a gift in honor of a tragic event and doesn't know whether to be happy for the gift or sorry for the tragedy. You understand me, don't you, he crushes my shoulders, I made love to her three times on this carpet, four times on that chair, two or three times on the desk, I'll be glad to demonstrate them all to you one day, maybe I forgot to mention another once or twice, so what does it mean, that we can be man and wife, she and I? That I should leave my children, break up the family I love so much, you tell me, what does it mean? What price am I expected to pay for my pleasures? I didn't rape her, you know, I didn't even seduce her, when it happened I did all I could to help her fix it and she was the one who refused, I went to your shelter and signed papers to say I was prepared to acknowledge paternity or consent to adoption, what more do you want, for me to love her? I'm sorry, that you can't compel me to do, you can't control my feelings, and I am surprised by the sharp transition but not afraid, there's something soft about him which doesn't endanger me, and I look at his shirt as his broad fingers button it up, how can it still be so white at the end of the day, and I draw his hands toward me, kiss his fingernails, every nail seems to me to have its own little face, and they all smile at me shyly, like his face bending down to me, and I lay his head on my chest, his thick fragrant hair covers my breasts, don't worry, I whisper to him, don't worry, everything will be all right.

When I drive home in the dark I laugh out loud, because right next to the car he said to me, you know that Hava would never have done such a thing, that's why I said I preferred you, and I giggled, poor Hava, she has no idea what she's missing, and I see him in the mirror looking after me, a big, grateful man who was granted an unexpected pardon, but as I get closer to home I force myself to think of poor Yael, I didn't help her at all, I only helped myself, in a strange and unexpected way, nobody would have believed it of me, and I myself can hardly believe that it happened, that at long last I had dared to finish what had been broken off then, in the rooftop studio on the day of the first rain, as if that was the real sin for which I'd been punished, that I didn't permit myself to stay with him there, and that now that the deed was done the sin had been wiped away.

When I come home I see them sitting in the living room, waiting for me tense and silent, my mother and Udi and Noga, as if they are my anxious parents and I their wayward child. Mommy, where were you, only Noga dares to ask, and I answer lightly, I had a few meetings, and Udi looks at me, hardly able to stop himself from interrogating me as usual, I haven't seen him for a week and his body seems to have shrunk and his gloom swollen, his eyes are red as if he hasn't slept since then, and my mother says, you look radiant, Na'ama, stealing a provocative look at him, and I feel like saying to her, that's exactly what you looked like when you came home from your meetings, looking at us in astonishment as if you didn't remember who we were or what we wanted of you, but I look at them in silence, it seems to me that they have all conspired against me to sabotage my modest happiness, and I won't let them, I mustn't let them. Noga, have you done your homework, I pounce on her, firmly changing the subject, and she as expected says no and shuts herself in her room, and my mother says grimly, I'll make something to eat, and retires to the kitchen, and Udi gets up slowly and stands facing me, his limbs locked in the tangle of his thoughts, I told you you'd be better off without me, he whispers in a sanctimonious tone, his eyes darting over my face, and I melt at the sight of his helpless frustration, so this is happiness, for years I've been seeking it in vain in the domains of friendship and lovingkindness, when all the time it was hiding here, in the cracks between victory and bitter defeat, between absolute emptiness and memory ceaselessly seeping in, this is happiness, to see an old enemy bound in chains, he has no right to ask where I was and what I was doing, he has no right to look for incriminating clues, and only his embittered steps going downstairs leave a demanding question in their wake, a question whose answer has always been there waiting.

Nineteen

That night she stands next to my bed, the still, breathing statue of a child, and I open my eyes and immediately close them again, and turn over onto my other side, his wife's tanned leg invades the bed, planting a rude kick in the heart of my dreaming groin, that's what women do to keep their husbands and only you give up without a fight, you haven't got the guts to fight for him, or maybe you don't think he's worth it, that's exactly what he would say, whenever we fell into the trap of so-called heart-to-heart talks, you don't really want me, you think you deserve something better, you only stay with me for fear of being alone, not for love, but I never really listened to him, I only waited for my turn, to sweep his arguments away like twigs on the tidal wave of my accusations, and now I remember his offended look on the stairs, barely one week has passed and you've cheated on me already, you've given me up more quickly than I thought.

Cool currents of air penetrate my bed, stepping hesitantly over my limbs, for the first time, as at the end of a shower when the water is still hot but your skin can feel the threat of the cold hiding behind it, I sense the approaching end of this hard summer, and I sit up to look for the blanket and I see her again, her eyes closed, asleep on her feet in the middle of her watch, what is she guarding with this mixture of dedication and negligence, and I touch her skin, Nogi, you're freezing, get into bed, and she says, Daddy doesn't love me. You're cold, I insist, can't you see that it's getting cold at night, and she says, I know he doesn't love me, and I pull her to me angrily, when I finally manage to fall asleep she has to come and wake me up, what harm have I done her to make her persecute me like this, and only then do her words sink in, and I don't say anything because I have nothing to say, perhaps she's right, I have no idea whom he loves. He hardly spoke to me, she goes on, he hardly listened to me, just looked at his watch all the time, as if someone was waiting for him, and I force myself to hug her, instead of the wave of pity I should feel I am seized by savage anger against both him and her, I feel like running away from the pair of them, let them solve their problems without me. Noga, let me sleep, I grumble, I can't be responsible for your father, I have no idea what he feels, I only know that I love you, but when she falls into a rebuked silence I wonder if even this is true, what did he say, buttoning his white shirt, you can't force me to love, and I bury my head in the pillow, I'm sick of loving, I admit it, all I want is for love to be given to me, and for nothing to be taken from me in return.

But in the morning when I find her sleeping by my side, I stroke her salty cheeks, where the tears of the night have left their transparent tracks, like the slimy trail of snails, and then she opens her eyes, fringed by long, lacy lashes, I'm his daughter, she says, he has to love me, and I cut her short, get up Nogi, it's late, stop brooding about it all the time, think about other things, and when she leaves the room, her lips pursed in frustration, I breathe a sigh of relief, how she loves telling me how miserable she is, but I have to push her away in order to be able to love her, when I load her pain onto myself it weakens me, and then I don't have the strength to love, only to hurl clenched fists of pity at her. When we're just ready to leave he phones, you're still at home, he asks dryly, as if we've always been in the habit of talking on the phone in the mornings, as if we haven't lain face-to-face in bed night after night, and I say, yes, I'm still here, even though I was on the point of leaving, and I tell Noga to hurry up and walk to school, I have a feeling that he wants to come home, and I pace the rooms triumphantly, smiling at the objects which saw me in my insult, if he comes back then it will be to a completely different life, I'll tell him, a life of independent adults who have chosen each other, not frightened children clinging to each other in hatred, but when he comes in the sharp claws of loss dig into my flesh, he was once yours and now he isn't, weep sore for him that goeth away, standing opposite me in a denim shirt and brown corduroys, tall and aloof, his face chiseled in miserly, pitiless precision. I came to get a few things, he says, I'm going away, and I curse him with clenched lips, you've won again, you were always bolder, crueler, for one happy day I thought I'd beaten you, now you'll humiliate me for weeks, I thought I could make conditions, it turns out that there isn't even anyone to make them to, and it seems to me that my face is falling, the force of gravity is growing stronger, pulling down the corners of my mouth, my shoulders, my breasts in their sweaty bra, my trembling knees, down, down, because he's leaving me again, when I thought he wanted to come back, that stupid Hava, how dare she delude me that I'm better off without him, again I trail behind him from room to room, my teeth chattering in insult, weep ye not for the dead, neither bemoan him, but weep sore for him that goeth away, for he shall return no more, nor see his native country.

Where are you going, to Tibet? I try my luck with a clumsy lunge, and he says shortly, something like that, and I exclaim, so suddenly, you didn't say anything yesterday, and he says coldly, I decided to go last night, I can't stay here anymore, and I say mockingly, is this another prophecy? Something like that, he says, but I know that it's more like punishment, he sensed that I'd been with another man and now he wants to punish me, the nerve of him, what gives him the right, and I announce to his back, I know that you're not going alone, but he doesn't answer, he drags a ladder from the porch to the bedroom and climbs to the snowy heights of the closet. I look with hostility at his shapely feet, toe after toe in a neat, disciplined slope peeping out of the brown strap of his sandal, inches from my eyes, and for a moment it seems to me that he isn't really going, just helping me take down the winter clothes in the familiar, reassuring, cyclical routine, this summer will finally end, after all, the first signs arrived last night, and we're getting ready for winter a little earlier than usual, but he cuts the illusion short, where did you put my blue windbreaker, he demands, as if it's still my role to help him, and his to disappear without saying where to and with whom, and I whisper to his feet standing on the top rung of the ladder, you're going with Zohara, aren't you, and his toes shrink abruptly, hiding behind the sandal strap, in a confession of guilt.

I'm going with her but it's not what you think, he blurts quickly into the depths of the closet, and I put my hands on the ladder rungs, in a minute I'll shake it the way you shake a tree trunk to make the fruit fall, and he'll fall broken to the floor and he won't go anywhere with anyone, but all this has already happened, he already lay here broken and paralyzed and we all suffered, I have to let him go, how small my power over him is and how easily it's turned against me, the sooner I get out of the picture of his life the sooner he'll see it as it really is. For so many years I let him use me to hide from himself, to blame me in order to clear himself, to turn everything into a personal quarrel between us, so that he could throw the whole mess of his frustration into my face, so long as he didn't have to examine himself, it isn't going to happen anymore, I vow, and in order to get out of the picture I leave the room immediately and after a few minutes he appears, the blue windbreaker in his hands, together with a woolen cap and thick socks, and I don't say a word, suddenly I understand that the more I say the less he'll say, and I see him taking a plastic bag from behind the fridge and putting his things into it, strange that he remembers where the plastic bags are, and he finds the tap easily too, pours himself a glass of water and sits down next to me. It isn't what you think, he says, I don't love her like I loved you, it's something completely different, she simply lets me live, she accepts me as I am, she doesn't expect anything of me, she doesn't try to educate me.

I find it difficult to console myself with these subtle distinctions, especially with the past tense deafening my ears, I loved you, I loved you, and the more he tries to explain the more I recede, I'm not sitting next to him on the sofa anymore but looking at him from a vast distance, a distance I've unconsciously traveled over the past few months, and I see how he's doing the wrong thing again, running away from every problem, taking the easy way out, is this what he calls a change? Judging himself by the eyes of others again, punishing himself by punishing others, how weak he actually is, it was only by virtue of his weakness that he controlled me for all these years, but I know I mustn't say anything, I can't save him, and he can't save me, each of us is on our own even though we lived in the same house for so many years, and have one name, and one daughter, and from a vast distance I put out my hand and stroke his hair, I feel as if he's my child, as if I gave birth to him, this is the only way that I can love him, and for some reason I prefer to love him, and for a moment I see the aftermath of this warped journey, the farther he runs the farther he'll get from real change, but I have no way of stopping him, as if he's a moonstruck child walking on a narrow balustrade and if I try to direct him he'll fall. I look at him with a new curiosity, he is no longer my husband, no longer Noga's father, he's a man neither young nor happy who believes he's trying to improve his life, his hair droops on his head, limp and thin, his eyes are lowered, his lips pursed, even the high cheekbones around which the rest of his face is structured have dropped down wearily under his skin, and his hands cling tightly to the plastic bag with the socks and woolen cap and blue windbreaker as if they're the last things he has left on earth, and I contemplate his dry hands, seeing them on baby Noga's stomach, tickling her ribs, while she chokes with laughter and I scold him, stop it, it's dangerous for her to laugh too much. What about the baby, I ask quietly, and he says, I try, and smiles apologetically, she's so small, and I bow my head, how easy it is for him to give when he isn't obliged to, all his resistance melts away, she's still small, there's no accusation in her eyes, no need to escape from them to the ends of the earth, it seems that it's only easy to make love to a stranger, to bring up a strange baby, and what of all the years when we thought the opposite, who will avenge their insult?

With rare composure I analyze his words, something I have never been able to do before, I was too busy defending myself from their implications about me, and all of a sudden I'm as cool as a cucumber, only a few months too late, when it can't help anymore, not the two of us at any rate, and when he stands up I look at the ridges of his corduroys, straightening out as if they have woken from sleep, and I remember how we bought them for him last winter, on his birthday, the three of us walking among the racks of hangers, and then I think with a pang about her approaching birthday, at the end of the month she'll turn ten, and I want to remind him to write or call to wish her a happy birthday, but all that comes out of my mouth is a dry cough, it's not my business, it's between him and her. Did you say something, he asks, and I whisper, nothing, have a safe journey, and I brush my lips quickly over his cheek, a faint smell of dust rises from it, of a lonely desert fire, and he hugs his plastic bag, sends me a crooked smile, and when I see him descending the stairs I think, how can the whole of life consist of a mighty battle waged between two people, and as soon as one of them retires it all peters out in a small, still voice, as if there had never been any point or purpose to the battle in the first place, and I had always believed that it was stronger than us, that it would live on after us, that we would be mercenaries in a war without end forever.

At the end of the bend I still see his narrow back, he seems to stop, hesitate for a moment, but I don't call him, we may be walking the same road but our lives have been completely separated, and I have no wish to fight for him, I let go like the sky, looking with silent surprise at the receding clouds, for so many years I have been trying to mend the tears, sewing them up with clumsy fingers, with crude ropes that only deepened the rent, and now it has become clear to me that this is not the point, the whole point is to learn to live with the flaw, to make friends with the lack, not to prettify the ugliness but to breathe it in, in lungfuls, to look down from above on the wasteland of life and to find a point in it, because what remains after giving up the fight, which seems to be harder than giving up the love, is only a terrible desolation, and any attempt to relieve it at night only makes it worse in the morning, and with this I have to live, and when he disappears round the bend I can't breathe for a moment, it's over, unbelievable that it should have ended before the end of life but that's what happened, and the fact that it happened doesn't mean that it had to happen, even that consolation is missing, only that it did happen, presumably it could have been averted, like most catastrophes, but now it is too late.

At the entrance to the shelter she's waiting for me, her stomach pressing against the bars of the gate, Na'ama, she calls out to me, how did you do it? I say in alarm, how did I do what, and she says, how did you persuade him, and I ask nervously, persuade him to do what? And she says, to be with me, to help me, he called this morning and promised to come and see me later. That's wonderful, Yaeli, I say with a sigh of relief, but don't build on it too much, you'll never get what you want from him, you'll always have to rely on yourself, and she says, that's not true, I believe that he'll change, and I rumple the spikes of her hair, you'll never change him, I say, you can only change yourself and even that will be difficult, and she looks at me in disappointment, so he isn't going to live with me? He isn't going to bring the baby up with me? And I say, no, he'll come to see you once in a while and he'll be so charming that you won't be able to love anyone else, but that won't last long either, you have to plan your life without him. But he'll come to the baby's birthdays, won't he, she asks, and I think about Noga's birthday, maybe I should have reminded him anyway, but what would have been the point, if it doesn't come from him she's better off without it, and I sit down close to her on the stairs, those damned birthdays, who needs them, but even if she gives the baby up they'll haunt her, what will she do every year on his birthday, bake a cake and eat it by herself, a teddy bear cake, a rabbit cake, a train cake, blow out the candles by herself, grow older with him, in separate houses, in different towns.

All morning he's been kicking, she murmurs, putting her hand on her stomach, he's trying to tell me something and I don't know what it is, if only I knew what was best for him, and I say quietly, so nobody will hear this heresy, even I can't believe the words that come out of my mouth, you know what's best for him, you have to be strong and admit it, it's got nothing to do with Mica, it's between you and your baby, I'm warning you, if you give him up you'll never recover from it, and she sighs, I think about it all the time and it doesn't lead anywhere, lucky I've still got two weeks to make up my mind, but when we stand up she utters a loud, deep cry, it seems as if the fetus is screaming from inside her stomach, look, the waters have broken.

Dripping water as if she took a bath in her clothes she stands and cries, and I run upstairs, her water broke, I say to Anat, gasping for breath, I'm taking her to the hospital, and Anat quickly packs Yael's bag, are you sure you want to be there, she asks, usually this is her job, and I say, yes, no problem, trying to hide my unprofessional overinvolvement. Does anyone need to be informed, she asks, and I rummage in my bag and take out the white note, tell him, I pant, agitated, as if I am the one suddenly starting a new family, to take the place of the old one that disappointed me so badly.

She lies sprawled on the backseat, exactly like the sick Noga a week ago, my little car has turned into an amateur ambulance, accumulating pain and sighs, on every journey there's somebody else groaning in the back and nevertheless I advance, driving slowly, almost at a walking pace, we'll be there in a minute, Yaeli, I say, everything's going to be all right, I'll help you, and she whimpers, I'm cold, I'm wet through. In spite of the blazing sun I turn on the heat, it feels as if the car is on fire but she is still shivering, her teeth are chattering, and I can hardly breathe, boiling-hot sweat streams from my forehead to my dry mouth, and I swallow it desperately, in the grip of a terrible thirst, I open my mouth and I feel as if jugs of liquid are pouring into it from the sky, murky, lukewarm amniotic fluid, and I gulp them down gratefully, my eyes are melting in the heat, it seems as if the built-up town is receding from us, and I am driving in the heart of the desert, searching for Udi, I know he's hiding here, and I have to tell him before it's too late, a new baby is knocking at the creaking doors of our hearts, what will we say to it and how will we greet it, but there isn't a living soul anywhere, only bonfires burning at the sides of the road, making the desert bloom with fiery yellow flowers whose smell is the smell of burning flesh, the smell of tender human sacrifices one day old.

When we enter the ward in a near swoon I remember how the nurse asked, can I help you, and Udi said, just get the baby out and we won't bother you anymore, and this time there's no need for questions, it's all perfectly clear, the dropped stomach and the wet clothes, and they snatch her away immediately, telling me to wait outside, and I walk up and down the corridor, throbbing with an unexpected joy, the whole world seems to be waiting with bated breath for the little creature to be born, holding out giant arms to receive precisely this baby that nobody wanted. I stand at the window with my eyes closed, instead of the boringly familiar urban landscape I am confronted again with utter desolation, bald hills protrude from the earth like growths with predatory beaks, and at their feet sudden oases, which only serve to emphasize the desolation. A heavenly hand pulls the hills up higher, and they rise aloft, salt mountains glittering like icebergs, Udi where are we, where are we driving to, but the driver's seat is empty, the wheel is steering itself into the chain of mountain ranges closing in on the desert plain, and from among the pale bushes of dust his figure emerges, what loneliness, he whispers, you have no idea how lonely I am, you never have.

A heavy hand shakes my shoulder, we only met yesterday and we're already expecting a baby, he whispers in my ear, his smile tickling my cheek, and I marvel, Mica, you got here quickly, and he says ingenuously, I decided to do whatever you say, and I laugh, really, why? And he says, just because I like making you happy. But Mica, I say sternly, you didn't come here for me, you came for Yael, and he grumbles, don't be such a spoilsport, there's no contradiction, can't I make two women happy at once? And I laugh again, we're so different that it's almost amusing, he'd never let anyone ruin his life and I'm just waiting for it to happen, how nice it must be to live with him, but then I remember that he hasn't even asked about her, he doesn't really care that she's suffering behind the wall, his love is charming and insubstantial, a passing affair, and I compare him to the tense, serious Udi, but his love didn't last either, what difference does it make if it passed after two and a half days or two and a half decades?

The nurse who comes out of the room glances curiously at our embrace next to the window, you can go in to her now, she says to me, but I prefer to send him, you go first, it will help her more, and when he disappears inside, nervously dragging his feet, I sit down on a dirty chair in the deserted corridor, before my eyes I seem to see their voices weaving to and fro like the strands of a shawl, her moans of pain, his attempted reassurance, and between them the echo of the baby's rapid pulse, like a divine oracle, thundering in the air, who will bring this baby up, who will push his carriage, who will get up at night when he cries, certainly not me, why am I clinging to their lives like this, I've done my job, I brought her here, and now I can go, I must go, and I try to stand up but I am overcome by exhaustion, as if I haven't slept for years, and I lean against the wall and close my eyes. The proximity of the new life, this new family painfully coming into being, envelops me in a childish security, as if someone is watching over my sleep, and I who struggle to fall asleep night after night in my own bed fall into a deep sleep on the plastic chair in the busy corridor, my ears assailed by snatches of conversation and shouts, hurried steps and cries of joy, sobs and scoldings, and nothing disturbs me like Udi's breathing by my side, the light of his reading lamp, and I feel like a little girl in a big house, the pampered youngest child of aging parents, with lots of brothers and sisters, fathers and mothers, with everything full of bustling life, abundant and benevolent. One of my beloved big brothers comes up to me and strokes my hair, his lips are on mine and he pushes a bittersweet marzipan tongue into my mouth, spreading the sweetness throughout my mouth, and I suck his tongue slowly, to make it last, feeling my body open, I'll lie with him here on the bench in front of everybody, we're all one family after all, but now footsteps approach and he lets go of my wet lips, sits down next to me and bows his head, and I put my hand on his shoulder, how is she, I ask as if we're talking about our daughter, and he says, she's okay now, the baby's born.

Congratulations, I say emotionally, and he looks at me doubtfully and sighs, if you insist, and I ask, how much does he weigh, who does he look like, and he grins, he looks like me but he weighs a little less, for the time being, and I laugh joyfully, exulting in the general breaching of boundaries, from the moment my closed little family broke up I have felt as if everything touches me, everything belongs to me, this baby is mine too, this man is mine too, the young woman inside is mine, and I am ready to contribute Noga to the pot, as far as I'm concerned she can be his too, for this is the way to alleviate the suffering of the world, to heal its wounds, thanks to me he was with her when she gave birth, and how will he be able to give up the baby after being present at its birth? For a moment I feel a gnawing doubt, I wonder what Hava would have to say about these innovations, but I immediately banish her from my thoughts, only those who have known sorrow know how to alleviate it, and I rise with difficulty to my feet, my fingers on his head, combing his hair in pleasant intimacy, I'm going to see her and the baby, I say, and he smiles, just don't stay there forever, we still have a lot of work to do, and I ask in surprise, what work? And he says, the house I'm building for you, we haven't finished working on the plans yet, and the smile I send him accompanies me into her room, a happy smile, surprised at its capacity for happiness.

Congratulations, Yaeli, I bend down to kiss her, a wet smell rises from her, a living, liquid smell of blood and soft, female inner organs, reminding me of the smell that came from Zohara, the smell that's accompanying Udi now, and she gives me a tired look, did your husband come home, and I say, no, whatever gave you that idea, and she says, you look radiant. I'm simply happy for you, I say quickly, I'm happy that it all went well, and she whimpers, it was awful, I thought I was dying, it was worse than I imagined, and I stroke her arm, still attached to the infusion, but it was very quick, hardly two hours, sometimes it can go on for days you know. Perhaps it's easier to bear when you want the baby, she whispers, for me it was completely hideous, and I look around, where is he, I have to see him, and she says, they took him to do some test, they'll bring him back in a minute. Did you try to feed him, I ask enthusiastically, peeking at the top of her breasts exposed by opening of her robe, and she says, not really, it's not for me, and puts her hand protectively on her breasts. It's difficult in the beginning, I say, but you get used to it in a couple of days, you have to try, and she sighs, her eyes are red with effort, her face as pink and soft as the robe she is wearing, reminding me of a flower I once saw, a flower that looked like a person.

But how do I know if it's the beginning or the end, she suddenly bursts out, I'm not at all sure if he'll still be with me in a few days' time, I don't know whether to start breast-feeding him or not, I haven't decided if I'm going to keep him at all, don't you understand? I am appalled, she's not going to destroy my new family, and rudely pushing aside all the careful questions I have been trained to ask I say firmly, almost sternly, what are you talking about, I thought it was all clear now, Mica was here for the birth, he'll be the baby's father, even if he doesn't live with you, he'll help you financially, and I'll help you too, you won't be alone, my daughter can baby-sit sometimes, and your parents will also get used to the idea in the end, it will be hard but believe me that it's much harder to give up your baby, it will haunt you all your life. I don't know, she wails, I don't know him yet, I won't even recognize him among all the other newborn babies, I could leave here tomorrow as if nothing has happened, a few weeks' diet and that's that, I could continue my studies and forget about it, and maybe in a few years, when the circumstances are right, I can have a proper family, I haven't got the strength to bring up a baby now, it's doesn't suit me at all, but I persevere, I can't stop myself, it's clear to me that I have to prevent a terrible mistake from happening, it seems to you now that you don't have the strength, you're still weak from the birth, you'll see that the baby will give you strength, you'll be able to continue your studies, you'll manage, think of the alternative, how every baby you see in the street might be him, and later on every child, every teenager, it will haunt you all your life, and when you have a family it will be even more painful, because then you'll realize what you gave up and you won't be able to forgive yourself, just think how whenever you see Mica you'll both be tortured by the memory of your baby, whom you could have loved together.

But I don't intend to see Mica anymore, she announces defiantly, and I turn pale, why, he came to be with you at the birth like you wanted, I'm not prepared to play down my achievement, and she says, it was actually seeing him here that opened my eyes, I saw that he really disgusted me, his whole being revolts me, I always thought it was difficult to guess what he really felt, but today I understood that he simply isn't capable of feeling, only of amusing himself, he wasn't here with me really, only nominally, I'm sick of nominally, and I listen to her astounded, I feel as if I'm hearing a poor evaluation of my son from his teacher, a stern warning, which threatens me too, with the taste of his marzipan still in my mouth, and just then the doctor comes in and asks me to leave the room, and I take a piece of paper out of my bag and write my home number down on it, call me if you need anything, I say, I'll come again this evening or tomorrow.

I rush out of the room, see him standing at the end of the corridor with a cup of coffee in his hand, shit, he says, I burned myself, these plastic cups melt in your hands, and I hold out my hand and in a strange kind of ceremony he deposits the boiling cup in it and I actually enjoy the sudden heat, which reminds me of the way here, the terrible, solemn way, eagerly swallowing the tasteless drink, and he says, leave that, let's go and have some real coffee, and I look at him disapprovingly, I haven't got the time, Mica, I have to get back to work, it's almost midday, the sentence she pronounced on him falls onto his head like pigeon droppings, wet and degrading. We still haven't summed up the situation, he tries again, give me an hour of your time, for the baby's sake, and I agree, walking next to him in silence, unable to make up my mind, hostile to him one minute and hostile to her the next, for being hostile to him, in a state of confusion I drive behind his car again, how quickly the harmony has collapsed even in my new family, I seem to have lost him and I swing between regret and relief, but at the junction he's waiting faithfully, waving his hand at me and immediately disappearing into a completely new street, it seems to have just been tarred, carpets of asphalt unroll before us, an old man with a tin of paint in his hand is painstakingly painting the white stripes of the pedestrian crossing. Where are we, I've never been here before, at the side of the road pale stone buildings are going up, some of them already capped with red roofs, but most of them bareheaded, bald, empty-eyed, sick skeletons, has he gone out of his mind, why has he brought me to this desolate, exposed building site, shadeless, treeless, only dug-up, ravaged ground, scaffoldings, huge cranes, and all around frightened virgin hills, waiting their turn.

At the end of a road which has not yet been tarred he stops, next to a half-finished building, and I open my window, is this an abduction, I ask, and he laughs, something like that, and pulls me out of the car, dragging me behind him into the building, an enormous dog appears from the back barking loudly and I recoil, cringing with the pain of my ankle which is about to be bitten, you had it coming, I say to myself, you had it coming, but all of a sudden the dog turns into a harmless pet, fawning at Mica's feet, begging to be stroked. Calm down, Elijah, he says and looks at me from the corner of his eye, enjoying this demonstration of his mastery, how can anybody call a dog Elijah, and I follow him into a naked, unpainted stairwell, narrow planks mark the stairs and we hold on to the ropes that in the fullness of time will turn into a steady banister, for a moment I am ready to believe that we are a young couple coming to see the progress on their new home, devoting profound thought to every floor tile. At the top of the stairs is a magnificent door, and he takes a bunch of keys out of his pocket and opens it wide and I look round in astonishment, in the middle of this wasteland a perfect doll's house has grown up, beautifully furnished, there's even a bowl of red apples on the living room table. What is this, I ask, who lives here, you? Where have you been hiding, he laughs, it's a model apartment, haven't you ever seen a model apartment before? I shake my head, stepping mesmerized between rooms offering me their perfection, this is Noga's room and this is the master bedroom, and next to it another furnished child's room, who will it be for, where will I get a child for this room, and suddenly my spirits fall, the presence of the child I never had stops my breath, what have I to do with this perfect apartment when I myself am still so imperfect and incomplete, and I go back to the living room overlooking the hills, where he is sitting and smoking proudly, do you like it, he asks, I built it, and I nod silently, she doesn't want him anymore, I remember, he isn't capable of feeling, only of amusing himself. So what are we doing here, I ask, a blood clot of hostility beginning its journey through my body, and he says, don't you think that at our age we have the right to a little privacy, or perhaps you prefer necking opposite the nurses' room, and I say, I don't know if I want to neck at all, I can't stand that word. Forget the semantics, he says, let me make love to your body, and he gets up and pulls me behind him into the vast bedroom, the parents' unit, he calls it, what a threatening word, almost military. Have you ever done it in a model apartment, he asks, and I say, never, and there's no chance I will either, and he smirks, never say never, I've got your number, you don't know what you're capable of, give me a month and you won't recognize yourself, and I stand lost in front of the magnificent bed, a fine layer of dust covers it like lace, giving the room a ghostly air, even his black hair is already becoming covered with pale specks, adding years to his age.

Mica, I say quietly, picking fleas of dust from his hair, you fathered a baby today, don't you realize that? And he sniggers, do I have a choice in the matter? Of course I realize it, and you're my present, I deserve a present, don't I, and I say, you're a baby yourself, you don't deserve anything, it's your turn to give now, not to receive. But that's all I thought of during the entire birth, he grumbles, I thought of how I would bring you here and you'd give me a present, you know that I was only there for your sake, and I sigh, she was right, she was right, only I am wrong all the time, and I sit down defeated on the edge of the bed, seeing his shoulders growing broader his face growing bigger as he comes closer to me, his smile is enormous, exposing strong canine teeth, in a minute a bark will escape from his throat, the giddy bark of the dog Elijah. Leave me alone, I push him away, and he says, offended, what's the matter with you, I thought we'd celebrate the baby's birthday together, who do you want me to celebrate it with, my wife? And I think again of the tanned foot kicking me right in the groin. Why are you crying, he asks in surprise, I promise you it will be all right, I'll go and visit the baby, I'll pay child support, I'm even prepared to go to bed with her occasionally if you insist, what else do you want of me? I look outside, the almost imperceptible movement of a withered branch fills me with sorrow, but it isn't a branch, it's a sharp iron rod covered with rust, how dangerous, I don't know what I want, but that's something else entirely, an inexpressible wretchedness floats in the air between us, the wretchedness of a baby nobody wants, of his mother who is too young, of the tanned leg that will never reach the edge of the picture, and I say, it's all wrong, Mica, don't you see? I should never have come here with you, I should never have made love with you yesterday, I've never slipped up so badly in my life.

He pulls away from me, an unpleasant expression on his face, cut the sanctimonious bullshit, if you're prepared to pay the price you can do anything you like, I'll pay the price when my kids find out they have a baby brother from another mother, when my wife finds out, it isn't easy but I'm not complaining, I prefer living my life the way I do, the main thing is to keep boredom at bay, and when I saw you yesterday with that hungry smile of yours I thought you were like me, I didn't think you'd drop out so quickly. But Mica, I say quietly, I have no idea if I'm like you, I have no idea if I'm like me, I lived for so many years with one man, I was shut up in our life, everything narrowed down to such an extent that all I could see was myself in relation to him, not as an independent being, you know how many questions I didn't even get to ask myself? And he looks at me doubtfully, you know, he says, yesterday when you told me that your husband had left you I thought he must be an idiot, but now I understand him completely, and I feel my cheeks burning as if a hundred matches have been lit inside them, you understand him? What's that supposed to mean?

Listen to me before you get insulted, he scolds, and I await his words as if my life depends on them, but he keeps me waiting, opens his mouth and immediately shuts it again, imprisoning the words behind the walls of his teeth, look how you try to control things, he says in the end, pointing in the air as if the proof lies here, in this apartment where nobody lives, you have some pious model in your head and you try to fit all of us into it, even me, Yael, people you scarcely know, you imagine that you're a model woman, and that you deserve a model life in return, but there's no such thing and never will be, and nevertheless we're entitled to live, and even enjoy life, you and me, and even your husband, he's entitled to live without feeling guilty all the time for not being a model husband or father or whatever the hell you wanted of him, because you're not perfect either, and you could even see that as an advantage, you're allowed to be jealous, to hate, to cheat, even to betray the trust of your self-righteous profession once in a while, as long as you're honest with yourself, instead of holding yourself up as some kind of saint, you understand what I'm saying, and he looks at me and grins, okay, end of lecture, we've reversed roles, now let's see you build a house like this.

I stare at the dust hovering in the air between us, soon it will cover us as it might the antique furniture in an enchanted castle, pieces of furniture that were once living, flawed human beings, and a wave of longing for Udi sweeps me up me so that I can hardly breathe, I feel as if a clenched fist in the depths of my body has suddenly relaxed, declaring a remission of debts, for one blessed, thrilling moment ledgers full of microscopic writing are wiped out before my eyes, and I get up quickly as if he's waiting for me at home and I have to tell him something important, something urgent that will make him very happy, where did I put my bag, but when I find it I stop in my tracks, because my house is empty, the good news will have to wait, and in the meantime I am left with the bad, with a strange man moving restlessly on the bed, flat out and helpless as a cripple knocked off his feet. Give me a hand, he requests, and I reach out to help him up but he pulls me down on top of him. Want a model fuck? he asks brightly, as if this is the first time the words have crossed his lips, and I say, definitely not, and he sniggers, I see I've offended you, let me make it up to you, and I say, you can never make it up to me, and he breathes hot air into my ear which shivers with pleasure, I'm making it up to you by making you sin, you have to sin in order to be able to forgive yourself.

I already sinned yesterday, I say sulkily, and he says, but yesterday you didn't know it, and I'm already giggling, his charm softens the harsh words still thundering in the air of this room which has no history, like Adam and Eve we are the first to laugh here, and the laughter turns into moans of pleasure, now he lifts my long skirt and finds his way, quickly and matter-of-factly this time, as if he has one point to clarify, and I hold on to his neck, he is a visitor in my life, I suddenly understand, come for a short visit, he can't be detained, why should I detain him. What's wrong, he asks, turning me round with a strong movement, and I look at the expanse of his face, growing misty in front of my eyes, we won't see each other again, I whisper, and he says, why not, it's up to you, and I shake my head stiffly, tears splash from my eyes, I have to go on, alone, no man will fill the void, and it isn't the void that Udi left behind him, but the void I myself left in my life, I who chose him and not me, I chose him in the dawn of my youth in order to exhaust my strength on him, to distract myself from my own being, from everything buried alive and begging inside me. What's the wonder that he left me, if I too had abandoned myself, many years before, an abandonment no less cruel, which in fact dictated his, and I look at the open mouth, the white teeth, the wrinkles between the eyes, engraved at a precise slant like ancient Hebrew writing, I will never

try to decipher my fate in this face, the vicissitudes of my life in the
waves of pleasure washing over it, this trap was not meant for me.
I'll have to leave you hungry, he laughs, so that you'll come again,
and he suddenly thrusts me away and hoists me up in the air, but I
cling to him, pulling off his shirt, the transience of the moment fills
me with sticky, vociferous lust, his chocolate shoulders break into
blocks around me, what's the point of building towers, they all collapse in the end, the higher they are the more painful their fall, and
I am content with random blocks of sweetness, and this too is more
than I deserve, and it's better this way, how pleasant it is to get rid
of one's burdensome sense of justice, how pleasant to surrender, to
live in absolute accord with the flaws of reality.

With sudden appetite I lick his stomach, his flesh is warm, our
teeth meet in a strong bite, a tooth for a tooth, what's the point of
pretending, only pain consoles, his teeth wander over my body, at
the bottom of the slender ankle where I imagined feeling the dog's
bite I feel a shiver of pleasure. His hands press my thighs apart,
making room for his fingers, his tongue, it seems as if he is trying to
split my body in two, why are you fucking me, he suddenly asks, his
hand hushing the stirring animal between my legs, go on, tell me,
I haven't got all day, I've got a new baby, I've got a wife and children, and I whisper, just because I am, I'm fucking you for no reason at all, and he smiles in satisfaction, stopping with his broad penis
the mouth of the animal that moans with pleasure, it seems to me
that I should weep, but instead wild laughter escapes my mouth, in
all my life I've never allowed myself to do anything for no reason, I
thought I was intended for other things, and he pants above me,
his face turned to the bare hills, which bathe it in a strange light,
the weak, disturbing light of the moon at midday, just because, he
whispers into my mouth, I like those words, and suddenly he freezes,
his face turns pale, as pale as Udi when he was sick, but then he
collapses on top of me with a sigh of relief, not bad, he groans, you
learn fast, Na'ama, there's hope for you yet.

In a minute we'll get up and gather up our bones, like picking up objects scattered about the house, we'll shake the cover of the model bed and spread it out with four hands, we'll separate the muddle of our clothes which are mixed up together like a ball of colored Play-Doh, we'll leave the new suburb to the mercy of the bulldozers and the banging of the hammers and the long shadow of the cranes, and at the door he'll say to me, when your husband comes back you should move into a new house, I'd be happy to design it for you, you'll see what a great bedroom I'll build you, and I'll say, he won't come back, why should he come back?

Twenty

Is she waiting for me or is it just a coincidence that she's standing at the entrance to the shelter, a formidable sentry, her clumsy body draped in festive black, her glasses magnifying her eyes, Na'ama, she spits out in a hurry, as if my name is disgusting to her, I have to go and get the new girl's signature, and I say in horror, get Yael's signature? But she decided to keep the baby!

Really? Hava twists her lips in sour, false surprise, how do you know? And I stammer, she told me right after the birth, I was there with her, and her voice pounces on me again, seizing hold of my body from the soles of my limp feet to the top of my steaming head, she told you? Are you sure she told you, or perhaps you told her?

We talked about it, I say evasively, it was quite clear in her case, don't you think? and she cuts in, her flabby cheeks quivering like a hungry bulldog's, it really makes no difference what I think, Na'ama, but it makes no difference what you think either, our role is to help the girl understand what she thinks, or have you forgotten?

I haven't forgotten, but I wanted to help her more, I falter, pressing my sunglasses to my eyes, in a minute the tears, my detestable enemies, will line up against me in transparent battalions, maliciously betraying everything I'm trying to hide. Helping more is helping less, she pronounces, overidentification is destructive, have you forgotten what our role is here? Unless we're able to step back we can't help them, your identification with her was destructive, because it stemmed from false motives, you were trying to solve your own problems through her, you were trying to help yourself, not her.

Stunned I stare at her surprising décolletage, lying right in front of my eyes, whitish, strewn with babyish pink freckles, skin that had aged in hiding, without seeing the sun, completely different from the rough texture of her arms, and in a crushed voice I say, even if you're right, she mustn't give up the baby, I have to go to her and try to repair the damage, but Hava puts out a sturdy arm and bars my way, I'm sorry, Na'ama, she specifically asked for you not to come, she doesn't want to see you again, she only wants to see me. Good, she glances smugly at her glittering gold watch, I'm late, wait for me here, I have a few more things to say to you, and she goes out of the gate, leaving my face on fire, and I watch her with hostility, is this what she got all dressed up for? Waddling like a goose on her high heels, cramming her fat into a cocktail dress with a ridiculous décolletage, to see Yael making the mistake of her life, a young, capricious girl, who would never forgive herself as long as she lived.

I hear her starting the engine indignantly, turning the back of her brand-new car toward me, maybe I should get in my car and follow her, what have I got to lose now, I can't let Yael sign those papers, but her arm has remained behind her, unequivocal as a red light, gluing me to the steps, I'm the one who made the mistake of my life, how could I have said those things to Yael, imposing my views on her, all I did was incite her against me, both by what I said and by what I did, and especially by what she still doesn't know I did. Everything I meant for the best has turned into the worst, and maybe I didn't even mean well, maybe I wanted to make her rebel so that she would remain as empty-handed as me, I tried at one and the same time to live her life and to empty it of content, I took her man and tried to lay my hands on her baby too, it's all my fault that she's giving it up, today she'll sign the papers and tomorrow she'll return to her previous life, what did she say, a couple of weeks' diet and that's that. I could have given Noga up too, those first months were so hard, day after day, night after weary night, surrender after surrender until there was nothing left of me, until I was a dried-up, empty shell, and sometimes from the depths of that prison of exhaustion, and boredom, and depression, I would have a vision of freedom, of kindly people reaching out to me with imploring hands, give her to us, in a single moment you'll be free, and she'll be happy, and I put her squirming body into their hands and wait for a divine silence to descend, all I want now is to sleep, but before I can change my mind her demanding wails wake me up, she hasn't gone anywhere, she's here forever, a heavy weight on my heart, growing heavier from day to day, our quarrels like wreaths around her head. Be more sensitive to her, I would scold him, spend more time with her, and he would immediately rebel, don't tell me what to do, you're not such a saint that you can preach to me, and she lost the most, robbed of all that should have been hers. You're right, Udi, I'm not such a saint, why was I so insistent that you love her if not to cover up my own dull, hesitant love, it was from her I escaped then to that rooftop studio on top of the tall building, from her never-ending demands, her hands clutching my neck, sitting there bathed in his admiration, wallowing in my own self-love, forgetting all about her. What kind of a family did I build, with what hollow, eroded building blocks, how could I have been so stupid as to believe that it would endure, and I stand up with difficulty, supporting myself on the bars of the gate, this was where I first saw Yael, her doe eyes fixed trustingly on mine, I didn't want to harm her, I only wanted her to love her baby, because I didn't succeed in loving mine. A car speeds past and I breathe a sigh of relief, it isn't Hava, not yet, but soon she'll be back, sweeping through the gate, the signed forms in her hand, a childless couple will win great happiness, wait for me, she said, I have a few more things to say to you, but I won't wait, Hava, I have to talk to myself first, every day I am assailed by astonishing, heartbreaking news, as if I am surrounded by prophets with the word of God on their lips, too many new truths are baring their teeth at me, if only I could calm them down like Mica calmed the dog Elijah on the deserted building site.

Hesitantly I open the shelter door, Anat sends me a worried look, she is sitting with the girls in a group discussion, all of them quiet as usual in the morning, pinned up on the notice board is their daily schedule, what does it have to do with me? I walk past them quickly and go upstairs to my office, saccharine pictures surround me provocatively, flaunting their hypocrisy, beautiful pregnant women hugging their bellies and looking serenely at the window, how did I stand it all these years, and in revulsion I strip the wall, tear up the pictures, and on one of the scraps I write a note to Hava, and put it quickly on her desk before I can change my mind.

In one of the cupboards I find a plastic bag and I empty the contents of my drawers into it, how little I have accumulated over the years, a few letters the girls sent me after leaving the shelter, rare photographs of babies in the proud arms of their mothers, it's only thanks to you that I'm a mother, someone wrote me on the back of a photograph, and I am terrified by the explicit words and the threatening opposite hiding within them. Without a word of good-bye I make for the door, casting one final look at the girls sitting round Anat, threatening her with their unhappy stomachs, and she is trapped between them, boyish, solitary, and suddenly my anger against her sharpens like a bayonet, you're the first one who abandoned me, I hiss, who gave you the right to judge me so severely, you were never my friend if you could treat me like that, and I open the shelter's gates wide, like Udi I'm leaving home, with a little plastic bag in my hands, leaving with nothing after so many years. In urgent haste I get into the car and begin to drive, without knowing where I'm going, all I want is to be in motion, subject to clear rules, stopping at the red light like everyone else, slowing down when children cross the road. Here's the road to the hospital, only yesterday I drove here burning with fever, frantic, Yael lying on the backseat, a baby knocking at her door, at the door of the world, while I struggled with the lock with all my might, as if I were the gatekeeper, and now there's nothing for me to do here, wrapped in her pink robe she sits and signs the papers, giving up the baby she gave birth to forever, and it's all because of me, it's all because I wanted a family.

Above my head the sun goes up in flames, burning with fire but not consumed, it seems to have grown arms and legs and they beat me about the head and I try to defend myself, letting go of the steering wheel, behind me cars honk their horns impatiently, and I escape into a side street, I don't believe it, in my distraction I've landed up outside his office, his car lies calmly anchored by the curb, all kinds of people are sitting there, treading on the red carpet, planning their houses, and he spreads out his promising designs in front of them, undisturbed by the fate of his new baby, by tomorrow he'll have forgotten him, and her, and me, and I don't stop, only slow down for a minute, continuing my journey through the exhausted town, the streets are as familiar and tedious as people I once met and now have nothing to say to, and I hurry past them, so they won't recognize me, so they won't say, look, here's Na'ama. Here's that street, long and curved, for years I haven't dared to visit it, not even in my thoughts, and exactly in the middle of the curve stands his building, stooped like a tower children build on the carpet, and I stop there, staring at the black street, the asphalt has recently been renewed, covering the traces of my panic flight, only in me nothing has been covered, everything remains fixed in an impossible interim state, like a dying which has no end, cut off from the annihilating salvation of death.

I get out of the car and raise my eyes to the top of the building, where is the spiteful window that exposed my nakedness, my
disgrace, a sharp radiance rises from it, a single sun ray is refracted
on it, long and slender as the blade of a heavenly sword, and I study
the sight in astonishment, what can anybody see from the street,
barely a vague silhouette, unidentified limbs, what did he see that
morning, the landscape of his feverish brain, the frontiers of his
mind, and I, like a trained circus animal, jumped through the hoops
of his flaming consciousness, cringing at his feet, expecting his
punishment as if it were a prize. He didn't see anything, he couldn't
have, I confessed before he asked, I turned myself in rashly, giving
him tremendous power, I was so afraid of my own.

This is how I remembered these steps, steep and crooked, trip-
ping up my excited feet, I'm coming back to you my dearest, empty-
handed, I was so afraid of remembering you that I never forgot you,
I was so afraid of loving you that I lost the ability to love. What
will I say to him when he opens the door, the paintbrush in his hand
and his eyes narrowed, hiding his surprise, show me that painting,
I'll ask, let me see myself beautiful for a minute.

Outside his door I stop, steady my breath, it was always blank,
mysterious, but now there's a sign stuck to it, Na'ama, it says in a
curly script, and I stare at it wide-eyed, for a moment I think it's a
letter meant for me, who knows how many years it's been waiting,
and I feel it in excitement, try to rip it from the door, but the sign
is blank, it hides nothing, only my name is written on it. He must
have left, he doesn't live here anymore, and some other Na'ama has
taken his place, my place, but I refuse to recognize her existence, it
seems to me that she must be me, and without any hesitation I knock
on the door, louder and louder, as if someone is sleeping in there
and I've been asked to wake them up, but no stir of life is heard from
the little apartment I loved so much, Na'ama doesn't open the door,
and I descend the stairs in growing disappointment and fall on his

mailbox, Na'ama Korman, it says, that's it, she isn't me, just a co-incidence that doesn't mean a thing.

Slowly I drive home, the car wheels groaning under the weight of my empty life, what's heavier, a sack of feathers or a sack of iron, there's nothing heavier than an empty sack, and I enter the stifling apartment, go straight to the bathroom as if I've returned from an exhausting journey and I'm filthy all over, fill the tub and sink into the water, letting my head fall back until it covers the roots of my hair. He didn't see me, everything could have been prevented, I brought it all on myself, I was so blind with guilt, how could I have failed to understand what was self-evident, that it was impossible to see someone standing at the window from the street, I was sure that if I recognized him it meant that he recognized me too, I didn't realize that we were two different entities, that my being was completely different from his, even though we were husband and wife. Dismayed by the freedom revealed to me among the paints and canvases, I preferred to live under a reign of terror, to pay the price of terror and not the price of freedom, and in return I paralyzed him with infinite anger, how suited we actually were, who but him would have succeeded so well at imprisoning me inside him, who but me would have succeeded so well at containing his weaknesses, with four busy hands we ruined our lives, in perfect harmony, while Noga looked on like a confused apprentice, observing our behavior with eyes like green grapes.

How I had enjoyed wallowing in his injustice to me all those years, even encouraging him to hurt me so as to experience its purifying force to the full, using Noga to make his life a misery, judging him, magnifying his guilt, paying him back with a terror of my own, coated with good intentions, don't preach to me, he said, you're not such a saint yourself. If only it were possible to rid life of guilt, that cunning secret counselor all of whose motives are malicious, to not bow beneath the burden of the other but to each peek from a different corner of the picture, and I drop my head and dive with my eyes open, coral reefs are hidden at the bottom of the bathtub, infinite riches, I could refuse to raise my head, ostracize my lungs, ignore my body's desire for the next breath, the primary desire, fiercer than any desire for a man, for the fruit of the womb, the desire to breathe, without expecting anything in return, to live in order to breathe, not in order to love, not in order to raise children, not in order to succeed, not in order to realize noble goals. I raise my head from the water and take a long, surprisingly joyful breath, gulping in the moist air, drunk on air I lift my foot and examine it forgivingly, the five short untidily arranged toes are happy to meet my face, this is the joy of the union between the two ends of the body, this is what remains to me, simply a body that wants to breathe, and all the rest is luxury, and it makes no difference if this man or that loved it, left it, just as the earth barely notices the footsteps of those who tread upon it, its only concern is for what is coming into being in its depths, the creeping of the boiling magma beneath its thin crust, the slow shifting, millions of years old, of continents yearning to be reunited.

Wrapped in a towel I go to the closet and absentmindedly take out the gray pantsuit, I wore it only once, when I went with him to the hospital, and it seems that the smell of that morning still clings to it, the smell of terror and surprise, and at the same time a secret anticipation of change, and to my surprise it fits me again, turning my body into an official, uniformed body, hard to hurt, and I comb my wet hair, spray myself with perfume, as if I am on my way to a decisive meeting, but without any oppressive tension. I enjoy making myself beautiful, taking pleasure in the body that has become attached to itself again, and when I go out into the midday heat I'm not sure where I'm heading, I follow snatches of conversation lingering in the street, the remains of a friendly smile, and suddenly I find myself in front of the café I haven't dared go into for years, walking past with stolen, slavish looks, but now I open the door, how it's changed, black tables sliding on a shiny marble floor, not a trace remains of the heavy, old-fashioned furniture whose charm lay in the very fact that it did not set out to charm, of the wood-paneled walls that soaked up the seductive words of courtship. I order a glass of red wine, even though I have no apparent reason to celebrate, I've lost my husband and now my job, years of effort gone down the drain, and nevertheless currents of gaiety animate me, pulses of enjoyable liberation, and I order another glass, my head is spinning, through the plate glass wall the world looks confidence-inspiring, cars stream through the street like blood through the arteries, and people stream through the veins of the pavements. Order has descended on the world, a modest, neighborhood order, and it seems that even I have some small place within it, and then I see a familiar figure advancing, her slow steps slightly upsetting the order, because walking uphill is hard for her, the couple behind her are obliged to pause, and then to separate in order to pass her, but she doesn't notice, sunk in a complicated daydream, her eyes fixed on the place where the street and the pavement meet, her lips seem to be moving, what is she muttering there? I stand up and press myself to the glass, to sense her being from close up, a tall, sloppy little girl, her beauty unformed, her feet tending to turn absentmindedly toward the street, but she corrects herself immediately and gets back on course, and I stare at her receding back, slightly stooped, incredible that we are so connected, live together, sometimes even sleep in the same bed, and only when she walks away do I remember to call her, an uninhibited tipsy cry leaps from my throat, and she turns round in surprise, enters the cafe and approaches me suspiciously, Mother, what are you doing here? Why aren't you at work? Why are you all dressed up?

I hug her shoulders and lead her to the table, you finished early today too, didn't you, I say, and she says, yes, today the summer program ended, the long vacation has begun. The long vacation has begun for me too, I announce gaily, I left my job today, and she asks, really, why, and immediately takes fright, then what are we going to live on, we won't have any money, and I say, don't worry, I'll get severance pay, and afterward I'll find something, and she asks, but why, Mommy, and I sigh, it sounds like a cliché, but I have to take care of myself before I can take care of other people. She gives me a deep look and says, actually it sounds logical, Mommy, and I laugh, yes, banalities are usually more logical than most things, and I immediately order a toasted cheese sandwich and a cola for her, it feels good sitting opposite her, her face is tanned, emphasizing her rich eyes, two bottles of colored sand, and her cute nose is almost amusing, and her lips are so beautiful when she smiles. What are we going to do during the vacation, she asks, and already I feel threatened, what have I got to offer her, all her friends are probably taking trips in the country and abroad, whole families, I can never compete with them. We'll go to the pool, I answer hesitantly, we'll see movies, we'll read books, maybe we'll go to that hotel in the north where I went with Daddy, it's lovely there, and she says, yay, let's go there! And then she falls silent, examining me apprehensively, a modest happiness has joined us at our table, and we are both very wary, careful not to chase our new guest away by talking too loudly.

With a sigh I watch her muddled movements, already she has dropped her fork, giving me an ingratiating look, and right after that a piece of tomato stains her shirt, her cheeks are covered with toast crumbs, how sweet and funny she is when she eats, her innocent confidence that she is entitled to this food, that it will always be available to her, chewing with unaffected naturalness, feeling wanted as she eats. I fall enthusiastically on her leftovers and afterward we walk home arm in arm, a couple going home after a particularly successful blind date, and on the way she says, it's my birthday soon, and I tense, right, what do you want to do? And she says, just an ordinary party, I'll invite the whole class, we'll play the games we learned at summer camp, and I am cheered by her enthusiasm, apparently she is happier with her classmates now, but I don't dare ask, afraid to show my anxiety.

No problem, Nogi, I say, there's still lots of time, but in fact the time passes quickly, sometimes I remember in astonishment how much I used to get done in one day, because now the days slip by so fast, like silent, slippery eels, impossible to hold. We wake up late, usually I get up a little earlier, go to the stores for fresh rolls and vegetables and make us breakfast, Noga watches television and sometimes I join her, looking enviously at the well-groomed heads on the screen, their fame guards them like a sheepdog, anybody whose existence so many people are aware of can't just disappear, like us, where it sometimes seems that if we failed to wake up one morning nobody would notice our absence. Maybe only my mother, who lives her hollow life not far from us, sometimes invites us to supper, looks at us in silence, her lips with their crown of wrinkles sealed, letting us make friends without interfering. At noon we go to the pool, sink into the water facing each other with our eyes open, sunspots trembling between us, sheets of glorious blue unfurling in front of us, from time to time children from her class wave at Noga with a lazy hand, and I see her approaching them timidly, trying to join in their games, but quite soon her bare, defeated feet return to me, and I clam my lips shut, not allowing them to disturb my rest, it seems that the gates have closed, the wall has tightened around me, not like once, when it was as full of holes as a sieve and every anxiety moved in to live inside my soul. Now I am almost impermeable, and it is only when confronted by a baby in a carriage that I become as startled as if I have seen a ghost, examining it with bated breath, wondering if it is the tiny adopted Mica, veils of sorrow choke me and I hide behind the newspaper or a book, what's happening to her now, how is she coping with the loss, and when I think of my part in her tragedy I sink again but extricate myself with all my might, there are too many denunciations condemning me from outside, why should I rush to join in the chorus, I have to balance them from inside, otherwise I won't be able to survive.

We hardly talk, so many words have already been said, we should leave them to sink before casting new stones into the water, and for the time being we are content with what is growing up between us, a quiet, relaxed comradeship, her troubles are clear to me and mine are clear to her and we exist beyond them, not at their heart, not jumping into the fire like we used to but standing on the fringes of the great conflagration, keeping out of the way of the sparks. Sometimes it seems to me that these opaque, empty days are the happiest of my life, because I hardly feel anything, as if I am lying in the dentist's chair with my mouth open after the anesthetizing shot, knowing that charges of pain are exploding inside me but not feeling their full force, and it seems to me that if I only ignore them they will ignore me in exchange.

So this is how you all live, this is the great secret of your survival, this is what Zohara tried to show me, this is how Udi tried to rescue himself, this is how you all walk serenely down the bypass roads, and only I insisted on feeling everything, marching down the exposed highway on my flat feet, not missing a single nuance, digging up the festering emotions to the roots, and I wonder what Udi would say about my new, dormant existence, a daring revolt against the tyranny of feeling, I think of all the things I could tell him if he were here beside me now, about the baby given up for adoption because of me, about the gates of the shelter that had closed behind me, but immediately I remember, he wouldn't have listened, everything turned into a contest between us, every mistake of mine proved that he was better than me, every achievement was enlisted and appropriated to the ends of the inner struggle, we never saw each other as independent figures with the right to lives of their own, to failures, moods, everything was narrowed down to the stifling circle of the connection between us, we looked at each other from such close quarters that we didn't see anything, and at the same time we were distant, he had to travel to Tibet for me to feel close to him, and when Noga asks, what are you thinking about, Mommy, I say, nothing in particular.

Sometimes I think, maybe this silence is good for me and not for her, maybe I should try to get her to talk, it's strange that she's stopped talking about him, as if she never had a father, but I can't bring myself to do it, it appears that there is such a thing as can't, for so many years I thought I could do everything I had to do, and it turns out that I can't, I'm comfortable with our silence, and that's enough for the time being, but one night I find her sitting up awake in bed, spreading a crumpled page out on her knees. What's that, Nogi, I ask her, and she says, the letter Daddy left me before he went away, and I fall silent immediately, once I nearly set the house on fire to get hold of this letter, and now it's boring, irrelevant, I have no need to read it. Do you think that Daddy's all right, she asks, and I make haste to say, of course, why not, and she says, it's strange that he hasn't contacted us, maybe something's happened to him, and I put my hand on her tousled head, Nogi, you prefer worrying about him to being angry with him. But maybe something really has happened to him, how do you know it hasn't, she insists, planting a muffled anxiety in me, and I can't fall asleep, and reach out for the Bible lying rejected by his side of the bed, perhaps he left a letter for me too, perhaps it's hiding between the lines, and I page through it, where are the prophesies of consolation that came to my rescue then like a chorus of good friends, why are they hiding from me, and suddenly a swarm of stinging words pounce on me from the page, awakening the memory of an unforgivable insult, what did he say to me then, in the blooming garden of the hotel, on the last moment of the spring, the rare moment of our happiness, if you could call that fragile, burdensome creature by the name of happiness at all. I can't go up to the hotel with you, he said, I can't eat and drink and return by the way I came, I have to escape from here before someone makes me sin like they did the man of God, and now the story he found so threatening confronts me in all its wickedness, the story of the man of God who came out of Judah to Beth-el and prophesied the burning of the altar and the destruction of the sinful Beth-el, and God had forbidden him to eat bread or drink water there or to return by the way he came, but an old prophet from Beth-el tripped him up on purpose, I too am a prophet, he lied to him, and an angel of the Lord told me to bring you to my house, to give you food and drink. The man of God, who was already hungry and thirsty, was tempted to believe him, and while they were sitting at the table, eating and drinking, the word of the Lord was heard, thy carcass shall not come unto the sepulchre of thy fathers, for thou hast disobeyed the mouth of the Lord, and indeed, after he left there a lion met him by the way and slew him, and the old prophet buried him in Beth-el and he asked his sons to bury him by his side after he died, lay my bones beside his bones.

I put the book down angrily, indignant at the bitter fate of the man of God, who failed to pass the test, how could he have known that he was being lied to, how is it possible to distinguish between the word of the Lord and a lie, before my eyes I see in sharp focus the picture of Udi kneeling among the trees and prophesying, prophesying the destruction of our little family, not knowing that the false prophetess is already waiting at the door to our house, her hair venomous snakes, words of encouragement and reassurance on her smooth tongue, you're holding on to him too tightly, she said to me, you're crumbling him like a clod of earth, you have to let go, but the minute I let go she grabbed hold of him, dragging him behind her, pulverizing us all into gray crumbs. I feel the sheet next to me, for a moment it seems to me that his long bones are lying on the bed by my side, fast asleep, I mustn't wake them, but suddenly they sit up and begin to dance a farewell dance before my eyes, bowing and curtsying, creaking hollowly, and I stifle a scream, he's going to die there, in distant Tibet, his carcass will not come unto the sepulchre of his fathers, we'll never see him again, a malicious false prophecy removed him from our home, I have to change my life, he said, I've been given a warning here, how could he have known that he was being tested, and I jump out of bed and go to the porch, and look at the silent street, the bathing suits dripping above my head, giving off a misleading smell of wet dust, like the smell of the first rains.

Here I saw him walking away, the knapsack on his back, with a hoarse throat I tried to stop him, casting stones of anger and insult at him, how did he suddenly turn into my sworn enemy, on that morning in the blooming garden of the hotel, strangling our infant happiness, but a new understanding slowly covers the porch like a canopy of peace, he didn't sin, he shouldn't be punished because he didn't sin, he didn't eat or drink, he didn't return to our beautiful room in the hotel, to the huge, seductive bed, he obeyed the word of the Lord for all our sakes, for the sake of the purity of our little kingdom, perhaps this was the test and he passed it, so what if our holiday ended in depression and disappointment, perhaps a completely different logic lay hidden beneath the events that upset us so much, a deeper, even completely contradictory logic, because if he ever does come back, he will have to return by another way, to be another person, and I go back to the bedroom and page quickly through the book, eager to reach the moment when the prophecy of the man of God comes true, his carcass may have been buried in the earth but his prophecy remained, and here is King Josiah gathering to him the remnants of the house of Israel and purifying the land of its corruption, the Topheth in the valley of Hinnom, that no man might make his son or his daughter pass through the fire to Moloch, taking the bones out of the sepulchres and burning them on the altar at Beth-el, but the bones of the man of God who came out of Judah he does not touch, and they let his bones alone, together with the bones of the old prophet that came out of Samaria.

Before my eyes I see the desolate Kingdom of Israel, strewn with the rubble of the altars and the high places, testimony to its sins, its people exiled, turning their stiff necks on their country, on their homes where strangers were housed, like Udi roaming in strange landscapes, a strange baby on his back, and I wonder if he has another Udi inside him, that I never knew, that I managed to miss all these years, perhaps by my side he withers and by hers he blooms, and for a moment I observe his blooming with an aching heart, see him turning his head and laughing, and she looks at him admiringly, but there's nothing real in it after all, like there was nothing real in the spring flowers surrounding the hotel, struggling to hang on, refusing to accept their destiny, to astonish for a moment and then withdraw into little bulbs under the earth. A gust of compassion shakes me, when he lay here sick and suffering on this bed I was unable to feel compassion for him, and now that he is healthy, covering vast distances on his strong legs, a new woman by his side, I fill with compassion, I see his heart trying in vain to stretch, a too-narrow bridge between two receding banks, soon its remains will be swept away in the rushing river, and then his guilt will pounce on him like a hungry lion, greedily devouring the feast that has come its way, leaving only disappointing scraps, a disturbing memorial to what was and will never be again. You wanted to be loved, you wanted to be reconciled, but as long as you go on running you'll have no rest, merely the snatched sleep of an escaped prisoner, only if you confront the guardians of your mind face-to-face will you be able to be happy, or unhappy, but it will be your unhappiness, or your happiness, not Noga's, not mine, I'm out of the picture already, not even the heel of my foot peeps from it, I even feel sorry for Zohara, she's holding the remains of a ruined kingdom in her hands, and she still doesn't know it, who am I to blame her, I too am culpable, I removed a day-old baby from his mother's arms. I close the book and put it down on his side of the bed, on the pillow that was once his, I'll never find those soothing prophecies of consolation again, but when I am about to fall asleep I remember the last prophecy, demanding and binding as the last words of a dying man: Behold, I will send you Elijah the prophet before the coming of the great and dreadful day of the Lord, and he shall turn the heart of the fathers to the children, and the heart of the children to their fathers, lest I come and smite the earth with a curse.

It seems that I have just this moment fallen asleep but the room is already dazzling, the whole sun has crowded through one narrow slit in the blind, and Noga bursts into my bed, Mommy, get up, tomorrow's my birthday and we haven't bought anything yet, and I get up and dress myself wearily, the fate of the man of God trailing behind me incomprehensibly, how could he have known that the old prophet was lying to him, the word of God can break forth even from the mouth of an ass. Absentmindedly I buy snacks and balloons and modeling clay and all kinds of cutouts and stickers, and a few discs that Noga says are absolutely essential, and at home we play them one after the other, our silent house fills with rhythmic, discordant sounds, which disturb me at first but gradually give me a sense of relief, as if this is no longer my house and whatever happens in it is not my responsibility. From time to time she looks out of the corner of her eye at the silent telephone, do you think Daddy will remember my birthday, she asks, do you think he'll call tomorrow, and I think of the man of God, don't return by the way in which you came, the obligation to change is a divine commandment, but who knows what change is required, and what it costs, you can only know when the false prophecy is refuted, when the lion is already sticking its teeth in your flesh. I stand at the window and look at the street, yellow leaves speckle it, giving it a new air of expectancy, is there another way to come here, not by this street, to enter the house not through this door, and she says, Mommy, why don't you answer me? And I say crossly, I don't know if it's even possible to phone from there, but she keeps on, do you think that he'll remember? How do I know if he'll remember, I say, and I stare at her distractedly, I imagine that if he remembers you'll know.

In the kitchen I surround myself with sugar and cocoa, eggs and milk and flour, silently preparing her birthday cake, a choco-late cake in the shape of a heart, like she requested, and the house fills with a pungent family smell, and only in the evening do I re-member that we forgot to buy decorations for the cake, and I hurry to the supermarket, vacillating in front of the shelf with the cake decorations, what should I get, colored candies, or marzipan teddy bears, or gilded hearts, maybe that would be too much, decorating a heart-shaped cake with hearts. A hard object suddenly pushes me from behind, so that my forehead bangs into the shelf, and I turn round to protest to the person who's just bumped me with a shop-ping cart, but then I see that it isn't a shopping cart, it's a baby carriage, and the baby begins to wail, and I drop my eyes, I can't see such things, they remind me of Yael, and suddenly I start, is it my imagination or is it really Yael, with her hair dyed a new color, a demure honey-brown instead of that violent red, with a body that has shrunk beyond recognition, is it really her, can it be possible that she changed her mind, that she took the tiny Micah home with her, to be his mother forever. I follow her stealthily, peeping in tre-mendous excitement between the shelves, afraid of being seen, where has she disappeared to, I scan all the aisles and she isn't there, and when I am on the point of giving up I suddenly see her next to the cash register, in tight jeans and a tee-shirt, slender as if she's never given birth in her life, putting dairy products on the counter one after the other, and next to them baby bottles, and diapers, and milk powder, is it her or isn't it, but when she looks in my direction I have no more doubts, those eyes can only be hers, and I freeze between the shelves until she moves away, and then I flee, running and crying all the way home, my arms fluttering in the summery air like broken wings, and when I reach our street I sit down on a bench, trying to calm down before I go home, my joy mixed with a wild fear, as if I have been saved from a traffic accident and only now can I permit myself to realize how terrible it could have been, she didn't give the baby up, she's going to raise it herself, the catastrophe I almost brought down on her head has been averted, Hava succeeded in repairing the damage, in changing her decision, why didn't she tell me, I might have finished my life without knowing.

I drag my feet upstairs, open the door to Noga's surprised face, what happened, she asks, and I mumble, nothing, and lie down on the sofa and burst into tears, actually something good happened, I was saved by a miracle, but she isn't convinced, tell me everything, Mommy, I'm going to be ten tomorrow, you can tell me. I made a mistake with one of the girls at the shelter, I was afraid that I'd caused her to give up her baby, and now I saw her with him, and she looks at me in astonishment, almost in contempt, I don't understand how you could blame yourself, even if she did give him up it couldn't have been because of you, it's such a big decision, no one person could have had such an influence on her, could anyone have persuaded you to give me up? And I sob, of course not, Nogi, but it's not the same thing, I was older when you were born, and I had Daddy. And now that you don't have Daddy would you give me up? she asks with brave, matter-of-fact seriousness, her face resolute, as if ready for any answer, and I say, are you crazy, without you my life wouldn't be worth living.

Was that the reason you left your job, she asks, and immediately announces happily, so now you can go back, and I shake my head, I don't know, Nogi, I'm not sure at all, and she asks, where are the decorations for the cake, and I hold my empty hands out to her, I forgot, I was so confused that I forgot, and she puts her hands in mine, never mind, we can do without the decorations, and I hug her, crushing her in my arms, my darling Nogi, I love you so much, and she says, and I love you, I'm glad you didn't give me up.

I take the telephone into the bedroom and close the door behind me, a crisp, authoritative voice answers my call, what strength that woman has, even at the end of the day she's brisk and energetic, and I sob, Hava, I wanted to thank you, I really appreciate what you did, you saved my life, and she says in surprise, Na'ama, I was just thinking about you, she doesn't even ask what I'm thanking her for, and I understand that we'll never speak of it again. What were you thinking about me, I ask, and she says, Hani just phoned to speak to you, she's not in good shape, she can't pull herself together, and I'm surprised that she should mention it at all, once the girls leave the shelter we always refer them to agencies in the area where they live for help, to distance them from us, from the living memory of what they have given up, and I remember Hani with sadness, the way she called me that night, the pink sweater unraveled in her hands, I didn't keep my promise to her, I didn't bring her a new sweater, and all of a sudden I feel an urgent need to see her, I have so many things to say to her, I should have been there for her after she parted from her baby, how can we send them on their way like that and never see them again, when the worst is still waiting for them, to live hour by hour in the shadow of the renunciation, we should help them, make sure that they don't punish themselves for the rest of their lives through barrenness or unhappy marriages.

So how are things at home, Hava asks, how's your daughter, and I am surprised that she of all people, who is always so busy, wants to continue the conversation. My daughter's all right, I reply, it's her birthday tomorrow, and she says emphatically, congratulations, as if this is some great achievement, and immediately asks, and what about Udi, and I say, Udi's gone abroad, I haven't heard from him for a long time, and she says, remember, you're allowed to look back only on the condition that your feet carry you forward, and I say, don't worry, Hava, he won't come back.

That's not the question, she scolds, the question is whether you'll let yourself go back to the same kind of relationship, and I interrupt her, you may not believe it but I hardly ever think about it, it sometimes seems to me that I haven't even reached my prime yet, and she sighs in satisfaction, I knew you were stronger than you thought, just remember that change is never completed, it's a daily battle, not to let anyone take over your life, don't forget it, she adds with pathos, as if she's parting from me forever, and I feel a sharp beak of anxiety pecking at my head, Hava, are you okay, I ask, is everything all right?

I'm going into the hospital tonight for surgery, she says calmly, I won't be here for a few weeks, and I say in a near shout, is it anything serious? And she says, something curable, you mean? I don't know, I'm always optimistic, and I press my lips to the receiver, I'm so sorry, Hava, I didn't know you were sick, and she says, nobody knew, it's been going on for a few years now, and I ask, is there anything I can do to help?

Yes, she says, I want you to come back to us, Anat won't be able to manage without you, we need your soul in the shelter, and I sigh dismissively, my soul has only brought me trouble, I'm trying to get rid of it, and she exclaims, don't even think of it, you mustn't despise a gift you've been given, even if it may sometimes seem a burden, and I say nothing, seeing before my eyes the beautiful, secret building, sad girls going up and down the stairs like angels, an extra heart beating next to theirs, how I've missed them, and I whisper hoarsely, I'll come back, Hava, of course I will.

In the morning I hear a strange rustling sound, as if dry bones are crumbling in my bed, and I see on the sheet next to me fragile yellow leaves that have blown in through the window, and I count them in excitement, unbelievable, exactly ten leaves, one for each year, because after all it's my birthday too, the birthday of my motherhood, and I arrange them round me and contemplate them, filled with triumphant joy, as if I have defeated the summer with my own hands and crowned the autumn, not because I prefer autumn but because only this stubborn cycle of change can bring us consolation, and I answer the summons of the telephone eagerly, and hear Amos saying clearly that he's going down to Eilat with his parents and won't be able to come to the birthday party, and Ron and Asaf won't be coming either because they're gone abroad, and when Noga wakes up Nitzan calls to announce that she has the flu, and we pounce nervously on the balloons, filling them with hot, angry air, tying them together like gangs of dangerous prisoners.

Noga is pale with tension and when she touches one of the balloons it bursts, and we both recoil in alarm as if a car bomb has exploded in our living room, and after another one bursts, all by itself, the brightly colored balloons become our enemies and we tread between them suspiciously, not daring to breathe. Noga takes a quick shower and allows me to comb her curls, and then she stands in front of the mirror, trying on one garment after the other, her entire wardrobe strewn on the floor, and then she comes to me imploring, her nipples opening in front of me like flowers awakened by the sun, I haven't got anything to wear, she's almost crying, did Daddy take all his clothes? It seems so, I sigh, look in our closet, and she kicks the doors angrily, how could he not have thought of me, how could he do this to me, she sits on the living room floor and cries, and I bend down to her, perhaps there's still something pretty among your own clothes, I can't believe that you've outgrown everything, but I immediately take myself back to the kitchen, I mustn't be dressing her and giving her advice now, it's her business. I only like wearing his clothes, she wails, kicking the sofa, which immediately responds with a thick cloud of dust, and I pretend to be busy, opening and closing the fridge, until silence falls and after nearly an hour she emerges from her room wearing a blue velvet blouse I once bought her, her wayward curls caught in a rubber band.

You look lovely, I exclaim, see how the color brings out your eyes, and how beautiful you are when your hair's off your face, and I can see that she's pleased, together we make the rounds of the rooms for a final checkup, scissors and glue and colored paper and beads and modeling clay in every corner, in the fridge the undecorated black chocolate heart waits, eleven candles stuck in its chambers, surrounded by bottles of soft drinks like armed guards. Plates

of snacks are dotted over the table and one of the discs is already
playing loudly, almost drowning out the sound of the telephone,
and I bite my lips, praying that it's not another cancellation, and
hear Noga saying in a dull voice, that's okay, never mind, another
time, as if she's having another birthday party tomorrow. Marva has
a soccer practice she can't miss, she whispers, and I think of the
children who don't even bother to call, and the closer the time
comes the more I clench my lips, should I say something or not,
lance the boil or let it fester, what would Hava do now, probably
nothing, for there is nothing I can do to comfort her. She tries to
look calm, but I can see how tense she is, blinking nervously, looking at her watch, and I go out to the porch with a cigarette, sit down
next to the balustrade in spite of the heat, from there I can keep an
eye on what's happening, see everything a minute before she does.

I hear laughter approaching and immediately look down, Shira
and Merav her childhood friends are coming down the street chattering vivaciously, and I breathe a sigh of relief, at least they're
coming, but to my horror they walk past our building and continue
on their way, and I almost shout after them, come to the birthday
party, don't ostracize her, but they disappear down the hill, perhaps
they're only going to buy a present and they'll be back right away,
I try to console myself, and again childish voices rise from the street,
and I bend down to see better, just a bunch of little kids who aren't
going to save us, and I scold myself, what did you think, that a birthday wipes out the problems? It only underlines them, it's been a year
since anyone called to invite her anywhere, a year since anyone
came to play with her, what did you think, that they would come
out of pity, out of politeness? There's no such thing with children,
and perhaps it's better that way, and I turn round and see her standing at the porch door, spying on me spying, no one's coming, she
whispers, so nobody will hear her shame, it's already half past four.

Why aren't they coming, Noga? I send her a miserable smile,
and she lowers her eyes, because they don't like me, and I ask, but

why? And she says, I don't know, what interests them doesn't interest me, what makes them laugh doesn't make me laugh, and I go up to her, what makes you laugh, Nogi? And she says, this makes me laugh, pointing to the tidy house, the balloons swollen with anticipation, the plates of snacks and the activity corners, and her laughter turns into a dry, barking cough, and I hand her a glass of water, and help her to drink it because her hands are trembling, and she groans, I don't feel well, I want to go and lie down. I lead her silently to her bed, lay her limbs between the scissors and the rolls of tape, kiss her high forehead, covered in sweat, and then there's a knock at the door, and she shrinks, hiding herself under the blanket, don't open the door, Mommy, she begs, I'd rather no one came than two or three to see that nobody but them turned up.

I agree with all my heart, who has the strength now to put on a show of merriment for the sake of one or two children, but the knocking doesn't stop, it gets louder, convinced that there's someone at home, and I hold out my hand, let's go and open the door, Nogi, we haven't got a choice, you invited them, you can't go back on it now, and she sits up apprehensively, tell them I'm sick, she urges me, say the party's off and I didn't have time to let them know, what do you care, but I insist, you tell them you're sick, I can't cover up for you.

Hand in hand we march to the door, Noga opens it apprehensively, and the balloons tied to it peep in like a flock of curious children, their foreheads touching ours, and among them a narrow, sandy eye blinks at us, with a tense, sunburned face gradually forming around it, and she advances toward him slowly, warily, as if she's afraid that like the balloons his face will suddenly explode into colored scraps, but then a smile appears on her lips, and gets broader and broader. I look at the narrow doorway filling up with his body, and beyond the hills of his sharp shoulders, beyond their long, silent embrace, solidifying before my eyes like a tableau of two wax dolls clutching each other, the simple light of a summer afternoon shines at me, a blessed, ordinary light, without glory, without expectations, bringing the message of the evening that is already on its way to us, with the cool night stirring the golden leaves of the poplar, and beyond all this there is nothing that can be known with certainty, and it seems that there is no longer any need for promises, neither from heaven nor earth, Daddy, she says in a steady, surprisingly mature voice, you remembered, I knew you would.